Hungry For You

LYNSAY SANDS

The right of Lynsay Sands to be identified as the author of this
work has been asserted by her in accordance with the
Copyright, Designs and Patents Act 1988.

First published in Great Britain in 2012 by
Gollancz
An imprint of the Orion Publishing Group
Orion House, 5 Upper St Martin's Lane, London WC2H 9EA
An Hachette UK Company

1 3 5 7 9 10 8 6 4 2

A CIP catalogue record for this book is available
from the British Library

ISBN 978 0 575 11086 1

Printed in Great Britain by Clays Ltd, St Ives plc

The Orion Publishing Group's policy is to use papers that are
natural, renewable and recyclable products and made from wood
grown in sustainable forests. The logging and manufacturing
processes are expected to conform to the environmental
regulations of the country of origin.

www.lynsaysands.net
www.orionbooks.co.uk

One

Cale was just raising his hand to knock at the door when it swung open. A tall fellow with short dark hair and a phone pressed to his ear peered out at him.

"Cale Valens?"

"Yes," Cale answered, knowing the guards at the front gate had called up to the house warning of his arrival.

"Come on in." The fellow stepped back to make way, pushing a button to end his call before offering a hand to Cale. "Justin Bricker. Most people call me Bricker."

Cale accepted the hand, shaking it politely as he stomped his feet on the welcome mat a couple of times to remove the worst of the snow on his boots. He then stepped inside. "I was told I should speak to Garrett Mortimer."

"Yeah, I know. The boys at the gate called the house and said as much, but Mortimer's down at the garage with Sam." Bricker shut the door and then turned to face him, waving the phone vaguely. "I was just calling down there to tell him you were here, but there's no answer. Hopefully that means they're on their way to the house."

"Hopefully?" Cale removed his brown leather winter coat.

"Yeah, well, they may have been getting busy in one of the cells," Bricker explained wryly as he took the coat and quickly hung it in a closet beside the door. "They've only been life mates for eight or nine months and are still pretty into each other." He closed the closet door, swung back to Cale, and then headed up the hall toward the back of the house. "Come on. I'll get you a bag of blood while we wait."

Cale followed, recalling what his uncle Lucian had said about these men. Mortimer and Bricker used to be partners, enforcers hunting rogues vampires, but now they ran the enforcer house together. Bricker was the younger man and backed up Mortimer, who was now in charge of all the rest of the enforcers.

"One bag or two?" Bricker asked, leading him into a large, cupboard-lined kitchen with an island in the middle.

"One is fine," Cale murmured.

The younger immortal immediately opened a refrigerator to reveal a large amount of bagged blood stacked up alongside various mortal foodstuffs. The sight was a bit startling. Cale hadn't eaten mortal food in more than a millennium and only ever had blood in his own refrigerator. The thought crossed his mind to wonder if it was really hygienic to have raw meat and vegetables so close to the blood.

"O positive all right?" Bricker asked, sorting through the bags in the fridge.

"Fine." Hygienic or not, he was hungry.

"Here you go."

Cale accepted the bag Bricker held out with a murmured thanks, waited the few seconds it took for his canines to descend, and then quickly popped the clear bag of crimson liquid to his fangs.

"Grab a seat," Bricker urged, using his foot to hook one of the wooden barstools tucked under the island and dragging it out for himself. He slapped a bag of blood to his own teeth as he sat on the stool.

Cale pulled a second stool out, but had barely settled on the high seat when the soft *shush* of sliding glass doors opening and closing sounded from the next room. He followed Bricker's glance expectantly to the open door across from them. It led into what was obviously a dining room. The end of a dark oak table was visible, as well as an end chair, but the door and whoever had entered were out of sight. However, their voices reached the two of them easily, and Cale found himself unintentionally eavesdropping on what he soon realized was a private conversation.

"Are you sure you're ready, love?" a man asked in solemn tones.

"Yes, of course, I'm sure," a woman answered, although she didn't sound all that certain in Cale's opinion. He wondered who she was and what she was claiming to be ready for.

Apparently the male speaker had noted the uncertainty as well. "Are you, Sam? It's been eight months and you—"

"I know," the woman interrupted. "And I'm sorry I've dragged my feet about it as I have. It wasn't because I don't love you, Mortimer. I do, but—"

"But you didn't want to leave your sisters," the man said with apparent understanding.

Cale felt his eyebrows rise as he recognized the names. Mortimer was who he was here to see, but so was Sam. She apparently had a sister named Alex, and Aunt Marguerite had a "feeling" this Alex might be the woman he'd waited for his whole life. Cale wasn't holding out much hope that Marguerite was right. As old as he was, he'd pretty much given up hope on ever finding a life mate. He'd pretty much resigned himself to being eternally single. But he also hadn't wanted to offend the woman, so had agreed to come meet this Alex.

Curious now to see the couple who were speaking, Cale shifted slightly on his stool, leaning to the side, but it was no good. They must have stopped at the door they'd just entered. They also obviously thought they were having a private conversation, and he glanced to Bricker, expecting him to make some noise to alert them to the fact they weren't alone, but the younger immortal almost seemed to be holding his breath as he waited for what they might say next.

Cale found himself frowning around the bag in his mouth and was about to scrape his stool back to warn the couple, but the woman's next words made him pause.

"It wasn't because of Jo and Alex."

Cale stilled curiously, hoping to hear more about this Alex.

"That was just an excuse, Mortimer. One I even had myself half convinced of," the woman admitted on an apologetic sigh. "But Jo said something to me after she met Nicholas that made me realize it wasn't the real reason."

"What was that?" Mortimer asked quietly.

"She pointed out that, after you turn me, I would still have ten years to try to find them life mates. She said I was just afraid, and I think—no, I *know* now she was right."

"Afraid of what, Sam?" Mortimer asked with quiet concern. "The pain of turning?"

"No . . . Although that's scary on its own," she admitted on a wry laugh. Her voice was more serious when she added, "But really I was afraid that you would wake up one day and realize . . . well, that I'm just me," she finished helplessly.

"I don't understand. I know who you are, Sam. What—?"

"I know, but—This is silly, but, while I'm smart, and hardworking, and basically nice, I'm not . . ." Sam's voice was slightly embarrassed as she said, "Well, I'm just not some sexy, gorgeous vamp type of gal who can hold the attention of a guy like you for eternity."

"Honey, you're beautiful. I—"

"I look like Olive Oyl, Mortimer." The words burst into the air on a breath of exasperation, as if she thought that should be obvious.

Cale tore the now-empty bag from his mouth and glanced to Bricker with confusion, his voice a bare whisper as he asked, "Olive Oyl?"

Bricker removed his own bag and explained in a hushed tone, "Popeye's girlfriend." When Cale continued to stare at him blankly, he rolled his eyes. "She's a cartoon character; dark hair, huge eyes, and spindly as a stick figure. Sam is—"

"Honey, I have eyes. I know you look like Olive Oyl."

Bricker stopped his explanation on a low curse and squeezed his eyes closed briefly. He then turned his head back toward the door, muttering with disgust, "You old guys are so bloody smooth. Honestly."

Cale would have liked to argue the point, but really, even he—who hadn't bothered with women in what seemed like forever—knew Mortimer's words had been the wrong thing to say. Obviously, Mortimer realized it too because he began to babble, "I mean, you're beautiful to me. I love your smile and the way your eyes twinkle when you're amused or teasing and—"

"But I still look like Olive Oyl," Sam said in tones that made it obvious she wasn't impressed with the man's efforts to save the situation.

"Not really." There was a distinct lack of conviction in Mortimer's voice, but it was stronger when he added, "Look, honey, the point is, I don't see you through rose-colored glasses. My love isn't based on some shallow fantasy image of you, and I'm not going to suddenly wake up one day and notice you have knobby knees."

"Knobby knees?" she cried.

"I—No," he assured her quickly, sounding a bit panicked now. "No, of course they aren't knobby. I just mean I know exactly how you look. I *do* see you, and you're what I want, not some silly fantasy like Jessica Rabbit was."

"Jessica Rabbit?" Sam echoed with disbelief. "You had fantasies about Jessica Rabbit? A *cartoon rabbit*?"

Cale's eyebrows rose at that. He'd been alive a long time and had fantasized about a lot of things, but never a cartoon rabbit.

"Well not as a rabbit," Mortimer muttered, sounding a bit chagrined. "And not as a cartoon character. I wasn't really—I mean, I didn't want to hook up with her or anything. She was just a representation of the type of woman I thought I might end up with."

"Voluptuous and sexy," Sam suggested.

"Exactly," Mortimer said, sounding relieved.

Cale didn't need Bricker's groan to tell him that was possibly the stupidest thing the man could say. Dark hair, huge eyes, and a stick figure didn't suggest voluptuous and sexy to him.

"Mortimer," Sam said, her voice hard, "I'm neither voluptuous nor sexy. If that's what you want, why spend eternity with me?"

"Honey, you *are* sexy. You're smart, and brains are really sexy as hell."

"Right," Sam snapped, obviously not buying that line.

"Gad!" Bricker barked.

When the younger immortal leapt off his stool and hurried toward the dining-room door, Cale followed.

He entered the room on the other man's heels, his eyes moving with interest over the couple peering toward them with surprise.

Bricker's description of dark hair, big eyes, and spindly as a stick figure fit Sam, Cale decided. It was probably also the most unattractive way to put it. The woman did have dark hair, but only in that it wasn't blond. There were tints of light brown and even red in her hair that made for a lush, almost auburn. As for her eyes, Cale had always found large eyes an attractive feature, but they did tend to dominate this woman's thin face. He suspected they would be lovely if she had a little more meat on her to round her cheeks out a bit. Actually, the woman could have done with a little more rounding everywhere. Her body was on the point of being emaciated. It made him wonder if she didn't have some ailment of the thyroid or something.

He shifted his gaze to Garrett Mortimer then, but barely got an impression of fair hair and a muscular body before Bricker paused before the couple, and snapped, "For cripes sake, you two! What are you doing? Sam, you love Mortimer, and he loves you, and that's what he's trying to tell you, he's just too stupid to get it out right. But he loves and wants you *just the way you are*." He shook his head with disgust. "You should be secure in that knowledge by now for God's sake. The two of you have been going at it like a pair of bunnies for months, with no sign of letting up."

"Bricker!" Sam squawked, flushing bright pink as she glanced from the enforcer to Cale with a mortification he suspected wouldn't be nearly as strong had he, a stranger, not been present.

"Oh, right," Bricker muttered, glancing back toward him with a sigh that suggested he'd briefly forgotten Cale's presence. "Sam, Mortimer, this is Cale Valens. Cale, this is Garrett Mortimer and Sam Willan."

"Cale," Mortimer said slowly, offering a hand, and then recognition lit his face. "Martine Argeneau's son."

"Yes." Cale shook the offered hand politely and then glanced again to Sam. Much to his surprise, the embarrassment that had been coloring her face a moment ago appeared to have slipped away, replaced with an interest that was sharp and focused.

"Are you single, Mr. Valens?" Sam asked as she moved forward to shake his hand as well.

Cale raised an eyebrow at the blunt question, but glanced to Bricker when he released a short, sharp laugh.

"I see your agreeing to turn hasn't dampened your determination to see Alex settled with an immortal, Sam," Bricker commented with amusement, then warned Cale, "Look out. She'll be holding a dinner party and introducing the two of you by week's end."

"Well, why not?" Sam sounded a touch defensive. "You never know. They might suit each other."

"Honey," Mortimer said on a sigh, "the chances of Alex's being a possible life mate for an immortal are pretty slim. It's amazing that Jo turned out to be Nicholas's life mate. It's very rare to find three mortal sisters who suit—"

"Chances shmances," Sam interrupted firmly. "Besides, there's no harm in introducing them and seeing if they wouldn't suit. Alex would make a good immortal. She's smart, successful, and already works nights. I'll just call her and see if she can come over for dinner." Sam started to turn away, but Mortimer caught her arm.

"Why don't we find out why Cale is here and see if he even has time to stay for dinner first?" he suggested quietly.

Sam hesitated, but then glanced to Cale. "Can you stay for dinner?"

When he nodded, she grinned and then whirled away again.

"Thank you for humoring her," Mortimer said on a sigh, as they watched her cross the room.

Cale shrugged. "I am not humoring *her* so much as Marguerite."

"Marguerite?" Sam stopped abruptly in the kitchen doorway and spun around, her already large eyes appearing even larger in her startled face.

Cale's eyebrows lifted. The woman was almost vibrating with an emotion he couldn't quite identify. He was about to read her mind when Mortimer captured his attention by echoing her exclamation in a deeper, though no less startled, voice.

"Marguerite?"

Cale glanced to the man, and then to Bricker, both of whom were now peering at him with intense interest. Grimacing, he admitted, "Marguerite seems to have a bee in her bonnet about me meeting Sam's sister, Alex."

"She does?" Sam breathed, taking several steps toward them.

Cale found himself shifting uncomfortably as he admitted, "Yes. She seems to think we might suit each other . . . I expect she's wrong, but it can't hurt to humor her and meet your sister to see one way or the other."

"I'll have Alex come over at once!" Sam spun away again, this time making it out of the room before anyone spoke.

A snort of amusement brought Cale's glance to Bricker as the younger immortal asked, "You're kidding right?"

"About what?" Cale asked, scowling. He didn't like being laughed at, and the younger man was definitely laughing. He was also eyeing him with a combination of pity and, strangely, what appeared to be envy.

"About not expecting Marguerite to be right," Bricker explained, and then slapped him on the back. "Buddy, if Marguerite is having one of her 'feelings' that you and Alex will suit, you're as good as mated. It's what Marguerite *does*. She finds life mates for anyone and everyone she can. She's hooked up every single couple who have found each other the last few years."

"Every *Argeneau* couple," Mortimer corrected firmly. "She was not responsible for Sam and me."

"Yeah, well I wouldn't be too sure about that," Bricker said dryly. "She probably suggested Lucian send us to that job in cottage country in the hopes that one of us would suit one of the sisters."

Mortimer rolled his eyes at the suggestion. "She couldn't have known about Sam and her sisters. I don't think she's even been to Decker's cottage."

"Oh, he didn't tell you?" Bricker asked with amusement.

"Tell me what?" Mortimer asked, suddenly wary.

"Marguerite helped him find the place. Since he was always so busy on the job, she vetted the available properties and suggested the one next to Sam and her sisters was the nicest."

"Christ," Mortimer muttered.

Bricker laughed, but Cale simply peered from one man to the other curiously. "Is she really that good at finding mates for immortals?"

"Oh yeah," Bricker assured him. "So, if Marguerite thinks Alex is the one for you, it's in the bag. It looks like your bachelor days are done, my friend. Bet you can't wait."

Cale found himself frowning at the suggestion, and said a bit stiffly, "Not all of us are lonely and in need of a life mate. Some of us manage to live relatively happy, busy lives without one."

"Yeah right," Bricker said with disbelief.

Cale scowled, but didn't argue the point further. Why bother? It wasn't really true anyway.

"You have to be kidding me." Alex Willan stared at the man standing on the other side of her desk. Peter Cunningham, or Pierre as he preferred to be called, was her head cook. He was also short, bearded, and had beady little eyes. She'd always thought he resembled a weasel, but never so much as she did at that moment. "You can't quit just like that. The new restaurant opens in two weeks."

"Yes I know." He gave her a sad little moue. "But really Alexandra, he is offering a king's ransom for me to—"

"Of course he is. He's trying to ruin me," she snapped.

Peter shrugged. "Well, if you were to beat their offer . . ."

Alex's eyes narrowed. She couldn't help noticing that he'd said "beat" rather than "match" or even "come close." The little creep really was a weasel with no loyalty at all . . . but she needed him.

"How much?" she asked sharply, and barely managed to keep from hyperventilating at the amount he murmured. Dear God, that was three times what she was paying him and twice what she could afford . . . which he knew, of course.

It was a ridiculous sum. No chef earned that, and he wasn't worth it. Peter was good, but not that good. It didn't make any sense that Jacques Tournier, the owner of Chez Joie, would offer him that much. But then Alex could suddenly see what the plan was. Jacques was luring the man away in a deliberate attempt to leave her high and dry. He'd keep him on for two or three weeks, just long enough to cause scads of trouble for her, then he'd fire him under some pretext or other.

Alex opened her mouth, prepared to warn Pierre, but the smug expression on his face stopped her. Peter had always been an egotistical bastard. It was bad enough when he was only the *sous-chef,* but in the short time since she'd promoted him to head chef, his ego had grown to ten times its previous bloated state. No, she thought with a sigh, he wouldn't believe her. He'd think it just sour grapes.

"I know you can't afford it," Peter said pityingly. Then with something less than sympathy, he added, "Just admit it so I can stop wasting my time and get out of here."

Alex's mouth tightened. "Well, if you knew, why even bother suggesting it?"

"I didn't want you to think I was totally without loyalty," he admitted with a shrug. "Were you to beat their offer, I would have stayed."

"Thanks," she said dryly.

"*De rien,*" he said, and turned toward the door.

Alex almost let him walk out, but her conscience got the better of her. Whether he'd believe her or not, she had to at least try to warn him that he was setting himself up for a fall. Once Jacques fired him—and she didn't doubt for a minute he would—Peter would be marked. The entire industry would know that he'd left her for them, and then lost that job. Even if people didn't suspect the truth of what happened and label him a putrid little weasel, they would think he'd been fired for *something*.

Alex had barely begun to speak her thoughts, however, before Peter was shaking his head. Still, she rushed on with it, warning him as her conscience dictated. The moment she fell silent, he sneered at her with derision.

"I knew you would be upset, Alexandra, but making up such a ridiculous story to get me to stay is just sad.

The truth is, I have been selling myself cheap for some time now. I've built up a reputation as an amazing chef these last several weeks while cooking in your stead—"

"Two weeks," Alex corrected impatiently. "It's only been two weeks since I promoted you to head chef. And you're cooking *my* recipes, not coming up with brilliant ones of your own. Surely you can see how ridiculous it is that someone would pay you that kind of money for—"

"No, I do not see it as ridiculous. I am brilliant. Jacques sees my potential and that I deserve to be paid my value. But you obviously don't. You have been trying to keep me under. Now I will get paid what I deserve and enjoy some of the profits produced by my skills." Mouth tightening, he added, "And you're not going to trick me into staying here with such stupid stories."

With a little sniff of disgust, Peter turned on his heel and sailed out of her office with his nose up and a self-righteous air that made her want to gag.

Alex closed her eyes. At the moment, she wanted nothing more than to yell a string of obscenities after the man, and suspected she would enjoy his fall when it came. Unfortunately, her own fall would come first.

Cursing, she pulled her Rolodex toward her and began to rifle through the numbers. Perhaps one of her old friends from culinary school could help for a night or two. Christ, she was ruined if she didn't find someone and quickly.

An hour later, Alex reached the W's in her Rolodex with no prospects when the phone rang. Irritated with the interruption when she was having a crisis, Alex snapped it up. She barked "hello," the fingers of her free hand still flipping through the cards one after the other in quick succession.

"I have someone I want you to meet."

Alex frowned at the strange greeting, slow to recognize her sister's voice. Once she did, a deep sigh slid from her lips, and she shook her head wearily. She really didn't need this right now. She was heartily sick of the parade of men Sam had been presenting her with over the last eight months.

It had been bad enough when she and their younger sister, Jo, had both been single and available, but now that Jo had Nicholas, Sam was focusing all of her attention on finding Alex a man. She supposed it wouldn't be so bad if even one of the men Sam had insisted on introducing her to had shown some mild interest in her, but after barely more than a moment, and sometimes as little as a few seconds, every single one had simply ignored her, or in some cases, even walked away.

It was giving her a complex. She'd even started dieting, something she'd sworn she'd never do, and exercising, a pastime she detested, as well as trying different makeup and fashion choices in an effort to boost her now-flagging ego.

This really was the last thing she needed, but Alex knew Sam's heart was in the right place and forced herself to hang on to her patience and even managed to keep her tone to only mildly exasperated.

"Sam, honey, my head chef just quit, and I have one

hour to replace him before the dinner set start to arrive. I don't have time for your matchmaking right now."

"Oh, but, Alex, I'm pretty sure this is the one," she protested.

"Right, well, maybe he is, but if he isn't a world-class chef, I'm not interested," Alex said grimly. "I'm hanging up now."

"He is!"

Alex paused with the phone halfway back to its cradle and pulled it back to her ear. "What? He is what?"

"A chef?" Sam said, but it sounded like a question rather than an announcement. It was enough to make Alex narrow her eyes.

"For real?" she asked suspiciously.

"Yes." Sam sounded more certain this time.

"Where did he last work?" she asked cautiously.

"I—I'm not sure," Sam hedged. "He's from Europe."

"Europe?" Alex asked, her interest growing. They had some fine culinary schools in Europe. She'd attended one of them.

"Yes," Sam assured her. "Actually, that's why I was sure he would be the one. He's into cooking and fine cuisine like you."

Alex drummed her fingers thoughtfully on the desk. It seemed like just too much good fortune that her sister wanted to introduce her to a chef the very day she was in desperate need of one. On the other hand, she'd suffered enough bad luck the last few months that a bit of good luck was surely in order. Finally, she asked, "What's his name?"

"Valens."

"I've never heard of him," Alex murmured, and then realized how stupid it was to say that. She didn't know every single chef in Europe. In fact, she only knew a few from her days in culinary school . . . and the names of the famous ones of course.

"Look, he's a chef, and you need one. What can it hurt to meet him?" Sam asked. "I swear you won't be sorry. I really think this will work out. Marguerite is never wrong. You have to meet him."

"Marguerite?" Alex asked with confusion, recognizing the name. She was the aunt of one of Mortimer's band mates, Decker Argeneau. Alex had never met her, but Sam mentioned her a lot. However, she had no idea what the woman had to do with any of this.

"Just meet him," Sam pleaded.

Alex sighed, her fingers tapping a rapid tattoo. She could sense that Sam was lying about something in her determination to get her to meet the man, and really, she didn't have time to waste at the moment. On the other hand, Sam hadn't hesitated to say he could cook and had even said it was why she'd thought they might hit it off, so Alex suspected that part of it was at least true. At least she hoped it was. The fact was, she was desperate. And, frankly, beggars couldn't be choosers. If the man could cook even half decently, she was definitely interested in him though not the way Sam was obviously hoping she would be.

"Send him over," she barked, and then slammed the phone back in its cradle before she could change her mind.

* * *

Cale was telling Bricker and Mortimer about the wedding he'd attended in New York for several of his family members and their life mates when Sam came hurrying back into the room. "It's all set," she announced excitedly. "You have to go to her restaurant right away."

Cale frowned. "You said you would have her come here."

"Yes, well, there was a change of plans. Alex has a small crisis at the restaurant and can't leave," Sam announced, catching his arm and urging him toward the door to the kitchen. "Actually that reminds me. Can you cook?"

Cale stopped, forcing her to a halt, and announced stiffly, "I don't eat."

"I didn't ask you if you eat," she pointed out. "Can you cook?"

"Why would I cook if I don't eat?" he asked dryly.

"Not doing one doesn't preclude your doing the other," Sam said impatiently, and then clucked with irritation and tried to urge him to continue forward as she pointed out, "Male designers don't wear women's clothing, but they design it."

"How do you know they don't wear it?" Bricker asked lightly, drawing Cale's attention to the fact that he and Mortimer had followed and now stood behind them.

Mortimer chuckled at the words, but Sam didn't seem to see the humor. Grinding her teeth together, she tugged at Cale's arm again. "Come on. You need to get to the restaurant before she changes her mind and takes off for the new place or something."

Cale tugged his arm free of her hold. "I do not cook food and have no desire to visit a place filled with the stench of it. You'll just have to arrange a meeting for a different day. I have no desire to go to her place of business."

Two

'I can't believe Sam told her sister I am a chef,' Cale muttered for probably the sixth time since finding himself bundled into the passenger seat of his rental car, and riding away from the enforcer house with Justin Bricker at the wheel.

"Believe it," Bricker said dryly. "Sam is desperate to see her sister settled with an immortal. She and her sisters are as thick as thieves. She'll do everything and anything she can to ensure that Alex doesn't have to be left behind at some point in the future."

"Hmm." Cale supposed he could understand that. He had often thought it must be hard for mortals to give up their families and friends to claim the immortals they loved. They gained a lot in return, of course: eternal youth and a love and passion most mortals could only dream of. Still, family was important to his clan, and to his mind it spoke well of Sam and her sisters that they deemed family important as well.

"Still . . . a chef? Just the sight of food makes my stomach turn, and the smell . . ." He grimaced and shuddered, growing nauseous at just the thought of it. His reaction to food was one of the reasons Cale didn't much bother with mortals anymore. Their very lives seemed to revolve around food or beverages. They did business over coffee or drinks and held feasts to celebrate every event. It was for that reason that Cale had funneled most of his business interests into areas where he need only deal with immortals. Of course, some of them ate too, those who were still young, or were mated. But he ran into the problem much less often when dealing with immortals than he would with mortals.

"This is the first time I've heard of an immortal with that kind of reaction to food," Bricker commented, and then cast him a curious glance, and asked, "Just how old are you?"

Cale scowled. The older he got, the more he detested answering that question and supposed he was starting to feel his age. Not physically, of course, but mentally. The truth was, lately, Cale was bored to tears. It was why he'd agreed to a long visit in Canada. He hadn't had any real change in his life for a very long time. Running companies that catered to immortals' needs and had mostly immortal employees meant he hadn't had to change his name or job for some time. He also lived on a country estate just outside Paris where there were no neighbors to notice his lack of aging. It had allowed him to avoid moving as well.

Cale knew that while doing so had been convenient, it had also allowed him to stagnate. Lately he'd been thinking that a major rearranging of his life was in order. He'd been contemplating leaving his company in the hands of one of his capable senior employees and taking up a different line of work, but he simply hadn't decided on what he wanted to do. He'd considered several things, but most of them necessitated attending university to gain the necessary skills, which meant being around mortals and their ever-present love for food.

Another option he'd considered was hiring himself out as a mercenary. Cale had enjoyed battle in his youth, and while he couldn't become a proper soldier because he couldn't risk daylight, he understood they still hired mercenaries to fight in third-world countries. He supposed it spoke of how low his mood had sunk that the idea of a bloody battlefield appealed to him.

"If you're Martine and Darius's son, you have to have been born before Christ," Bricker said thoughtfully. "Your father died in 300 B.C. or something, didn't he?"

"In 230 B.C.," Cale said tightly. It was not a time he liked to recall. He had lost not only his father but several brothers that year, all in the same battle. Actually, "slaughter" was the better word since they'd been lured into a trap by an immortal who vied for the same mercenary contracts they did and had decided to eliminate the competition. Cale's father, Darius, had been a great warrior and raised his sons with the same skills, and then made a living by hiring himself and his sons out for battle.

Including Cale, his mother had borne eleven children with his father, all sons. The pair had met and become life mates in 1180 B.C., when his father was two hundred years old and his mother three hundred. While they had adhered to the rule of one child every century, they'd also had two sets of twins, and—so far—the council didn't punish parents for having twins by making them wait an extra century to have another child. Of those eleven sons, only three still survived. The rest had died alongside their father on a bloody battlefield in 230 B.C. Cale still ached at the memory of the mammoth loss.

"Well, then maybe your reaction to food is because you're so old," Bricker murmured with concern. Apparently, the idea of having such an extreme distaste for food was bothersome to the younger immortal. Shrugging, he said more cheerfully, "But if Marguerite's right about this—and she always is—once you meet Alex, you're going to find yourself craving food."

When Cale merely peered at him dubiously, he chuckled, and added, "Trust me. By tonight, you're going to be stuffing your face like a mortal after a weeklong fast."

Cale scowled, not pleased at the suggestion. Really, he wasn't any more pleased to find himself trapped in a vehicle with the younger immortal. Food eaters always had a similar stench. Normally that smell didn't bother him so much, but then he wasn't normally trapped in an airless car with one. Wrinkling his nose, he sighed, and asked, "Why are you driving me there again?"

"Because you don't know your way around Toronto,

and Sam didn't want to take the chance of your getting lost," Bricker reminded him with amusement. "She also worried you might crack up your car on the icy roads and didn't want to risk that either. Since Mortimer wanted to discuss her turning and wouldn't let her drive you herself, she reluctantly decided I should deliver you to Alex. I'm to report back to her on every word that passes between you," he announced with amusement.

"Right," Cale muttered, beginning to wonder what he'd gotten himself into here. Perhaps it really wasn't worth it to humor Marguerite after all. Not if it meant going to a restaurant where he would be surrounded by the stench of mortal food . . . and this Alex woman thought he was a chef for God's sake! What on earth had possessed Sam to claim he could cook? He didn't know the first damned thing about cooking and didn't want to. On the other hand, if it turned out Marguerite was right, and this woman was his life mate . . . Well, he supposed that might make it worth it . . . and he really might start to like food again then.

"Here." Bricker reached blindly into the backseat to retrieve a book. He offered the large volume to Cale, saying, "Sam thought it might help if you gave this a quick once-over on the way."

"Cooking for Dummies?" Cale read with something akin to horror as his gaze moved with distaste over the picture of the dead, headless, featherless, and trussed-up roasted chicken on the plate next to a bunch of equally roasted vegetables.

"Well, it can't hurt," Bricker said with amusement. "Alex is expecting a world-class chef."

Cale tossed the book back on the seat behind him with disgust. "I have no intention of cooking. I'll just go there, meet the woman, see if I can read her, and leave when I can."

"Or," Bricker drawled, "you're going to go there, discover Marguerite was on the mark *again,* that you can't read Alex, and you'll be desperate for an excuse to stay close to her as you try to lay claim to her as a life mate."

Cale snorted. "If I can't read her, and she is my life mate, I won't need an excuse to stay close to her. She'll want me there."

"Oh, man, do you have a lot to learn about mortal women," Bricker said dryly.

Cale glanced at him sharply. "Surely, if she is my life mate, she will—"

"What? Drop into your palm like a plum, ripe for the picking?" Bricker tore his gaze from the road to glance at him with obvious amusement. When Cale merely scowled, he shook his head and turned his attention back to the road. "You weren't paying attention back there at the house, were you? Didn't you catch the fact that Mortimer and Sam are life mates, have been together for eight months, and yet she's only now agreeing to the turn? Mortal women do have free will, you know."

Cale's eyes widened as he realized that was true.

"And contrary to what the movie claims, Earth girls *aren't* easy."

"What?" Cale asked, completely bewildered by the reference.

"Never mind," Bricker muttered with disgust. "The

point is, while *we* grow up with the knowledge that someday we will meet that special someone who can't read us and whom we can't read and so will, therefore, be our perfect life mate, mortal women *don't*. They grow up being taught that men are cheating, lying bastards and being told that they will have to kiss a lot of toads before they find the one who will be their prince. And *then* they're taught to be cautious because some princes are actually wolves in princely clothing."

Cale peered at the younger immortal with dismay. "Are you serious?"

"You don't watch much TV, do you?" Bricker asked dryly, and then suggested, "Get a clue, watch a movie or two tonight. It will bring you up to date on the state of the war of the sexes."

"War?"

"Yes, war," Bricker said solemnly. "Women aren't the sweet little biddable gals pleased just to have a bit of attention anymore. If they have a man in their lives, it's because they want him there, not because they need him to take care of them. Today's women can take care of themselves. At least a lot of them can. And as a successful businesswoman, Alex is one of the ones who can. In fact, dragging her attention away from her business is most likely going to be more of a struggle than anything. Especially right now," he added grimly.

"Why especially right now?" Cale asked.

"She's in the midst of opening a second restaurant," Bricker informed him. "She started with this little hole-in-the-wall. It was fancy," he added, in case Cale got the wrong impression. "But small. Only she's one hell of a cook, and it was a raging success. You had to book months ahead to get a table. So she decided she needed a larger venue, only from what Sam has said, that's been one problem after another, and Alex has been running in circles trying to get it together in time for opening night."

"When is that?" Cale asked.

"In two weeks," Bricker said dryly. "Trust me, she'll be running around like a chicken with her head cut off and—life mate or no life mate—you'll be lucky if she gives you the time of day if she finds out you're *not* a chef."

Cale was silent for a moment, and then undid his seat belt and shifted around to reach in the back for the cookbook. It seemed to him it was better to be safe than sorry.

"There's absolutely no one you can think of who's even a halfway-decent cook and presently unemployed?" Alex asked unhappily, and then listened to the voice over the phone as Gina, a dear friend who was also a chef, told her no. Alex grimaced, and murmured, "Well, thanks for trying, anyway."

Alex set the phone back in its cradle with a weary sigh. She'd spent the last forty-five minutes since talking to Sam making calls, but there didn't appear to be any chefs out there in search of a position . . . which was just ridiculous considering the state of the economy, but it was also just her luck lately.

Growling with frustration, Alex scrubbed her hands over her face, and then dropped onto her desk chair with a groan. She'd continued with her calls in case the chef whom Sam was sending over was completely unsuitable, but it seemed he was her only hope at this point. If he wasn't up to scratch, she would have to cook here herself tonight, which meant she couldn't see to the things she needed to do to get the larger restaurant opened on time at the new location.

Why on earth had she set herself up for this hell? Alex wondered miserably. It had seemed such a simple and easy plan at the time. This restaurant had been going like gangbusters, always full, the money rolling in. She'd been the fat, happy cat enjoying the cream of her success . . . and then some little devil had whispered in her ear that she should expand and, like an idiot, she'd rushed impulsively forward with the idea.

Originally, Alex had hoped to purchase the storefront next door and simply knock down the wall between and make this restaurant larger. But then she'd realized it meant canceling several bookings to get the work done, and then someone suggested simply opening another restaurant at the other end of the city. She might bring in a whole new clientele.

With visions of a chain of La Bonne Vie restaurants dancing through her head, Alex had set out to find the perfect building in the perfect location. Then she'd settled down to decorate and market the opening of the second La Bonne Vie. Everything had gone smoothly at first, and then bad luck had begun to plague her. The perfect spot had been an old Victorian house at the edge of a busy shopping area. It was newly renovated, charming, and perfect—until an electrical fire had broken out late one night shortly after she'd started decorating it.

Fortunately, Alex had already had an alarm system put in, and the fire department had gotten there quickly. Unfortunately, while the fire itself hadn't spread far, there had been smoke damage throughout the entire building. Suddenly, instead of some light redecorating, Alex had found herself faced with the necessity of gutting the interior and fully restoring it.

Her luck hadn't gotten any better from there. The last few months had been spent putting out fires of a different sort: chasing down shipments that were delayed or just seemed to have disappeared, workmen who suddenly quit or simply didn't show up, orders that had somehow gotten confused so that the wrong products arrived. In a couple of instances, the workmen had started to install the wrong items before she got there, and the companies refused to reimburse her for "used" products.

Soon the money had started to run out, and she'd had to dig into her private savings. That was when Alex had begun to panic. With the opening date already set and promoted, she'd fired the project manager who had been overseeing the redecorating and promoted Peter from *sous-chef* to head chef at the original La Bonne Vie, so that she could be on site at the new building all the time to ensure that there were no more foul-ups . . . which had apparently convinced the little weasel that he was a world-class chef worthy of scads of money.

"The ass," she muttered to herself, her glance sliding unhappily to the clock on the wall. Dinner bookings started at five, and it was nearly that now. If Sam's chef didn't show up, she'd have to start cooking herself. Not that she minded. Cooking was Alex's first love, all she'd ever wanted to do. It had been a terrible wrench to her when she'd had to pass the head-chef hat to Peter so that she could oversee the renovations at the new restaurant. But she'd had no choice.

Normally, Alex wouldn't even have been here today when Peter arrived with his announcement. She'd only popped by the restaurant to check on things and grab some paperwork she was hoping to go over later tonight. Her intention had been to head back over to the new restaurant in time for the delivery of paint the painters were supposed to get on the walls before the dining-room tables and chairs arrived tomorrow. At least that had been the plan before Peter had turned up with his announcement that he'd been offered that ridiculous sum of money to go to work for Chez Joie.

Alex scowled at the very thought of the nasty trick being used by her biggest competitor, Jacques Tournier. They had always been competitive, their respective restaurants vying for the same upscale clientele, but this was going too far. Not only could he ruin her, but he was definitely going to do Peter and his career some damage. But then Jacques had always been a jerk.

She glanced to the clock to find that while she'd sat fretting, time had continued to crawl forward. Alex could no longer put it off; she had to get out there and get to work. The first guests would have arrived by now, and their orders were no doubt already appearing in the kitchen. She would just call the painters at the other restaurant and—

A tap at the door sounded as Alex reached for the phone. Calling out for whoever it was to enter, she started to punch in the number to the new restaurant but paused as the door opened, and Justin Bricker appeared, his usual cheerful smile in place as he stepped into her office.

"Hey, Alex. How are tricks?" he greeted easily.

Alex stared at him nonplussed, and then groaned. "Dear God, surely you aren't the chef Sam was talking about?"

"No," he said with a laugh, and gestured behind him with a thumb. "Cale here is."

"Kale?" Alex echoed blankly, her eyes sliding to the still half-closed door. She didn't see any evidence of a second man. Frowning, she set the phone back in its receiver and leaned to the side, trying to see out into the kitchen as she muttered, "Kale is a vegetable."

"Not kale. Cale . . . with a C," Bricker explained, and then glanced around and frowned when he saw that the second man hadn't entered. Scowling, Bricker stepped out of the room briefly, and she heard him mutter, "What are you doing, man? Get in here and try to read her."

Alex's eyebrows rose at the words, and she briefly wondered what they meant, but then Bricker reappeared, dragging a man in a charcoal-colored suit into the room as the fellow said, "I was looking for something to cover my nose and mouth with. Dear God, how anyone can work around all this food is beyond me. The stench is unbearable. I—"

Alex arched one eyebrow as the man spotted her and came to an abrupt halt just inside the door. She'd opened her mouth to snap that her kitchen did not stink, but the words never made it past her lips. She found herself simply staring at the man. He was . . . interesting. Not handsome in the classical sense, but definitely interesting, she decided and *GQ* worthy in that suit. Her gaze quickly slid over his tall, muscular build, clothed in what she was sure was a designer original. Then her eyes paused at his face to take in the strong, angular features, silver-blue eyes, and clear complexion.

What was it with all these friends of Mortimer's? she wondered with a frown. Every single one had perfect skin and arresting eyes.

"Well? Can you read her?" Bricker asked impatiently.

"What?" Cale glanced toward him with a confusion that seemed to clear quickly. "Oh, right."

His gaze shifted back to her, and Alex found herself sighing as he focused on her with a concentration she recognized from every other male Sam had introduced her to since hooking up with Mortimer. It was the look that usually preceded the man's then completely ignoring her or even walking away, the look that was giving her a complex.

"Great! Another one of your and Mortimer's weirdo friends," she muttered with disgust, and turned an angry glare on Bricker as she asked, "Are they all crackheads, or has listening to your music too loud made them all mentally deficient?"

"I know they don't do crack, so it must be the music thing," Bricker said with amusement.

Alex rolled her eyes. "I don't have time for this, Justin. Can he cook or can't he?"

Bricker glanced to Cale. "Can you read her?"

"Read what?" Alex asked irritably, her gaze shifting back to Cale to see that his expression had become even more concentrated, focusing on a spot in the center of her forehead.

"You can't, can you?" Bricker said with what sounded like glee.

"No." The word was barely breathed, and the deep concentration on his expression faded to be replaced by a slightly stunned expression.

Alex frowned. Cale wasn't walking away like all the other men had after that look. Instead, he was staring at her as if she was some rare and exotic creature. She would have preferred the walking away, Alex decided as discomfort began to slither through her. Shifting impatiently, she glanced to Bricker again. "What is—?"

"He can cook," Bricker interrupted cheerfully.

Alex narrowed her eyes, sure there was something here she was missing but completely clueless as to what that could be.

"Ms. Willan?"

Alex glanced to the door with a start. Bev, whom she'd promoted to *sous-chef* to replace Peter when she'd raised him to head chef, was standing in the doorway, an anxious look on her face. "Yes?"

"The orders are coming in and Peter—I mean Pierre," she corrected herself with a grimace, "hasn't come back from wherever he went. Should I—?"

"Peter," Alex emphasized the name, "isn't coming back. He only showed up today to quit," she added abruptly, recalled to her present problems. "Get started on the orders. I'll be there in a moment."

Wide-eyed, Bev nodded and backed out of the office, leaving Alex to glance back to the two men. Cale was still staring as if she were the crown jewels, but Bricker was grinning like the idiot she was beginning to suspect he was.

Sighing with exasperation, she shifted her full attention to Cale. "Where did you train?"

"He's from Paris," Bricker announced.

"He is?" she asked with surprise. Sam had said Europe, but Cale's accent wasn't exactly French. Actually, she couldn't place it at all, it held hints of French, with some English intonations and even Germanic ones as well. Realizing that what accent he had wasn't really relevant, she pointed out, "I didn't ask where he was from, but where he trained. Was it La Belle Ecole, Le Cordon Bleu, or—"

"Cordon Bleu," Bricker interrupted, and Alex narrowed her eyes on him briefly. When he merely beamed at her, she glanced to Cale to note that he was still staring at her. For some reason, that stare was starting to wear on her, making her feel like she had a booger hanging out of her nose or a smudge on her face or something . . . which just annoyed her.

Refusing to give in to the urge to run her hands over her face and nose to check, she ground her teeth together and snapped, "Fine. He trained at Le Cordon Bleu. Where has he worked since then?"

When Bricker hesitated, Cale said, "I work for myself."

Alex's eyes widened slightly though it wasn't at his words so much as the sound of his voice. She hadn't noticed that sexy, sort of husky tone to his voice the first time he'd spoken, but then perhaps she'd been too upset at the suggestion that her kitchen stank to pay attention then. Irritated with herself for noticing it now, she scowled, and asked, "If you have your own restaurant, why would you want a job here?"

"He doesn't really," Bricker spoke up when Cale hesitated. "He's here visiting in Canada for a while, but offered to help out until you can find a replacement chef."

"*Oui*. What he said." Cale nodded with satisfaction and smiled at her, making Alex catch her breath.

Had she thought he was just interesting and not handsome? What was wrong with her, she asked herself, and then frowned as she noted how hot it was in her office. She would have to check the thermostat before she left and see about turning it down, Alex decided, avoiding the urge to tug her sweater away from her chest and fan herself. She then frowned at that thought. Before she left? She was thinking as if she'd already decided to hire the man. That wasn't right. While she appreciated that he was willing to help out when he was here on his vacation, for all she knew he couldn't cook spit.

Forcing herself to regather her thoughts, she cleared her throat, and asked, "Are you any good? Is your restaurant successful?"

"Alex," Bricker said dryly. "The man's wearing a designer suit. His watch is diamond-encrusted. He's *very* good at what he does."

Alex blinked and glanced from the suit—which really

looked very nice on him—to the watch he now appeared to be trying to hide by tugging his sleeve down over it. Despite the discomfitted reaction to Bricker's pointing out his outer signs of success, she caught a glimpse of the sparkling watch face and acknowledged that the man had money, which suggested some level of success at what he did.

A curse and the crash of shattering glass from the kitchen made up Alex's mind for her. She would test him out, and if he could cook, she would accept his help. It would at least give her some more time to find a replacement for Peter while allowing her to make sure the renovations to the new restaurant didn't run off course again.

"He can cook something to reassure you if you like," Bricker announced suddenly.

Alex nodded at once, and then raised her eyebrows in surprise as she noted the horror on Cale's face and the sharp way he turned on the other man.

"You can," Bricker said insistently, then in tones that suggested a meaning that she didn't understand, he added, "Trust me."

Three

'All right, this will be your station.'

Cale came to a halt behind Alex and managed to drag his eyes off her rear and to her face when she half turned to glance at him. My life mate. The words drifted through his mind with a lot of wonder attached. Marguerite had been right. He couldn't read Alex Willan. She was his life mate. The knowledge kept rolling through his brain, but Cale was having trouble wrapping his mind around it. He'd finally met his life mate. After all these centuries, he would have a life mate. He need no longer be alone. He would be mated.

Nope, Cale thought on a small sigh, no matter how he presented it to himself, his brain appeared numb and unable to take it in.

"Or I suppose you're used to the French term *mis en place*," Alex added, drawing his attention again.

Cale nodded stiffly.

"Really, as head chef you'll no doubt be all over the kitchen," Alex went on, turning stiffly away from him to wave over the area she'd led him to. "But this is where you'll mostly be working when you aren't riding herd on the others."

Cale managed another stiff nod when she glanced back at him and tried to look like he knew what she was talking about, but his gaze slid blindly over the gleaming metal services before him, his mind taken up with the litany running through his head. Life mate. Life mate. Life mate.

"This is a small enough operation that the head chef does triple duty, acting as the *saucier* and fish chef as well," Alex explained almost apologetically. "That's what you call the sauté chef and *poissonnier* in France."

Cale pursed his lips and nodded again, her words not really making it past his thoughts about spending eternity with her.

"As I mentioned, Bev is the *sous-chef,* your right hand. Go to her if you have any questions. But she too does triple duty and takes on the jobs of roast chef and grill chef or what the French call the *rôtisseur* and *grillardin.*"

"*Grillardin,*" Cale echoed, managing a nod for the attractive redhead named Bev when she glanced over to smile at him curiously.

"And then Bobby over there is the vegetable chef and roundsman, the *entremetier* and *tournant,*" Alex added, apparently translating it to French out of concern that he might not know the English terms. She needn't have worried—he didn't understand the French ones either.

While Cale knew what the words themselves meant, he wasn't sure what it meant the fellow did exactly, but he tried to look knowledgeable as he gave the young, blond male mortal a nod of acknowledgment.

"Rebecca over there," Alex pointed to a woman coming out of a small room at the back of the kitchen. She was short and a bit round, with rosy cheeks and dark hair pulled back into a ponytail. "She's the pantry chef and pastry chef, the *garde manger* and *pâtissier*. She's a dream at sweets," Alex assured him with a smile.

"Ah, sweets," Cale said with another nod of feigned understanding.

"Right." Alex smiled at him brightly and gestured to the wall, where several sheets of paper with typing on them had been taped up. "The recipes we use here are all mine. When I raised Peter to head chef . . . or *chef de cuisine,* I had to put the recipes up here for him to be able to use . . . which saves me having to do that now."

Alex smiled at him again, and Cale thought that she really had a very nice smile. While he could see the resemblance to Sam, Alex had a full figure, her large eyes complementing her pretty face rather than dominating it, and her hair was shorter, a shiny brown bob that fell below her ears and swung around her face as her head moved. He found himself wondering if the dark tendrils were as soft as they looked and had to stick his hands in his pockets to resist the urge to find out.

"So if you want to just take one of the orders waiting"—she gestured to several smaller slips of paper caught in clips on the metal shelf beside his station—

"and get started, I'll stay just long enough to be sure you've got a handle on things, and then get out of your way."

Cale stared at her blankly, sure he'd missed something while he'd been staring at her. Was she suggesting he actually cook? Of course she was. It was what he was supposed to be here for, he reminded himself, and glanced over the foreign objects surrounding him. He didn't even know where to start.

"Perhaps he should take off his suit jacket. You have an apron he can use, right?" Bricker asked, stepping into the void.

"Oh, yes of course." Alex shook her head. "I'm sorry. Everything's so topsy-turvy right now I wasn't thinking. Here give me your suit jacket. I'll hang it in my office and get you an apron and hat."

Cale muttered a thank-you, helping when she began to tug his jacket off, then watched silently as she hurried across the kitchen to her office. The moment she disappeared inside, he turned sharply on Bricker and grabbed him by the front of his T-shirt. "What have you done? I can't do this. I don't know the first thing about cooking."

"Hey, whoa, buddy, I didn't do this. Sam is the one who told her you were a cook," he reminded him.

"Well, I'm not," he said sharply, turning back to his station. "Look at this. What is all this? These knobs"— he twisted one of them, bringing on a quiet hiss, then grabbed up a shiny silver rod with one flat end—"and this . . . thing."

"Christ, what are you trying to do, blow us up?"

Bricker muttered, reaching past him to return the knob he'd twisted to its resting place. Cale noted that the hissing immediately stopped. Bricker then snatched the silver thing from his hand. "This is a spatula. You use it to . . . well, sauté I suppose," he muttered, then glanced at Cale's expression and sighed. "Look, these are the controls for the grills. These knobs turn the gas on, but you have to turn them all the way to ignite them." He twisted the knob, and the hissing Cale had noted earlier started again. It was followed by a *click click click,* and then a whoosh as a ring of flames suddenly exploded to life.

Bricker turned the knob back a bit and the flames lessened, then he grabbed up one of several pans on a shelf beside the grill and set it on the stove. "See, you sauté things in the pan over the fire and spread them around or turn them with the spatula."

Bricker moved the spatula to emulate what he was describing. "This isn't as difficult as you seem to think it is. Just read the recipes and follow them. You'll do great. Trust me."

Cale scowled with displeasure but quickly pasted on a smile as Alex returned with a white apron and hat in hand.

"Here we are." She handed him a ridiculous, large white hat and then quickly tossed the top of the apron over his head. Alex then grabbed the strings and reached around him, intending to tie them up for him, but then flushed and stepped back when she realized the position she'd put herself in. Avoiding his eyes, she muttered something under her breath and hurried around him to tie the strings from the back. Cale had liked it better when she was doing it from the front.

"There. All set. I guess you'd best get to it. The orders are waiting."

When Cale stared at her blankly, Bricker snatched up one of the orders and shoved it in front of his face. "This is the first one. Trout Amandine. Mmmm."

Cale snatched the slip of paper from him irritably and peered at the writing.

"Ms. Willan?"

They all paused and glanced toward the girl who suddenly hurried into the kitchens. Dressed in black dress pants and a wine-colored shirt, the woman obviously wasn't kitchen staff. She was also upset about something, a frown marring her plain face.

"What is it, Sue?" Alex asked, moving a little away to speak to her.

"What do I do?" Cale asked Bricker sharply the moment she was out of hearing.

"Make the trout," Bricker said dryly.

"How?" Cale growled. "And what trout?"

Bricker glanced around. "Oh. Right. Hang on, I'll find it."

Cale shook his head with disgust as the man hurried off, and then turned to glance toward Alex, catching some of the conversation going on. It seemed one of the waitresses hadn't shown up for work and they were short-staffed in the dining room. Alex looked stressed at this news.

"Here, I already coated both sides with flour," Bricker announced, appearing at his side again to distract him, and Cale turned to find him holding out a plate with two slices of floured fish on it.

"What do I do with it?" he asked, accepting the offering.

When Bricker glanced to the sheets of paper, Cale followed his gaze, but all the recipes were for sauces, and there didn't appear to be a recipe for Trout Amandine. He supposed chefs were expected to know how to make it.

"Hang on, I'll pick Bev's brain again," Bricker said on a sigh.

"Again?" Cale asked as he started to move away.

"How do you think I found out where to get the fish and to coat it with flour?" he muttered before hurrying away toward the redheaded Bev. It didn't take him long before he was at Cale's side again. "Right. Brown the trout in three tablespoons and one teaspoon butter for four or five minutes, and then turn them and brown for another two minutes. Then you sprinkle them with lemon juice and cook another minute or two while you brown the almonds in another pan, no butter, then sprinkle the almonds and some parsley over the trout and send it out."

As he spoke, Bricker was dumping butter in a small frying pan and setting it on the grill. He turned the flame on under it, then reached for the plate of trout. Cale took it from him at once.

"I'm supposed to be doing it," he reminded him grimly.

"Right. You do it," Bricker said at once, releasing his hold on the dish.

Grunting with satisfaction, Cale took the plate and turned it over the pan so that the fish dropped on top of the pats of butter. The other man immediately sucked in a dismayed breath.

"What are you doing? You're supposed to wait for the butter to melt before you put the fish in," he said with alarm.

"You didn't say that," Cale snapped, and reached to grab the fish back out, but Bricker caught his arm.

"Never mind. Just leave it."

"A problem?" Alex asked, turning to peer in their direction with worry.

"No," Cale and Bricker said as one, both of them shifting to hide the fish from her view.

Alex frowned slightly, but then turned reluctantly back to Sue, who, Cale was guessing, was in charge of the waitstaff.

"Here."

Cale turned to see that Bricker had found a fork somewhere and was sliding it under the fish, trying to mash the butter, presumably so it would melt faster. The action scraped away a good portion of flour from the fish, however, and judging by the man's curse, that wasn't a good thing. Frowning, Cale glanced around, spotted a plate with a powdery white substance on it he thought was what Bricker had used to coat the fish, and picked up a handful. Turning back to the pan, he dumped it on the fish, bringing a squawk from Bricker.

"What are you doing?" the man cried with alarm.

"Cooking," Cale said with irritation.

"That's not—"

"Is there something wrong?" Alex asked, and Cale glanced around to see she was coming toward them.

"No," he said quickly.

"Everything's fine," Bricker assured her in strained tones. "You go on and take care of . . . whatever."

Alex hesitated, but then her expression went briefly blank before she nodded and moved back to Sue.

Eyes narrowing, Cale glanced to Bricker, not at all surprised to see that his expression was concentrated. He'd given Alex a mental nudge to make her return to her conversation. The younger immortal was controlling his woman.

"Stop glaring at me," Bricker muttered, turning his attention back to the frying pan and starting to scrape off most of the flour Cale had just put on the fish.

"Stop controlling my woman," Cale countered.

"I'm just trying to help," Bricker said grimly, and then cursed.

"What's wrong?" Cale asked, glancing worriedly at the pan. The butter was melted now. It was also turning brown and bubbling angrily around the fish.

"I put the fire on too high," Bricker admitted on a sigh.

Cale pursed his lips. He suspected there was more wrong than that the heat was too high. The butter had become a thick, flour-filled soup. He didn't think it was supposed to be. And, while he was no cook, he was pretty sure the fish was burning. Clearing his throat, he suggested, "Perhaps I should turn the fish now."

"Yeah," Bricker agreed, his mouth twisting with dissatisfaction. "Go ahead."

Cale took the spatula he handed him, quickly slid

it under the strips of fish, and turned them. He and Bricker then both sighed unhappily at the result. The fish was covered with blackened flour in places and bald in others, half of the flour coating left behind and stuck to the pan.

"Maybe we should start the almonds," Bricker suggested on a sigh.

"Hmm," Cale murmured.

"I'll find them."

The man was off at once, and Cale immediately glanced toward Alex again, only she wasn't where she'd been when last he'd looked. Sue was now gone, and Alex had moved into her office. He could see her through the open door, talking on the phone. No doubt trying to find a replacement for the missing waitress, he thought.

"Here we go."

Cale glanced around as Bricker returned and dumped a handful of sliced almonds into a fresh pan.

"Just brown them over this flame," he instructed, twisting the knob to get the flame going. "And I'll get the lemon to squeeze over the fish."

"Right," Cale murmured, thinking that sounded easy enough. A moment later, staring down at a pan full of half-burned and half-raw almond slices, he revised his opinion.

"This cooking business isn't as easy as it looks," Bricker commented with disappointment moments later as they peered at the charred trout speckled with parsley and blackened almond slices they had just set on a plate. "Eating is easier."

"Hmm," Cale said, shaking his head with disgust.

"How are we doing?"

Both men jerked upright and shifted to hide their efforts as Alex suddenly appeared beside them.

"Good, good," Bricker assured her quickly. "The first dish is pretty much done."

"Just one?" Alex asked, her eyes widening with alarm. Her gaze shot to the shelf beside them and the alarm grew by leaps and bounds, making Cale turn to peer at it as well. He frowned when he noted that the number of slips on the shelf had more than doubled. He'd been vaguely aware of people moving past them but hadn't realized that more orders had been arriving. He'd been too distracted by trying to cook and listening to Alex and Sue.

"It's all right. Everything is in hand here. You should just go about whatever it is that needs doing," Bricker said firmly.

Cale wasn't surprised to see the concentration on the other immortal's face when he glanced his way. He was controlling Alex again, Cale knew, but this time was grateful for it. The woman had enough problems on her plate without his adding to them. He would never win her that way.

"You obviously have everything in hand here. I should go about what needs doing," Alex agreed woodenly and turned away, only to come to an abrupt halt when Sue suddenly pushed through the kitchen doors.

"Did you find anyone?" the other woman asked hopefully as she hurried over to slip even more orders onto the shelf.

"No," Alex admitted, her shoulders slumping with defeat.

"What are we going to do?" Sue asked with alarm. "We're getting behind on taking orders. Every table is full, Alex. We only have two girls on tonight, including myself."

Alex reached up to run a hand through her hair with an agitation that brought a frown to Cale's face. "We'll just have to—"

"Bricker will wait tables for you," Cale interrupted.

"What?" Bricker squawked.

He turned on the younger immortal, his expression grim. "You will wait the tables."

"The hell I will," Bricker said at once.

"Bricker," Cale growled, and then caught his arm and urged him along the row of shelving and counter-tops until they were out of earshot. "I can't cook."

"I noticed," he said dryly.

"Well, it's not going to improve," he assured him grimly. "And Alex's customers aren't going to be pleased with my offerings . . . unless someone helps them think they are," he added meaningfully.

Bricker raised his eyebrows. "You want me to control the customers?"

"You got me into this," Cale pointed out grimly.

"Oh, hey, no." Bricker held up his hands, palms open. "That wasn't me. Sam is the one who told her you were a chef."

"Sam just said that to get her to meet me; she wasn't the one in Alex's office telling her I was from Paris and had my own restaurant," he countered grimly, and then frowned when he noted Bev listening wide-eyed. Scowling, he took a moment to quickly wipe her mind of what she'd overheard and to make sure she didn't continue to listen.

"I didn't say it was a restaurant," Bricker defended himself quickly. "She just assumed—"

"Semantics," Cale snapped, cutting him off. "You will do this. I won't see Alex ruined because of your 'help.'"

Bricker hesitated, but then whipped out his phone.

"Who are you calling?" Cale asked with a scowl.

"Mortimer," Bricker answered quietly. "I do have a job, you know. I can't just disappear for the night without checking with him first."

Cale relaxed a bit, relieved that the man was at least willing. This was one hell of a debacle, one he wasn't even sure how he'd landed in, but he was confident that between the two of them they could handle things. He'd do his best at cooking, and Bricker would ensure that the customers thought they were happy. Then, the minute he was away from here, he'd start calling around to find someone else to take his place, or better yet, find someone to take the original chef's place permanently. Alex would think him a hero, and Cale could woo her . . . and explain later that he wasn't really a chef and didn't own a restaurant.

He was just relaxing, thinking his problems mostly resolved if he could just get through this night without poisoning anyone, when a gasp from Alex drew his attention. She'd moved to his "station" to look at his Trout Amandine and appeared rather horrified by his and Bricker's efforts. Cale instinctively tried to slip into her mind to control her, but of course he couldn't. He turned to Bricker in a panic. Fortunately, the man had already noticed. He muttered something into the phone, and then lowered it briefly and slid into Alex's thoughts to steer her away from the dish. He left her standing blank-faced in the center of the kitchen as he turned back to his call.

Cale sighed and then took a moment to glance at the others in the kitchen. None of them seemed to have noticed. The other cooks were all bustling around, getting their dishes together under Bev's eagle eye. He suspected he was the one who was supposed to be overseeing the other cooks, but the *sous-chef* had taken over the chore without prompting, ensuring that the rest of the kitchen ran smoothly. The woman definitely seemed to know what she was about. Perhaps he should suggest Alex promote Bev to *chef de cuisine,* and then hire another *sous-chef.* Surely those were easier to find than a head chef.

"Right." Bricker snapped his phone closed and urged Cale back toward Alex. "Mortimer says it's all right for me to stay tonight, but we're going to have to work something else out for tomorrow."

Cale merely nodded. He had no intention or desire to be doing this two nights in a row anyway. He would find a replacement chef for Alex if he had to call in every favor owed him, he thought grimly, and then turned his attention to Alex as Bricker said, "Everything is in order here, Alex. I will help out and wait tables tonight, and Cale is an excellent chef. Everything will be fine.

You should really just go about whatever it is you need to do and leave things to us without worrying."

Cale wasn't terribly surprised when Alex woodenly agreed and turned to walk into her office. Sighing with relief, he turned to his station and the waiting orders. "So, what's the next order?"

Bricker snorted at the question. "That's your problem, buddy. I'm waiting tables now, remember?"

Cale glanced at him with alarm. "But—"

"Just follow the recipes. If it's something like the Trout Amandine and you don't know what to do, slip into Bev's mind and get the answer," he suggested, heading for the door to the dining room.

Cale opened his mouth to protest again, but both he and Bricker halted as Alex suddenly came out of her office, shifting her purse and a stack of papers from hand to hand as she shrugged on a winter coat.

"Where are you going?" Cale asked with surprise.

"To the new restaurant," she explained hurriedly, heading for the door at the back of the kitchen. "You and Bricker have everything in hand here and there's nothing to worry about, so I need to get back to the new restaurant. They were waiting on the paint when I left and I have to be sure the right color arrived. I'll check back here at closing time. See you then."

Cale gaped after her as she pushed through the back door. A gust of wind rushed into the room, and then the door closed, and she was gone. He stared blankly for a minute, and then turned sharply on Bricker.

"Hmm," the younger man said with a frown. "That's a rather startling development."

"Startling?" Cale ground out with fury. "The only reason I let you convince me to try to cook was to be close to her, and she's not even going to be here."

"Yeah. That's kind of ironic, huh?" Bricker said with a shake of the head. Cale was just winding up to blast the immortal, when Bricker commented, "On the bright side, you don't look as green as you did when we first got here. I take it the smell of food isn't bothering you anymore?"

Cale stiffened and took a moment to check himself. There was no nausea, no distaste for the smells wafting in the air around him. He inhaled a deep breath to be sure, but no, it appeared the scent of food no longer repulsed him. Actually, some of the smells in the room even seemed slightly pleasant, he realized with surprise.

"I told you," Bricker said smugly. He chuckled and turned toward the door to the dining room, adding, "Welcome to the land of the living. Now get cooking."

Alex felt incredibly relaxed for the first time in weeks as she drove from one restaurant to the other. She had a real and very hunky French chef serving up her recipes, Bricker was filling in for the missing waitress, and all was right with her world. She continued to feel happy and worry-free right up until she arrived at the new restaurant and entered to find the painters busily painting the dining area.

The papers Alex was carrying slipped from her fingers, and a curse slid from her lips as she peered in horror at the three lime green walls already done.

While the curse she'd used was one that would have made her mother wince, the painters didn't react to it at all and carried on working.

"Stop," she said finally. "Stop dammit!"

One of the painters shifted on his ladder to dip his roller in more paint, and it was only then Alex noted the earbuds in his ear. Her gaze slid to the other two painters to see that they wore them as well. All three were listening to iPods or some other small MP3 player and hadn't heard her.

Cursing colorfully again, Alex rushed forward to tug at the pant leg of the nearest man. Startled, he nearly tumbled from the ladder but caught himself at the last moment. Ripping the buds from his ears, he scowled at her furiously. His name was Bill, and he was a big burly guy, intimidating as hell . . . or he would have been if she weren't in such a temper.

"What the hell are you trying to do? Kill me?" he barked.

"No, but you're killing me," Alex snapped back and waved toward the painted walls. "What is this?"

"It's paint, lady," he growled, glaring at her. "You hired us to paint and we're painting."

"I told you to wait until I got back," she reminded him grimly, and silently berated herself for not completing that phone call she'd been starting when Justin and Cale had arrived. She could have asked them what color the paint was or insist they wait until she returned. Instead, she'd put the phone down and forgotten all about it until now. Not that the painters probably would have heard the ringing with their iPods on anyway.

"We did wait," Bill snapped. "You've been gone more than four hours. We finally decided we'd best get started, or we'd be here all night."

Alex ground her teeth together. She'd only intended on being gone an hour at the most, but with everything that had happened, the time had gotten away from her.

"When an hour and a half passed with no sign of you and not even a phone call, we started painting," Bill snapped angrily.

"The wrong color," she shrieked back. "Does this look like White Sand to you?"

"No, it looks like walls," he snarled.

"I mean the color," she said furiously. "The paint is supposed to be a soothing off-white called White Sand, not lime green."

He frowned at her, and then glanced around the room briefly, before shaking his head. "This is the paint they delivered, so this is the paint we used."

"It's the *wrong* paint," she said grimly.

"Well, that's not my problem," he said stiffly. "Call the store you bought it from and complain to them."

"You're damned right I will." Alex whirled away in a temper, slipping her bag off her shoulder to dig inside it for her cell phone as she paced across the room. When she realized the other two men, earbuds in and oblivious to what was going on, were still painting, she snapped, "Make them stop."

Grunting with displeasure, Bill climbed down off his ladder and moved to the nearest man. Alex then turned her attention to her phone but paused as she realized she didn't know the number. She needed a phone book, or the bill, she thought, and rushed through the dining room and then the kitchen to get to the office.

Alex found a copy of the delivery invoice lying on top of her otherwise empty desktop. She snatched it up, noted that yes, the receipt did say White Sand paint and that the store number was at the top.

Alex plopped her purse where the invoice had been and punched in the number to the paint store, her temper simmering, but she managed to maintain her cool as she explained her problem to the efficient-sounding woman who answered. She even managed to keep her temper under control when the woman said she would fetch the manager and put her on hold. However, after fifteen minutes on hold, she was practically foaming at the mouth. When the manager finally picked up, Alex tore into him over both the mix-up and being on hold for so long. The manager started out trying to soothe her, explaining that he'd taken so long because they'd had to get the delivery papers from the driver.

Unfortunately, Alex wasn't in the mood to be soothed. She barked out that someone should have let her know rather than leaving her hanging, and was angry enough she feared she might have thrown in an insult about the ineptitude of the woman who had answered the phone and himself for not thinking of that. Whatever the case, that's when the manager stopped being soothing. He announced coolly that according to the delivery papers six cans of White Sand paint had been ordered *and delivered* and he had a signature on the papers indicating that this was the case and all was in order.

Alex immediately snapped that it certainly wasn't

White Sand on her walls. Unfortunately, she might have included another insult or two there. She certainly wasn't very diplomatic. Really, it had been a very stressful couple of months, and she was feeling a bit like a woman on the edge at that point.

Her attitude won her a moment of chilly silence that was followed by the manager's announcing coldly that he would be more than happy to replace any unopened cans of paint remaining. However, she would have to look to the painters for reimbursing her for the paint already used since they had signed for it . . . and thank you for shopping with us.

It was the dial tone that sounded after he hung up that snapped Alex out of her hysteria. She listened to it dully, all her anger running out of her like air draining out of a balloon. She sat on the desk, staring bleakly at the unpainted walls of her office and then slowly hung up. Alex knew she'd reacted badly to this latest problem, but dammit, there hadn't seemed to be a day that had gone by without one problem or another cropping up in the months getting this restaurant ready. She was starting to think the damned thing was cursed.

Taking a deep breath, Alex held it briefly, and then slowly let it out and tried to focus on what needed doing rather than what had happened so far. The tables and chairs were arriving tomorrow, so the dining room had to be painted tonight. She had the painters, she needed paint . . . and quickly since she doubted the painters would be pleased to sit about kicking their heels for long.

Fine, Alex thought grimly, she would rush to the

nearest paint store, buy the proper paint, as well as primer since the lime green was bright enough she doubted the White Sand would cover it, bring it back, and set the men back to work.

Feeling somewhat calmer, she headed out of her office to find the painters. They were in the dining room where she'd left them, but the ladders were gone as well as the rest of the painting paraphernalia and the men themselves were heading out, carrying the rolled-up drop cloths.

"Wait a minute," she cried, hurrying after them. "Where are you going?"

"To grab a beer," Bill announced, stomping to the van parked in front of the restaurant and tossing the drop cloths in the open back door.

"But what about the restaurant?" Alex asked with renewed panic. "You have to finish painting."

The man slammed the truck's back door and turned to her with irritation. "You said it was the wrong paint and we were to stop painting."

"Well, yes, but I'm going to go get the right paint and—"

"Nope." The man spun away to walk around to the driver's side door.

"Nope?" Alex echoed, and then hurried after him. "What do you mean, no? I need the restaurant painted tonight. The tables arrive tomorrow."

"Lady, it's Friday night. We ain't sitting around twiddling our thumbs waiting on you to buy paint, and then working our arses off until midnight to get the job done."

"But the tables come tomorrow," she repeated plaintively.

"Then I guess you'd best get painting, because we aren't." He dragged the door open and climbed up behind the steering wheel. He then tried to pull the door closed, but Alex was in the way. Pausing, he scowled at her. "This job has been nothing but a pain in the ass from the start. We were nearly done here and ready to go when you came in and stopped us."

"It was the wrong paint," she pointed out with disbelief.

He ignored that and continued, "On top of that, we were actually supposed to do this job last week, but you rebooked and we nearly killed ourselves finishing other jobs over the last couple of days to make time to come here today."

"The wrong carpet was installed, I had to have it redone, and the only day the installers had available was the day you guys were supposed to come," she explained quickly, glancing past him as the other two men climbed into the van. Neither of them would even meet her gaze. It seemed they weren't eager to get stuck here either.

"And now you're claiming the wrong paint arrived," Bill continued dryly, drawing her eyes back to him. "It seems to me either you're the one making mistakes, or the Big Guy upstairs is trying to tell you something."

"But I need the restaurant painted," she said, almost pleading now.

"Then I guess you'd best get painting cause we're

going for a beer. Now get the hell out of the way or I'll close the door on you."

Alex stared at him for a moment, but knew from his hard expression that she wasn't going to convince him to finish the job. Sighing, she stepped out of the way.

He tugged the door shut with a grunt and then gunned the engine to life before rolling down his window to peer out at her. "Sorry about your problems," he said almost gruffly, and then added, "We'll send you a bill for the painting we did today."

Four

'If you guys are done with your cleanup, I'll let you out and lock up now."

Cale glanced to the *sous-chef,* Bev, who stood in Alex's office doorway. The woman was eyeing them all uncomfortably. He didn't need to read her mind to understand that it was because they were in Alex's office when Alex herself wasn't. However, they'd been exhausted after finishing, and there were no seats in the kitchen, so they'd made their way to the office to get off their feet for a few minutes.

Ignoring the *sous-chef*'s reprimanding gaze, he said, "Alex said she'd come back at the end of the night. We're waiting for her."

Bev immediately shook her head. "She called earlier. There was a snag at the new restaurant and she's going to be there all night. She asked me to close and lock up. If you don't mind, I'll let you out the back door. I don't have keys to the front and have to lock it from the inside."

Cale frowned, but then glanced to his aunt Marguerite as she shifted on the couch, digging in her purse to retrieve her cell phone. Marguerite and Leigh, his uncle Lucian's new bride, had plopped themselves there with relief once the last order had been filled and the *chef de cuisine*'s station had been cleaned. He grimaced at the weary expression on both their faces, feeling guilty for causing their exhaustion.

Cale had lasted a little more than fifteen minutes after Alex left before calling Marguerite in a panic, begging her to come help him. That was after managing to produce two burnt fish dishes and one sauce that had bubbled over, caught fire, and made one hell of a mess on the grill. He hadn't known what else to do. Feeding the customers nasty, burnt food and letting Bricker twist their minds so they left thinking they'd had the best meal ever was bad enough, but burning down Alex's restaurant was another.

He'd called Marguerite. As it had turned out, she and Leigh were in town for dinner and a movie and were only ten minutes away. The two women had headed over before he'd even finished explaining the situation.

However, it hadn't been Marguerite who had ended up saving his bacon, but Leigh. He'd learned at the wedding that she owned a restaurant but hadn't realized she could cook too. She could. She'd taken his place tonight at the head chef's station and manned it like a pro. Cale and Marguerite had alternately backed her up when necessary as she scrambled to catch up with the orders, and spent the rest of their time controlling the minds of the cooks in the kitchen as well as the waiters and waitresses, who were continually popping into the room with orders. They'd kept them from noticing what was happening and calling to tattle to Alex. It seemed, however, while they'd prevented anyone's calling out, Alex had called in. Fortunately, a quick read of Bev's mind told him that she hadn't said anything about the help he'd had here tonight.

"Well then," Marguerite murmured, snapping her phone shut and getting to her feet as Leigh stood up. "I guess we may as well head home."

Cale stood at once and moved to hug each woman with gratitude. "Thank you for your help."

"You're welcome," Marguerite murmured as he stepped back. She then smiled wryly, and added, "I'll see if I can find someone to take your place tomorrow night."

Cale thanked her again. He then hesitated, his glance moving to Bricker as the younger immortal stood. "Would you mind—"

"Certainly," Marguerite interrupted. "The enforcer house is on our way. We'll drop Bricker off."

"I'll get our coats," Bricker offered.

Cale murmured his thanks and watched as the man headed out of the room.

"Cale."

He shifted his gaze back to Marguerite to see a troubled look on her face. After a sigh, she said, "I think it may be best if you tell Alex the truth about your lack of cooking ability as soon as you can. Perhaps not until she gets to know you a little better, but don't leave it too long. A relationship started on lies has a shaky foundation."

Cale nodded solemnly, knowing she was right. As immortals, they had enough secrets to overcome to enjoy a relationship. Unnecessary lies just added to the burden. "I will."

"Here's yours," Bricker announced, appearing at the office door. He was wearing his own winter coat and holding out Cale's. "So are you heading to a hotel or something?"

"Or something." Cale accepted the coat, and then glanced around to see where Alex had put his suit jacket earlier. Spotting it on a coatrack in the corner, he grabbed it and tugged first it, and then the winter coat on before turning to urge Bricker and the women out of the office.

"Do you need the address?" Bricker asked, pausing in the doorway and forcing Cale to a halt as well.

"What address?" he asked warily.

"To the new La Bonne Vie," Bricker said dryly and shook his head. "Don't bother trying to keep secrets for a while. Your mind is an open book at the moment. Alex is definitely the one."

"I think he realizes that, Bricker," Marguerite said dryly, taking his arm to urge him forward so Cale could get out of the room. "And I have already given him the address."

"You have?" Cale asked, his surprise distracting him from the irritation Bricker's words had stirred in him.

Marguerite nodded, continuing to tug Bricker across

the kitchen toward the back door. "Check your phone. I texted it to you."

Recalling her fiddling with her phone earlier, Cale dragged his own out of his pocket and quickly checked his text messages. Sure enough, there was one from Marguerite with a street address on it. Cale grinned to himself and then hurried after the trio.

"Thank you, Marguerite," he murmured, pausing to press a kiss to her cheek before opening the back door for the three of them. Leigh smiled at him wearily as she led the other two out, then Cale glanced to Bev. Reading the anxiety in her mind about locking up and making her way to her car in the dark parking lot alone, Cale held the door for her, and murmured, "I'll wait and walk you to your car before I go."

"Thank you," she said with obvious relief. She quickly locked the door, and then nearly jogged to a small Toyota parked by the Dumpster. "Is your car far? Would you like a ride? It's cold out tonight."

Cale smiled faintly, but shook his head. "My car isn't far. I'm fine. Have a good night."

"Good night." She pulled the car door closed, starting the engine as he turned away.

Cale immediately headed around the side of the restaurant. Marguerite, Leigh, and Bricker were already turning out of sight at the front of the building, en route to whatever vehicle the women had arrived in. Cale followed just as swiftly, eager to get to the restaurant and see Alex again. He'd help her with whatever problem it was she'd run into and get a chance to woo her a bit. Well, he would help so long as it wasn't cooking, Cale thought wryly. While he'd learned a thing or two from watching Leigh tonight, Cale didn't think he'd ever be offering himself up as a chef again . . . or allow anyone else to either.

Grimacing to himself, he hurried to his car and got in, his key in the ignition almost before he even had the door closed. Immortals could better bear more extremes of temperature, but it was damned cold out tonight. Cold enough that Cale was feeling it and couldn't get the engine started and the heater going quick enough. Leaving the car to heat up, he turned his attention to the rental car's GPS system and entered the address Marguerite had texted him. By the time he had a route mapped out, the car windows had defrosted. He shifted into drive and set out, trying to come up with an excuse to give for seeking her out there.

Alex was humming the tune playing in her ears and doing a little dance to the beat as she dragged the ladder several steps to the right and then climbed back up to resume her painting. She'd decided the painters had the right idea and fetched her earplugs to listen to music on her iPhone as she worked. She had always found music soothing. It often helped her be creative as well. She'd come up with some of her best recipes while rock music blared in her ears. Still, she was surprised it had managed to lift her out of the hellish mood she'd been in after watching Bill and the boys drive away.

She'd been low enough at that point that Alex had almost given up and just gone home to bed to sleep the rest of her life away. However, she'd always been a fighter, and the mood hadn't lasted long. After allowing herself a few minutes to indulge in a self-pity party, she'd managed to gather herself, grab her purse, and head for the paint store. As Bill had said, if she wanted it painted, she would have to do it herself. Certainly, there was no way she was going to get another painting company to send men out past dinnertime on a Friday night. She was it.

After hitting the paint store for primer and painting paraphernalia, Alex had swung by the hardware store for a ladder before returning to settle into doing it herself. Oddly enough, she found the experience rather soothing. There was something about emptying your mind and simply letting it drift while your body worked . . . it did wonders for her stress level. Unfortunately, once the tension had left, other sensations had started to make their way to the surface . . . like hunger . . . and thirst. Sadly, food was the one thing she hadn't thought to buy while on her shopping trip.

Grimacing at her hunger pangs, Alex turned to run the roller through the tray, only to find she'd used up the last of the paint in it. Pausing, she glanced toward the ground and the paint can waiting there, and then back to the wall. She was no professional but thought she was doing a pretty good job so far. She'd gotten the primer up and was now working on the first coat of White Sand, with two walls and part of a third done. Despite the primer, it was going to take two coats to finish the walls properly, and she'd hoped to get at least the first coat done before going out in search of food.

However, her stomach felt like it was taking an acid

bath and, frankly, she was running low on energy. Her legs had actually started shaking a couple of times as she'd worked on this third wall. Shaky legs and ladders just didn't seem like a good combination to her. It would be more sensible to take a break now and finish after she'd hit a fast-food joint or something.

As a chef, Alex would never admit to anyone that she enjoyed anything as pedestrian as rubbery burgers with reconstituted onions and processed, half-wax cheese on them, but at times like this, cheeseburgers were a fast treat that would hit the spot.

Smiling at the thought, Alex set the roller in the tray, picked it up in one hand, and carefully backed down off the ladder. She'd bought several rollers so didn't bother washing this one. Instead, she left it to dry, closed the paint can, and then headed toward the back of the restaurant. After washing her hands, she ducked into her office to retrieve her purse and coat. A moment later, she was letting herself out the back door, and then nearly jumping out of her skin when something brushed her arm.

Alex whirled to see what it was, shrieking when she saw the dark figure looming over her. Wielding her purse like a weapon, she instinctively began to thrash her attacker with it, slamming it over his head with one hand as she punched at his stomach, his arm, and anything else she could reach with her other.

Fortunately, her earplugs got jerked from her ears with the action and she became aware that her "attacker" was shouting her name between efforts to block her blows. Ending her assault, she stepped warily back, eyeing the dark figure. Her voice was shaky as she asked, "Who are you?"

"Cale Valens," he answered with a sigh, straightening from the slightly hunched position he'd taken when she started assaulting him.

"Cale?" Eyes widening with disbelief, she asked, "My chef, Cale?"

"Sort of," he muttered.

Alex was digging in her purse for her keys and silently berating herself for not turning on the outer lights and checking the small parking lot behind the restaurant before stepping out. She found her keys and pulled them out, then quickly flicked on the attached tiny flashlight to run over him. It was definitely Cale, her chef, she noted, and frowned at the way his eyes seemed to glow in the darkness. A trick of the light, she told herself, and glanced around uncertainly. The parking lot was empty except for her car.

"Where's your car?" she asked.

"Parked out front. I was originally at the front door, but couldn't get your attention. When I saw you head for the back of the restaurant, I came around back, hoping you were coming out," he explained quietly, and then urged her hand holding the flashlight away so it was no longer shining in his face. "Would you mind? That's very bright."

"Sorry," she muttered, shutting it off. Alex shifted from one foot to the other, her gaze sliding to her car as she contemplated the meal she had been heading out to collect, but then sighed, and asked, "What are you doing here?"

"Bev mentioned you had run into a problem and I wondered if I might help," he said quietly.

"Why?" she asked with surprise, drawing a short laugh from him.

"Do Canadians not believe in helping others when they are in need?" he asked rather than answer the question.

"Well, yes, but you don't even know me," she pointed out dryly.

"I'd like to," he responded, and Alex stilled in surprise. She'd become so used to men simply walking away or ignoring her lately that his words quite took her breath away. It was a bit stunning . . . and—if she was honest with herself—tempting. Cale was a good-looking man, and at another time she might have been pleased to let him get to know her, but this wasn't the time. Alex had a restaurant to get up and running and another to keep from floundering. Flirting with a coworker or—even worse—an employee just wasn't smart.

Shaking her head, she said quietly, "I'm afraid I don't have time in my life right now to get to know anyone. Excuse me."

Alex turned to cross the short distance to her car but was only halfway to it when Cale was at her side again.

"Where are you going?" he asked, matching his step to hers as she walked around her car.

"Home," she lied, hoping that would get rid of him, but instead she caught him shaking his head out of the corner of her eye.

"I don't think so. You left the lights on in the restaurant and you haven't finished painting yet," Cale commented.

Alex stopped at the driver's side door and glanced at him sharply. "You were looking through the windows?"

"I have been here quite a while. I did knock several times, but you apparently couldn't hear me with your headphones on," he said wryly. "Besides, it is a business, not a private home. You needn't make it sound like I am a Peeping Paul."

"Peeping Tom," she corrected absently, wondering how long he'd been watching her. Deciding it didn't matter she hit the button to unlock her car and pulled the driver's door open. "Fine, I'm not going home, I'm heading out to get something to eat. But I have a lot on my plate and really don't have time for men right now, so good night."

Alex then quickly slid into her car and pulled the door closed before he could say anything else to tempt her. Fortunately, he didn't make a pest of himself but backed a couple of steps away from the car. Breathing out a little sigh of relief, Alex stuck her key in the ignition and quickly cranked it forward, only to freeze as all she got was a *click click click*.

"Oh, you've got to be kidding me," she muttered, cranking the key again with the same result. She was no mechanic, that had been her father, and while he'd tried to teach her the fundamentals about cars when she was young, she hadn't paid much attention. Still, she knew that sound couldn't be a good sign. Alex tried a third time with the same result, and then groaned and let her head drop to rest on the steering wheel in despair. This was the living end. She just could not handle all these problems hitting her one right after the other. What the hell had she ever done to deserve this ridiculous run of bad luck? She was a good person, generally nonjudgmental and nice to everyone she met. She also gave to charity. What the hell had she done to deserve this?

A tap at her window made her raise her head to peer out at Cale. To give him credit, he looked concerned rather than smug about her latest problem, which was nice since she'd just basically told him to hit the road in a very polite way. Alex heaved out a breath and straightened in her seat. Forgetting that the engine hadn't started, she hit the button to unroll the window, realized her mistake when nothing happened, and instead opened the door.

"Can I help?" he offered quietly.

Alex felt her lips twist and asked, "Do you know anything about cars?"

"No. It is not my area of expertise," he admitted apologetically. "But I have my rental car here and can take you where you wish to go."

Alex stared at him silently, debating the matter. She suspected most men would have wasted her time banging around under the hood, and then simply given her some spiel about not having the parts to fix it rather than admit they didn't know how. She appreciated his honesty, but she'd just told him she didn't have time for a man, and she didn't. Would accepting his help now constitute using him? Would he expect something from her in return? Did she care? Frankly, Alex was so hungry she would start eating paint chips if she didn't find some food.

"No strings attached," Cale added solemnly, and that was enough for her.

"What the hell," she muttered, grabbing her purse and quickly getting out of the car.

They were both silent as they walked around the building. For her part, Alex was too tired to come up with anything to say. She wasn't even considering what she was going to do about her car. She was simply concentrating on putting one foot in front of the other and not falling on her butt on the icy concrete. As for Cale, she had no idea why he was so silent.

She'd half expected him to redouble his efforts to convince her to let him "get to know her." However, he didn't and was also silent as he ushered her to a Lexus parked on the street in front of her restaurant.

Alex murmured her thanks as he opened the door and took her elbow to aid her in. He then closed the door for her before hurrying around to the driver's side, and Alex wondered if good manners were a European thing. She had never had a Canadian man see her into a vehicle like she was spun glass that needed coddling.

She quickly did up her seat belt, and then glanced to Cale as the driver's side door opened. He got into the car on a cold breeze carrying a combination of citrus and a woodsy aroma she couldn't identify. Toronto air had never smelled that good. Alex was pretty sure the scent was his, some designer aftershave she guessed, and found herself inhaling deeply with appreciation.

"Where would you like to go?" Cale asked, starting the engine before doing up his own seat belt.

Alex opened her mouth, and then hesitated about admitting she'd planned to hit a fast-food joint. He was a Parisian chef, for heaven's sake, and would no doubt sneer at the thought of fast food. On the other hand, she wasn't interested in him and shouldn't care, Alex reminded herself and spat out the name with defiance.

"And where is that?" Cale asked, not even arching a supercilious eyebrow at her choice.

Alex found herself relaxing and gave the directions. It wasn't far, and she hadn't considered that it was past midnight, so was relieved to see that the restaurant had a twenty-four-hour drive-thru.

It quickly became obvious Cale had never gone to a drive-thru before. Alex found herself biting her lip with amusement when he rolled the window all the way down and leaned half out of it to talk directly into the speaker. Her eyebrows rose with surprise, however, when he gave her order, hesitated, and then said, "Double everything please, it's for two."

Alex now suspected she was going to have company for her meal. She'd been hoping he'd simply drive her back and drop her off with her booty, allowing her to get on with her business. But if he asked to join her to eat, it would really be rude to refuse after he'd taken her to the restaurant and back . . . and even paid for the food, she added with silent irritation when he waved away the money she offered to pay for both meals.

Alex spent the ride back to the restaurant ignoring the scents emanating from the bag on her lap and concentrating on figuring out the best way to get rid of Cale once they were done eating. A polite, "Well, I have to get back to work now, so thanks for everything," seemed the best way to go. At least that was the best she'd come up with by the time they'd reached her restaurant again.

Rather than risk a ticket for parking on the street, Alex directed him to park around back and was out of the car almost the moment he stopped. She was walking toward the back door of the restaurant, the bag of food in one hand and searching her pocket for her keys with her other when Cale called her name. Pausing impatiently, she glanced back to see him coming around the car with one of the drinks in hand.

He smiled almost painfully as he approached, and then said, "I doubled the order intending to eat as well."

"Yes, I figured that out," Alex assured him, and when he hesitated, she recognized the significance of his only carrying one drink and realized he hadn't intended on joining her as she'd feared. "Oh, I'm sorry," she said, flushing, "I thought you expected to eat here with me."

She started to shift the bag in her hands, intending to retrieve her half of the food, but he said, "Well I hadn't intended to because you'd said you were busy, but since you are inviting me, I will be pleased to join you."

"Oh, I—" Alex started to tell him that it hadn't really been an invitation, but he was already hurrying around his car to shut off the still-running engine and fetch the other drink.

Sighing, she shook her head at her own inept tendency to get herself into these ridiculous situations, and then turned and continued on to the back door of the restaurant. By the time she had unlocked it, he was behind her, and Alex pulled the door open and then held it for him to enter with the drinks. She followed him inside, but Cale paused after only a couple of steps to peer around.

A low whistle slid from his lips as he took in the setup. "It's huge."

"Three times as big as the original La Bonne Vie," Alex acknowledged proudly as she paused beside him to peer over the kitchen herself. She was rather pleased with what she'd done here. She'd designed the layout herself and thought it was perfect. There was plenty of room so people wouldn't be tripping over each other, and yet no one was so far away that they would have to raise their voices to be heard.

"You are planning for more kitchen staff, obviously," he said, glancing over the various stations.

"More than double the staff at the original restaurant," she acknowledged, "They're already hired and trained and ready to go."

He glanced at her curiously. "I am surprised you simply did not have one of them step in and take Peter's place tonight then."

Alex shook her head. "I've had them training with my staff at the other restaurant for the last month, but released them yesterday for the next two weeks so they could get themselves and everything else in order before this restaurant opens. Most of them went on vacation or headed home to move their families here this week."

When Cale raised an eyebrow, she explained, "Several were from out of town and we had an agreement to wait for the training to end before making the hiring permanent. It was in case we couldn't work together," she explained with a shrug.

While Alex had been careful about whom she hired, people presented a different side during an interview than they did in the workplace. Peter was a case in point. He'd been charming and obsequious when she'd hired him but had become an egomaniac in the kitchen. She'd wanted to avoid making that mistake again so had put the temporary clause into the agreement to try to ensure she did. Fortunately, they'd all seemed to work out very well . . . so far.

"The head chef I hired is from British Columbia, and flew home this morning to help his wife move house here. Otherwise, I'd have asked him to take over at the original restaurant until I could find a replacement."

"Aren't you going to be head chef here?" Cale asked with surprise.

Alex felt her mouth twist with displeasure as she led the way into the dining room. "That was the original plan. I'd hire a business manager to take care of the business end of both restaurants and be head chef here."

"But?" Cale prompted, following her to the center of the dining room, where she set down the bag of food and her purse and then shrugged out of her coat. Dropping that to the floor too, she plopped down to sit on the drop cloth and began to open the bag holding their food.

"But I ran into a few snags and the money started running out," she said dryly as she set out the burgers and fries. Glancing his way as he set aside his coat and settled across the food from her, she added, "Business managers are expensive."

"And head chefs aren't?" he asked with surprise.

"Really good head chefs can be expensive if they are ambitious and want to use their own recipes and eventually start their own restaurants. But the man I hired is easygoing, not very ambitious at all. He's more than happy just to cook my recipes in my restaurant and has no aspirations to be the next Gordon Ramsey." She began to unwrap a burger. "He's also originally from this end of the country, and eager enough to return that he was willing to work relatively cheaply . . . at least at first," she added on a sigh. "I've agreed to increase his pay after the first six months. By then I'm hoping the restaurant is paying for itself."

"But you would really rather be head chef yourself," he said slowly, watching almost curiously as she bit into her burger.

Alex chewed and swallowed, just managing not to murmur with pleasure as the first bite dropped into her empty stomach. She then reached for a french fry and nodded. "Of course. Cooking has always been my first love. I'd rather do that than anything in the world. And, really, if I'd known that opening this second restaurant was going to be such a pain in the ass and force me to give up cooking, I'd never have started it."

"I see." Cale carefully unwrapped his own burger.

Alex took another bite and peered wistfully around the unfinished dining room. She'd had such high hopes for this expansion, fantasies about manning the lovely new kitchen, creating amazing new recipes, serving world-class meals, and maybe even earning a much-sought-after Michelin star if Michelin ever did a travel guide for Canada. She'd heard rumors they were considering or even producing one, and it would be the highlight of her career to earn a Michelin star or two or three.

But those were just fantasies. The grim reality was that, thanks to all the problems she'd run into with opening this restaurant, she had gone through all her savings and had to take out a loan secured by her house to finish the renovations. Alex would now be happy just to get this restaurant up and running and supporting itself. The hope that it would do well enough that she could pay off all of her debt and hire a business manager so that she could return to cooking was just that, a hope. And it was starting to look like something not likely to happen until sometime in the very distant future . . . if at all. Alex now sincerely wished she'd never started this project. She'd been happy in her own little kitchen at the original La Bonne Vie with a nice little nest egg. Why hadn't she simply been content with that?

"This is good."

The surprised exclamation from Cale drew Alex away from her thoughts. She glanced curiously his way to see him lifting the top bun of his burger to peer at what was underneath as he enthusiastically chewed the food in his mouth. Smiling slightly, she said, "It's just a cheeseburger. Have you never had one before?"

Cale shook his head, too busy biting into the burger again to actually answer with words.

Alex chuckled softly and took another bite of her own burger, watching with amusement as Cale once again opened his burger to look at the fixings.

"A burger is beef, *oui*?" he asked, peering at the patty.

"Yes," she said with a laugh.

"And these little white things?" he asked, poking at the fixings on top.

"Reconstituted onions," she answered.

"Reconstituted?"

"They dry them out and ship them to the restaurant, where they're soaked in water to reinflate them before putting them on the burgers."

"Why?" he asked with surprise.

Alex shrugged. "Perhaps they feel real onions would be overpowering on the little burgers. They use real, fresh onion on the larger burgers."

"Hmm." Cale took another bite, apparently not bothered that these onions had been dehydrated and then rehydrated before landing on his burger.

Alex watched him for a moment, surprised by how much he seemed to be enjoying the simple meal. He was eating like a starving man, she thought, and then shook her head and turned her attention back to her own food.

"So," Cale murmured as he swallowed the last bite of his burger and turned his attention to the little packet of fries. He took one of the pale sticks out and peered at it curiously, then continued, "If you found someone who would manage both businesses at a low wage, you could return to cooking?"

"In my dreams," Alex muttered, and popped a fry into her own mouth. A good business manager to oversee both restaurants would cost at least twice what she was paying either of her head chefs, who while carrying the title head chef, were actually working as *sous-chefs* or even station chefs. She herself was still making all the decisions, creating the menu, managing the staff, handling scheduling and payroll and doing all the other things a head chef usually dealt with. She just wasn't getting to cook anymore.

"This would make you happy, *oui*?" Cale asked, and his accent was thicker than usual.

Alex glanced up to see that he was watching her solemnly as he awaited her answer. That, as well as the fact that his accent had thickened, made her suspect that her answer was important somehow.

"Of course it would," she answered honestly. "I hate the business end of things. I am not an organized type person by nature. I'm more a creative sort, used to chaos."

"Chaos?"

Alex nodded. "Flour and other ingredients everywhere, the clang of pots and pans, the clack of dinnerware, the smell of Italian seasonings or spicy herbs from the entrées competing with the vanilla and lemon from the dessert area." She shrugged. "It's usually controlled chaos in the kitchens every night, and I love it. Sitting in an airless little office trying to make the debit and credit columns balance is like some sort of torture to me." She sighed. "Besides, while I've always thought of myself as an easygoing, diplomatic sort, I've found that I'm really not very good in a crisis."

Alex grimaced, and told him, "I'm afraid I've been reduced to shrieking a couple of times this last week when things went wrong. I guess the stress is getting to me."

"Hmm." Cale cleared his throat and said, "Then I think I can help get you back to cooking, Alex."

"How?" she asked with surprise.

"I am not really a chef."

Five

'What? What did you just say?'

Cale considered Alex's expression, and said more slowly, "I'm not a chef. I am a businessman."

"But you—I hired you to—Oh my God!" Panic on her face now, Alex stood up and began to search her pockets.

When she came up with her phone and began to punch in numbers, Cale frowned and stood up as well. "Who are you calling?"

"Bev," she snapped. "I have to see if you've ruined me or not."

"I haven't ruined you," he assured her quickly. "Please, Alex, put that away and hear me out."

"No. I—" She paused and peered at him narrowly. "You cooked the Trout Amandine. It was perfect."

"Er . . . yes . . . well . . ." Cale frowned, trying to decide how best to handle this. Obviously, he should

have taken a moment to think this through before opening his damned mouth. His only thought had been that
she loved cooking and he enjoyed business, so why not
switch and let him help with managing things rather
than the cooking? Cale had thought she'd be pleased
to get back to cooking and leave the business issues
to him. And he suspected she would be, but starting
with "I'm not a chef" probably hadn't been the clever-
est way to go. Alex wasn't ready for the "I'm not a chef
but a vampire" speech, and he couldn't explain that he
wasn't really a chef without explaining how he had then
managed to keep from ruining her restaurant's reputation tonight.

Jesus, I'm obviously not on my game tonight, Cale
acknowledged, and suspected it was this life-mate
business that was at fault. Despite Marguerite's "feeling" and Sam's excitement, and even Bricker's taunts,
he really hadn't been prepared to walk in there and
discover Alex was indeed his life mate . . . and he
wasn't handling the situation with his usual aplomb. He
needed to turn this around and quickly, or he suspected
she'd be tossing him out on his ear at any moment.

Before Cale could quite decide how to save the situation, Alex stopped glaring at him to concentrate on the
phone as it was obviously answered on the other end.

"I'm sorry I woke you, Bev," Alex said grimly. "But I
need to know what happened at the restaurant tonight."

Cale didn't have to hear the woman's voice to know
what she would say. They had made sure that neither
she nor the other staff was aware of Marguerite and
Leigh's presence in the kitchen. Still, he was relieved

as he listened to Bev assure Alex that everything had gone like clockwork and Cale had been a great success. Everyone had raved about his food, the woman told her, and one of the city's most respected food critics had been a diner at one of the tables and had been so pleased he'd revealed himself and promised a very complimentary review in Saturday's food section.

Alex was looking more and more confused as the woman spoke, and when she ended the call, she turned that confused look on Cale. Her expression shifted to grim, however, as she slid the phone back into her pocket. "Was that your idea of a joke? Bev said everything went well tonight. Better than well. What—?"

"Just sit down, Alex," Cale interrupted quietly. "I'll explain everything."

She hesitated, but then settled back where she had been. Cale immediately sat across from her, wondering how the hell he was going to explain this . . . and then inspiration struck. "I fear my English isn't as good as I would wish, and I occasionally misspeak when trying to explain things."

He was just congratulating himself on coming up with that when she said dubiously, "It sounded pretty clear to me. *I am not a chef* is pretty plain."

Cale grimaced. "Yes, well, I meant to say that I am not a chef like you. You said cooking was your first love, while business is not. I am the opposite, I love managing the business end of things and would rather not be cooking." When her eyes narrowed, he added, "Unlike you, I was not following a dream when I got into cooking."

But he was actually following a dream when he'd agreed to be the chef Alex needed tonight, he realized. The dream of getting close to and claiming his life mate. It was a lifelong dream, really. One every immortal had.

"I got into cooking due to family pressure," he said. It wasn't exactly a lie. Sam had gotten him into this, and she was Alex's family. If he were lucky, she would be his family soon as well.

"Ah," Alex murmured, nodding solemnly. "I see. A family restaurant . . . pressure from the folks to train as a chef and take over the business . . ." She nodded again, apparently sure she had it all figured out. "Cooking isn't in your soul, but your blood."

"Blood certainly has a lot to do with my situation," Cale muttered.

"What was that?" Alex asked.

"Nothing," he said quickly. "The point is I really dislike cooking. I prefer the simple logic of business and would much rather tend that end of things for you and leave you to the cooking."

Alex tilted her head slightly, uncertainty on her face. "I really didn't expect you to spend your entire vacation helping out at the restaurant. I thought—well hoped really—that you would be willing to cook for just a couple of nights until I could find someone to replace Peter."

"I am happy to help for as long as it takes," he assured her. "And as the business manager, I would be pleased to take care of the matter of a replacement for Peter if it is necessary."

"If it's necessary?" she asked with surprise.

Cale hesitated, but then decided it might be pushing his luck to tell her he was hoping for a much more permanent situation with her. Besides, if he did manage to convince her to be his life mate, he didn't know what that might mean for both their lives. He had been feeling the need for a change and would be happy to leave his companies in Europe in the hands of his managers, merely overseeing it from Canada as he helped run her restaurants, but Alex might change her mind about the direction of her life. It wasn't uncommon for new life mates to do so.

Shrugging, he merely said, "I will look into available people for the position and leave the final decision up to you."

She relaxed and nodded slowly. Her expression turned thoughtful, and he was sure she was about to agree, but Alex was a businessperson and apparently had learned some caution when it came to such decisions. It seemed that, as tempting as the idea of returning to cooking must be to her, she wasn't going to leap at the opportunity because she said, "I need to think about this."

"Of course," he murmured.

"And I don't have time for that right now," she added with a glance toward the waiting walls. A little sigh slid from her lips and she moved toward the tray and roller she'd left earlier. "I appreciate the offer, but I won't just let the first handsome face convince me to hand over my business."

"You find me handsome?" Cale asked with a grin, kneeling to open the can of paint for her.

Alex flushed, but rolled her eyes and ignored the question, merely taking the now-open can from him to pour the thick liquid into the tray, as she continued, "I'll need to know your qualifications and what experience you have. I hate to ask for a résumé, but it would really help me with the decision."

"I shall give it to you orally while I help you paint," he said solemnly, and Alex set the can down and glanced to him with a frown.

"That isn't necessary. I don't expect you to help with this. It isn't under the job description of either a chef or a business manager. Besides, you aren't exactly dressed for it," she pointed out.

Cale glanced down at his designer suit, and then shrugged and began to remove the jacket. "I have several of these and this one is old anyway. Besides, in my experience, a good business manager does whatever needs doing. As you have done."

Alex grimaced. "I didn't really have much choice when the painters took off."

"There are always choices," he said solemnly. "Not always good ones, but there *are* choices, and here you made the responsible one."

"That's me, responsible Alex," she said with a little self-derision, and turned to start back up her ladder with the tray. She set it on the holder at the top of the ladder and then glanced down to him. "Can you hand me the roller, please?"

"Certainly." He picked it up and passed it to her, watched briefly as she began to run it through the paint in the tray, and then glanced around. "Is there another tray and roller?"

Alex paused and glanced down to him. "You really don't have to—"

"I want to," he interrupted firmly.

She stared at him for a moment but then shrugged and pointed to a corner near the front of the room. "There's another tray and roller there. I don't have another ladder though, so you'll have to do the lower half while I do the top."

"You're the boss," Cale said lightly, and moved to find the extra tray and rollers. He had set himself up with paint and was starting on the lower half of the wall beside her when she asked her first question.

"So, I gather you run the business end of the family restaurant in Paris as well as cook there on occasion? Or have you managed to get away from cooking altogether?"

Cale frowned at the wall he was painting, knowing he would have to be careful here. He suspected Marguerite was right, and a relationship based on lies was not a good thing, so he really didn't want to lie any more than necessary. Finally, he said, "Until tonight I have not cooked for a very long time."

That was true enough, he *had* cooked before. He had roasted meat over an open fire several times in his youth. It wasn't exactly Cordon Bleu cooking, but was cooking nonetheless.

"So you just run the restaurant now?" Alex asked curiously over the quiet shush of her roller running up and down the wall.

Cale grimaced, his hand automatically moving his own roller over the wall as he thought. He didn't run a restaurant at all, but didn't think saying that would be too smart, so instead said, "I run several businesses in Europe, most of them having to do with the travel industry and transport of goods."

"Travel and transport? How did you go from a restaurant to travel and transport?" she asked with surprise.

"They are not that dissimilar," he said, and thought that was true. Argentis Inc. and Argeneau Enterprises held sway in Canada and the US, as well as the UK, but Cale had his own version of the company in France, Italy, and Spain called Valens Industries.

He ran blood banks and saw to the blood's distribution, feeding the masses . . . at least the immortal masses. He also catered to immortals' needs in other ways. One company was purely for travel, with flights that started and ended in the evenings so immortals needn't travel with mortals if they did not wish. It also assisted with recommending and booking places for them to stay at their destination, transportation while there, the supply of blood during their stay, and provided them with booklets of the local haunts catering to their kind.

Cale also had another operation that aided with ID and other things immortals needed when they changed names and moved house.

He couldn't tell Alex that, though, so said, "I deal with a special-needs clientele who doesn't wish to utilize the usual transport available and travel with the masses."

"Ah, rich folk who want special attention," Alex said dryly. "We get a lot of those at my restaurant too."

"Yes, I'm sure you do," Cale murmured, and thought she would be surprised to know that a good many of them were immortals. According to Leigh and Marguerite, several of the family who had found their life mates and were eating again frequented La Bonne Vie and adored the food there. Leigh had been ecstatic about gaining access to the recipes for the sauces she'd been creating in his stead last night. Although she'd been quick to assure him that it wouldn't prevent her and Lucian from frequenting the restaurant, claiming that food always tasted better when someone else cooked it.

"What goods do you transport?" she asked, drawing him from his thoughts.

Cale sighed to himself. This not-lying business could be quite tiresome. After taking a moment to debate, he continued vaguely, "These special clientele often have needs they wish filled that are not the usual items that can be bought at a grocery store."

"Please don't tell me you're talking prostitutes here," Alex said, tipping her head to look down at him with worry.

"No. Merely exotic beverages or unusual items," he assured her with a laugh. You didn't get more exotic than blood as a beverage, or the occasional coffin to sleep in for old-timers who disliked giving up the old ways. At least, they would certainly be exotic and unusual to mortals.

"Exotic beverages," she murmured, shaking her

head. Alex then wrinkled her nose, and asked, "And you really enjoy the business end of things?"

Cale chuckled at her expression. "It is not all as tedious as you seem to find it. There is the challenge of resolving problems, the excitement of new projects, the—"

"Yeah, yeah, I'll take your word for it," she interrupted with disgust. "Frankly, problem solving is not one of my strong suits . . . unless it's a problem like reducing the acid content of a tomato-based sauce, or how to get a soufflé perfect. I'm better with food than people. People tend to piss me off."

He glanced up at her with surprise. "But you own a restaurant. You must deal with people day in and day out."

Alex waved that suggestion away. "I deal with my kitchen staff, who are intelligent and good at what they do. I don't have to deal with whiny customers who order something they've never heard of like gazpacho, and then complain that it's cold, not knowing that's how it's to be served." She clucked with irritation. "And I certainly am not used to dealing with the ineptitude of salespeople who write down the wrong numbers and get completely inappropriate and unwanted goods sent to me like lime green carpet and paint, and screaming orange bathroom tiles."

"Did that happen?" Cale asked with surprise.

Alex set her roller in the tray with a sigh, and then stretched her back and nodded. "Why do you think I'm painting? I hired men to do this, but by the time I got back from the old restaurant tonight, the wrong paint had been delivered and the painters had almost finished painting the walls with it," she explained with disgust and shook her head. "The walls looked like someone had puked green slime all over them."

Cale glanced at the unpainted portion of wall and noted the green tint to the white primer they were covering. He ran his roller through the paint in the tray again and continued painting as he asked, "And the green carpet?"

"The same deal. I had a project manager then and was working at the other restaurant training the new crew. I stopped in here to check on things after closing and found the floor carpeted in a sea of pea green rather than the shade I had chosen. I nearly had a heart attack, and it was too late at night to do a damned thing about it. I spent most of the next morning making calls trying to get it straightened out."

"Obviously you did," Cale commented, glancing down at the dark carpet visible through the drop cloth.

Alex snorted. "Yeah. But it cost me. The project manager had signed for the carpet, and it couldn't be returned because it had already been laid. Basically, I had to buy it all over again to get the right color installed."

"Is that when you fired the project manager?" Cale asked, shifting his tray further to the right to continue painting.

"No," Alex said on a sigh. "He said he'd forgotten what color it was I'd chosen and I hadn't shown him. I thought it was just a one-off. So I bit the bullet on that one, but then the same thing happened with the tiles for the bathroom and kitchens."

"Screaming orange?" he asked, recalling her earlier words.

"Yes," she said with displeasure. "And that time I had reminded him of what color the tiles should be that morning. I even called the store the night before delivery and made the store clerk read the numbers out to me to be sure they matched the ones on my receipt."

"They did?" he asked.

"Oh yeah, so I went to work in the old restaurant sure everything would be fine, only to arrive to the orange tiles covering the kitchen and bathrooms that night."

"The project manager allowed them to be installed?" Cale asked with a frown.

Alex snorted with disgust. "Turns out my project manager was a raging alcoholic and apparently off-site more than he was on. That day he arrived with a hangover, let the installers in, then left them to sign for the tiles and went to pass out in my office." She shook her head with a sigh. "But I wasn't about to bite the bullet this time. The tiles I had ordered were a ridiculously expensive Italian import. They cost as much as everything else put together."

"What happened?" Cale asked.

Alex's mouth twisted bitterly. "The head tile guy was smarter than the carpet installers. He thought the orange might be wrong and tried to wake up the project manager, but he was out cold. So he double-checked the tile numbers on the receipt against the numbers on the boxes before accepting them, and the numbers were the same so he just decided I had bad taste and went ahead with it."

She glanced down and smiled wryly when she saw Cale's surprised expression. "I checked the numbers myself, and they were indeed the same. It seems the salesman had mistakenly reversed two numbers when writing them down, and the orange tiles were what were on the order . . . and I'd signed the damned thing without double-checking. I'd gotten exactly what I'd signed for."

Cale winced and guessed, "The supplier wouldn't replace them?"

Alex snorted and turned back to her work. "The orange ones had been installed. They had to be torn out and didn't come out intact . . . and like I said, they were superexpensive. He wasn't taking that kind of loss if he didn't have to. Unfortunately, my signing the order with the wrong numbers got him off the hook. Legally, it was my fault. Buyer beware and all that."

"And now the paint," Cale murmured, frowning as he continued painting as well.

"Yes, well, after the tiles, I fired the project manager." She scowled at the wall, and admitted, "It was too late though. Replacing the tiles, even with less expensive ones, pretty much wiped me out financially and I couldn't afford to hire another manager. But I needed someone here to make sure there were no more errors like that. I certainly couldn't afford another mistake, so I promoted Peter to head chef two weeks ago, so that I could be here at all times and double-check everything."

"But?" Cale prompted, knowing something had gone wrong or they wouldn't now be repainting the walls.

"I ran over to the old restaurant today to pick up some papers, and the paint showed up a little early. Plus, I was much longer than I intended to be thanks to Peter quitting and my having to find a replacement. By the time I left you at the restaurant and got back here, more than four hours had passed." She shrugged unhappily. "In the meantime, the wrong paint had arrived and the men started painting."

"Ah," Cale breathed. He worked in silence for a minute, and then asked, "Are you having to swallow the expense for this mix-up as well?"

Alex shrugged unhappily. "Probably. The men signed for the paint. And it was used, or most of it was. The store manager said to bring back any paint that hadn't been opened, which is one can," she added dryly.

"I'm guessing you checked the receipt to be sure you'd ordered the right one this time?" he queried gently.

Alex nodded. "Both the billing receipt and the delivery invoice say White Sand."

"And the cans?" Cale asked.

Alex stopped painting and glanced down at him with surprise. She obviously hadn't thought to check the cans. Setting her roller in the tray, she hurried off the ladder and moved to the used and unopened cans of paint she'd set in the corner. Cale immediately set down his own roller and followed.

Pausing at her side, he quickly glanced over the cans. The lids to the used ones were off and lying on their tops on the drop cloth, but the full one still had its top on.

"That one says White Sand," he pointed out, gesturing to the unopened can. His gaze slid to the half-used can. The lid had been replaced, but a smudge of green paint covered the label. Cale knelt and began returning the other lids to their cans. A few also had their label obscured, but two were readable, and said "White Sand."

Cale shifted to take the unopened can in hand. Spotting the opener, he grabbed it, caught it under the lid and tore the top off the paint can. They stared at the thick green liquid revealed.

"It looks like someone mixed them wrong," Cale said quietly. "The store will have to reimburse you for this."

"And for the painter's time," she said, beaming at him as if he'd revealed a small fortune in gold dubloons in the can. Cale had no idea how much painters cost, but felt sure he hadn't saved her that much money. He suspected she was just happy to have at least one reversal of fortune, one instance where she wasn't having to bite the bullet and swallow the expense. She proved him right by saying, "Maybe this is a sign that my luck is changing. You may just be my good-luck charm, Cale. Thank you."

"My pleasure," Cale assured her, putting the lid back on the can. Straightening, he said, "I shall have it taken care of in the morning, if you like?"

Alex smiled wryly. "It would be worth it to hire you just to not have to deal with the store manager again."

"Then hire me," he said. When she hesitated, he

added, "You could return to cooking and stop worrying about all of this."

"You're like the devil whispering in my ear with temptation," she said with amusement.

"Good. Hire me," he repeated firmly.

Alex hesitated. Finally, she frowned and shook her head. "You're from France."

Cale's eyebrows shot up. "Is that a problem?"

"Well, only to the government," she said dryly. "You won't have a SIN number."

"A sin number?" he asked with confusion.

"A Social Insurance Number," she explained. "They call it a social security number in the States. I'm not sure what they call it in France, but you can't work in Canada without a Canadian SIN card . . . or at least a work Visa or something."

"I have a Social Insurance Number," he lied. Arranging for such things for immortals who wished to relocate to Canada was one of the things his companies did.

"How can you have a Social Insurance Number? You're from France," she said with confusion.

"I have dual citizenship," Cale said blandly, thinking he'd have to call his office and have his assistant arrange for a SIN card to be sent to him. Realizing she was staring at him wide-eyed, he added, "A good portion of my family lives here. It is why I came."

She tilted her head, "Is Mortimer family?"

"No. He works for my uncle, though," Cale said, and that just seemed to confuse her more.

"How can he work for your Uncle? Mortimer, Bricker, and Decker are in a band."

Cale stiffened. No one had told him that Alex thought the men were in a band. Smiling a bit stiffly, he said, "Work is perhaps the wrong term, but my uncle books their . . . er . . . concerts and appearances. They play where he sends them."

"Oh, you mean he's their agent or manager or whatever," Alex said nodding.

"Yes, that's it. He is their manager," Cale murmured, leading her back across the room. He picked up a roller, and then noting that she had finished painting the area where the ladder allowed her to reach, he took a moment to move the ladder for her.

"Thank you," Alex said as she began to climb back up it.

"De rien," Cale murmured, wondering how Lucian would feel about his new cover.

"So you're here visiting family," Alex commented as she set back to work, and then gave a slight laugh. "I'm glad to hear it. I thought maybe you weren't too bright, vacationing here during the coldest season."

Cale smiled faintly, but said, "I'm sure there is a lot to do here in the winter."

"Oh yeah," she agreed with amusement. "Ski, snowmobile, or huddle inside by a warm fire until the cold passes. I tend to prefer the latter."

"You don't like to ski?" he asked, wondering what she did for fun, or if she even took the time to do anything fun. He suspected Alex was a workaholic. Successful people usually were.

"I've never been," Alex admitted with a shrug. "I've always wanted to try, but never really had the opportunity or time . . . Snowmobiling sounds like it might be fun too, but I've never tried that either."

Cale was thinking that perhaps he should arrange an outing for her to try both activities, when she said, "I'm sorry about roping you into work tonight when you're here to visit family."

"Not at all," he said at once. "I merely would have been sitting in my hotel tonight anyway." It wasn't true of course. Cale probably would have been having a powwow with Marguerite and Lucian, and most likely Sam and Mortimer, trying to figure out a different way to get close to Alex. In fact, her bad luck had actually been his good fortune . . . even if he couldn't cook.

"I doubt you would have been sitting in a hotel," Alex said at once. "Your family is probably eager to see you and . . ." She paused and quit painting to frown down at him. "Working for me would prevent your seeing them."

"They all have jobs," he said quickly. "Working would fill my time while they were unavailable."

"Oh, yes, I hadn't thought of that," she said, but her hand had slowed and she glanced down to ask, "You're staying in a hotel rather than with your relatives?"

Cale chuckled at the question. "I had several offers to stay with relatives, but since most of them just got married, I thought they might not really appreciate my intruding."

"Most of them just got married?" Alex glanced down at him sharply. "You aren't related to that family Sam is always talking about, are you? The Argeneaus? They just had some big multicouple wedding in New York last weekend."

Cale nodded. "I flew to New York for the wedding, stayed in the city for several days to do some business and see a Broadway show or two, and then flew up here."

"When are you flying home?" she asked.

Cale paused. He hadn't actually set a date. He'd left his return date open because he hadn't been sure how long he'd wish to stay. He'd wanted to look into business opportunities here while visiting. Mind you, he hadn't expected to be taking on a job in such short order but was happy to go with what fate was presently offering if it allowed him a chance to win Alex. The question was, how long would that take?

Frowning, he rubbed his stomach absently as he tried to figure it out. He knew mortals expected a courtship. But how long would that take? A week? Two weeks? Months?

"Two months," he answered, just to be on the safe side.

"You can take that much time away from your businesses?" Alex asked with surprise.

"Good bosses understand that working themselves to exhaustion does no one any good," he said meaningfully, glancing at his watch. When Alex grimaced at the gentle reprimand, he added, "I have good employees working for me, ones I trust to handle the day-to-day issues. They will call if anything important comes up, but otherwise, probably won't even miss me."

"Huh," Alex muttered. "It must be nice."

"You have good people working for you," Cale said quietly. "I suspect Peter wasn't, but Bev is a jewel, and Bobby and Rebecca seem quite competent."

"They are," she agreed. "Bev has been a surprise. She held Bobby's job before, and I've always known she was good, but she's slid into the *sous-chef* position as smoothly as if she's always been doing it. I actually considered promoting her to head chef and looking for her replacement."

"Why didn't you?" Cale asked.

Alex hesitated, then admitted wryly, "Because I'm hoping to return to the position of head chef myself eventually and would feel bad about demoting her when I did."

"Ah," Cale said with understanding. Rubbing his stomach, he paused to peer at their work. He was finished with the lower portion of the wall all the way to the end and ready to start on the next wall. Alex was a little further behind, but that was a good thing. He could get started on the next wall and be out of the way of her ladder by the time she got there. He shifted his tray to get started.

"So, what got you into cooking?" Cale asked as he set back to work.

Alex smiled faintly and admitted, "Believe it or not, it was my grandfather."

"Really?" he asked with interest and glanced around to see her nod.

"He was a cook in the army when he was young, and then a line cook when he came back. He loved to cook and sort of infected me with it." She paused to run her roller in paint and then said, "He was my best friend."

Cale raised an eyebrow. "Your grandfather?"

"Yeah." Alex laughed at his expression, and then shrugged. "My family moved every year until I was about ten. It made it hard to make and keep friends."

"Why did your family move so much?"

Alex blew her breath out, but said, "My dad was a mechanic who wanted his own shop and was also handy around the house, and my mom was a secretary with a good eye for interior design who supported his dream. The year I was born, they bought an old heap of a house, spent a year fixing it up around their jobs, and then sold it and bought another. They did that every year until I was about ten, when they finally had enough money to start Dad's garage.

"That's when Gramps, my mother's father, moved in. Mom and Dad worked long hours to make a go of the garage, and Gramps had just retired. His health wasn't very good, so he moved in to help out with us kids. I have two younger sisters," she paused to explain. "Sam you've met, and the baby of the family is Jo, who's traveling in Europe right now with her boyfriend."

"Anyway, the years Gramps lived with us were the best ever," she said with a fond smile. "Every day after school, we'd come home to find him whistling as he pulled cookies or some other small treat from the oven. He'd say, 'Do your homework, girls, and you can have one . . . But only one each. We don't want to spoil your appetite for dinner.'" She chuckled. "We used to rush through our homework in record time, and then he'd bring the treats out and sit down with us at the table, and we'd all eat one with a glass of milk while we told him about our day."

"He usually sent us to watch television then while he started dinner, but I'd leave Jo and Sam watching cartoons and go into the kitchen to bother Gramps. I'd ask what he was doing, and why he was putting this or that in, and he'd explain patiently and give me a small task to do. By the time I started high school, he was letting me do larger tasks and even letting me cook while he assisted me. I've loved cooking ever since, and when I graduated from high school, I decided to train as a chef."

"Your grandfather must have been proud," Cale said, and frowned when he saw sadness claim her face.

"I'm afraid he never knew. He died of a heart attack toward the end of my last year at high school."

"I'm sorry," Cale said quietly, absently rubbing a hand over his stomach.

"So am I." Her tone was solemn. "He was a wonderful man."

"What about your other grandparents?" Cale asked.

"Oh." Alex sighed. "My father's parents died before I was born, and my mother's mother, Gramps's wife, died of brain cancer when I was little. I don't even remember her. Gramps was it."

"Well, I'm sure he would have been proud to know you went on to become a chef."

"He would have been bursting with it," she said with a laugh. "Especially since I trained in Paris. He always used to tell me Paris produced the world's best chefs. He would have been impressed that I went there."

"You trained in Paris?" Cale stopped painting at the news that she'd been so close geographically so many years ago. If not for fate, he might have met her then.

"Nothing but Paris would do," she assured him on a wry laugh. "I was determined to be the best chef in the world."

"Did you like Paris?" he asked, wondering if she would like his home.

"I loved it," Alex assured him. "The smells, the sights, people watching . . . It's the only place I know where absolutely everyone seems to be wandering around with baguettes in hand." She grinned and admitted, "I was almost sorry to come home when I was finished training."

"But you did," he prompted when she fell silent.

"Oh yes. I managed to get a job as a line cook in a good restaurant, then worked my way up to *sous-chef,* but my dream job was head chef. It probably would have taken another four or five years to find that kind of position anywhere if I hadn't opened La Bonne Vie."

"Did you make the money for that the same way your parents did? Renovating houses?"

"No. I'm neither handy like my dad, nor do I have a good eye like my mom," she said. "I started La Bonne Vie with my share of the inheritance when my parents died in a car accident."

"I'm sorry, but I'm sure they'd be pleased with your success. The one is doing so well you're opening a second," Cale praised.

"Yeah, if I don't go bankrupt before opening night," Alex said dryly. She glanced down and suddenly asked, "Are you all right?"

The question and her concerned tone of voice made Cale look up to see her backing down the ladder.

"Jesus, you look awful," she murmured, stopping beside him. "You've been rubbing your stomach intermittently for the last little while, and I thought something might be wrong, but you're pale as death, Cale."

He glanced down to see that he was indeed rubbing his stomach. He was also suddenly aware of the gnawing sensation troubling him. He needed to feed, Cale realized unhappily. He hadn't fed since . . . well, actually he'd only had the one bag at the enforcer house in the last forty-eight hours. Cale had unexpectedly entertained a couple of cousins in his hotel in New York last week and had used up more than he'd planned during his stay. His supply had run out yesterday, but he'd decided that rather than send for more, he could hold out until he got to the hotel in Toronto, where a cooler of blood should be waiting.

Unfortunately, Cale hadn't yet made it to the hotel. He'd received a message from Marguerite asking him to stop in once he'd landed and had headed straight to her home after claiming his rental car. As it turned out, that had been something of an ambush. He'd arrived to find Marguerite, her husband Julius, and Lucian and Leigh waiting for him.

Cale hadn't even gotten through the door before

Marguerite was telling him about her certainty that Alex was the one. He'd heard her out, taking in Lucian's solemn face and crossed arms the whole while, and had known instinctively that Lucian was there to back Marguerite and would just pester him until he agreed to meeting the woman. That being the case, the first chance he'd gotten to get in a word, Cale had agreed to go to the enforcer house and arrange to meet the woman. He suspected he'd surprised everyone by agreeing so easily, but the moment he had, Marguerite had insisted he should head over at once. Lucian had spoken up then, giving him a quick rundown of the people there. He'd then given him directions before sending him on his way to the enforcer house, where he'd managed to get in one bag of blood before being hustled off to the restaurant.

That one bag hadn't been nearly enough, he acknowledged as Alex raised a hand to feel his forehead. The gnawing sensation in Cale's gut immediately intensified in response to her scent. He definitely needed to feed, he thought, and didn't realize he'd said it aloud until Alex frowned and said, "We just ate."

"It was a very small burger," he muttered and moved away, ostensibly to set down his roller, but really to get away from Alex and the blood he could actually smell pulsing under her skin.

"Yes it was," she said almost apologetically. "I always get the little cheeseburgers rather than a proper burger. It's those reconstituted onions. I really like them. Still—"

"And it's the only thing I've eaten all day," he interrupted as he straightened.

Her eyebrows flew up, and she was suddenly moving. "Okay. Time to go."

"You don't have to come with me," Cale said with alarm when she grabbed her purse and coat.

Alex shrugged her coat on. "How long have you been in Toronto?"

"Today," he admitted with confusion.

"That's what I thought. So you don't know where the nearest twenty-four-hour grocery store is. I do."

"Yes, but I can find my way back to that restaurant we visited earlier," Cale assured her, thinking he'd make a quick run to the hotel, drop off his suitcase, grab a bag or two of blood, and hit the drive-thru again on his way back. He'd enjoyed the food they'd had earlier and wouldn't mind more of it.

"No way," Alex said firmly. "There's absolutely no nutritional value to that stuff, and you haven't eaten all day. We'll go to the grocery store and gather the fixings for a nice healthy picnic."

"But I thought I'd stop and check into my hotel on the way back and drop off my luggage," he said desperately.

Alex turned to peer at him wide-eyed. "You haven't even checked into your hotel yet?"

"No. I'm afraid not. I went straight to my aunt's from the airport, then on to the . . . er . . . well Mortimer's place, and then wound up at your restaurant and now here," he finished.

"Oh, well we should head straight to the hotel first then, and we should get moving. They could give your room away," she said worriedly, rushing out of the room.

"Right," Cale muttered wearily, collecting and shrugging into his own jacket. This complicated things.

Six

'This is nice. I've never been in this hotel, but the rooms are lovely."

Cale glanced around as he followed Alex into his hotel room. It had been twenty years since he'd stayed at this particular hotel. It was owned by an immortal who ensured that the windows had blackout curtains and the closets had outlets for special travel refrigerators. That thought in mind, Cale paused to open the sliding glass door to see if his blood had been delivered. The closet was empty.

"What's wrong?" Alex asked coming up beside him.

Cale forced away a frown. "Nothing. I was just debating whether to change or not."

She looked him up and down. "Well, I guess that depends on whether you were planning to help me finish the painting or not . . . I mean, you don't have to if you—"

"I'm helping," he interrupted as she began to babble.

"Thanks," Alex said softly, and then cleared her throat. "Then you should probably change. You seem to have managed to avoid getting any on your suit yet, but I wouldn't want you to tempt fate." She glanced around and then said, "I need to go to the washroom. You could change out here while I—" She paused suddenly and frowned. "Or did you want to shower or something?"

"Why? Do I stink?" Cale asked with amusement, and she flushed.

"No, of course not. I just thought, well I always feel like showering after a flight, and you did spend all those hours over a hot grill and—"

"I'm good. A shower would just delay eating. I'll shower after we finish painting. You go ahead and go to the washroom, and I'll change."

Alex nodded and moved to the bathroom door. "I'll take my time."

Cale wheeled his suitcase to the bed, opened it, and rifled through the contents in search of a casual shirt and jeans. He then quickly stripped off his clothes and began to dress. He'd pulled on his jeans, done them up, and picked up the long-sleeved maroon shirt he'd taken out when a knock sounded at the door. Taking the shirt, he crossed the room to answer it and released a relieved breath when he saw the man on the other side holding a large cooler in hand.

"Come in," he said, and glanced toward the closed bathroom door as he made way for the man to enter.

"Where do you want this?" the deliveryman asked, moving into the room.

"Here." Cale opened the closet door.

"Nice setup," the man said as he paused beside Cale and peered into the unusually deep closet with the plug socket against the back wall. He set down the cooler and plugged it in, explaining, "This is the newest model. Portable. You can hook it into your car lighter if you need to take it on the road."

"Great, thanks." Cale tipped the man and saw him out. He then immediately moved back to the waiting cooler. Squatting in the closet door, he flipped the lid open. One glimpse of the bags of dark red blood inside was enough to make his teeth start to drop, and Cale immediately grabbed a bag and popped it to the sharp tips. He then simply squatted there as the liquid was sucked up into his teeth and body.

Cale hesitated after the first bag, wondering if he had enough time for another, but the fact that his stomach cramps had barely lessened made him decide to take the chance. The bag was only half-empty, however, when the bathroom door began to open.

"Knock knock. I'm coming out. Are you decent?" Alex's voice sang out teasingly, and Cale reacted with all the aplomb you'd expect from a man of his considerable age: He half stumbled and half fell into the closet, pulling the door closed behind him with panic.

"Cale?" he heard Alex say uncertainly from the room. "Where are you?"

Cursing silently, Cale stood up in the closet, and then cursed aloud as his head slammed into the clothing rod.

"Cale?" there was a nervous quality to Alex's voice

now, but it was also drawing closer. She'd heard him banging around and was coming to investigate, he realized with alarm, and immediately tore the half-full bag from his teeth. Big mistake, he realized at once as cold blood splashed across his face and down his chest. Cursing again, he dropped the now-hemorrhaging bag in the cooler, slammed the lid down, and then quickly mopped at his face with his maroon shirt.

He'd barely started on his chest when the closet door began to slide open. Cale instinctively jerked his shirt up in front of his torso to hide any remaining blood as light splashed over him.

"What on earth are you doing in the closet?"

"I wasn't quite dressed yet," Cale blurted.

"Oh," Alex said nonplussed, her gaze sliding over the shirt he held defensively before him, and then to his jeans-clad legs beneath. She was obviously a bit perplexed as to why he was acting like a Victorian virgin when he was only lacking a shirt, but she backed away. "Well, I'll give you another minute then."

Cale sighed as she moved out of sight. He quickly wiped away the remaining blood on his chest, not stepping out of the closet until he heard the bathroom door close again.

Cale took a moment to inspect himself in the mirror-fronted sliding closet door, relieved to see he'd gotten all the blood. He then threw the shirt into the closet on top of the cooler and rushed to his suitcase to retrieve a fresh one, this time a green T-shirt. As he pulled it over his head, he called, "You can come out now."

"Are you sure?" Alex called through the door. "I wouldn't want to catch a glimpse of your bare chest. I might not be able to contain myself."

"I wish," Cale muttered, grimacing at her obvious amusement as he tugged his T-shirt into place. He so wasn't impressing this woman yet. Shaking his head, he walked over and opened the bathroom door, and then stood aside and held his arm out in a gesture for her to exit. "I'm ready to go if you are."

Alex grinned and then walked past him, murmuring, "I applaud you for your courage."

"Courage?" he asked with confusion.

"Hmm." She headed for the door to the hall, swinging her purse gaily as she went. "Many men find it difficult to come out of the closet."

Cale was sure she was making a joke at his expense but didn't understand it. Shaking his head, he grabbed his coat from the bed and followed her out of the room.

Grocery shopping was an incredibly interesting experience for Cale. Food had certainly changed since he'd last indulged in eating. Instead of having to hunt it down, slay, clean, and cook it yourself, you could now buy it already prepared or even cooked for you and ready to eat. He'd known this, of course—he wasn't completely ignorant of the world he lived in—but he'd never actually had a reason to be in a grocery store and never seen one for himself. That made it all much more interesting, and he found himself hanging over counters, dawdling in the aisles, and picking up almost everything he saw. And absolutely everything looked good.

"Good Lord," Alex said with exasperation, grabbing his arm to urge him away from the baked-goods section. "One would think you'd never been shopping."

"I haven't," he muttered without thinking. When she turned on him sharply, he quickly added, "Not in a North American grocery store."

"Oh, right," she said relaxing. "I suppose everything here is different from what you're used to, different brands, different packaging, etc."

"*Oui,*" Cale murmured, eyeing the deli counter as she urged him past it. There were some wonderful smells coming from it.

"I think that's everything," Alex murmured, selecting several packages of sliced meat and cheese and setting them in the cart. "Let's get out of here."

Nodding, Cale pushed the cart after her as she led him to the front of the store. His mind was on the problem of getting her to agree to his being her manager rather than her chef. Aside from the fact that it would make her much happier to cook than manage, it would definitely be better for him, and yet she seemed to be resisting the idea. At least, she hadn't yet agreed to it.

The ringing of his cell phone distracted him as they reached the cash register, and Cale pulled it out with a frown. Recognizing Lucian's number, he hesitated, his gaze sliding between the phone and the counter Alex was presently unloading their groceries onto.

"Go ahead, I can handle this," Alex said quietly. "At this hour it must be someone in France calling about a business problem."

Cale didn't correct her but nodded and pressed the

button to take the call, moving away from the cash register as Lucian growled, "Bricker said you were heading over to the restaurant to see Alex. What's happening?"

Cale smiled wryly at the greeting. Lucian wasn't known for "Hello? How are you?" type greetings.

"We're at the grocery store, shopping for a snack." He paused out of earshot and glanced back to watch Alex.

Lucian grunted at this news. "Marguerite's trying to find a chef to replace you, but no luck so far. I understand Leigh and Marguerite gave up their night at the movies to help you out. It won't happen again. I'll not allow it, so if you know a chef that might help, speak up now, or you're going to get a crash course in cooking tomorrow night."

Cale sighed, now understanding the reason for the call. Lucian was pissed about Leigh's helping. He didn't really blame him. Leigh was pregnant, and since she'd lost the last child she'd been carrying, Lucian was extra protective of her. An immortal only lost a child if there was a genetic flaw, something that was rare, and he knew it had upset both of them.

"I may not need a chef," Cale said, and then quickly explained his hope of taking over the business end of things and leaving Alex to cook.

"What's the problem then?" Lucian asked sharply. "She should be jumping at that offer. You're one hell of a businessman."

Cale pulled the phone from his ear to peer at the number again just to be sure it was his uncle. He'd never known the man to give compliments. Leigh was definitely having a beneficial effect on the man. Putting the phone back to his ear, he said, "She's resisting. I suppose after the trouble she had with the project manager, she's afraid to trust someone else."

Lucian grunted, was silent for a minute and then announced, "I'll have Bricker meet you at the new restaurant and help you convince her."

Cale sighed at the suggestion, knowing Lucian meant he would have Bricker use mind control on Alex. The idea was tempting. It would certainly make things easier, but he didn't like the idea of taking the decision from her in that way. "I'm not sure that's a good idea. This is her business, Uncle. She—"

"She isn't aware of all the facts," Lucian interrupted. "And she can't be told. She can't make a proper decision with only half the facts, so I'll make it for her."

"But—"

"She's your life mate," Lucian said grimly. "Your winning her over and convincing her to take up that role will make you happy, her happy, and Sam and Jo happy, which in turn will keep my enforcers happy. I'm sending Bricker."

The announcement was followed by a *click,* and then dead air. Lucian had hung up.

Muttering under his breath, Cale pocketed the phone and turned to head back to the register in time to stop Alex from paying for the groceries.

"I'm the one who was hungry," he reminded firmly when she appeared about to protest allowing him to foot the bill. Alex hesitated, but then nodded solemnly and didn't argue further.

"Are you all right?" she asked moments later as they drove back to the restaurant. "You seem a bit quiet."

Cale forced a smile. "Just hungry," he assured her, but the truth was he was fretting over Bricker's meeting them at the restaurant to use mind control on Alex. Part of him was irritated at his uncle's underhanded tactics. The man really had no business in their relationship. Not that something as insignificant as it being none of his business had ever stopped Lucian. However, another, much larger, part of Cale was rather relieved at the idea. It would certainly simplify things. That way, Alex would be happy, and he could stay close and woo her.

"Is that Justin?" Alex asked, as they pulled into the parking lot.

"Yes," Cale murmured, spotting Bricker seated in his SUV.

"I wonder what he's doing here," Alex said with a frown. "I hope there isn't something wrong with Sam."

"He's here to help with the painting," Cale said to keep her from worrying unnecessarily. He then decided he'd bribe the man into helping to ensure what he'd just said wasn't a lie.

A loud and rapid banging dragged Alex from sleep. Yawning, she opened her eyes, sat up in bed, and peered around with confusion, slow to comprehend what had woken her. When the banging came again, she tossed the bedsheets and cover aside and got hurriedly to her feet, nearly tripping over her own feet as she stumbled out the door of her bedroom. She managed to make it downstairs and to the front door without breaking her neck and yanked the door open just as a third round of rapping started.

The young man on her porch caught himself mid-knock, smiled uncertainly as he took in her flannel pajamas with pandas on them, and said, "Ms. Willan? Alexandra Willan?"

Alex nodded and then shifted to stand on one foot, covering it with her other foot against the cold rushing in at her.

"Here are your keys," the fellow said, raising a hand to dangle them before her.

"My keys?" Alex echoed with confusion.

"Yes ma'am. Your car's all fixed up. Turns out the battery connection had somehow come loose. She's good now. Can you sign here that you received the car?"

"Oh, yes, of course." Alex took the pen and clipboard he offered and signed where he pointed. As she handed the clipboard back, her gaze slid to her vehicle now parked in her short driveway. It looked like it had been cleaned as well as fixed. The salt stains that had marked it were gone. Alex shook her head slightly. She'd left the keys with Cale last night. He'd promised to have someone look at her vehicle for her. Apparently, he'd done as he promised.

"Have a good day."

Alex glanced back to the young man to see that he was heading off her porch. Frowning, she switched feet to warm the one that had been on top of the other, and asked, "What about the bill?"

"Oh, Mr. Argeneau said to send the bill to the restaurant. You should get it in a few days," he said with a wave over his shoulder as he hurried toward a truck idling at the curb.

"Thank you!" Alex called as he slid into the vehicle. He nodded again and gave another wave as he closed the door.

Alex immediately closed the door, very glad to be able to do so. As one would expect for late February, it was cold, but it was also windy, making it seem colder still.

Shivering, she headed back upstairs, thinking she should shower, dress, and head over to check on the new restaurant. Somehow last night she'd found herself agreeing to Cale's taking over as business manager, leaving her to cook. Alex had been leaning that way anyway, bending under the weight of temptation, but she didn't recall actually deciding it for certain.

She'd just suddenly announced that he was hired as they were sharing their picnic with Bricker. Then she'd allowed herself to be convinced to give him the keys to the new restaurant, as well as to her car, and found herself being driven home and leaving the rest of the painting to the two men. Alex wasn't really sure how that had happened.

"I must have been seriously exhausted," she muttered with a shake of the head as she crossed her bedroom to the attached bathroom. It was the only explanation she could come up with. Alex wasn't the type to shirk a job and go home to bed leaving others to do it.

The cold air when she'd answered the door had

woken her up properly; now the shower warmed her, but Alex knew she wouldn't be fully awake until she'd had coffee. However, she didn't want to take the time to make a pot. She'd pick up a couple of coffees from Tim Hortons on the way to the restaurant, she decided as she washed and rinsed her hair: one for her and one for Cale, who had somehow convinced her that he should work today and be at the restaurant to accept the furniture delivery.

She never should have agreed to that, Alex thought irritably as she stepped out of the shower. The man was going to burn himself out by week's end at this rate. The possibility was a bit worrying, and Alex decided she'd pick him up a breakfast sandwich on the way to help keep up his strength.

Or normal sandwiches, she decided as she walked back into her room and saw the time. It was late afternoon. Cripes, Cale had probably received the tables and chairs and headed to his hotel by now. Still, she wanted food, and she'd double the order just in case he was still around.

As it turned out, Cale was still there when Alex arrived. At least his car was, she noted. Not wanting the food to get cold, she parked as close as she could to the door, then scrambled to get inside. She would definitely be glad to see the end of winter, Alex thought as she set the coffees and food down to remove her coat. Tossing the long winter item across the nearest counter in her lovely new kitchen, Alex left the coffee and food where they were and hurried to the dining room.

A small sigh slid from her lips as she stepped into

the room. The painting was finished, the walls a warm, off-white with burgundy trim along the top. She smiled faintly as she recalled trying to explain how she'd planned to do it and her frustration because she knew she wasn't describing it properly. Bricker had insisted he understood, however, and she'd found herself relaxing and believing him. He had been right. While Cale had looked uncertain, Bricker had apparently understood exactly what she wanted. It was exactly as she'd envisioned.

Her gaze slid to the tables and chairs next, and a little shiver of pleasure slid through her. They were the right ones and absolutely perfect. Her luck really was turning, Alex decided as she moved forward, drawing her fingers lightly over one table, and then another. It looked good. Things were shaping up.

"It's coming together."

Alex turned to see Cale standing in the doorway between the kitchen and dining room. She beamed at him, grinning so wide it almost hurt. "Thanks to you," she said, and then rushed past him to get into the kitchen.

"I can't believe you're still here," she said as she crossed to the coffees and bag of food. "But just in case you were, I brought you an apology."

"Apology?" he asked, and she could hear the surprise in his voice.

"Yes." She turned with a coffee in hand. "I'm so sorry about your staying here to paint, and then being here to accept delivery of the furniture. I never should have agreed to that."

"I offered," he reminded her quietly, moving forward when she held out the coffee.

"Yes, well, I should have said no," Alex announced, as he took the coffee. She turned to retrieve one of the two bacon, lettuce and tomato sandwiches next, and then offered him that as well, saying, "You must be exhausted."

"Actually I'm good," he said, taking the sandwich. "It must be jet lag. My internal clock is probably all messed up."

"Hmm," Alex said doubtfully, finding it hard to believe he wasn't completely wiped.

"Shall we sit in the dining room?" he suggested.

Smiling at the very thought, Alex collected her own coffee and sandwich and followed him out to settle at one of the tables near the kitchen door.

"I gather your car was fixed then?" Cale asked as he unwrapped his sandwich.

"Yes. Thank you. You must have called them first thing."

"Oui, first thing," he acknowledged. "What was wrong with it?"

"Nothing serious in the end," Alex assured him. "I think he said the connection to the battery had shaken loose or something." She shrugged.

"That's all? A loose wire?" he asked.

Alex nodded, unable to answer verbally since her mouth was full of warm sandwich at the moment. They were both silent for several moments after that, concentrating on their food.

"I should have picked us up two coffees each," she said with a sigh as she balled up her sandwich wrapper and pushed it into her now-empty coffee cup.

"There's fresh coffee in the office," Cale announced as she replaced the lid on her cup, and when she glanced at him with surprise, he explained, "Bricker is addicted to the stuff. He insisted on stopping to pick up a coffeepot, cups, and—as he put it—all the fixings on the way back here."

"Where did you find a store that sold coffeepots at that hour?" Alex asked with surprise.

"The grocery store where we got the items for the picnic," he answered, collecting his own empty wrapper and coffee cup as he got to his feet. "It has a whole line of small appliances, as well as books, and whatnot."

"Oh, yes I'd forgotten about that," she admitted as she followed him back through the kitchen and into her office. "I'm used to the grocery store by my place. It only carries food."

Cale nodded as he took her cup and moved toward the small garbage can by her desk. He gestured over his shoulder as he went. "I set it up in the corner there. No table of course, so I made do with the floor."

Alex immediately moved to the coffeepot, cups, and fixings lined up in the corner and knelt to fix them both a cup.

"Mmm, it is fresh," she murmured, taking a sip of hers, and then straightened to carry them both to the desk.

"I had just finished turning it on when I heard the back door," Cale assured her, accepting the cup she held out. He took a sip, sighed with pleasure, then moved to the desk.

"You got a chair," she said with surprise, noticing the desk chair behind the desk. *Her* desk chair, she realized, recognizing the dark brown leather model she'd ordered and been told was back-ordered and wouldn't show up for six weeks.

"I happened to find the bill for the chair as I was organizing your papers. When I saw that it was back-ordered, I called and made arrangements to have the display model brought over until your own chair arrives. It makes it easier to work than sitting on the floor."

"They agreed to that?" she asked with amazement.

"Oui. Once I pointed out that according to the receipt it was supposed to be delivered last week, and that delays and disappointments like this were bad business and might not make good press," he added with a devilish grin. "When I then suggested they bring the display around for you to use in the meantime, the manager agreed readily enough."

"Bad press?" she asked with amusement.

Cale shrugged. "I was tired of sitting on the floor. Besides, I could get it mentioned in an article easily enough if I put my mind to it."

"Hmm," she murmured, peering at the chair with a little sigh of pleasure. It looked as good as she'd thought it would, and her own model would look even better since it would be minus the few scuffs and scratches this one had.

"I took care of the paint matter as well," Cale announced, moving around the desk to begin sorting through papers on it. She recognized the bill for the paint when he pulled it out of the pile. "After the table and chairs arrived, I took the paint cans into the store and showed them that the cans read White Sand but obviously weren't White Sand. The manager agreed they'd been mixed wrong. He's going to reimburse you for the paint, as well as the cost of the painters, and asked me to give you his apologies."

"Wow," Alex murmured, peering down at the receipt he handed her. It had a bunch of incomprehensible scribbling on it now and what appeared to be a signature. Probably the manager's, she guessed, and then glanced to Cale as he began sorting through the papers again.

"Unfortunately, I couldn't do anything about the carpet. Your project manager signed for that despite its being the incorrect color. However, I stopped at the store where you bought the tiles. I pointed out that the fault was the salesman's, and that you shouldn't be expected to double-check his numbers. I also pointed out that while the numbers were wrong, the color written beside the numbers was correct, and that would have been what you checked. I suggested a judge would probably agree." He paused to smile at her, and then held out that bill as well, and said, "He agreed to reimburse you for the tiles."

"He did?" Alex breathed as the threat of bankruptcy receded in her mind. Dear God, with the return of the money for those damned expensive Italian tiles, she'd even have money in her savings again. Not much, but something.

"*Oui*. He did . . . with a little persuasion and a couple of threats," Cale added dryly, and then cautioned, "You still have to eat the cost of both installations. He wouldn't bend on that, but since he was taking a big hit on what was essentially a mistake by his sales guy, I didn't push too—"

Cale's words died on an "oomph" of surprise as Alex suddenly launched herself at him with a squeal. She hugged him hard, then caught his face in both hands, kissed him on both cheeks, and proclaimed, "You are a god!"

Cale chuckled at her excitement and slid his arms around her waist. "Well, I'm glad you're satisfied with my work, ma'am."

"Satisfied?" she asked with a laugh. "I've never been this satisfied in my life. Getting reimbursed for the tiles is better than . . . well, better than sex even."

"Then you've been having sex with the wrong people," he assured her solemnly, and Alex was suddenly conscious of several things. That she was his boss and he an employee, that they were in her office, and that she was in his arms . . . and shouldn't be. Geez, he could charge her with sexual harassment.

Suddenly flustered, she pulled away from him, aware that her face was flushing a bright red. He frowned but let her go without protest. Alex immediately turned toward the door, saying in tones as businesslike as she could manage, "I guess I'd better get to the old restaurant to prep before the dinner hour starts. And you should go home—well to your hotel and catch some sleep. You must be exhausted." She stopped walking suddenly and turned back with concern. "This is Saturday. You didn't have to give up any plans to visit family today to stay here, did you?"

"No," Cale assured her quietly as he moved to turn off the coffeepot. As he straightened, he added, "In fact, I had the day clear with only plans for a late supper with my cousin Thomas and his wife Inez."

Alex sighed unhappily at this news. "And thanks to me you've been up all night and day and will probably be too exhausted to enjoy the visit."

"I'll catch a nap before I meet them," he assured her as he retrieved his coat from the back of the desk chair. "It's going to be a very late dinner, and then I'm driving them to the airport. They came for the wedding," he explained, "but Inez needs to get back to work, so they're flying back to Europe tonight."

"Europe?" she asked with surprise.

"England," he clarified. "While it's only a two-and-a-half-hour journey there from Paris, and wouldn't seem far to a Canadian, to us it's considered an overnight trip, so we don't see each other much despite his being in Europe."

"Ah." Alex nodded with a faint smile, relaxing a little. "I remember that from being there. You guys have a different view of travel than we do."

Cale nodded. "Anyway, I'm visiting with them tonight, but I'll check in at your other restaurant at closing time and see that all is well."

Alex clucked and shook her head. "Don't be silly. You're not expected to work all hours of the day and night. Which reminds me, what days do you want to work?" When he hesitated, she pointed out. "This is Saturday, and normally I wouldn't think you'd be working Saturdays because the banks and most businesses are closed on weekends. You'll probably want to work Monday through Friday. Yes?"

Cale nodded. "That sounds fine."

"But you should also get a full weekend, so if you want this Monday off—" she began.

"No, no. I'll work Monday," he assured her. "I've been on vacation this last week, remember."

Alex hesitated, but then nodded. "Okay. I'll see you next week then."

Cale frowned and hesitated, but then said, "I suppose you'll be cooking tomorrow as well?"

"Yes." Alex nodded. "We're open Wednesday through Sunday, with Mondays and Tuesdays off. Surprisingly, a lot of people book for Sunday dinners, but Mondays and Tuesdays are slow, so it seemed best to take them as our weekends."

His frown deepened. "Then I'm off on Saturday and Sunday and you're off on Mondays and Tuesdays?"

"Yes." She grinned. "So don't be surprised if I drop in to see how things are going here once in a while on those days."

Cale nodded and relaxed a little. "I'll look forward to it."

Alex snorted. "Yeah right, cause everyone enjoys their boss hanging over their shoulder."

He smiled faintly. "You can hang over my shoulder anytime."

"I'll remind you of that when you complain that I

don't know how to delegate and hover too much," she said with a forced laugh, and then did up her coat. "Now, come on, you need to go catch a nap before you meet your cousins. I feel guilty enough about your lack of sleep. Besides, I need to get to La Bonne Vie, the other La Bonne Vie," she added, and frowned and muttered, "I should have called it a different name. It gets confusing in conversation."

Cale stood to shrug into his own coat, and suggested, "Call them Bonne Vie One and Bonne Vie Two."

"Good idea." Alex turned to lead the way out of the office. But she paused in the door and turned back to smile at him. "Thank you, Cale. For everything. For a guy named after food, you're pretty brilliant."

He paused abruptly, a startled expression claiming his features. "What?"

She grimaced, "Just teasing . . . well mostly. I do think of the vegetable every time I say your name."

"The vegetable?" he asked in a choked voice.

Alex grimaced. "Yeah. Kale with a K is a green leafy veggie, a type of cabbage as I recall," she murmured, turning to head out the door.

"Call me Cal," he said grimly, following her.

Alex smiled faintly, but was searching her mind for something else to say. For some reason she had a terrible urge to babble around the man now, and knew it was out of discomfort over what had happened in the office. Finally, she blurted, "Is Cale short for anything?"

"No."

"It's Scottish, isn't it?" she asked as she crossed the kitchen to the back door and pushed it open.

Cale hesitated, and then admitted, "My mother loved poetry, and Calliope was the muse of eloquence and epic poetry. She hoped if she named me for the muse, I'd grow up to be a poet rather than a warrior like the rest of my brothers. She thought that Cale would be a good male version of the name."

"Warrior?" Alex asked, glancing at him with surprise as she turned back to watch him lock the door.

"My English," he excused himself, sounding oddly grim. "I meant soldier. My brothers all grew up to be soldiers."

"Oh, your brothers are older than you then?" When he turned from locking the door, she added, "I'm pretty sure you have to be eighteen to be a soldier. If they were soldiers when she named you, then they had to be at least eighteen or so when you were born."

"I am much younger than my brothers, *oui*." He took her arm to walk her across the parking lot. It was only four o'clock, but the sky was already starting to darken with the threat of nightfall. That was one thing Alex hated about winter. She didn't mind the cold so much as the short days.

"Well, have a good dinner," she said with forced good cheer as she unlocked and opened the driver's door.

"Yes, and you enjoy your cooking." He held the door as she slid in behind the steering wheel.

"Oh, believe me, I will." She assured him, then said, "See you Monday," and pulled the door closed.

Alex started the engine, gave Cale a little wave, and pulled away, smiling happily to herself.

Cale Valens was awesome. She couldn't believe her luck. He'd done more to turn things around in one day than she could ever have managed at all. Getting re-imbursed for the tiles was the bomb! Alex could actually breathe again. She'd felt like she was drowning for weeks now, but right that minute she felt on top of the world, and it was all thanks to Cale.

God, he was good. And she got to cook again. She really had to call Sam and thank her for sending the man her way. He was an answer to a prayer. He gave her hope that this having two restaurants would work out after all. Now all she had to do was keep her hands off the man and avoid a sexual-harassment suit.

Seven

Alex set to work prepping for the night ahead with a pleased sigh, setting out the pans and utensils she was most likely to need, and then lining up ingredients she would use. It was Friday, a week since Cale's arrival in her life, and it had been an awesome week. The man was a blessing, accomplishing more in that time than she could have.

Cale had managed to get all of her paperwork in order, had overseen countless deliveries without a hitch—or at least, if there had been hitches, he'd taken care of them and kept the aggravation from her. The new restaurant was now furnished, including her office, which had also been painted. After the fiasco with the tiles, Alex had intended to leave her office unfinished until she could better afford it; but once Cale had arranged the refund for the tiles, she'd decided to splurge and gone out to buy the paint. She'd bought it Monday and painted the office Monday night . . . much to Cale's chagrin. He'd been upset that she hadn't told him and let him help, but he worked hard enough during the day and she hadn't wanted to bother him on his time off.

Besides, Alex thought it might be best to avoid spending too much time alone with the man. He was just too attractive for her peace of mind. On top of that, he was working for her, which might only be temporary, but that was another problem altogether. She didn't need to fall for the guy when he was leaving in a month or two. She feared he would be easy to fall for.

There was now only one week to go until the opening of the new restaurant, and Alex found she was actually looking forward to it instead of panicking every time she thought of it. This, the old La Bonne Vie, was being shut down for that night so that she and her staff could attend the opening. They'd also be on hand to help if necessary, and it might be since Alex was expecting quite a turnout on opening night. She was looking forward to that too.

"Which reminds me," Alex murmured to herself, and glanced over her shoulder to Bev. The woman was checking a roast duck she'd popped in the oven earlier.

"Bev, will Mark be able to get Friday night off to attend the opening?" Alex asked as the woman eased the oven door closed and straightened. The young woman's boyfriend, Mark, worked at Chez Joie. Friday night was a busy night for most restaurants, and he hadn't been sure he'd be able to get the time off to attend . . . especially considering what it was for.

Bev glanced her way and smiled widely. "Yes, much

to my amazement, Jacques didn't even give him a hard time over it."

Alex raised her eyebrows, surprised at such decency from Jacques, or Jack as she'd always known him before he'd started Chez Joie and changed it to Jacques. What was it with men and their need to put on airs, she wondered. She didn't know any women chefs who took on fake French names to make themselves feel or sound more important. But Jack had actually had his name legally changed to sound French . . . the pretentious twit, she thought, and then considered that he and Peter/Pierre might be getting along like gangbusters. Both were egocentric weasels. Which was why she was surprised he'd not given Mark a hard time about attending the opening of a competitor's new restaurant.

"That reminds me," Bev said suddenly. "Mark told me this morning that Jacques fired Peter last night." The younger woman wrinkled her nose. "I guess Peter didn't take it well. He—" She stopped suddenly, her face paling as she peered toward the door.

Expecting someone to have entered, Alex turned, but there was no one there. She didn't understand what had caused Bev's reaction until she peered through the window into the restaurant and spotted Peter walking quickly through the tables toward the kitchens.

"Speak of the devil," Alex muttered. It didn't take a genius to figure out why the man was here. He'd been fired and hoped to gain back his old job, she guessed, and sighed unhappily, not really needing this tonight. Fridays were always busy, and she didn't want to start the night in a bad mood . . . although to be honest, she didn't want to start any night in a bad mood and would have been happy to bypass the coming conversation altogether.

Grimacing, she glanced back to Bev, noting the resigned look on the other woman's face as she ducked her head back to her work. It didn't take a genius to figure out what was bothering her. Bev was afraid Alex would actually take Peter back, which meant Bev would be demoted.

Before Alex could reassure the woman, Peter pushed through the door into the kitchens and headed straight for her.

He hesitated briefly, and then—in humble tones she wasn't at all used to from him—said, "Alex, can I have a word with you, please?"

She considered simply saying no and avoiding what she knew was coming, but then feared he would simply say it out here and decided perhaps the office was better.

Sighing, she led him across the kitchen, saying, "I only have a minute, Peter. It's Friday night."

At the door to her office, Alex paused and gestured for him to enter, then followed, leaving the door open. She didn't want him closing the door and trapping her in the room with him, she wasn't stupid. Peter had a hair-trigger temper, and she wanted someone to know if he suddenly tried to throttle her.

"Sit down," she said quietly, moving around behind her desk. Alex settled in her seat, and then waited a touch impatiently as Peter peered down at his hands and swallowed repeatedly. She now just wanted to get the unpleasantness over with and get on with her life. She was so eager for that she almost blurted that he couldn't have his job back before he asked for it, but he began to speak as she opened her mouth.

"You were right," he announced grimly. "Jacques fired me last night." He raised his head, expression furious, and said, "He was just trying to ruin you by hiring me away from you."

"I did try to warn you," Alex murmured, not bothering to feign surprise.

"He was furious with that five-star review in the paper last week when you had that French guy cooking," Peter went on, his tone rabid. "And he tried to hire away your new head manager when he heard that you'd hired him. When that didn't work, he just lost it."

Alex's eyes narrowed. Cale hadn't mentioned anything about Jacques approaching him.

"He called me into his office and ranted and raved at me like it was my fault," Peter continued with outrage. "He said hiring me was useless and . . . and then he fired me."

"I see," Alex murmured.

"Do you know he hadn't even fired his previous head chef?" Peter asked with disgust. "The guy was only on vacation."

She wasn't terribly surprised at this news. Alex also wasn't surprised that Jacques had hired a chef rather than cook himself. He was a horrible cook. The only way he'd managed to get as far as he had in the culinary school they'd both attended was by cheating. He'd been tossed out when he was caught and disappeared for a while, only to pop up in Toronto and open Chez Joie shortly after she started La Bonne Vie.

"So I've come to ask for my position back," Peter announced stiffly, reclaiming her attention as he hurried on. "I realize you are head chef again, so I would have to take the *sous-chef* position once more, but I'm willing to accept that humiliation as punishment for not heeding your warnings and—"

"Peter," Alex interrupted quietly.

"Pierre," he corrected with a flash of the old arrogance she suspected was boiling under the humbler facade he was presenting.

Alex just shook her head, and said, "I'm sorry you've lost your job at Chez Joie. And yes, I did warn you, however—"

"Yes, I know, but—"

"However," Alex repeated firmly. When he got the message and fell silent, she continued, "I'm not willing to demote Bev and fire Bobby. I won't rearrange everything to suit you when you'll simply do this again the first chance you get and leave me in a lurch once more."

"I wouldn't. I swear it," he said passionately.

"I don't believe you," she said quietly. He started to say something again, but she held up her hand and added, "And I'm not willing to take the chance."

"But I don't have a job now," he said, as if that might have slipped her notice and realizing it should make her change her mind.

"That's not my fault or problem, Peter," she pointed out quietly. "I asked you to stay at the time. I explained what I thought Jacques was up to, and you chose to leave. I'm afraid you'll have to live with that decision."

Peter stared at her blankly, apparently having been sure she'd be pleased to accept him back. The fact that she wasn't forgiving all and welcoming him back wasn't what he wanted to hear, and she felt herself tense as anger began to replace his surprise.

"You arrogant bitch," he hissed coldly. "I suppose you're pleased to see me here groveling?"

The night he'd left, Alex had thought she would enjoy his fall, but now that it was here, she found she wasn't enjoying it at all. Not even a little. Instead, she actually felt sorry for the little weasel and said so. "No, actually I'm sorry for you."

"Sorry?" Rage covered his face and he leapt to his feet. "Don't you dare feel sorry for me. I am Pierre. I am a brilliant chef. Certainly too good for this little shit hole. You're the one who's going to be sorry!" Turning on his heel, he stormed out, nearly running over Bev on the way.

"Jerk," Alex muttered as he slammed out of the kitchen.

"You didn't hire him back."

Alex glanced to the door where Bev now stood, staring at her wide-eyed. Frowning, she said, "Of course I didn't. Why would I? He was difficult to work with at the best of times, and you're a better *sous-chef* than he ever was. And someday you'll make a better head chef than he could ever dream to be."

Bev flushed at the compliment. "Thank you."

"Don't thank me, it's the truth," Alex said solemnly,

and then glanced to the phone on her desk when it began to ring. Recognizing Sam's number, she glanced to the clock, frowning when she saw what time it was. The front doors would be opening in a couple of minutes and the first people arriving. She didn't really have long to talk, and Sam would know that. For her to be calling at this time of the day, it must be something important.

"I'd better get back to prep," Bev murmured.

Alex nodded. "I'll be along in a minute. Can you close the door for me?"

"Sure." Bev pulled the door closed as Alex reached for the phone.

"How is Cale?" Sam asked the moment Alex said hello.

She raised her eyebrows at the unconventional greeting, but then found herself smiling and saying, "He's brilliant. Awesome. Thank you for sending him my way."

"I'm so glad." Sam sounded truly delighted, but then asked, "How awesome?"

Alex sat back in her seat, her eyebrows rising. "What do you mean?"

"I mean . . . well *how* exactly is he awesome?"

Alex considered the question, and then simply said, "He's the answer to my dreams, Sam. Or maybe my prayers."

"Has he told you about his family?" Sam asked at once.

"Not much," she admitted. "I gather he has brothers who are soldiers. And he learned to cook for the family restaurant, but prefers the business end of things. That's about it really."

"That's it?" Sam asked, and Alex could hear the disappointment in her voice.

"Yes, that's it," Alex said with a laugh. "Why would he tell me any more than that? I'm his boss, not his girlfriend."

A low groan came down the line. "Alex, don't you—I mean, what do you think of him as a man?"

"Is he a man?" she teased, and peered out the window above her couch at the bustling activity in the kitchen.

"Alexandra!" Sam snapped impatiently.

She sighed. What did she think of him as a man? In her mind's eye Cale rose before her, Cale smiling, Cale frowning, Cale painting, Cale sitting at her desk. Finally, she admitted, "I think he's gorgeous, smart, funny, smells divine, and he probably has the sexiest accent I've ever heard."

"And?" Sam prompted.

"And what?"

"What are you going to do about it?" Sam asked impatiently.

Alex sat up in her seat, her voice firm as she said, "Absolutely nothing."

"What?" her sister gasped with what sounded like horror. "But—"

"Sam, honey," she interrupted gently. "I know you're deliriously happy with Mortimer and want the same for me, but Cale is the best business manager I could ask for. I'm not messing that up by getting involved." She let that sink in, and then added, "Besides, I'm not like you. I don't need a man to make me happy. Cooking and my restaurant make me happy."

"But it doesn't keep you warm at night," Sam said at once.

"That's what electric blankets are for."

"You can't talk to electric blankets," Sam argued.

"That's what friends are for," Alex responded at once.

"Friends can't give you sex," she snapped finally.

"Friends with benefits can," Alex said with a grin, actually enjoying her sister's frustration.

Sam sounded surprised when she asked, "Do you have a friend with benefits?"

"No," Alex admitted, her smile fading. Truly, her love life was a barren wasteland at the moment and had been for a while. It was depressing to even think of it. Forcing her shoulders straight, she added, "But a BOB fills in nicely until I get one."

"Who is Bob?" Sam asked with confusion.

"Not a who, a what," Alex explained dryly. "A battery-operated boyfriend."

"What?" Sam sounded completely lost now.

"A vibrator, Sam," she said dryly. "Geez. You've heard of those, haven't you?"

A long sigh came down the line, and then Sam said, "Alex, please . . . Just give Cale a chance. If you don't, you could be passing up on the greatest happiness of your life."

Alex was silent for a moment, wondering if she *was* passing up on a good thing with Cale. But then she reminded herself that he was only here for a short time and would be returning home eventually.

"How is Cale taking your . . . reticence," Sam asked garnering her attention again.

Alex felt her eyebrows rise, and said slowly, "He said he'd like to get to know me better, but I made it plain I don't have time for men right now and he's respecting that."

"What an idiot," Sam muttered, making Alex smile with affection. Her sister loved her and *would* think the man an idiot for not pursuing her ardently. It was sweet, Alex thought, but her smile faded as she glanced out to the kitchen and saw Sue placing orders on her shelf.

"Honey, I have to go," she said apologetically. "The orders have started rolling in now."

Sam sighed, but said, "That's all right, I need to call Marguerite anyway."

"Marguerite Argeneau?" Alex asked with surprise. It was the only Marguerite Sam had ever mentioned to her.

"Yes," Sam muttered, sounding grim, and Alex felt her curiosity stir. She hadn't realized the two women knew each other that well. Sam always talked about the woman like she was some sort of goddess or someone high above their social standing, but it sounded like she was making friends with her.

Sue rushed into the kitchen with more orders in hand, and Alex grimaced. "Right, you call Marguerite then, but first I want to tell you . . . thank you thank you thank you for sending Cale to me. He's working wonders and keeping me from bankruptcy. You saved my life. I love you, Sam."

Alex barely waited for Sam's depressed "I love you

too" back before hanging up and hurrying out to her station.

Cale had just rung the doorbell of Marguerite's large house when the door was opened. The woman had obviously been watching for him.

"Cale," she said happily, and stepped forward to hug him. "Right on time. Now we're all here."

"Who is we?" Cale asked with a frown, as he hugged her back. He'd taken to keeping mortal hours now that he was helping out at the restaurant. It meant consuming a little more blood than usual to make up for the damage the sun could cause; but he'd minimized that as much as possible, bundling up against the sun as well as the cold and working mostly from Alex's office at the new restaurant, where there were no windows.

Unfortunately, it meant his hours were at odds with that of his relatives, and he'd played telephone tag with most of them this last week. Marguerite had called several times Friday, the last message sounding so urgent that Cale had arranged for an early wake-up call this morning so that he could get ahold of her before she and Julius retired at dawn. Cale had been more than a little surprised when all she'd wanted was to invite him to dinner that night. Since it was Saturday, and Alex would be working anyway, he'd accepted.

"I invited a few others," Marguerite said evasively as she urged him inside.

"Who?" Cale asked as she set to work helping him remove his winter clothing as if he were a child.

"Oh, Julius is here of course," she murmured, hanging up his coat.

"Of course," Cale said with a faint smile. The only time he'd seen Marguerite without Julius was when she'd helped him at the restaurant. In New York and then here, the man seemed attached to her side like a Siamese twin. "Who else?"

"Come and see," she said gaily, and took his arm to urge him into the living room.

Cale came to a halt the moment he reached the door and saw the people seated inside. Julius was there, crossing the room to join Marguerite as if the few minutes apart had been unbearable. The man slid his arm around Marguerite and pressed a kiss to her forehead as he hugged her to his side, but Cale's attention had turned to the others in the room. Lucian, Leigh, Mortimer, Sam, and Bricker all stared back, and he got a distinct sense of déjà vu. This reminded him of the day he'd arrived and stopped here at Marguerite's behest to find Lucian and Leigh waiting with Marguerite and Julius. He'd felt ambushed then, and did again now.

"Oh no, dear. This isn't an ambush," Marguerite said at once, and he glanced at her sharply, realizing that she'd read his thoughts. He didn't feel any better when she said, "Actually I'm not so much reading them as you are shouting them. It's this new life-mate business. It makes it hard for you to guard your thoughts and even seems to amplify them. We've all been through it," she added sympathetically, and urged him to take a seat across from the sofa where Lucian, Leigh, and Bricker were seated. Mortimer and Sam were seated on a love seat on his right, and Marguerite and Julius now settled onto the love seat on his left, leaving him feeling like he was surrounded and under interrogation.

Cale shifted uncomfortably in his seat, glancing over the people staring back at him, and then ran one hand wearily through his hair. "So if this isn't an ambush, what is it?"

There was a moment of silence as glances were exchanged, and then Marguerite said, "We just want to help with Alex."

"I don't need help," Cale said stiffly.

"Oh? It's going well then?" she asked gently.

Cale felt his mouth tighten, he wouldn't say well exactly. He hardly saw the woman. He worked at the new restaurant, she at the old. She had Mondays and Tuesdays off and he Saturday and Sundays and while he'd dropped by the old restaurant several times and she'd dropped around at the new restaurant as well to check on things, she'd kept the talk strictly to business. Cale had tried to steer it into more personal conversation several times, but Alex always steered it firmly back to business. It was incredibly frustrating, and he hadn't a clue what to do about it; but he wasn't willing to admit that.

Forgetting that they could read his mind and would know all this, he said stiffly, "It's going very well."

"Have you slept with her yet?" Lucian asked abruptly.

"Luc," Leigh reprimanded, slapping his shoulder. "You'll embarrass Cale."

"Honey," Lucian said gently, "Cale is over two thou-

sand years old. Nothing should embarrass him anymore."

"Are you that old?" Sam asked with amazement.

"He was born in 280 B.C.," Lucian informed her, and
Sam blanched. Cale got the distinct impression she was
reassessing him as a mate for her sister and finding him
wanting now that she knew how old he was.

"You haven't answered my question," Lucian pointed
out, reclaiming Cale's attention.

"No," he said at last. "I haven't slept with her yet."

"And you won't," he announced firmly.

Cale frowned at his certainty. "What makes you
think—?"

"She doesn't sleep with employees."

Cale scowled at the title employee. He was a business
owner in his own right in France. Actually, he had his
own miniempire. The idea of her thinking of him as a
mere employee rather than an equal who was helping
her out was a bit distressing to him. "I am a coworker.
Not an employee. And that's only temporary anyway.
I'm just—"

"Fine. She doesn't sleep with coworkers either,"
Lucian interrupted dryly, and added, "She told Sam
that on Friday night. Sam immediately called Marguerite for advice, and Marguerite got us all here tonight
to help you."

Cale sat back in his seat with defeat. He'd known it
was an ambush. "Fine. What do you suggest?"

There was a moment of silence, and then Marguerite
said, "I wish Lucern was here. His Kate had issues with

the idea of getting involved with one of her writers, but they managed to get past that. He could tell us how."

"Dream sex," Lucian said abruptly, drawing all eyes his way.

"Dream sex?" Cale said uncertainly.

Lucian nodded. "It's hard to avoid temptation when you're having shared wet dreams."

"Yes, it is," Sam agreed excitedly, and then flushed when everyone glanced her way. "Well, it is. I was pretty into my career and not looking for a relationship when Mortimer came along, but those dreams . . ." She shook her head, blood rushing up her throat and into her face as she recalled them. "They made it pretty hard for me to resist Mortimer. Every time I looked at him, I was remembering those damned dreams."

"Thank God for that," Mortimer murmured, hugging her close.

Sam smiled and melted into him.

"You haven't turned yet," Cale commented, and when Sam and Mortimer glanced his way with surprise, he pointed out, "Sorry, but Bricker and I overheard your conversation when I came to the enforcer house last week. You were agreeing to the turn. But you haven't yet?"

"Mortimer's a little shorthanded at the moment with everyone away on their honeymoons," Sam said shyly. "We plan to do it this week, though."

"You've agreed to turn?" Marguerite asked, beaming on the woman. "How lovely. What day are you doing it? I'll come help Mortimer oversee it if you like."

"I will too," Leigh offered.

"You will not," Lucian said at once. "I'm not having her kick you and possibly damaging the baby."

"I would never kick Leigh," Sam said with surprise.

"You wouldn't mean to," Lucian said. "But in that kind of pain, you won't know what you're doing."

Sam blanched. "I know Jo went through a lot of pain when she turned, but I thought that was because she was wounded. Won't it be easier for me?"

"I thought we were here to discuss Cale and Alex," Mortimer said, no doubt worried that if Sam knew just what she was in for, she might have second thoughts about turning.

"Yeah," Bricker said at once, backing his friend. "We were talking about wet dreams."

"Right, wet dreams," Cale said dryly. He grimaced at the group of them. "Just how am I to make Alex have wet dreams about me when I can't get into her mind?" When Bricker opened his mouth to speak, he added sharply, "And please don't suggest one of you give them to her. There is no way in hell I am allowing that."

Lucian snorted and shook his head. "Didn't your mother explain the facts of immortal life to you?"

"Of course," he said impatiently, scowling at the man.

"Then why don't you know about shared wet dreams?" he countered.

When Cale glared at him, Marguerite said quickly, "They aren't something anyone gives to her, dear . . . except maybe you. Life mates who sleep under the same roof tend to share their dreams . . . erotic dreams about each other."

"Sam and I weren't even under the same roof," Mortimer announced. "We were in neighboring cottages and experienced it."

Sam flushed but nodded silently.

"Then we need to get you two closer," Marguerite murmured thoughtfully. "Under the same roof would be best, but somewhere nearby might work."

Cale scowled at the suggestion, and said, "I don't see why you think sharing dreams would convince her to bypass her rule not to date coworkers and go out with me."

"He's never had them," Mortimer pointed out to Lucian when the older immortal began to look annoyed.

"Then he should trust us to know what we're talking about," Lucian growled.

It was Marguerite who said gently, "Cale dear, right now Alex is just seeing you as the answer to her business dreams. She's noticed that you're handsome and is attracted to you, but it's like seeing a lovely dessert you've never tried before when you're on a diet. It may look delicious, but because you don't know for sure how delicious, it's easier to deny yourself. Whereas, if it were a lovely slice of cheesecake that you have tasted and do know will be delicious, it would be harder to resist."

"I see," he murmured. "Then couldn't I just kiss her? She would experience our attraction that way and—"

"Kisses are nice, but she might pull away before you could get very far," Sam pointed out. "Alex is pretty stubborn when she sets her mind to something. A shared dream really would be better, so that she could experience all the passion. A kiss would be like just sampling the first course, and we want her to get the full meal to know what she could have."

Cale ran a hand wearily through his hair. "Right."

"How long has it been since you had sex?" Lucian asked, drawing another reprimanding look from Leigh. Sighing, he patted her hand and explained, "If it's been a while, he may need a refresher course. Or one of those books I bought."

"You said you didn't read those books," Leigh said with surprise.

"Well, no, but I've always been exceptional at everything I do and managed to get along without them. However, Cale is not me."

Cale rolled his eyes. "I'd forgotten just how arrogant you could be, Uncle."

Lucian shrugged. "That's a skill too, and, as I say, I'm exceptional at everything."

Leigh laughed and kissed the man on the cheek as if she thought he was joking. Cale suspected he wasn't.

"All right, I think we're agreed the best way to deal with this is to somehow get Alex and Cale under the same roof or at least nearer each other so they can experience the shared dreams," Marguerite said firmly, and then glanced around the room. "Does anyone have ideas?"

"I could take him over to her place in a van, park on the road, and have him sleep in the back," Bricker suggested. "That might be close enough for their minds to meet."

"No goddamned way," Cale barked, blanching at

the very suggestion. Lying in the back of a van having erotic dreams about Alex while Bricker sat in the front seat able to read what he was experiencing was just not something he was willing to even consider. Dear God!

"I thought you said that after this many years nothing should embarrass him?" Leigh said with gentle amusement.

Lucian grunted. "I guess he's more sensitive than I thought."

"I am *not* sensitive," Cale snapped, irritated by the very suggestion.

"It's probably his mother's fault," Lucian said, ignoring him. "Martine named him after Calliope, the muse of poetry. Between that and his father dying when he was only fifty, he's probably suffered under Martine's namby-pamby influence."

When Cale began to growl deep in his throat, Marguerite spoke up quickly to keep the peace. "Perhaps we should move to the dining room. Dinner is probably ready now, and we can think about a solution while we eat, and then talk about this some more."

"Food is always a good idea, Marguerite," Lucian announced.

"Great," Cale muttered as everyone got up with murmurs of agreement. It seemed he would have a break before they continued with this torture they called help.

Eight

"Do you want some help?"

Alex glanced up from the grill she was scrubbing and smiled at Bev. "No, I'm almost done. You go ahead with the others."

Bev nodded gratefully and hurried to collect her coat and purse and follow the others out the back door. Alex took a moment to enjoy the cold breeze that wafted through the room as the door opened and closed. It was always hot in the kitchen by the end of the night, hours of cooking tended to raise the temperature several degrees despite the top-rated ventilation system she'd had installed. The breeze felt nice.

Sighing, she turned back to finish cleaning her station. As the owner, she could have made someone else perform this chore, but Alex was rather possessive of her station. It had been hell for her to see Peter working at it, switching things around and touching her tools. She was glad it was her own again.

Smiling to herself as she finished, Alex put away her cleaning gear, and then removed her hat and apron as she headed into her office. It was Saturday night and they closed later on Saturdays. Still, normally she would have sat down and done a little paperwork before heading home; but now that Cale was handling the paperwork, there was nothing for her to do, and she was glad of it. She didn't know if it was because she'd gotten out of the routine during those few weeks she'd been overseeing the new restaurant, or if she was fighting off a bug, but she was incredibly tired tonight and eager to head home.

Alex hung her apron from the tree in the corner of her office, shrugged into her coat, and then paused to cover a yawn that left her eyes watering. Dashing away the moisture, she grabbed her keys and purse and headed for the back door, hoping that the blast of cold air that awaited her outside would wake her up for the drive home.

As much as she'd been expecting it, the frigid wind that slapped at her as she stepped outside had her gasping breathlessly. Squinting her eyes against it, she quickly locked the door, and then gasped with surprise when she was suddenly grabbed from behind. She managed a half shout before an arm snaked around her neck, cutting off the sound even as another arm banded around her waist. When she was then lifted off her feet and carried away, her surprise turned to panic.

She dropped her keys and clawed at the arm around her neck even as she began to kick, aiming for the man behind her.

When neither action had any effect, Alex reached behind her head and dug her nails into the first flesh she found. A shouted curse was her reward, and then the arm around her throat pulled out from the curve of both of hers, which were now over it. Something cut into the side of her face as it did, and she gritted her teeth at the pain. Her assailant tried to grab for her hands while maintaining his hold around her waist. But she had two free to his one, and he finally gave that up and punched her in the head.

Alex moaned as lights exploded behind her eyes, and then the arm around her waist was suddenly gone. Her feet hit the ground with a jarring impact, and immediately slid out from beneath her. She crashed backward onto the icy tarmac, and there was a second explosion of pain, this time one that seemed to start at the back of her skull and vibrate forward through her brain.

For a moment, all Alex was aware of was that pain, and then she realized she was being dragged across the icy ground by one arm. She was trying to gather herself to struggle again when bright light suddenly splashed over her. She heard what sounded like the skidding of car tires and then a loud horn blaring before her hand was released and she flopped loosely to the ground. Moaning, Alex curled into a ball on the frozen ground and grabbed for the back of her skull, trying to hold her exploding head together.

The blaring horn stopped abruptly and was followed by the faint sound of a door opening and rapid footsteps approaching. "Alex? Are you okay?"

She forced her eyes open to see Bev squatting beside her, looking her over with concern, as she muttered, "Thank goodness I forgot my glasses and came back. That guy was attacking you."

"Yes," Alex agreed, though she couldn't have said if she was agreeing it was good Bev had forgotten her glasses and returned, or that, yes, indeed, that man had been attacking her.

"Can you get up?" Bev asked, glancing nervously around.

Realizing that the girl was worried her attacker might return, and that it was a distinct possibility, Alex forced herself to uncurl and sit up. Bev immediately moved to help her, taking her arm over her shoulder and clutching her about the waist as she stood upright. Working together, they managed to get Alex upright and on her feet just as second car pulled into the parking lot.

Alex glanced toward it, frowning when she recognized Cale getting out of the vehicle and hurrying toward them.

"What happened? Did you fall on the ice?" he asked with concern, moving to her other side.

"I'm fine," Alex said rather than explain.

It was Bev who blurted, "Someone attacked her."

Alex grimaced, and then waved her hand when Cale turned sharply on her. She repeated, "I'm fine. Bev forgot her glasses and came back and scared him off."

Cale glanced around as if prepared to chase after the

culprit, but apparently not seeing anyone, he turned back, then paused to bend down, and she heard the jangle of keys. He'd found hers, she realized, as he straightened with them. Holding them in one hand, he used his other to catch her chin and tilt her face up to his. "You're bleeding."

Alex didn't know how on earth he could tell in the darkness surrounding them, then frowned as she realized just how dark it was. She glanced toward the light over the door that usually lit up half the parking lot.

"What's wrong with the light?" Bev asked, glancing that way now herself.

"I don't know. I'm sure I turned it on," Alex muttered, and then started to shake her head but pressed a hand to her forehead at the pain that caused. "We'd best go in and get your glasses, Bev, so you can get home."

Not waiting for an agreement, Alex started toward the door, grateful for Cale's supporting hand at her arm. Her legs were a bit shaky still. At the door, he used her keys and unlocked and pulled it open, then ushered her inside.

"Where's the light switch?" Cale asked, pausing inside the door.

"I've got it," Bev said, and the overheads suddenly flashed to life, making Alex wince as the bright light knifed right through her eyes and into her head. She heard the other woman flip another switch several times. "You did have the outside light on, Alex, but it's not working. It was on when I left though," she added, a frown in her voice. "Maybe the bulb burnt out."

"I'll look at it before we leave," Cale said grimly,

urging Alex forward. She moved willingly enough, but was grateful when he drew her to a halt in the kitchen and didn't make her walk all the way to her office. Movement seemed to just exacerbate the pain radiating from the back of her head, and she couldn't hold back a moan when Cale suddenly caught her at the waist and lifted her to sit on the counter.

Of course, he didn't miss the sound, and she noted the concern that crowded onto his face as he peered her over. When he then began to move his hands through her hair, Alex guessed he was looking for a bump, and said, "It's in the back."

Cale immediately moved to her side and began to feel around the back of her head. He paused at once when Alex sucked in a sharp breath as his fingers found the lump.

"It doesn't appear to be bleeding," he muttered.

"Your cheek is bleeding though," Bev said, peering at her worriedly.

"I think it was his watch, or a ring," Alex said, recalling the sharp pain as his hand had dragged across her face in the struggle.

"You need to go to the hospital," Cale decided.

"Is the cut that bad?" she asked, reaching instinctively to her cheek, worried it might be some horribly disfiguring wound that would scar.

"No, but the bump on the back of your head is huge and still growing," he said grimly, and then glanced to Bev. "Could you get some ice and put it in a towel or plastic bag or something?"

"Of course," Bev murmured and moved off at once.

"I don't need to go to the hospital," Alex said quietly. "I didn't lose consciousness or anything. It's just a bump."

"You could have a concussion," Cale said firmly. "It's better to have it checked to be sure everything is all right."

"He's right," Bev agreed, returning with ice in a baggie. "Better to be safe than sorry."

Alex rolled her eyes as Cale took the bag, but then winced as he pressed it to the back of her head, sending pain radiating outward through her skull again. She bit her lip until it eased a bit, and then let her breath out on a sigh. "Fine. I'll stop at the hospital and have it checked out on my way home."

"I shall take you, and then deliver you home if the hospital says it's all right," Cale said firmly, and added, "We can call the police about the attack from there."

"Why?" Alex asked dryly. "The guy is long gone, and I didn't see who it was. I also don't particularly feel like filling out a stack of reports about some mugger they'll never catch."

"Was he mugging you?" Bev asked doubtfully. "It looked like he was trying to drag you behind the Dumpster. I thought it was a rapist when I pulled up."

Cale glanced to her sharply. "Did you see his face?"

"No," the woman admitted apologetically. "It was dark and it all happened so fast." She shrugged, and then added, "But it could have been Peter."

"Peter?" Cale asked sharply.

"The head chef who quit," Alex said on a sigh. "I don't think he'd have done this though."

"I don't know," Bev said with a frown. "He was pretty upset the other day when you refused to hire him back. And he did say you'd be sorry."

Alex frowned at the suggestion.

"Come on." Cale caught her by the waist again and eased her off the counter to stand. "I want to have you checked out."

"I'll come too," Bev said, hurrying to her station to grab her glasses. The steam in the kitchen tended to fog them up on her, and she always took them off and set them on the shelf above her station before cooking.

"You don't have to come with us Bev," Alex said as Cale began to urge her toward the back door. "I'm sure I'm fine. You go on home and relax."

When Bev hesitated, Cale added, "I'll call after we've seen the doctor to let you know if everything is all right or not."

"All right then," Bev said reluctantly, and moved past them to open and hold the door for them to exit. She waited with them while Cale used Alex's keys to lock both doors, and then walked with them across the parking lot to where Bev's car still stood, engine running, lights on, and driver's side door open. *She's lucky someone didn't drive off with it,* Alex thought on a sigh.

"At least it will be warm," Bev muttered, as they stopped by the open door. She then paused, and said, "Please don't forget to call me. I'll be up all night worrying if you don't."

"I won't," Cale assured her solemnly. "Go on. We'll wait until you set off."

When Bev glanced to Alex, she caught her hand and gave it a squeeze. "Thank you."

Bev smiled faintly. "And here it usually annoys you when I forget my glasses and come back."

"Never again," Alex assured her wryly.

"Yes it will, but that's okay," Bev said with a chuckle, and gave her a quick hug, then turned and slid into her car. They waited until she'd started her vehicle and set off, then Cale urged Alex to his rental car. She didn't bother arguing that she could drive herself to the hospital. Truthfully, her head ached so badly the idea of squinting against the lights of oncoming night traffic was an unpleasant one. She was grateful to leave the driving to Cale.

Cale paced the hall outside Alex's bedroom for the four hundred and fifty-third time, and then paused before the door and listened. This time rather than miserable sighs or restless rustling, he heard a steady, deep breathing that indicated sleep. He immediately reached for the doorknob and eased the door open just enough to peer in. She was definitely asleep. She lay curled on her side, her hair a mess about her face and her mouth open, a thin line of drool leaking from her mouth.

Cale smiled faintly, relieved to see that the lines of pain no longer carved her face. After arriving home, Alex had twice assured him she felt fine, and he needn't stay, but those pained lines had told him she was suffering. He eased the door closed again, and then headed downstairs, pulling his phone from his back pocket as he went.

By the time he turned into the kitchen on the main floor, he was punching in Bricker's number. Cale had called Bev before they'd left the hospital to let her know Alex was okay and he was taking her home. Alex had been standing beside him when he'd made that call; but this call was trickier, and he'd wanted to be sure she was sleeping and wouldn't overhear before making it.

"Yo, Cale," Bricker greeted, answering on the second ring. "To what do I owe the pleasure? Don't tell me you've decided to go ahead with my idea of sleeping in the van in front of Alex's house? If so, say the word and I'm on the way, Buddy."

"No I haven't changed my mind about that," Cale said grimly. "And please tell me that tonight was not some bright plan of yours to get Alex and me under the same roof."

"Tonight?" Bricker asked, sounding uncertain. "No, I don't think so. Why? What happened?"

"You didn't get one of your buddies to attack Alex so that she'd be concussed, and I'd have to stay here the night to watch over her?" Cale asked, not really thinking he had but wanting to be sure. Bricker seemed to have some wild ideas. He was young enough to forget how fragile mortals were. And while the thought had just been a passing idea of possible culprits behind the attack, once it had slid through his mind, he hadn't been able to shake it. However, Bricker's horrified gasp and true shock now were hard to feign, he decided as Bricker cursed volubly and quite prolifically over the phone.

"No! Of course I didn't have Alex attacked just so

you could get your groove on. Christ! What kind of man do you take me for? She's Sam's sister! Not to mention the best damned cook around! Jesus! She— Is she all right?" he interrupted himself to ask.

"She has a mild concussion. She'll be fine. She's supposed to take it easy for a couple of days though."

Bricker grunted and then returned to his rant. "I can't believe you'd think I was behind her being attacked. Sitting in a van twiddling my thumbs while you bone up is one thing, but attacking her? No way."

"Bone up?" Cale asked uncertainly.

"Get a boner," the man explained, and then added, "Or an erection to those of us too damned old to know modern lingo . . . not to mention be able to judge character anymore. You've spent too damned much time alone if you thought I'd—"

"I didn't really," Cale said quickly, hoping to bring his rant to an end. "It's just that since it achieved what everyone was so eager to have happen, it occurred to me it might not be an accident."

"Well, of course it's not an accident," Bricker snapped, still apparently annoyed. "You don't accidentally attack someone, but I can promise I wasn't behind it. And I know Mortimer wouldn't do something like that either. As for Julius, I don't know him all that well, but I don't think he would . . . Now, Lucian might," he added dryly. "That old hard-ass isn't above doing anything so long as it achieves the wanted end. He'd think nothing of clubbing a gal over the head and dragging her to his cave."

"How did you know she was dragged?" Cale asked

suspiciously, drawing a return of anger and another curse from Bricker.

"I was speaking metaphorically," Bricker spat. "Christ, you really do think I'd do that kind of thing. What kind of guy do you take me for?"

"The kind of guy who suggests burning her house down so she has to come stay at my hotel," Cale said dryly. It had been one of Bricker's many very bad suggestions earlier that night.

"It was a joke! I was joking. Man, you old dudes are as lacking in humor as you are in wooing skills," he snapped.

A small silence fell. When Bricker spoke again, Cale could hear the frown in his voice and knew the man had thought of something.

"I gather you didn't see who it was?" he asked.

"No," Cale admitted.

"But it was an immortal?"

Cale hesitated. "I can't be sure of that. I didn't see him, and Alex didn't say anything that might reveal that it was. What are you thinking?"

Bricker was silent so long Cale didn't think he'd answer, but then he said reluctantly, "We've been having some trouble with a particular rogue. A no-fanger," he added grimly.

Cale stiffened. His cousin, Decker, had mentioned this at the wedding reception in New York. A no-fanger named Leonius had kidnapped and turned Decker's life mate, Dani, as well as her teenage sister, Stephanie, and seemed to want them back.

"I know about Leonius from Decker," Cale said now.

"But what would make you think he'd wish to harm Alex?"

"Well, one of his sons attacked Alex and Sam's younger sister, Jo, planning to take her back to his father. He seemed to think Leonius would enjoy gaining a little revenge on us through her." He let that sink in and then added, "It's possible this is the same thing. Not likely," he added quickly, "But possible."

Cale frowned. "I don't know. She has had an awful run of bad luck lately, and I've been wondering if it was all connected."

"Yeah, she has," Bricker agreed, and then said, "But I don't think Leonius or his sons would bother with the little problems she's been having."

"Those *little* problems damn near ruined her," Cale murmured, thinking about all the wrong deliveries and defecting employees.

"Maybe, but Leonius isn't the kind of guy who seeks revenge by ruining people. His type of revenge is more a rape-and-torture-type deal."

"Bev said Alex's assailant was trying to drag Alex behind the Dumpster."

"Trying, huh?" Bricker said thoughtfully. "Not likely an immortal then. Any one of us could pick her up with one hand and take her wherever we want her to go. Hell, we wouldn't even have to pick her up, we could make her go where we want with mind control . . . well, the rest of us could. Not you, of course."

"Hmm," Cale murmured, but the revenge business was still in his head. Now that he was thinking it, this whole situation reminded him a great deal of the events leading up to the deaths of his father and brothers. They'd suffered a lot of accidents prior to the ambush as well: defective weapons, suddenly wild horses throwing their riders, and fires. They later realized that those "accidents" were all due to his father's competitor, who had been working himself up to the ambush that killed Cale's father and so many of his brothers.

"I'll talk to Mortimer and see what he thinks, and then get back to you tomorrow. In the meantime, you should really get to sleep and get those shared dreams going."

Cale grimaced at the suggestion, and reminded him, "She has a splitting headache, Bricker."

"I thought that was a married woman's complaint?" Bricker responded quickly, and then laughed at his own joke as he hung up.

Cale shook his head and snapped his phone closed with a sigh. Justin Bricker was an annoying little punk. And Cale was actually starting to like him.

Running a hand through his hair, he glanced around the kitchen. Alex had said to make himself at home. It was a good thing since he was now hungry . . . and for more than food. Unfortunately, Alex wouldn't have a couple of pints of O positive around. She would have food though. Cale would settle for that for now. He wasn't sure how much of the cramping in his stomach was for food and how much was a need for blood. If the food helped, he'd hold out until morning. If not, he'd have to call and see if a special delivery could be made.

Cale moved to the cupboards and began opening them. There was loads of food, but it all seemed to be in boxes or cans with cooking involved. He wasn't in the mood to try that again, so tried the refrigerator next. He'd struck gold. There were several premade meals inside, all merely needing a moment or so in the microwave. Cale had seen Alex use the microwave at the new restaurant several times. She'd brought him lunch every day this last week when she'd checked in to see how things were going, and he'd watched her pop them in the microwave and punch buttons to set it working. He could do that.

Cale chose a plate of lasagne, set it in the microwave, and then peered at the panel. It took him a couple of tries, but then he figured out that he had to hit cook, how long he wanted it to cook for, and then the start button to work the machine. Sighing with satisfaction as the microwave began to hum, Cale stepped back, and then reached for his phone when it rang.

"Yeah," Bricker said as soon as Cale said hello. "So Lucian happened to come in as I was telling Mortimer about Alex's being attacked, and then Sam overheard part of the conversation, and now they both want— Hey!"

There was a rustling, and then Lucian barked, "I'm sending Bricker over to read Alex's mind and see if she caught a glimpse of her attacker. If it's an immortal, I want to know."

"She said she didn't see him," Cale said calmly.

"She's a mortal with a head wound," Lucian said dryly. "She doesn't know what she knows."

"Right," Cale said on a sigh, and then thought to ask, "If Bricker's coming over, have him bring some blood."

Lucian grunted what might have been agreement, and then apparently handed the phone to Sam because her voice was the next to speak.

"Bricker said Alex was all right. She is, isn't she?" she asked anxiously.

"She's fine," Cale said soothingly, glancing toward the microwave when a small popping sound came from inside. The Saran Wrap covering the dish had swollen like a balloon and now had tomato sauce splashed inside as if the sauce were boiling and bubbling, though it didn't appear to be.

"Bricker said she had a concussion," Sam said, reclaiming his attention.

"A mild concussion, yes," he admitted. "But she never lost consciousness, so they said it was all right for her to come home so long as she took it easy for the next couple of days, and there was someone here to keep an eye on her, which I'm doing," he assured her. "I've checked on her several times already and intend to continue checking on her through the night. I'll also stick around and keep an eye on her tomorrow."

"Good," Sam breathed, and then asked worriedly, "She's supposed to take it easy the next couple of days? What about the restaurant?"

"I guess I'll have to find someone to cook for her tomorrow night," Cale said with a sigh, wondering who the hell he would find for that.

"Good luck with that," Sam said dryly, and then warned, "Even if you do find someone to replace her at the restaurant, I don't envy you trying to make her take it easy. She's not a good patient. She'll fret at staying in tomorrow."

"Well, the doctor said she was to take it easy, so she'll just have to take it easy," Cale said grimly. "We can stay in and watch movies or something."

"Yes, well I recommend you start with that, but if she gets stubborn, suggest antiquing," Sam told him.

"Antiquing?" he asked with surprise.

"Yes. Just look around you. Alex loves antiquing, and it's not very strenuous. She'll walk slowly through the shops to look at everything, and you can recommend breaks for coffee and lunch between each place."

Cale didn't have to glance around. He had noticed several antiques when he'd followed Alex in earlier. He'd never heard of antiquing before, but guessed it was buying old stuff and supposed he could bear it to keep Alex from doing anything too strenuous.

"Bricker's ready to head over, and he wants his phone back, but would you mind calling me tomorrow to let me know how she is? Or have her call?" Sam asked.

"Yes, of course," Cale said, giving a start as a much louder pop sounded from inside the microwave. Turning, he saw that the plastic had burst and tomato was now splattered on the door's glass window. He started toward the microwave, but paused as Bricker's voice sounded over the phone.

"I'll be there as quick as I can, but it will probably take forty-five minutes or so to cross town," he announced.

Cale grunted in response and continued on to the microwave, peering in with worry at what was supposed to be his meal.

"Is there anything you want me to bring with me or pick up on the way?" Bricker asked.

Cale peered at the mess inside the microwave, but shook his head, and said, "No thanks. There's plenty of food and coffee here."

"Right. See you soon then," Bricker said.

Cale nodded and hung up before he realized his nod wouldn't have been seen. Shrugging, he slid the phone into his pocket and peered at the microwave panel, searching for the button to shut it off. He'd check his lasagne, clean the inside of the machine and put it on for another ten minutes if it wasn't done. He'd put a different cover on it though. Unfortunately, while he'd watched her press buttons, he hadn't really paid much attention to what Alex used to heat things up in the microwave, but it seemed obvious he needed something heavier than that plastic wrap. Maybe a plastic lid would be better, he thought as he spotted a button labeled clear/stop and pressed it.

Nine

Cale had just set the microwave running again for the sixth time when he heard the knock on the door. Knowing it would be Bricker, he hurried out of the kitchen with relief and strode up the hall to open the front door.

"Hi," Bricker greeted cheerfully. "I brought—"

He stopped abruptly when Cale flipped open the lid of the small cooler he'd just lifted and snatched out a bag of blood to slap to his teeth.

"Hungry I guess," Bricker said wryly, following him into the house when Cale turned and led the way back up the hall to the kitchen. "I only brought four bags. I figure you can't keep it in the refrigerator here anyway, and I can bring more by tomorrow if you can't get away to get your own."

Cale grunted agreement around the bag in his mouth as he went through the kitchen door, then cursed around it as well and rushed for the microwave when he spotted the sparks flying off the pan inside.

"What the hell are you doing?" Bricker asked with horror, setting the cooler on the kitchen table and rushing to his side in front of the microwave. The minute Cale hit the clear/stop button, Bricker jerked the door open and then glanced around for a towel to pull out the pan. "Cripes, you never put metal inside a microwave."

"Well the plastic kept melting," Cale muttered, tearing the now-empty bag from his teeth as the younger immortal dropped the pan in the sink.

"Jesus, you don't put plastic inside either unless it's microwaveable," he said with disgust, then stopped talking and turned slowly, his mouth dropping open as he peered at the various plates around the room. He moved to the closest one and asked, "What's this?"

"Exploded lasagne," Cale said on a sigh.

"Exploded?" Bricker asked, arching an eyebrow.

"The plastic wrap burst and the lasagne kind of exploded all over the inside of the microwave." He grimaced with disgust. "It was a hell of a mess."

"Ah," Bricker murmured and gestured to the next dish. "And this?"

"Melted meat loaf," Cale admitted, moving to take a second bag of blood from the cooler.

"Melted? It looks fine." Bricker poked at it. "The cheese feels kind of weird though."

"That's not cheese, it's a plastic lid that melted when I microwaved it," he explained unhappily. When Bricker raised an eyebrow, he added defensively, "I plan to re-place the container tomorrow."

"Hmm." Bricker moved on to the next dish. "And this?"

"Rock-hard penne. Since the plastic wrap exploded and the Rubbermaid melted, I tried cooking without either. I thought maybe you weren't supposed to cover the food at all, but it came out all shriveled and hard as rock," he pointed out grimly. "That's why I tried the pan for the next one. I figured you must have to cover it with something more solid than plastic."

"How long did you cook it?" Bricker asked.

"Only ten minutes."

"Oh man." He laughed. "You're lucky it didn't burst into flames. It only takes a minute or two to reheat dishes when you have it on high."

"Well, that explains things," Cale said, and slapped the second bag to his teeth.

Shaking his head, Bricker moved to the refrigerator and opened the door. "There's still some kind of pasta dish in here. It looks like an Alfredo of some sort. I'll heat it up for you if you like."

Unable to speak with the new bag in his mouth, Cale nodded.

"Before I forget, Lucian found a cook to replace Alex tomorrow night," Bricker announced as he pulled the Alfredo from the fridge. "Is she sleeping?"

Cale nodded again and watched as Bricker removed the plastic wrap at one corner of the dish, and then set it in the microwave.

"You only use microwaveable plastic wrap, which I'm pretty sure this is," Bricker explained as he began to push buttons. "But you have to leave an opening for the steam to escape."

Cale grunted his understanding around the bag, and then tore it from his teeth as it finished emptying. "Who did Lucian find to replace her?"

"Actually, it was Lucern who got the guy. Lucian called everyone to set them on the task and Lucern called back to say he'd gotten—you won't believe this—Chef Emile agreed to take Alex's place."

"Is he any good?" Cale asked, moving to set both empty bags back in the cooler.

"You're kidding, right?" Bricker asked with amazement. "He's a famous chef, Cale. He has his own show and everything. *Emile's Kitchen.* He's not only good, but this will have the media rushing to La Bonne Vie for interviews and such. It will be good press for Alex, probably get coverage of the opening of the new restaurant too since Lucern invited him to that as well."

Cale narrowed his eyes. "He agreed? Or was convinced?"

"Agreed," Bricker assured him, moving to the microwave when it dinged. "Lucern and Kate are in Toronto for a couple of weeks and Emile is in New York. You can't control a mortal's mind over the phone. Besides, I gather he and Lucern are buddies. Emile did a cookbook for Kate's publishing house. It's how they met. They're always talking online." He shrugged and took out the Alfredo. "So when Lucian called him, Lucern called Emile, and we got lucky. He apparently just finished shooting this season's show and has a couple of weeks off. Lucern asked him to come cook for Alex and stay with him and Kate for a week or so, maybe attend the restaurant opening, and get in relaxation time . . . and he agreed."

"Hmm, I'll have to thank Lucern," Cale murmured. He glanced toward the Alfredo Bricker was now stirring. "Is that ready?"

"No. You put it in for a minute and a half, then stir it and cook it for another forty-five seconds," Bricker explained as he replaced the plastic wrap.

Cale nodded and turned to head for the door. "I'm going to go check on Alex again while that cooks."

"I'll come with you." Bricker set the dish back in the microwave and pressed the buttons to get it going again. When he turned to find Cale had stopped to glare at him, he reminded, "Lucian wants me to read her."

"Right," he muttered, and turned to lead the way upstairs.

Cale paused outside the door, listening to be sure her breathing was slow and steady, and then eased the door open a crack to see that she was indeed sleeping. He turned to Bricker to whisper, "From the door, I don't want her to wake up and find you in her room."

"I'd control her if that happened," Bricker assured him and then quickly added, "From the door is fine."

Nodding, Cale stepped back and waited as Bricker peered in and focused his gaze on Alex. It didn't take long for him to read her. After a moment, he shook his head and eased the door closed.

"He grabbed her from behind, so she didn't see anything," Bricker said as he led the way downstairs. "It didn't feel like an immortal attack though."

"Why is that?" Cale asked as they returned to the kitchen.

"He didn't control her, not even when she went for his eyes with her nails, and he didn't have our strength."

"I see," Cale murmured, moving over to the microwave to retrieve the now-done Alfredo. He set it on the counter to cool and then moved to the cooler of blood to finish off the last two bags as he waited. Before slapping the first to his teeth, he asked, "So you don't think it could be connected to Leonius?"

"Doubtful," Bricker decided. "It just doesn't have the feel of an immortal. Although I suppose Leonius could have spawned a mortal child or two. The son who went after Jo was immortal rather than no-fanger, and while it's rare for a mortal to be impregnated by an immortal or no-fanger, it isn't unheard of. I guess he could have a mortal son trying to win his approval by bringing him someone connected to the family."

Cale pondered that as he waited for his bag to empty. He'd just removed it from his mouth when Bricker spoke again.

"Maybe it was just a mortal mugger or rapist," he suggested.

"Bev suggested it might be that Peter guy who quit on Alex the day I arrived," Cale admitted, setting the empty bag in the cooler with the other two. He then moved to search the drawers for a fork and set it on the table beside the cooling pasta dish.

"I thought his name was Pierre," Bricker said with surprise.

"An affectation," Cale said dryly. "His real name is Peter. And I guess he showed up recently looking to get his job back and wasn't happy when Alex told him no." He slapped the last bag of blood to his teeth. It was better to use them up and send the empty bags with Bricker than to risk Alex finding them in her garbage and asking questions.

"Huh," Bricker said. "I met him a couple of times when I went to the restaurant for dinner with Mortimer and Sam. We always went in back to see Alex before leaving, and that guy was a straight-up-arrogant prick. You haven't happened to come across his address while straightening out Alex's paperwork, have you?"

Cale frowned around the bag in his mouth, forced to wait until it was empty before he could ask, "Why?"

"Because I'll stop by his place on the way home and give him a read, see if it was him or not," Bricker said as he watched Cale set the last empty bag in the cooler with the others, and then move to sit at the table.

"I don't recall his address, but I did see his last check and know his last name. We can probably look it up in the phone book if it's listed," he said, and scooped some Alfredo into his mouth, then paused and simply held it there as the flavor exploded on his tongue.

"Good, huh?" Bricker said enviously.

Cale nodded and swallowed. "Alex has brought me lunches at work and I knew she was a good cook, but this is manna from heaven."

"Yeah." Bricker sighed. "She's one hell of a cook." He turned and walked to where the phone sat on the kitchen counter and opened the drawer below it, then smiled and lifted out a phone book, saying, "Bingo. So what's Peter's last name?"

"Cunningham," Cale answered, and continued eating as Bricker began to leaf through the book. It took several moments, but then he made a triumphant sound. Cale glanced his way in question. "Find it?"

"Yeah, several, now I just have to figure out which one he is." Bricker said dryly as he closed the book. As he put it away, he said, "I saw in Alex's memory that the light wasn't working outside the door when she left but had been earlier in the evening. Do you want me to take a look at that too?"

"Someone smashed the lightbulb," Cale announced quietly.

"Alex didn't know that. Why didn't you say anything to her?"

"Because they couldn't see that and would wonder how I could," Cale pointed out dryly.

"Ah." Bricker nodded in understanding. "It was that dark?"

Cale nodded. "Whoever attacked her probably did it so she wouldn't recognize him if she got a look."

"Which suggests Pierre/Peter is our guy," Bricker said grimly, his gaze on Cale's meal. "I'll go have a meeting of minds with him. I think I'll hit a fast-food joint on the way. The smell of that has made me hungry."

"Thanks for bringing the blood . . . and for the help with heating up dinner," Cale said, standing up to walk him out when Bricker picked up the cooler and headed for the door.

"No problem. Give me a shout if you need anything else. If I can't get away, I can always have one of the other guys swing by."

"Thanks," Cale repeated as the younger immortal opened the front door.

Bricker nodded and paused to glance back. "Good luck with dreaming. Hopefully her headache is gone now and you'll be able to experience the shared-dreams business."

"I'm not counting on it. She took a pretty hard knock. Even if she doesn't have a headache, she might not be up to something like that."

"You weren't counting on her being your life mate either," Bricker pointed out with a grin as he continued out the door. "Good night."

"Good night." Cale watched him walk to an SUV parked in the driveway, get in, and start the engine. He closed the front door and locked it as the SUV began to back out of the drive.

Cale returned to his meal then, savoring every bite of the tasty dish. Once it was finished, he dumped all the meals he'd ruined with his microwaving efforts and cleaned the dishes before heading back up to check on Alex again. Finding her sleeping peacefully, he went downstairs to the living room, and then just stood there for a minute, unsure what to do. It had taken them a lot of time at the hospital, and it was now after three. Cale had been keeping normal hours and should have been tired, but felt wide-awake.

His gaze landed on the television, and he shrugged and grabbed the remote off the coffee table, then settled on the couch and turned on the TV. Cale didn't have a television at home, but he'd taken Bricker's advice and watched some TV at the hotel before dropping off to sleep and knew how to work the remote, which was a bonus. He flicked through the channels until he found something that looked interesting, and then settled in to watch.

Alex woke up thirsty. Shifting sleepily, she sat up and peered around the room in the dim light creeping from the partially closed door of the bathroom. Cale had left the light on and the door slightly open in case she woke in the night, and she now appreciated his thoughtfulness, as she slid from the bed. She considered donning her robe for this trek down to the kitchen in search of water, but then decided her overlarge flannels were more than decent.

A light was on in the living room as she came down the stairs. Alex glanced toward it curiously but headed into the kitchen for the water. After gulping down two glasses, she ran herself a third, and then headed toward the living room, curious to see what Cale was doing.

She found him sleeping on the sofa seated upright, his chin on his chest. Alex grimaced at the thought of the crick he was sure to have in his neck after sleeping like that and moved closer to the couch. She considered waking him, but he looked so peaceful, so she took one of the decorative pillows from the end of the couch, and then moved in front of him. After a hesitation, she stepped between his legs, moving forward until her knees pressed against the couch. She then leaned forward to set the pillow on the sofa back behind him and tried to ease his head to rest on it.

Alex was just about to straighten and head up to her room when his eyes suddenly opened. She froze at once as if caught doing something she shouldn't, and then smiled wryly at her own reaction, and explained, "I was afraid you'd get a crick in your neck from sleeping like tha—"

Her explanation died on a small gasp of surprise as he suddenly reached up and caught her by the back of her head. Before she could do more than blink, he'd tugged her head down over his and pressed his lips to hers. It was so unexpected, Alex didn't react as she should have and pull away. By the time she recalled that she was trying to avoid getting involved with him and that she shouldn't allow this, it was too late. His tongue had slid between her slightly parted lips and into her mouth, stirring up an immediate maelstrom of responses within her. Rather than push him away, Alex found herself opening her mouth wider for him and bracing her hands on the back of the couch on either side of his head.

Cale immediately deepened the kiss, his hands coming up to run along her arms. A shiver of desire slid through her at the simple caress, and then she moaned as his hands slid to clasp her breasts through the flannel of her pajama top. Alex leaned into the caress, giving him some of her weight as he kissed her most thoroughly. When he began to urge her upright, she went with some confusion, and then glanced down with surprise as she felt a cool breeze brush across her chest. Her eyes widened when she saw that the buttons of her flannel top were now undone, leaving it gaping open, her breasts on display.

She swallowed when Cale sat forward on the couch and reached to caress the revealed bounty. Her gaze slid to his face, and she watched his expression through drooping eyelids as he squeezed and kneaded the round orbs. When he then caught her nipples between thumbs and fingers and tweaked them gently, she moaned and covered his hands with her own, her eyes closing briefly as pleasure rolled through her.

"Open your eyes," he whispered, and Alex forced them open in time to see him shift forward to the edge of the couch and close his mouth over one now-hard nipple. She watched with fascination as he alternately suckled, nipped, and flicked the hard tip with his tongue even as he continued to caress her other breast with one hand. Her body was humming with sensation, and she was hardly aware of his other hand's moving until it slid between her legs, rubbing the cloth against her there.

Alex gasped then, and reached for his shoulders, to help her stay upright as he caressed her, sending wave after wave of pleasure sliding through her. She couldn't bear the onslaught for long, however, and soon clasped the hair at the back of his head and pulled it away from her breast so that she could bend to kiss him again. He answered the silent request, mouth rising to hers and tongue sweeping out to plunge into hers, but he continued to move his hand between her legs, the action faster now and more insistent.

Alex groaned into his mouth, and then began to suck on his tongue, her fingers scraping across his scalp with demand. She groaned again, this time in protest, when his hand slid from between her legs. But it was back quickly, slipping between the waistband of her pajamas and her hot skin to touch her again, this time without the cloth between them. The explosion of need within her then was so all-consuming, she was hardly aware of his tugging her pajama bottoms down to pool around her ankles. She only became aware of losing them when he stopped caressing her again to catch her by the waist, lift her out of them, and then set her down to straddle his lap.

The rough material of his jeans brushed against her bare thighs as Alex settled on him, and then he pushed the top off of her shoulders so it could join the bottoms on the floor. Cale broke their kiss and leaned back slightly to peer at her through sleepy eyes, and Alex found herself staring at them with fascination. They seemed more silver than gray now, the silver molten and growing in his eyes as his hand slid between her legs once more. She bit her lip and dug her nails into his shoulders as his fingers danced lightly along her flesh, then Alex moaned and tipped her head back, eyes closing as his fingers dipped in to find the core of her.

"Look at me," he ordered quietly, and she forced herself to lift her head. His eyes appeared almost to be on fire now, and she stared into them as he worked her flesh, her breath coming in small pants that grew more shallow as her excitement mounted. When he slid one finger into her while still caressing her, she couldn't help it, Alex's eyes squeezed closed, her mouth opening on a gasped "Oh" that turned into a moan as it withdrew, only to plunge back in again.

Alex was sure an orgasm was about to rip through her when he suddenly stopped. Opening her eyes, she blinked down at him with confusion, and then gasped in surprise when he caught her at the waist again and lifted her off him. She turned to peer at him, and then saw that he'd stood to remove his own clothes. She rose at once to help, but got distracted by his chest as he lifted his shirt off over his head. Alex couldn't resist running her hands over the wide expanse, but then let them drop to the button and zipper of his jeans, undoing each in quick time.

Despite being tight, his jeans fell away like butter sliding off a roasting turkey, and his erection spilled out, swollen and wanting. Alex instinctively reached for it, but Cale caught her and turned her away from him so her back was to his chest. He then wrapped his arms around her from behind, his mouth pressing to the side of her neck as one of his hands began to caress her breasts and the other slid between her legs again. This time he cupped her, using the hold to press her back against his erection so that her bottom rubbed against him as he then continued his earlier caresses.

"Cale, please," Alex moaned, pushing back into him almost roughly. She was positive she couldn't take much more of this and wanted to feel him inside her, wanted him filling her and driving her to the apex they were headed for. Much to her relief, he heeded her plea. But he didn't draw her down to straddle him on the couch again as she'd expected. Instead, he urged her to kneel on the couch and lean forward so that she could brace herself on the back of it.

Alex cried out as he thrust into her, her nails digging desperately into the back of the couch as her legs trembled. Cale paused then and pressed a kiss to the side of her neck, then withdrew slightly and pressed back into her again. She felt his teeth scrape across the tender flesh of her throat, and Alex turned her head to kiss him with all the passion he was stirring in her; but that made him stop, so she bit down into the back of her couch as he began to pound into her in earnest. When he reached around with his hand to caress her again, she couldn't bear it anymore and cried out as her pleasure exploded around him.

Alex must have slept after that. When next she opened her eyes, she lay on Cale's chest on the couch. Unsure if he was awake or not, she lifted her head slowly to peer at him and managed a smile when she saw that his eyes were open, and he was peering back.

"Hello," she whispered shyly.

"Hello," he said solemnly.

Alex stared at him for a moment, but then her shyness swelled, and she started to rise, but froze as she felt his erection beneath her. Her eyes shot back to his face with shock. "Didn't you—?"

"Yes," he assured her with a wry smile. "But it seems I want you again."

Alex glanced down to his chest and hesitated, unsure

what she should do. She'd already made the big mistake of sleeping with him. Would it make it worse if she did it again?

Deciding that if she had to ask herself that, it probably would, she slid her right foot to the floor, intending to get off him, but as she shifted, she rubbed against his returning erection. The excitement that sent tingling through her made her pause again.

"I don't think I'll ever get enough of you," Cale whispered, shifting his hips so that he rubbed against her once more.

Alex peered down at his solemn face, and muttered, "Oh, what the hell." She reached between them to clasp his erection, and then steered it back inside of her as she settled on top of him. As she did, Cale smiled at her sexily.

"Welcome back," he murmured, and reached for her breasts.

Alex closed her eyes with a little sigh as his hands caressed her, and began to raise herself again, but the ring of a phone had her blinking her eyes open and peering around with confusion.

Frowning, she sat up abruptly as she realized she was in her bed, fully dressed in her flannels, and completely alone. What the hell?

The phone rang again, and Alex reached out to grab and silence it. She pulled it to her ear, and barked, "Hello?"

"Congratulations! You've won a free trip to Las Vegas. All you have to do to claim your prize is—"

"Pay you thousands of dollars," Alex muttered with

disgust and slammed the phone back in its holder. Her gaze slid to the bedside alarm clock as she did, and she sighed when she saw that it was eight thirty in the morning. "Damned telemarketers," she muttered, dropping back in bed.

There was supposed to be a list you could put your name on to avoid getting such calls. She'd have to look into how to get on it, Alex thought, and then glanced around the room again. She really was still dressed and in bed. Had that whole episode with Cale been a dream? It must have been, she realized, and muttered, "I knew those jeans came off way too easy."

Cale stared toward the ceiling overhead, wondering who had called. He'd like to slice them up and fry them slowly for interrupting him and Alex. Hell, these shared wet dreams were something else. They were also definitely wet, he realized, a cool damp sensation at his groin drawing his attention to the darker spot over the erection still raging there. He'd obviously spent himself, and then "boned up" again as Bricker had called it. Thank God he hadn't agreed to the sleep-in-the-van idea.

"Someone could have warned me," he muttered with disgust. He would have brought a change of clothes with him, but all he had was what he was wearing. Cale dropped back onto the couch with a sigh, and then stiffened as he heard movement overhead. Alex was up. Great, now she was going to come down here and—

Cursing, he scrambled off the couch and hurried into the kitchen only to pause in the center of it, unsure what to do. The padding of light footsteps coming down the stairs, however, drove him to action. Rushing to the fridge, he tugged the door open, snatched a half full carton of orange juice from the top shelf and promptly tipped it up to his mouth.

"Good morning, I—"

With his back to her, Cale jerked as if startled and allowed orange juice to splash down over his chin, chest, and then his jeans. He damn near emptied the whole half carton to make sure it got to his jeans before jerking it upright and turning to Alex with feigned surprise.

"Oh, geez, I'm sorry, I didn't mean to startle you." Alex rushed forward. She grabbed the dish towel he'd left to dry beside the sink and hurried to his side to begin mopping up the worst of the juice from his face and chest. "The phone call just woke me up and then I tried to go back to sleep, but I was thirsty, so I came down to get a drink of water and I—"

Cale bit his lip. She'd been mopping at his face then chest as she babbled, and then automatically knelt to continue on to his jeans, but had apparently realized what she was doing and paused. Fortunately, his panic had cooled his passion, and his original erection had gone away; however, watching her mop at him, her hair tousled as it had been in the dream and wearing the adorable flannel pajamas he'd so enjoyed stripping from her in their dream . . . well, he hadn't been able to stop himself from growing half-erect again as the sight brought the dream to mind.

"Oh," she breathed, staring at the bulge in his jeans. "I . . . Maybe you should—"

Alex raised her head and hand, holding the cloth

out and peering up uncertainly from where she knelt before him. That brought a whole new set of images to mind, ones they hadn't tried in the dream. Cale's eyes widened in horror as he completely "boned up" now, his erection pushing against his jeans and creating a very noticeable bulge.

"Yes, yes, of course," he said, taking the towel in one hand and her arm in the other to quickly urge her to her feet when she started to lower her gaze to his growing bulge again. Once he had her on her feet, Cale turned away and moved to the sink, using washing his hands as an excuse to keep his back to her as he waited for his erection to recede.

"I really am sorry," Alex murmured, moving to the cupboard now to retrieve a glass. "I guess I should have made some noise or something to let you know I was coming."

"It wasn't your fault. The phone call roused me from sleep, but I wasn't fully awake. I was just startled," he said quietly, wondering how long he was going to have to wash his hand. This particular erection seemed rather persistent. "How's your head?"

"Pretty good." She moved to a watercooler in the corner and ran cold water into her glass. "A little achy still, but I think more sleep would cure that. It was late when we got back from the hospital."

"Yes," Cale agreed, reluctantly turning off the tap and shaking his hands over the sink to remove the worst of the water as he tried to think of how he was going to keep his back to her. Not coming up with anything, he said a bit abruptly, "You should go back to bed."

"I will after I've had something to eat." She appeared at his side with a fresh dish towel, and Cale murmured a "thanks" as he took it but stayed facing the sink as he dried his hands.

"Geez, where did all the food go? Did you have a party or something last night?"

Cale glanced around to see her standing in the open refrigerator door, frowning over the now-barren shelves. "Oh, I . . . er . . ." Sighing, he set the towel down and moved to the door into the hall. "I need to go get a change of clothes from the hotel anyway. I'll pick up something on the way back."

"Cale."

He heard her feet padding after him and moved a little more quickly to the closet by the front door, managing to retrieve his coat before she caught up.

"Keys." She offered her keys as he turned with the coat held in front of his groin. "So you can get back in."

"Right." He smiled and took the keys, then backed toward the door, the coat still held at his waist. "I won't be long. Any special requests when it comes to food?"

"I'll leave it to you."

"Right." He turned away, pulled the door open, and headed out with relief.

"Put your coat on," she said with a laugh, catching the door when he tried to pull it closed. "It's freezing out there, and you're wet. You'll get frostbite."

Cale quickly shrugged the item on as he jogged down the steps and rushed to the car.

Ten

The house was silent when Cale returned almost two hours later. He'd been as quick as he could be, grabbing a bag of blood from the cooler as soon as he stepped into his hotel room, and then actually feeding on it as he jumped in the shower. It had been the fastest shower in history, he was sure. The bag at his teeth hadn't even been empty by the time he got out, but he'd dried himself one-handed, and then begun to dress in fresh clothes as it finished.

After that Cale had only taken the time to throw more clean clothes into a bag to take back with him before rushing down to his car. Both the stop at the hotel and then hitting the Tim Hortons drive-thru on the way back had probably taken him less than twenty minutes. However, Alex's house was a good forty-minute drive from his hotel, which was where most of the time had gone.

Now he closed the front door, engaged the lock, and carried the food and coffee into the kitchen before removing his outerwear. He quickly put them away in the hall closet, and then moved quietly upstairs. Cale heard her slow, deep breathing before reaching her door, but eased it open anyway to be sure. He smiled widely when he spotted her curled up on her side with her back to him, sleeping peacefully away.

Cale eased the door closed, turned on his heel and rushed back downstairs. She was sleeping! The thought raced madly through his head. *They could share another dream!* The thought had him already half-erect before he'd even reached the living room and the waiting couch. Diving onto it, he settled himself on his back and closed his eyes, eager for sleep to claim him and the dream to start as it had earlier.

"Hello?"

Cale's eyes popped open and he sat up to peer toward the empty doorway with a frown. This wasn't a dream. He'd barely closed his eyes before Alex had called his name. He must have woken her closing the door. Sighing, he called, "Yeah?"

"I thought I heard you come in," she called from the top of the stairs. "I'm just going to grab a shower. I'll be right down."

Cale's shoulders slumped. It seemed there would be no more shared dreams for now. Damn! He'd been looking forward to it. Sighing, he stood up and moved back out to the kitchen. The food and coffee still waited on the table. Cale collected plates and silverware for two. He had poured their coffees into cups and unwrapped and set the food on the plates by the time Alex entered the kitchen. Her hair was damp but brushed, she was dressed in jeans and a blue sweater, and she smelled of oranges and spice as she joined him at the table.

"Wow, it's still warm," she said with pleasure, pressing a finger to the top of her sandwich.

"*Oui.* I got it at the coffee shop just around the corner." Cale settled in a seat across from her. "And you were fast in the shower."

Nodding, she sat down. Both of them were unusually quiet while they ate. Cale didn't need to think hard to figure out why. Every time he glanced at her, their shared dream rose in his mind, stealing any ability to speak. Judging by the way Alex flushed every time she glanced his way, Cale suspected she was suffering from the same problem. It was almost a relief when they had both finished.

They worked together in that same silence as they cleaned their cups and plates, and then Alex glanced at him, flushed, glanced away, and murmured, "I'm thinking I might head over to the restaurant and check that light over the back door, change the bulb. If I don't, I'll forget and end up having to leave in the dark again."

"The doctor said you were supposed to take it easy today," Cale said quietly.

"I know, but I have to cook tonight and—"

"No you don't," Cale interrupted. "My cousin arranged for Emile to fly in and take your place tonight."

Alex looked at him fully for the first time since coming downstairs. She definitely wasn't thinking about their dream this time. Her eyes were wide and uncertain. "Excuse me? Your cousin arranged for who to take my place?"

"Emile," Cale said, smiling wryly at her stunned expression. Apparently she recognized the name where he hadn't. "I gather from a purely business perspective it's a very good move. Not only is he supposed to be a good chef, but they're expecting the press to be all over your restaurant once they hear . . . and if I know my family, there have already been several calls made to the different newsrooms in the city. This should be very good press for the restaurant, as well as the opening next week."

"Damn," Alex breathed, leaning weakly against the counter. "And here I was afraid the attack was a sign that my streak of bad luck hadn't ended like I'd started to think."

Cale smiled incredulously. "You're now thinking your getting attacked is good luck?"

She peered at him as if that were a stupid question. "If it makes Emile cook in my kitchen and garners a lot of press, you're damned right it's good luck. Heck, the kind of press this will bring in is worth broken bones and stitches, maybe even a short coma. A little bump on the head is nothing."

Cale chuckled with disbelief.

"Oh geez," Alex said suddenly straightening. "I need to clean the restaurant."

"I thought you cleaned it every night after closing." Cale followed when she headed out of the kitchen.

"I do, but this is *Emile,*" she said over her shoulder,

speaking the name as if it were synonymous with King or God. "It has to be spotless."

"Would it pass a health inspection?" Cale asked, already knowing the answer. He had noticed the night he'd worked at the restaurant and then again the few times he'd stopped in at closing time, that Alex was very conscientious about that aspect of her business and had trained her people to be as well.

"Of course. I keep a clean kitchen," she said almost indignantly, stopping at the closet and dragging the door open.

"Then it's good enough for Emile," he said reasonably.

"That's different. I want to make sure there isn't even a speck of dust to be found. He's—"

"Alex," Cale said quietly, taking her coat from her when she dragged it off a hanger.

Scowling she turned on him. "Cale, give me that. I have to get to the restaurant and start cleaning. I want to scrub it from top to bottom, use bleach and a toothbrush in every crack and cranny." She frowned and added, "Maybe I should buy a new apron just for him."

She had been grabbing at the coat as she spoke, but Cale just kept shifting it out of her reach. Now he caught her arm, forcing her to a halt. "Scrubbing the kitchen today is not relaxing. In fact, it's more 'not relaxing' than if you were to cook tonight."

"Yes, but this is *Emile*," she emphasized with frustration. "I need to make sure everything is perfect."

Cale stared at her silently, and then sighed and lowered her coat. "Very well, if you insist that Emile's presence means cleaning all day, then I shall call my cousin and tell him to contact Emile and cancel his replacing you."

Alex had snatched her coat from him the moment he lowered it and immediately started to shrug into it, but froze now to turn shocked eyes to him. "What?"

"Well," he said reasonably, "the man is only coming up here to help out because you've been injured and are supposed to take it easy. How do you think he would feel if he went to all that trouble, and then arrived to find that the woman who was supposed to take it easy had worked herself like a dog today cleaning for his arrival . . . Cleaning a kitchen which, by the way, was perfectly spotless when I saw it last night," he added grimly.

"He doesn't have to know," Alex protested.

"He would feel like he'd been taken advantage of, used for his reputation," Cale continued firmly, and then added, "And even if he didn't find out, I would know and not feel right. If you insist on this, I would rather cancel his replacing you, and let you cook, which is surely less strenuous than scrubbing a floor on your hands and knees. The doctor said you were to take it easy."

"But . . ." She stared at him with frustration, but apparently unable to find a valid argument, sagged with defeat. Alex sighed, and her voice was resentful as she muttered, "I guess you're right. He'd probably be pissed to find out I'd been cleaning when I was supposed to be too sick to cook."

"You *are* too sick to cook," Cale said firmly. When she made a face at the claim, he added gently, "Alex, I know you feel fine right now, but your brain suffered a trauma last night. According to the doctor, it took a hard knock and was tossed around inside your skull when you fell. There could be bruising, or damage that isn't showing so far. Please do as he said and just take it easy? Just for one day?"

"Fine," she muttered, shrugging out of her coat and tossing it on the closet floor before slamming the door shut and marching off to the kitchen.

Cale stared after her with amazement, wondering if there really was some damage done. She was acting like a spoiled child who hadn't gotten her way. Fascinated by a side of her he'd never seen before, Cale followed her into the kitchen to find her leaning against the sink, staring out the window above it. When she sensed his arrival, she sighed and turned around muttering, "Sorry."

"I understand," Cale said quietly.

"So"—she forced a bright smile—"I guess I'll just putter around here today and rest. You can leave if you want, though I appreciate your staying last night. It was very sweet of you."

Cale narrowed his eyes, suspicion rising in him. His voice was easygoing when he said, "I'll leave if you like. I need to take your keys over to Lucian anyway."

"My keys?" she asked warily, her smile fading.

"He's going to take Emile to the restaurant. Probably a little earlier than is really necessary, but the man should have the chance to familiarize himself with the setup," Cale lied. No one had mentioned plans on who should let the chef into La Bonne Vie, and he'd decided that morning that he'd do it himself. But he wanted Alex to know that she wasn't going to be rid of him and sneak off to the restaurant as he suspected she was planning. "And of course, I need to take your car keys as well to arrange to have it brought here to you. We were in my car last night, and you'll be without a vehicle until I can have it moved here, but since you plan to stay in anyway . . ."

"Crap," Alex muttered, her smile definitely gone now. It seemed obvious she had been planning to sneak off to the restaurant.

"Or . . ." he began, but paused to consider the plan that had just occurred to him. Cale was now worried Alex was annoyed enough with him that she might send him home out of irritation. But if he could tempt her with an antiquing trip . . . If he left, she would be here without a car, so might be tempted, and he could see to it that she took it easy.

"Or what?" Alex asked scowling.

"Or you and I could do some antiquing today," he suggested, and then cautioned, "We'd have to take it easy. No gallivanting about."

"Gallivanting?" she asked dryly.

"Frequent breaks for coffee or food, and not on your feet for too long," he said firmly.

Alex stared at him for a very long time, but then sighed and pushed away from the counter again. Her tone was sulky when she said, "I guess that's better than being stuck here all day."

"You really are a bad patient, aren't you?" Cale said with amusement as he followed her out of the kitchen.

"Who said I was a bad patient?" Alex asked, glaring over her shoulder.

"Sam."

"Like she's any better," Alex snorted as she opened the closet door and bent to retrieve her discarded coat. She then tugged his coat off its hanger and turned to hand it to him.

"Thank you," Cale murmured.

Alex nodded and shrugged into her coat, before adding, "Besides, I'm not a bad patient."

"No?" Cale asked dryly, pulling on his scarf, hat, and gloves.

"No," she assured him, and then added with a touch of chagrin, "I just like to get my own way."

Cale laughed outright at that admission. He wasn't surprised. She owned her own home, ran her own business, and pretty much was used to getting her own way in matters. But then so was he, and Cale suspected that if he ever did succeed at wooing her into agreeing to be his life mate, there would be some fireworks for the first year or so as they struggled to learn to live as a couple. But the makeup sex would definitely be hot.

"Warm enough?" Alex asked with amusement as she took in the way he'd bundled up. The hat was pulled low on his forehead, and he'd wrapped the scarf around his neck and face so that the only portion of skin the sun would reach was the bit around his eyes.

"I'm European," he said through the scarf. "Not used to this cold."

"Hmm." Alex turned to open the front door. "This from the same man who didn't even pull his coat on before running out to his car this morning."

Cale didn't comment but followed her out of the house, locked the door, and pocketed her keys. He planned to hold on to them until at least tonight. There was no way she was going to ditch him and take off to the restaurant to clean. Crazy woman, he thought with a sigh. She obviously didn't know how fragile she was as a mortal. He would have to look after her until she agreed to the turn, Cale decided, and hoped it didn't take too long to get her to that point now that they'd shared a dream. He didn't know how Mortimer had managed Sam's not turning all these months. The guy must have worried himself sick.

Cale had felt like he'd swallowed his own heart last night when he'd gotten to the restaurant and seen Bev helping a bleeding Alex to her feet. He hadn't been able to get to her fast enough. He needed to up his game on the wooing front and get her to agree to be turned, and that was that.

"This should add some color to the office," Alex said with a pleased smile as she peered down at the framed eight-inch-by-eight-inch print on her lap. It was called *Food Prep,* and showed a chef in a bright Italian-style kitchen slicing a parsnip. Despite the fact that she'd found it today in an antiques store, Alex was pretty sure it wasn't an antique. At least she recalled seeing this print and three others being sold in a set in one of the restaurant catalogues she had. It looked much better live than it had in the tiny picture in the catalogue, and she thought she might order the other three prints that went with it when the restaurant was making a profit.

"It's charming." Cale glanced briefly toward the print, and then quickly returned his eyes to the road as he suggested, "Would you like to stop at the restaurant and hang it before we head over to the old La Bonne Vie for dinner? We're a bit early anyway."

"Yes, please," Alex said happily. They had headed north of the city to hit antiques stores in the small towns there and would drive right past the turnoff leading to the part of the city where the new restaurant resided. In fact, they were already approaching that off-ramp, Alex noted as Cale put on the blinker to take it. She watched him make the maneuver, and then asked curiously, "How does this car handle?"

When Cale glanced at her in question, she explained, "My car's kind of on its last legs and I'll need to replace it in the next six months to a year . . . if I can afford it," she added wryly, and then continued, "I was considering a Pontiac Solstice, but this seems to ride nice."

"It handles well," he assured her, and offered, "You can try it for yourself when we leave the restaurant if you like."

"Ooooh, that rare and exotic animal, a man willing to let a woman drive his car," she teased. Her mood had improved a great deal while they were antiquing. Alex still wished he'd let her give her restaurant kitchen a once-over, but understood why he hadn't. She'd also had fun this afternoon, enjoying wandering through the various antiques stores with him and looking at this and that.

"This is just a rental," he reminded her, and then added, "Though I'd be happy to let you drive my own vehicle. Of course, you have to come to France to do it."

"Like that will happen," she said with a laugh.

"I am sincerely hoping it will," he said solemnly.

Alex glanced at him sharply, her eyes following the outline of his profile. It was the first time anything had been said to suggest he hoped to continue their friendship beyond the two months he was to be here. If it was a friendship. She wasn't sure how to classify their relationship. He worked for her at the moment, had stated a desire to get to know her better, but hadn't tried to kiss her or anything. Well, except in that wild dream she'd had last night, but that was her mind torturing her with what she couldn't have. She couldn't lay that at his door.

Not that she wanted him to kiss her, Alex told herself firmly as she realized the direction of her own thoughts. She hadn't even allowed their conversations to dip into the personal area since the night they'd painted the dining room together. She didn't want to get involved, Alex reminded herself firmly, and turned her face forward as Cale turned into the parking lot behind the new restaurant. Her eyebrows rose when she spotted the SUV parked where she normally parked her own car. "Is that Justin Bricker?"

"Hmm." Cale nodded, his expression serious now.

"I wonder what he's doing here."

"So do I," Cale said dryly as he parked the car.

The moment the vehicle had stopped, Bricker moved to the passenger door and opened it for Alex. Grinning brightly, he greeted, "Hello, beautiful. I see you managed not to kill Cale during your enforced relaxation."

Alex smiled wryly as he took the print from her with one hand and reached out his other for her to hold as she got out of the car. "It was a close one when he wouldn't let me go clean the restaurant, but I managed to control myself."

Bricker chuckled at the claim as he closed the door for her. His gaze then shifted to the print he held. "For the new restaurant?"

"The office," she answered, peering at it again herself.

"Nice," Bricker decided. "I like the colors, and it suits a restaurant perfectly."

"That's what I thought too," she said with a laugh, taking the print back.

"So to what do we owe this visit?" Cale asked, coming around the car to join them.

"I came in search of keys to the restaurant for Lucian. He and Lucern are taking Emile over early so he can familiarize himself."

"Oh, right, I forgot about the keys." Cale began to search his pockets.

"I'm surprised you didn't call," Alex said to Bricker.

Bricker shrugged. "I was in the neighborhood so just swung by. When I realized you weren't here, I was going to call his cell number to see where the two of you were, but then you pulled in and saved me the trouble."

"Here." Cale handed the keys to Bricker. "We're coming by for supper once it's open."

"I'll let your hostess, Sue, know so she saves you a table," Bricker promised.

"If it's too busy, just tell her we'll eat in my office," Alex said, not wanting to put pressure on the woman. They were almost always booked to capacity, but if word of Emile's cooking there tonight had gotten out, she was sure it would be a madhouse, with tables originally ordered for two suddenly sporting four or more as people called friends and invited them along. A certain amount of that happened each night anyway, and they generally tried to accommodate such things, but she suspected tonight would be worse than usual.

"Will do," Bricker assured her.

"Alex, why don't you go inside and decide where you want your print? I'll hang it after I have a word with Bricker," Cale said quietly.

Alex raised her eyebrows curiously, wondering what he wanted to talk about that he couldn't say in front of her, but nodded and turned to make her way to the back door.

"Did you pay Peter a visit last night?" Cale asked the moment Alex disappeared inside the restaurant.

The younger immortal nodded with a grimace. "Yeah. He's an unpleasant little jerk, but he wasn't the attacker. He was pissed at Alex for not hiring him back, though."

"He *was* pissed?" Cale asked, one eyebrow lifting.

"I removed those feelings for him," Bricker said dryly. "He was really bitter, and he's the vengeful sort.

I figured it was better than leaving it and his causing problems later."

Cale nodded. "Good thinking. Thanks."

"So?" Bricker raised an eyebrow of his own now. "Did you have sweet dreams last night?"

Cale scowled. "That's none of your business."

Bricker chuckled, not at all offended by his short tone. Turning away, he headed for the SUV, saying, "That would be a yes then. I'll let Sam know. She's really fretting over the two of you."

Had he thought he was starting to like this guy? Cale asked himself with irritation as he watched the younger immortal get into the SUV and start it up. If so, he was definitely revising that opinion. Shaking his head as Bricker gave him a cheery little wave as he pulled out, Cale turned and headed inside.

The sound of pounding reached him the moment he entered the back door and Cale knew at once that rather than wait for him, Alex had gone ahead with hanging the print herself. The woman was entirely too independent. She seemed determined to prove she didn't need him for anything except the job he'd agreed to do. At least that was how it seemed to him. She was always trying to pay for their meals, always shunning help for the smallest task. She just didn't seem to know how to accept help. It made him feel kind of useless at times.

Sighing, Cale let the door close behind him and headed for the office, his eyes widening with horror when he saw what she'd gotten up to. Rather than drag out the ladder they'd used while painting, she'd pulled the desk chair over, and was now standing with one foot on the seat, and one on the arm of the chair as she pounded the nail of a picture hook into the wall. Alex seemed completely oblivious to the way the chair teetered with each blow, not to mention the fact that the damned thing was on wheels and could roll out from under her at any moment.

Cale hurried across the room as—finished with her pounding—she dropped the hammer on the chair seat and picked up the print to hang it. She'd just released the print when he reached the chair, and said sharply, "Jesus, Alex. You'll break your—"

Breaking off with a curse, Cale reached out to catch her as she gave a start, slipped, and then lost her balance as the chair shifted under her. He caught her close to his chest, closed his eyes briefly with relief that he'd been there to do so, and then snapped them open when she said with irritation, "For heaven's sake, Cale. I nearly broke my neck. You shouldn't startle people like that."

Cale stared down at her scowling face with disbelief. "You—I—"

Alex raised her eyebrows when Cale gave up trying to say whatever it was he was trying to get out and simply stared at her with frustration. She had no idea what had upset him so much. He was the one who had nearly scared her silly. And he was still holding her pressed tightly to his chest too, which was kind of discomfiting for her. She had the most ridiculous urge to slip her arms around his shoulders and press even closer, but managed to resist. Instead, she forced herself to stare back into his face and wait for him to set her down.

Okay, it wasn't really his face her gaze was focused on. For some reason she had zeroed in on his lips and couldn't seem to drag her attention away from them as her mind replayed scenes from her dream the night before. Images of those lips moving across her skin and closing over her nipple ran through her head, and she was just thinking that it seemed terribly hot in her office all of a sudden, when she realized that those sweet lips she was staring at were drawing closer.

He was going to kiss her, some part of her mind yelled in warning, and Alex knew she should turn her head away, or kick her legs to be set down, but found she was unwilling to. She wanted him to kiss her, wanted to know if it would be as wonderful as it had been in her dream.

Surely nothing could be that good, Alex thought faintly, and then his mouth drifted softly over hers, brushing across them as lightly as a butterfly's wings, once, then twice before settling so that his tongue could slide out to urge her lips apart. Alex wasn't aware of giving her brain the order to do it, but her mouth parted willingly enough, allowing his tongue in, and she had to revise her belief that no real kiss could compare with those from her dream. This was definitely as good or better, she decided, as his tongue swept in to tangle with hers.

Cale tasted of lemon meringue pie and coffee, the snack they'd had during the last break he'd insisted on while they'd been antiquing. But it was combined with another taste entirely his own, and Alex found herself moaning and shifting slightly in his arms so that her hands could creep up around his neck. Cale immediately deepened the kiss, his mouth becoming more demanding, and she found she was actually clutching at him and turning her upper body so that she could press closer.

She wasn't aware of his moving until he set her down. Alex was vaguely aware of the desk top suddenly beneath her bottom, but that was all the attention she could manage to spare. Her focus was on the hands now sliding over her body, and then playing over her breasts through her sweater.

Alex groaned and arched into the touch, then gasped when he broke their kiss to trail his lips to her ear. She immediately turned her head into that caress with a gasp, her body shuddering as he nipped at the lobe. She opened her eyes with confusion when he pulled back, and then she glanced down to see that he was working on removing her sweater and had already pushed it up her chest to reveal her bra. Alex instinctively raised her arms to help him, emitting a little sigh when he tugged it up over her head and off, then shuddering when his hands immediately moved to cover the silk triangles over her breasts. He began to kiss her again then, his tongue thrusting into her mouth as he kneaded her through her bra. She felt cool air touch the nipples he'd caressed to points, and she glanced down when he broke the kiss again to see that Cale had tugged the cups under her breasts, leaving them exposed. Not for long. She'd barely realized what he'd done when one hand covered an exposed breast while his mouth bent to the other.

Alex gasped and planted her hands on the desk top, leaning on them to arch her back. Cale immediately caught her by the hips and pulled her closer to the edge of the desk until her legs were framing his hips, the center of her pressing against his groin. She groaned as he repeatedly rubbed against her while continuing to suckle and nip at first one breast, and then the other. Alex had never experienced anything like the passion it sent reverberating through her. It came in waves that rolled through her body one after the other, the first seeming to join with the second, and then the third, building up to an unbearable level.

She wrapped her legs around his, pressing him tight against her in an effort to stop his thrusts. Alex then shifted her weight to one hand and tangled the other in his hair, dragging his head away from her breast and up for a kiss. She had never experienced the depth of sensation he was causing, and it terrified her, but her action didn't help much. In fact, it just made it worse; now he was seducing her with his mouth while one hand took up the torture at her breasts, and the other slid between them to caress her through her jeans.

"Oh God," Alex moaned, tearing her mouth from his and turning her head away. She needed some cessation, some air. She was sure she was going to faint from the pleasure building within her. But Cale simply trailed his mouth across her face to her ear and set up a whole new clamoring as he nibbled industriously there.

When his hands left off caressing her, Alex felt a moment's relief that turned to confusion when he caught her by the hips and lifted her off the desk to stand on her own legs. For a moment she feared he intended to stop, and it left her torn. While these sensations were overwhelming her, she was loath to see them end . . . but stopping was not on his agenda. By the time she realized his hands had shifted to work on the button and zipper of her jeans, they were both already undone, and his hand was slipping inside.

Alex clutched at his shoulders and went up on her tiptoes with a gasp as he now began to caress her through her panties without the heavy cloth of the jeans in the way.

"Cale," she gasped, hearing the desperation in her own voice, and then twisted her head to catch his mouth again, sucking at his tongue when it slid past her lips. Becoming aware that he was tugging at her jeans with his free hand, she reached blindly to help, pushing them off her hips and shimmying slightly to urge them down her legs, then groaning as that shifted her more fully into his caresses.

Her head was spinning now, and Alex was beginning to fear there had been some damage from her head injury after all. No man had ever affected her like this. It couldn't just be because of passion, she thought dazedly, clutching at the front of his shirt as he tore her panties from her. In the next moment, his fingers slid across her moist flesh, and Alex decided she didn't care. The fear was fading under a burning need he was bringing to raging life inside her, and she reached blindly for the front of his jeans to undo his button and zipper, but found the job already done and his erection half-exposed as he shoved his own jeans down his hips.

She barely got to remove him fully from the cloth and clasp him in hand before Cale gave up on the jeans and lifted her onto the desk. Alex gasped at the contact as her hot flesh met the cold wood, and then she was crying out into his mouth as he caught her under the thighs and drove into her, still fully dressed.

Cale paused then, his body filling hers. Alex wasn't sure why until he broke their kiss to peer down at her. Recognizing the uncertainty and question in his eyes, she reached up to press a kiss to his lips, then clasped his behind and dug her nails in, urging him to move.

They both groaned as he slowly withdrew partway, then groaned in unison again as he slid back in, and then his mouth covered hers again and his hips started into the rhythm of an age-old dance . . . It was a very short dance. Already on the edge of orgasm when he entered her, Alex lasted perhaps four more thrusts before her world exploded. She was vaguely aware of his accompanying shout and then darkness swept into her brain eliminating everything else.

Eleven

Alex woke up to find herself lying on Cale's chest on the couch. He must have moved them after she'd lost consciousness, she realized, and then frowned at the fact that she apparently hadn't even stirred when he'd moved her.

Biting her lip, she lay still for several minutes, trying to figure out what had just happened and what it meant. Not that she didn't know she'd just had mind-blowing sex on the desk in the office of her new restaurant with her business manager, there was no denying that. What she didn't understand was how powerful and overwhelming it had been.

Was it just the aftereffects of her head trauma? Sex wasn't normally that all-consuming for her, and she had never before blacked out like an alcoholic after a three-day binge. More important to her than all of that, however, was the question of how she was supposed to face him now.

"I'm awake. You don't have to lie still for fear of waking me."

That whisper from Cale was accompanied by his hand smoothing over her back, and Alex stiffened where she lay. He had completely misconstrued her stillness . . . And that was probably a good thing, she decided. She was supposed to be a grown-up modern woman, not some shrinking violet afraid to face up to what she'd done. Forcing herself to move, Alex braced her hands on either side of him, shifted her knees up on either side of his hips, and started to push herself up. But she froze halfway when the action had her straddling and sliding along the erection that apparently had been cuddled between their bodies.

"I've been awake for a little while," he said wryly when her eyes shot to his with surprise.

Alex blinked as she recalled a very similar scene from her dream. In the dream, that had been enough to make her decide on another go-round and take him into herself. In reality, she didn't think it would probably be that smart a move. She'd already made one huge mistake by sleeping with an employee, she wasn't going to compound it by—

Her thoughts scattered as Cale suddenly lifted his head to catch the nipple of one of the breasts she'd left unintentionally dangling in his face. Eyes locked on his, Alex simply knelt there, unable to force herself off him as she'd intended, not when that small action had reawakened all of her earlier passion. Dear God, how had he done that? she wondered dazedly, and then his hips shifted beneath her, rubbing his erection against her core, and her eyes shot open.

"Ride me," Cale whispered, allowing her nipple to slip from his lips. His hands moved to her hips then, and Alex found herself doing as he asked, shifting herself back and down to take him inside her. She then relocated her hands to his chest to brace herself and began to move over him, still not understanding how the passion had erupted to full-blown life as it had, but no longer caring.

The distant sound of knocking stirred Cale to wakefulness. He frowned briefly, wondering who it could be, but then recalled that he'd called Bricker after waking from the first round of lovemaking with Alex and asked him to bring him blood. It had seemed a good idea at the time. He'd only managed the one bag that morning and had found himself fighting not to bite her as his lips had played over her sweet skin. But he hadn't wanted to slip out and get it himself for fear that Alex would wake and scurry off to her house or the restaurant, and then do her best to avoid being alone with him again.

Actually, their first time together had been so quick and almost violently overwhelming that he'd feared it would scare the hell out of her and she'd do her level best not to see him again. Having the blood brought to him had been the only way he could think to avoid both the possibility of her scampering away and his biting her.

Bricker had agreed, but warned that it might take

some time for him to get there, so Cale had carried Alex to the couch and settled there with her to wait, not terribly surprised when she woke before the other man's arrival, and he'd again had to steel himself against biting her.

Fortunately, that session had been even shorter than the first, mostly due to the fact that Cale had been lying there for a very long time, holding Alex in his arms, inhaling her scent, and thinking of all the things he wanted to do to her. By the time he'd sensed she was awake, Cale had been as turned on as if he'd spent the entire time doing what he'd imagined, and that passion had quickly flooded her.

Another round of knocking forced Cale to action, and he carefully eased Alex off his chest, and then got up to answer the summons. He was out of the office and half-way across the kitchen before he recalled that he was naked. His footsteps slowed then, but afraid Bricker would knock again and wake Alex, he eschewed returning for his clothes and hurried to the door.

"Finally," Bricker muttered when Cale pushed it open. "I was beginning to think—" He paused abruptly as he noted Cale's state of undress, and then began to grin. "I guess that answers one question. You two finally got it on, huh?"

Cale scowled and snatched the cooler from him. He'd started to close the door when Bricker said, "Do you really want to keep that in there? Alex might—"

Cale cursed and pushed the door back open. "Get in here. I'll have a bag or two, and then you can take it away."

"Actually, I brought several bags this time. I was thinking you could put it in the trunk of your car," Bricker said, stepping in from the cold. "Just in case this turns into a three-day marathon session or something, and you need more."

"Good idea," Cale decided, pushing him back out the door again.

"Hold on." Bricker laughed. "Geez, if I were the sensitive sort, I might be hurt by your eagerness to be rid of me and just leave. Then you'd never even see the other delights I brought for you."

"What delights?" he asked suspiciously.

Bricker held up the bags Cale hadn't noticed he held in his other hand. "Food and drink. A meal à la Emile made especially for you two. As well as enough groceries to tide you over for a day or two."

Cale stopped trying to push him out the door and sighed. "Thank you. It was thoughtful."

"I'm a thoughtful guy," Bricker said lightly, and carried the bags over to the counter. "I got you wine, fruit, sandwich stuff, and chips." He paused in unloading the food to grin and say, "I didn't buy any dessert, but I did get whipped cream in case you wanted to make a dessert of Alex . . . or vice versa."

"Just when I was starting to like you again, you come out with a crack like that," Cale said dryly, setting the cooler on the counter.

"Oh, now, Cale, you'll make me blush with bromance talk like that," Bricker taunted, continuing with his unpacking.

"Bromance?" Cale asked with disgust. "What the hell is that?"

Bricker opened his mouth to answer, but then shook his head and returned to unloading groceries. "I think I'll let you fret over it until you can look it up online."

"God, you are an ass sometimes," Cale muttered, reaching for the lunchmeat, intending to put it in the fridge. He never got the chance; Bricker slapped his hand, startling him into dropping the package.

"What are you doing?" the younger immortal snapped. "Get away from the food. God, you're naked as a baby, and I know where your hands have been. Get over to the sink and clean yourself up. I'll put this stuff away."

"You're worse than my mother," Cale muttered, but instead of heading to the sink, he moved back into the office. Alex was still sound asleep on the couch as he passed through on the way to the attached bathroom. She'd explained to him the night they'd painted the dining room that her office used to be the master suite with an attached bathroom. She'd considered ripping it out and making her office bigger, but then had decided it might come in handy and left it, figuring she could always have it removed later if it never got used.

It was getting used now, Cale decided. The shower he took was very quick, and Bricker was just putting the last of the food away when Cale returned to the kitchen, hair damp and a towel wrapped around his waist. Dressing had seemed a waste since he intended on waking Alex with kisses and caresses as soon as he was rid of Bricker.

"That's everything except the meals Emile made. They're in insulated bags so should stay warm a bit longer," Bricker commented, stepping out of the walk-in refrigerator. "Now, why don't you down a couple bags of blood, then I'll take the cooler back out and put it in your trunk for you before I go."

"You go ahead," Cale said. "I can take the cooler out to the car when I'm done."

"Fancy a frostbit dick, do you?" Bricker asked, peering pointedly at his undressed state.

Cale grimaced and walked to the cooler to retrieve a bag of blood. He'd just slapped the bag to his teeth when he heard movement from the office. His eyes widened, and he started to instinctively pull the bag away, but Bricker was suddenly in front of him, staying his hand.

"Don't panic," he hissed, keeping Cale from removing the bag and making one hell of a mess. "You may not be able to control Alex, but I can."

When Cale glared at him over the bag, furious at the thought of his controlling her, Bricker sighed.

"I'll just put it in her mind to have a shower like you did. That will give you time to finish feeding before she comes looking for you," he said reassuringly, and then when Cale relaxed, he muttered, "You guys all get so touchy about anyone reading or controlling your women. What did you think I was going to do? Make her do naked cartwheels out of the office and into the kitchen?"

When Cale glowered at the very thought, Bricker laughed and turned his head toward the office door.

Cale couldn't see into the office from where he stood,

but Bricker was in a better position to do so, and he knew the younger immortal must be able to see Alex because they had to be able to see mortals to read their minds and control them. That fact had him reaching for the bag at his teeth again. He was not having Bricker looking at Alex naked.

"Settle down, hoss," Bricker muttered, reaching out to stay his hand again. "I'm looking at her face and nothing else."

Cale reluctantly forced himself to relax and waited.

"Man, Alex is one mixed-up chick at the moment," Bricker muttered, apparently reading her thoughts. "By the way, Sam said to warn you that some guy really messed with Alex's head in culinary school and that she's dated casually but hasn't had a serious relationship since."

Cale frowned at this news. Alex hadn't mentioned anything like that, but then other than the night they'd painted the dining room, she'd been very reticent about herself, determined to keep their relationship on a professional footing.

"Yeah, that whole professional footing thing is just what she's telling herself," Bricker informed him, obviously reading his thoughts as well as Alex's mind. "The truth is, she's afraid of getting hurt again, and she sensed from the start that you were the first man she'd met in a long time who could do that."

Cale's eyes widened. That was good news . . . sort of.

"I'll just send her to the shower, and then veil those fears of hers a little so she doesn't run screaming into the night before you can win her over."

Cale frowned again, not at all sure he wanted Bricker to veil her fears. It seemed unfair.

"Yeah, but you really want me to because you desperately want her to be your life mate," Bricker announced.

Cale admitted guiltily that the man was right. He did want him to, but that didn't mean he should let him.

"Too late," Bricker announced, relaxing. He glanced to Cale. "She's in the shower, and your bag is empty. Get a fresh one. Then give me your car keys."

Cale ripped the empty bag from his teeth and stalked over to the cooler to get another. He then slapped it to his teeth as he stomped across the kitchen and into the office. Not only did Cale like to get his way as Alex did, he also disliked taking direction, even if those directions were sensible.

Alex stepped out of the shower, dried herself off, and then strode back into the office naked. Once there, she picked up Cale's shirt and pulled it on, wondering even as she did it why she wasn't pulling on her clothes. That had been her first intention on awaking alone in her office. This time Cale hadn't been there to tempt her with a throbbing erection, and her first instinct had been to scramble off the couch and into her clothes, and then make a hasty retreat to figure out what the hell she was doing.

However, Alex had barely finished pulling on her sweater when she'd suddenly found herself tugging it back off and heading for the shower. Now a part of her brain was again urging her to pull on her clothes and make her escape, but it was less urgent, and more a suggestion. She found herself merely doing up the buttons on the front of the shirt and heading out into the kitchen.

Cale was at the back door when she stepped into the room. Dressed in only a towel that was barely wrapped about his waist, he was saying something to someone outside. Curious, Alex started toward him, but he finished his conversation and closed the door before she reached him.

"Who was that?" she asked.

Cale whirled from the door almost guiltily, but then quickly recovered and smiled as he crossed to meet her. His arms slid around her, drawing her close as his head lowered and despite the confusion in her mind, Alex found herself lifting her face for his kiss, and then closing her eyes when his mouth covered her. A small sigh slid from her lips when it ended, and he pulled back to answer her question.

"Bricker. He brought over a meal Emile put together for us."

"Really?" Alex asked, her eyes blinking open with surprise. When he nodded, Alex slid from his arms and, spotting the bag on the counter, she rushed over to peer inside. All there was to see was an insulated pack. Two insulated packs, she realized as she pulled the top one out.

"I take it you're hungry?" Cale asked with amusement, following her.

Alex glanced at him with surprise. "Aren't you? It's

well past dinnertime," she pointed out as she unzipped the pack. She then added in an embarrassed mutter, "We must have slept for a while."

"A little while," he said gently.

Alex felt herself flush and tried to ignore it as she lifted the lid of the insulated bag and let it drop open. She couldn't hold back her "Mmmm," of pleasure as the most incredible smell wafted up to tease her nose.

"Smells good." Cale leaned closer, lured in by the smell. "What is it?"

"I don't know," she admitted on a laugh as she lifted the covered container out. "But it smells to die for."

"Yes, it does," Cale agreed.

Alex set the first dish on the counter, and then moved to retrieve the second insulated pack from the carrier bag. This one emitted a different aroma when she unzipped it and took out the dish.

"They're different," Cale commented, glancing from one to the other.

Alex shrugged as she set the second container down. "He probably sent two different kinds of dishes in case one or the other of us didn't like one of them."

Cale nodded and began to open the first container as she took the lid off the second. They then took a minute to examine each dish.

"That's coq au vin, and some sort of salad," Alex announced, pointing to his dish.

"Chicken in wine?" Cale murmured, then glanced to her dish, and asked, "And that one?"

"Gratin Dauphinois and Basque chicken," she said

after a moment, and then explained, "Basically cheesy potatoes and chicken cooked with ham, peppers, tomatoes, and garlic."

"I don't recall those being on your menu," Cale said with a frown.

"No." She smiled slightly. "But the ingredients are in the kitchen anyway. He probably wanted to make something different than what everyone was ordering."

Cale nodded and then raised an eyebrow. "So which one do you want?"

"Both," she admitted with a laugh. "Let's share."

"Sounds good," he decided and moved away to find silverware as he asked, "In the dining room?"

"Sure." Alex picked up both dishes and headed for the door to the dining room, but paused when Cale suddenly went rushing past her.

"Let me get the blinds."

"Oh." Alex paused in the doorway, thinking it was a good thing they'd arrived and been hung this last week. The moment the last one was closed, she moved to one of the tables closer to the kitchen door and set down the plates.

"Good choice," Cale complimented as he rejoined her. "This way we don't have to bother with the lights."

"My thoughts exactly," Alex murmured, glancing around. The light splashing through the kitchen door and the long opening above the counter that the orders would be passed through gave off enough light for them to eat without having to turn on the overheads. It was actually nice, good ambience.

A moan from Cale drew her gaze around, and she smiled when she saw him chewing. He'd started without her.

"This one is very good," he announced after swallowing.

"Well, Emile didn't get famous by cooking bad food," she said with a sigh.

"Would you like to be as famous as he?" Cale asked curiously as he watched her lift a forkful of Basque chicken to her mouth.

Alex paused to consider the question, and admitted, "Probably every chef wants to be the next Emile, but . . ."

"But?" he prompted.

"But I don't think I'd care for the kind of fame he suffers," she admitted. When Cale raised his eyebrows in question, she shrugged. "The man lives in a fishbowl. Papparazzi follow him around like he's an actor, all of them just hoping and praying to catch him having one of his famous tantrums. He's forever landing in the news for one thing or another." She shook her head. "I wouldn't like that."

"Hmm. No I guess not."

Alex could feel him watching her as she ate and was suddenly incredibly self-conscious.

"How is it?" Cale asked.

Alex saw the hungry way he was watching her collect more food on her fork and nearly laughed aloud. It seemed her self-consciousness had been for nothing. It was the food he was lusting after now, not her.

"Here," she said with a smile, and held the forkful of food out to him.

Cale closed his hand around hers and helped steer the food to his mouth, the action forcing her to rise up slightly out of her seat. His eyes were on her as he did it, and little silver flames seemed to dance in their centers as he closed his lips over the forkful of food, and then slowly eased her hand back to remove the clean fork.

Her hand still caught in his, Alex found herself watching with fascination as he chewed and swallowed. Then his tongue slid out to run over his lips, and he smiled. "Delicious. The only thing that would make it better was if I were eating it off your body."

Alex's eyes rounded at the images that brought to mind. When he then released her hand, she dropped back into her seat with a little bump, her gaze still locked with his.

"You should eat," he said solemnly. "You're going to need your energy."

Alex opened her mouth, closed it again, and then dropped her gaze almost desperately to her plate. She was trying to regain her composure when he said, "Try this."

She lifted her head reluctantly to find that he was holding out a forkful of coq au vin. Swallowing, Alex hesitated, and then leaned forward and opened her mouth to accept the offering. Cale slid it in and her mouth closed automatically, but she was terribly aware of his eyes watching her as she did. When he began to withdraw the fork in a slow, leisurely fashion, her mind meandered its way into the gutter, thinking of his body withdrawing from hers during sex.

"Is it hot in here?" Alex asked faintly as soon as she'd swallowed. She managed to drag her gaze from his with some effort and return it to her plate.

"*Oui*. A little," he murmured, and then suggested, "If you're uncomfortable, why don't you take off my shirt?"

Her eyes shot to his again. He'd said it so smoothly, as if it were the most reasonable thing in the world. And considering that she'd had sex twice with him, Alex supposed she shouldn't be so shocked at the prospect of being naked again. Actually, she really wasn't. What was shocking her was that she wanted to do it. She wanted to stand up, move in front of him, and slowly undo every button of his shirt, shrug it off, and then jump on his lap and ride him like a cowgirl.

So much for a professional footing, she thought wryly, and then admitted that that had gone out the window hours ago.

"Come here."

Alex raised her head as he scooted his seat back and held out his hand. She hesitated, but then took the hand he offered and stood, allowing him to tug her gently around the table as he turned in his seat so that he sat it sideways. Once he had her where he wanted her, Cale released her hand and reached for the front of his shirt, quickly releasing button after button. He then eased the two flaps apart, the soft material brushing over her suddenly erect and very sensitive nipples.

"Mmmm," he murmured, running a hand up over the skin of her belly to cup one full breast. "Even Emile can't compete with Chef Alex."

A small burst of nervous laughter slipped from her lips at his teasing, but it ended on a gasp as he leaned forward to press a kiss to her stomach. Swallowing, she laced her fingers into his hair and cupped his head as his hands slid up the outside of her legs to smooth over her hips. His lips moved across her stomach from one side to the other, nibbling and tickling in a way that made her muscles jump and her toes curl into the carpeting.

"Beautiful," he whispered against her flesh, then he slid one hand around to cup her behind and urge her closer as his lips moved down to run over her hipbone. The other hand, however, was trailing up her inner thigh, and Alex bit her lip and closed her eyes as it skated across her skin toward the core of her. It never went there, however. Instead, it shifted under her thigh and raised it even as he slid from the chair to kneel on the floor.

Alex blinked her eyes open, clutching at his head a little desperately as he slid her one leg over his shoulder and ducked. When his tongue rasped over her tender flesh, she moaned and shuddered violently, the leg she was standing on beginning to tremble madly.

The man had a very talented mouth. She'd thought him a skilled kisser, but it was nothing compared to what he was doing now. It was as if he knew exactly where to touch to best pleasure her, when to exert pressure and when not to, when to go fast and when to slow down. Within seconds, Alex found herself a sad trembling mass and was sure she wouldn't even still be standing if not for his hands bracing her thighs. Afraid she was going to collapse on the poor man, she tugged at his hair to make him stop.

Cale leaned back to peer up at her, hesitated, and then started to stand. Relieved, Alex reached for him then, and started to drop to her own knees, intending to earn herself a break by pleasuring him. But her knees had barely hit the floor and her mouth had only just closed around him when he caught her arms and dragged her back to her feet. Alex allowed it more out of shock than anything. As brief as the contact between her mouth and his erection had been, it had sent a shock of pleasure through her as if she had been experiencing the caress herself.

"I—" Alex began, but her attempt to tell him of her strange experience ended on a gasp as Cale lifted her onto the table beside theirs. He moved between her legs and slid into her before that gasp ended. By the time they'd both cried out, and then passed out moments later, Alex had already forgotten the strange incident.

Twelve

Alex shifted sleepily, and then gasped in surprised
pain as her knee banged into something hard. Blinking her eyes open, she peered about, a sigh slipping
from her lips as she stared around her kitchen from
a perspective she'd never thought she'd have. She was
on the cold ceramic tiles that covered the floor, somewhere between one of the grills and one of the food-
prep tables. The table was what her knee had hit.

She rubbed the spot to ease the soreness, and then
glanced toward the man collapsed half on top of her.
Cale Valens, an amazing chef, incredible business
manager, and extraordinary lover. The man appeared
to be exceptional at everything he did. She could vouch
for that. She also couldn't seem to get enough of him.
All he had to do was touch her, and she melted like
warm chocolate.

In the last—she didn't even know how many hours—

they had made love in her office, the dining room, the office again on the couch, and, finally, the kitchen. The last time hadn't been any more planned than the others. They'd come in here in search of food, but their desire for each other had derailed their attempt to enjoy the groceries Bricker had brought them. Which was how she now found herself waking up on the cold kitchen floor, half-covered by Cale and surrounded by the remains of their attempted picnic.

Her gaze slid over the half-eaten fruit strewn on the floor around them and the nearly empty can of whipped cream. Aware that her nipples were growing hard again as she recalled how that can had gotten emptied, Alex decided it was time to move. While making love in almost every room of her restaurant had been fun, she'd had enough of hard surfaces. A nice soft bed with warm blankets and clean sheets would be her first choice from now on.

Alex sighed faintly at the thought as she eased out from under Cale. She had given up thinking that they could return to a more professional relationship. Actually, Alex didn't even want it anymore. The idea of giving up the pleasure they'd shared tonight was no longer one she even wished to consider. The man had gotten under her skin . . . and in her skin. And she wanted him there again, and again, and again for as long as possible. Alex suspected it would break her heart when he left, but there was nothing she could do about that at this point. She'd already fallen for the guy, and the only thing she could do was make as many memories with him as she could before he left.

Cale sighed sleepily and shifted onto his side, and Alex froze briefly, half-upright; but when his breathing returned to a slow, steady rhythm, she finished standing, and then tiptoed across the room to her office and through it to the bathroom. She leaned into the tub and turned on the taps, deciding she would take a quick shower to remove the sticky film the whipped cream had left behind. Then she would get dressed before Cale woke and wake him to suggest they head to her place.

Alex adjusted the knobs until the water was nice and hot without being scalding, and then hit the button to send the water through the showerhead rather than the taps. She stepped into the tub, pulling the door closed before too much water could escape. As she turned under the warm spray, Alex had to admit that leaving the bathroom in place rather than making her office larger had been a brilliant move. It had certainly come in handy tonight. She just wished she'd thought to buy more than the liquid hand soap they'd been forced to use tonight. She pressed the pump to squirt some of the vanilla-scented soap into her hand and began to work her hands to make a lather.

Some shampoo and a proper bar of soap, or even body scrub would have been nice too, she thought as she spread the lather over her body, washing away the sticky whipped cream. Getting some proper bath towels in here would be nice as well. The overlarge hand towels she'd bought for the bathroom were still really too small to be of much use, it had barely reached around Cale's hips. Recalling how skimpy the item had been on him, Alex felt heat flow through her and immediately turned into the spray to rinse the lather away.

"Mmm. Warm and wet Alex, my favorite meal."

Alex glanced over her shoulder with a start. Her eyes widened with alarm when she saw that Cale had the door open and was stepping in to join her.

"Oh, no," she said, backing into the corner to avoid his touch when he reached for her. She knew from experience that if he even so much as brushed against her, she'd fall into his arms. If that happened, she'd find herself waking up on top, or under, him in the bottom of the tub. If she woke up at all, Alex thought grimly. With her luck, she'd pass out on her back on the bottom of the tub and drown from the water spraying into her mouth.

Realizing that Cale had frozen and was now peering at her uncertainly, she smiled wryly, and explained, "I was hoping we could try a bed next time. Maybe go to my place?"

Cale relaxed and nodded, his voice solemn when he said, "*Oui.* I'd like that."

Alex let out a relieved breath, but knew she wasn't out of the woods yet. Now that it had been unleashed, their passion for each other was volatile enough that they still might end up a soggy puddle in the bottom of the tub should they brush against each other even accidentally. She glanced down at herself and saw that the water had rinsed the soap away.

"Then I'll get out and get dressed. I was done in here anyway," she said, easing toward the sliding panel at her end of the tub.

"Are you sure? I can get out and wait if you—"

"No, no, I'm sure." She slid the door open and stepped out. "You go ahead."

Alex quickly eased the door closed, shutting him inside alone, and only then released a little sigh of relief. She'd grabbed one of the towels and begun to dry herself when Cale spoke from inside the tub.

"Maybe we should collect your car on the way so you aren't trapped at the house after I leave for work."

Alex paused and grabbed her wristwatch off the sink counter where she'd left it before her first shower that evening. She frowned when she saw the time. "It's almost two in the morning, Cale. Surely you don't plan to work today when you've had so little sleep?"

"Not right away, no. But I don't sleep as much as most people. I could come back later in the day while you're resting and get at least a couple hours' paperwork done. I wouldn't want to shirk my work and disappoint my boss," he added with a chuckle.

"Trust me, I don't think it's possible for you to disappoint your boss," Alex said dryly, and smiled when he laughed again. Shaking her head, she added, "And your boss thinks that having spent Saturday night and Sunday babysitting her after her head injury, you deserve a day off."

"Well, I might have to make a run to the hotel for fresh clothes at some point, and you'll need the car eventually. We might as well stop and collect it on the way."

The old La Bonne Vie restaurant wasn't exactly on the way. In fact, it was quite out of the way. However, at this hour the traffic would be light on the highway, which probably cut the time it would take to get there in half, she realized.

"Okay, we'll stop and pick up my car," Alex said finally, and then stiffened when the sound of rushing water suddenly died. When the sliding door then began to open, she dropped the towel she'd been using and rushed out of the bathroom to retrieve her clothes from where they still lay strewn on the office floor. Alex had her panties, jeans, and bra on and was just pulling her sweater over her head when Cale came out of the bathroom. She took one look at his proud naked body as she tugged her sweater into place and immediately headed for the door, muttering, "I'll get your shirt."

Alex found his shirt in the dining room, lying forgotten on the floor between the two tables they'd used, only one to eat on. She then wrinkled her nose and collected their forgotten meals from Emile, stacking the containers one on top of the other to carry into the kitchen.

"Ah, you found it," Cale said, entering the kitchen as she crossed it. He moved toward her, his gaze sliding to the containers she held and a grimace claimed his features. "Emile's meals don't look nearly as tasty cold."

"No," she agreed, handing him his shirt, careful to be sure that her hand didn't touch his. Alex then continued on to the garbage and dumped the plastic containers of food while he finished dressing.

"I'll get our coats," Cale said, tucking in his shirt as he turned to head back to the office.

Alex started to follow, intending to get her purse, but

then recalled the food on the floor from their last session and instead walked around the counter. However, there was no food on the floor when she got there. Cale must have collected and discarded it all before following her into the shower, she realized with surprise, and thought the man was just too good to be true. There just had to be some horrible flaw she didn't yet know about. No one, man or woman, was this perfect.

"I brought your purse too," Cale announced, returning to the kitchen with his coat on but undone and his scarf around his neck. "Was there anything else I should have grabbed?"

"Thank you. No, that's all I had," she murmured, accepting her coat and purse, noticing as she did that he too was careful that their hands didn't touch.

"You said you wanted to try my car, do you want to drive it to La Bonne Vie One?" Cale asked as he did up his coat, and then retrieved his hat and gloves from his pocket to don them as well.

"Okay." Alex smiled at the offer, surprised he remembered. Her smile faded though as she led the way to the back door and the thought occurred to her that he really was too perfect.

"Here." Cale held out the keys to her as she turned from locking the back door of the restaurant moments later, and Alex held out her hand for him to drop them into. They then quickly walked to his car, both of them hurrying to get out of the cold. It was bad enough during the day, but at that hour it was absolutely frigid. At least there was no wind today to make it even worse, Alex thought as she scrambled into the driver's side.

She started the engine before doing anything else, and then adjusted the seat before glancing to Cale with surprise as he opened the back door rather than the front.

"Turn on the defroster," he said as he retrieved a scraper from the backseat, and then the door closed and he began to scrape the windows.

Alex did as he suggested, and then glanced around the backseat to see if there was another scraper. Not seeing one, she picked up her purse and quickly retrieved her air-miles card. After taking a moment to crank up the heat, she slid out and began to scrape the driver's side window.

"Where did you get a scraper?" Cale asked with surprise.

Alex held up her air-miles card and laughed at his surprised expression. "We hearty northerners learn to improvise while quite young."

"I guess so," he said with amusement.

"Credit cards work too," she informed him as she finished with the side window and moved to the back. "But it can be inconvenient if you damage them so I prefer to use my air-miles card."

"I'll keep that in mind."

Alex smiled faintly and moved to the rear window. As quick as the job was with them both working, she was still relieved when they'd finished and could get back into the car, especially since it was much warmer than it had been when they'd first come out.

"Do you want to grab a coffee at a drive-thru on the way?" Alex asked as she steered the rental car out of the parking lot.

"Sounds good," he said, and then asked suddenly, "Don't you have any gloves?"

Alex heard the frown in his voice and glanced over to see the concern on his face as he eyed the way she was holding the steering wheel. While the car interior was warm now, the steering wheel still felt like a block of ice, and she was holding it with as little contact as possible. Biting her lip, she closed her fingers around it properly, and said, "I do have gloves . . . somewhere. But I seem to forget to grab them all the time. It doesn't matter, though. I'm fine."

"Here." His gloves suddenly appeared in her peripheral vision as she stopped at a light.

Alex hesitated, but the steering wheel really was cold. Sighing, she accepted the gloves and tugged them on, murmuring, "Thank you" as she did.

"I'm buying you gloves for Christmas," he decided, and then teased, "The kind with the connecting string between them so that they're always in your coat, hanging out your sleeves waiting for you . . . and I'll insist you wear them."

"That threat doesn't scare me," she scoffed. "Christmas isn't for another ten months, and you're leaving in less than two."

"Maybe," he murmured.

His tone was so soft she'd almost missed the words, and Alex glanced at him sharply. "What does that mean?"

"It means I like it here and might be willing to make this my permanent home. It just depends."

Alex swallowed and turned her eyes back to the road before asking, "Depends on what?"

"On you."

Alex jerked to a halt at another set of lights and turned to peer at him with something like awe. The man was talking about a future with her. At least she thought he was. Wasn't he?

They were both silent for a minute, simply staring at each other, and then Cale turned to glance out the front window and said, "The light has changed."

Alex glanced to the light to see that it was green and eased her foot off the brakes.

Neither of them spoke again for the rest of the trip. She didn't know what Cale was thinking, but her own mind was so busy running around in circles that she was hardly able to give driving the proper attention. Alex even forgot to stop for the coffee she'd suggested when they'd started out as she pondered the possibility of a real, permanent-type relationship with him. Cale was the kind of man every woman was looking for, smart, sexy, considerate, and an incredible lover. The fact that she found him attractive was just the icing on the cake, because frankly, even a not-so-attractive man started to look like a supermodel when he had all those other traits. And he might be hers, she thought, her head whirling . . . and then the more cynical side of her spoke up, saying there had to be some huge flaw to the man, or he surely would have been scooped up by some other woman years ago. He probably liked to dress up in women's clothing on the weekend and pick up men, she thought . . . or maybe he was a serial killer.

"You go ahead and drive this car," Cale said as she

pulled in next to her own, still waiting in La Bonne Vie's parking lot. "Your car will still be cold."

He was out of the rental before she could respond, but Alex was quick to follow.

"Get back in the car." Cale scowled at her over the hood of the rental. "There's no need for both of us to be cold."

"I can help. Two scrapers are better than one," she said lightly, and started to tug off his gloves. When he came around the car protesting, Alex kept one on and handed him the other as she slid her now bare hand into her pocket. "I only need one hand to scrape."

Cale hesitated, but then smiled wryly and accepted the glove, commenting, "Compromise is good."

"Yes it is," she agreed softly, and turned to her car to retrieve her own scraper.

"Here."

Alex straightened to see him holding out her keys.

"Get the engine going while I start scraping."

Nodding, she took the keys and slid behind the wheel, starting it quickly. As she had in his car, Alex then turned on the defroster and cranked up the heat, but she also took a second to adjust the seat back to accommodate his long legs before grabbing her scraper and getting out.

With both of them working, they had the windows scraped in no time. Cale then opened the door of his rental for her.

"Here take your glove back, this steering wheel is warm now, and mine won't be." Alex removed and handed him the second glove as she slid into the driver's seat of the rental. As Cale took it, she added, "You should probably take the lead on the way to my house. You have to pull into the driveway first; otherwise, my car will be blocking yours."

"Good thinking." Cale pushed the door closed, and then jumped quickly into her car. A moment later they were both buckled up, and she was following her own car out of the parking lot.

Cale paused at the corner and glanced in the rearview mirror as Alex eased up behind him. A small smile claimed his lips as he recalled her reaction to his words that whether or not he stayed depended on her. She hadn't looked put off or horrified by the suggestion, and he was feeling good about how things were going, hopeful for the future.

Now that he'd put the idea of permanency in her head, Cale intended on spending every possible moment he could with her and bringing it up again and again until she not only got used to the idea but wanted it as much as he did. Today and tomorrow were Alex's days off, and Cale decided he would put them to good use. He'd make love to her until she couldn't stand, work while she was sleeping, and then return and make love to her again. It would mean consuming a lot more blood. He could go without sleep for quite a while so long as he upped his intake, and—

Cale let these plans go and frowned as he noticed a dark pickup pulling out of a side street behind him. Alex had fallen back about two car lengths, and the vehicle took advantage and slid between them. Not that there was that much traffic at this hour, but there was some.

Cale scowled into the rearview mirror, considering taking control of the driver's mind and making him shift into the other lane or something so that Alex would be behind him again, but then decided not to bother. No doubt the pickup would turn off soon enough. Besides, Alex knew the way to her own house.

Turning his attention back to the road, Cale wondered if he shouldn't hit a coffee shop and pick up some of that coffee Alex had mentioned stopping for. He suspected his comment about staying in Canada had pushed the plan from her mind, but he wouldn't mind a nice hot coffee about now . . . and maybe a sandwich. They hadn't eaten much of the food Bricker had brought them, managing just a bite or two of Emile's meals.

And probably half the can of whipped cream, he thought, a smile curving his lips. Alex was the one who had discovered the dessert topping. She'd been nibbling a strawberry as they'd surveyed what Bricker had brought them when she'd spotted the whipped cream. She'd grabbed it up with an oooh of pleasure and squirted some on the strawberry in her hand. Alex had then offered him the can and strawberries. Cale had taken the whipped cream, but recalling Bricker's suggestion about making Alex his dessert, had bypassed the fruit. Moments later the two of them were rolling around on the cold ceramic floor, covered in whipped cream.

Cale's smile faded somewhat as he recalled the sticky

moment or two it had led to when she'd tried to lick some of the whipped cream off him and experienced his pleasure along with him. Fortunately, he'd realized what was happening pretty quickly and intensified his attention to her body, managing to distract her from what she'd just experienced. There was no way to explain how they could feel each other's pleasure without revealing what he was, and Cale didn't think Alex was ready for that talk yet. It was why he'd stopped her in the dining room when she'd startled him by dropping to her knees to take him into her mouth.

He knew it was going to be a recurring problem. But it was one he would have to deal with until she knew what he was. So long as he was the only one doing the caressing, she would simply think their combined pleasure was hers alone. But if he let her pleasure him as she wanted to, she would definitely twig to something being different, Cale thought as he took the ramp onto the highway to cross the city.

He had heard countless tales of the merged mind and joined pleasure that existed between life mates, but it had still taken his breath away to experience it. It made all his other sexual experiences, both with mortals and immortals alike, pale in comparison. They were like the flicker of a lighted match next to a roaring inferno. It was addictive. Even now, his body was crying out for her, part of his mind wondering how quickly he could get her out of her winter coat and clothes and sink himself inside her body when they got back to the house.

Cale sighed as the thought caused a semi-erection that pressed insistently against the zipper of his jeans.

He was nothing but a walking, talking erection at the moment, and from what he'd heard, he could expect that to be the case for a good year.

Grimacing, Cale reached down and tried to adjust himself to a more comfortable position, then glanced in the rearview mirror to see that while the pickup had followed him onto the highway, it was now in the passing lane, allowing Alex to steer the rental up behind him. Despite his night vision, all he could make out was her silhouette in the vehicle's dark interior, and he knew that as a mortal, she wouldn't even be able to see that much of him.

That thought had barely drifted through his mind when the car he was driving suddenly jolted to the right. Cale gripped the steering wheel, and glanced to the side to see that the pickup in the outside lane had suddenly swerved and rammed into him. Thinking the driver had lost control for some reason or other, Cale tried to focus on him or her, intending to take control and steer the vehicle safely off the highway; but he'd barely touched on the driver's mind when Alex began to honk her horn.

Cale instinctively glanced to the rearview mirror to see that she was no longer directly behind him but to the side. Cale swiveled to peer out the front window again, gasping as he saw that the pickup had forced him out of his lane. He was straddling the right lane and an off-ramp . . . and headed straight for the concrete divide.

Cursing, he hit the brakes and tried to swerve off the road, but his vehicle was apparently hooked on something on the pickup. Cursing again, Cale hit the gas instead, wincing at the high shriek of metal on metal as he drove up the side of the pickup. Much to his relief, whatever was holding the vehicles together suddenly released, and he went veering onto the off-ramp, scraping along the side of the concrete divide before managing to right the car. He was free, but Cale now had another problem. He was going too damned fast for the curve.

Thirteen

'Oh God, oh God, oh God,' Alex half prayed and half chanted as she slammed Cale's rental car into park on the side of the off-ramp. Her own car was a crumpled mass ahead, mangled against the dividing rail. There was no sign of the pickup that had hit him. When Cale had crashed, it had gunned its engines and taken off. Probably a drunken idiot fleeing the scene before the cops could show up, Alex thought grimly as she shoved the driver's side door open and stumbled through the snow toward her car.

She hadn't been able to believe her eyes when the pickup had suddenly swerved into Cale and begun to force him off the road. Alex had instinctively begun to slow to stay out of the way, but the moment she'd realized that the impact had steered the little car toward the concrete divider and that Cale was staring at the pickup and didn't yet realize it, she'd laid on the horn of the rental car to try to warn him. Much to her relief, he'd jerked his head around, apparently spotted the problem and managed to pull away from the pickup. But she'd known at once that he was going too fast. Her ears were still ringing from the horrible crash as the car had hit the rail, but there was also a rushing in her ears as adrenaline pumped through her, helping her slog through the snow to get to Cale.

Alex had a terrible feeling she would get there only to find him dead. She just wasn't lucky enough to be given a gift like him and be allowed to keep it. Her parents and grandparents had been taken from her, why had she thought for even a minute that she could have him?

Tears blurred her eyes, and Alex dashed them impatiently away as she reached the driver's side door. The front end of her car looked like a squeeze box with the driver's side taking the worst of the damage. The windows had shattered, and she cut herself on the broken glass chips still embedded in the frame of the door as she grabbed the cold metal to lean in. All Alex could make out was Cale's still form lying across the seats, his head in the passenger seat. He wasn't moving.

Despair sliding through her, Alex released the window frame and immediately began to stumble her way through the snow to get to the passenger door. This side had a lot less damage, and much to her relief the door still worked. She was able to pull it open so that she could lean into the car to examine Cale. Alex glanced over his dark form, then opened the glove compartment and reached in for the emergency flashlight she kept there. She flicked it on with fingers now stiff from cold, and then shined it on Cale, a small sob slipping from her lips when she saw the damage.

His eyes were closed, and he was as pale as death, his chest and face covered with blood. Alex moved the light beam down to his legs and closed her eyes briefly against the sight of metal crushing them against the seat from the knees down. If it was as bad as it looked, they would need the Jaws of Life to get him out, she thought with despair, and reached into her coat pocket for her phone, but it wasn't there. She hadn't thought to grab it before leaving to go antiquing, Alex realized. It would still be in her charger at home, where she'd put it after returning from the hospital.

Cursing, she glanced to Cale, and then switched off the flashlight and set it on the floor so that she could lean in and search his pockets for his phone. She had just started on the first pocket when Cale suddenly jolted slightly upward with a loud, deep gasp as if she'd just hit him with defibrillator paddles.

"Cale?" she said with disbelief, her hands moving to his face as he fell back on the seat. "Can you hear me?"

When he moaned and turned his face into her hand, Alex sighed with relief. Tears began to fall down her cheeks in earnest, and she pressed a kiss to his forehead, whispering, "Thank God."

"Blood," he moaned.

"Yes, I know baby, you've lost a lot of blood. I need to call for an ambulance." She started to withdraw her hands from his face, but he caught her hand weakly and returned it to his face.

"No . . . phone," Cale groaned, nuzzling her hand.

She thought she even felt his warm tongue slide across her cold palm, but was more concerned about what he had said.

"You don't have your phone either? But I thought you called Bricker—you must have used the restaurant phone. I hadn't realized it was hooked up yet." Frowning, she turned her head to peer out the front window, wondering how far it was to a building or house where she could use a phone or at least get someone to call for an ambulance.

Pain shot through her hand, and Alex instinctively jerked it away from Cale with an "Ow!"

"Sorry," Cale sounded as miserable as he was weak, and she sighed and kissed his forehead again.

"It's okay. I cut it on the broken window when I first came up. It's a little tender." She half straightened to peer around again, hoping someone would take the off-ramp and stop to help. She didn't see anyone. Traffic wasn't completely absent on the highway, but apparently this wasn't a popular off-ramp. She'd have to go for help.

"Cale." She turned back to him and frowned at the rustling he was making. Picking up the flashlight, she turned it on and bit her lip when she saw the way he was twisting on the seats. He was obviously in terrible pain.

"Oh, God, Cale," she whispered, and then reached out to touch his cheek again with her free hand, and said in stronger tones, "Honey, I have to go for help. I'll be as quick as I can but—"

Cale moaned and turned his face into her hand again,

and this time she could see his tongue slip out to lick across her bloody palm. Despite the situation, the caress sent a shiver of excitement through her, and that raised a maelstrom of shame inside her. The man was delirious and half-dead, and she was standing there getting turned on. Her attention shifted back to Cale as he suddenly pushed her hand away.

"The trunk," he gasped.

"Trunk?" she asked uncertainly.

"The rental. A cooler," Cale got out in hoarse tones.

He was definitely delirious, Alex decided. "Honey, this is no time for a beer. You need help."

"The cooler," he insisted, sounding desperate, and then a tearing sound drew her eyes toward his legs and she shifted the flashlight beam there to see that he was trying to pull his legs free of the twisted metal as if to get out and get the cooler himself. Another tearing sounded, but this time she suspected it wasn't cloth. The man was doing himself damage in his desperation.

"Okay, I'll get the cooler," she said quickly, trying to calm him. "Just stop moving. You're only hurting yourself."

Much to her relief, he sagged and went still, merely murmuring, "Need it."

"Okay. I'll get it. Just don't move," she pleaded, and then backed out of the car and straightened to hurry back to the rental. The snow along the side of the ramp was a good two feet deep. Already knowing how hard it was to wade through, Alex risked the ramp itself but found it wasn't much faster. The road was icy, and she couldn't move too quickly for fear of slipping and hurting herself in a fall that would stop her from being able to get Cale the help he so desperately needed.

Alex was slowed down again when she finally reached the car. She'd left the keys in the ignition and the engine running in her rush to get to Cale and now had to wade through the snow to get to the driver's side and the keys. She was panting with exertion by the time she got to the open door. Alex reached in and hit the button on the black fob hanging from the key in the ignition. She then hit it again until she heard all the doors unlock. Straightening, she hurried around to the trunk and opened it to reveal a small cooler inside. Alex grabbed the handle and jerked it out, then slammed the trunk closed and hurried back to her car and Cale.

"Here, I got the cooler," Alex said soothingly as she bent to lean into the passenger side. She set the cooler on the front passenger floor, and then shined her flashlight over Cale, almost moaning when she saw that he'd continued trying to free himself while she was gone. He'd succeeded somewhat. His legs were half-out of where they'd been crushed against the seat, but it wasn't pretty. The front of his lower legs resembled hamburger, and she thought she saw bone in a spot or two.

"Oh, God, Cale, I have to get you help," she moaned, wondering if he'd ever walk again.

"In the cooler . . . blood," Cale growled, and she shifted her eyes and the flashlight beam to his face. He looked even paler than he had the first time she'd seen him. He was almost gray from lack of blood, but still struggling to pull himself across the seat, his eyes now a burning silver and focused on the cooler she'd set down. "Open it."

The words were almost a snarl, and Alex automatically shifted the handle out of the way and opened the cooler. Her eyes widened when she saw the stacked bags of blood inside. She stared at them with confusion, and then lifted one out to look at more closely. "What—?"

He suddenly snatched the bag from her, and her eyes widened with horror as she saw fangs suddenly slide out of his mouth. When he tore into the bag with them, she took a panicked step back, bumped into the car door, lost her footing, and landed on her butt in the cold snow. But the flashlight beam and her eyes never left Cale. He had closed his eyes, whether against the light shining on him, or with relief or pleasure she didn't know, but she could see that the bag was emptying, the plastic shriveling in on itself as its contents were removed.

"Another," he gasped, ripping the first bag away as soon as it was empty.

Alex didn't even glance to the cooler, but simply stared at him.

"Alex," Cale growled. "Please."

"What are you?" she asked shakily.

Cale closed his eyes. "I didn't want you to find out like this."

"Find out what? That you're a *vampire*?" She heard the hysterical note in her voice and snapped her mouth and eyes shut, thinking this then was the flaw. He was perfect . . . except for being a bloodsucking demon. Jesus, could she pick 'em or what?

A rustle and more tearing brought her eyes open to see that Cale had dragged himself a little farther along the seat, doing himself more damage as he did. But then he didn't have much choice, she supposed. If he was a vampire, he couldn't afford to have EMTs and firemen seeing him like this.

"Please," Cale repeated, panting.

Alex hesitated, but when he pulled himself another half an inch closer, she quickly snatched another bag of blood and shoved it at him to keep him at bay. He took the bag of blood but didn't thrust it to the fangs she could see so clearly.

"Alex, it's okay," he said.

A little burble of disbelieving laughter slipped from her lips, and she covered her mouth with dismay at the hysterical sound.

Cale sighed, a sound filled with despair, and finally shifted the bag to sink his teeth into it.

Alex watched, and suddenly wondered if he'd bitten her. She hadn't seen any marks, but there were places on her body she couldn't see without the use of a mirror or bending herself up like a pretzel . . . and he'd given a lot of attention to one specific such place. Dear God, maybe that was why she'd been passing out, she thought suddenly. He wasn't just licking and nibbling, but biting and sucking as well. She was probably a couple of quarts short on blood right now. Jesus!

She stared at Cale wide-eyed, wondering how he'd managed to keep her from feeling the pain. Man, she'd thought the pleasure he'd given her was like nothing she'd ever experienced. Now she knew why, he must be able to make her think she was enjoying it . . . which meant he could somehow control her mind, Alex realized. That explained why she'd suddenly gone from scrambling to get her clothes on to blithely going in to take a shower when she'd woken alone in the office.

Seeing that the bag at his teeth was almost empty, Alex snatched another from the cooler, but then hesitated. Maybe she shouldn't be giving him blood. He was weak and in pain now, but what if the blood healed him? She knew what he was now. He wasn't trying to control her at the moment, but that might just be because he was too weak from blood loss to do it. If she kept giving him blood and he got stronger . . . then what? Would he make her forget what he was? What else could he make her do? Would he keep her as a pet, a walking blood supply and sex slave until he tired of her? Again, then what? Would her body be found by the side of the road, drained of blood? He'd gotten the bagged blood in the cooler from somewhere. Did he find victims, drain their blood, then bag it and keep it for future use until he found another victim?

"Christ," she breathed.

"Alex?" Cale pulled the bag away and peered at her worriedly. "What are you thinking?"

She glanced to him as another thought suddenly struck her. "You're a friend of Mortimer's. He's not . . . like you?" she managed.

Cale didn't speak, but she could see the answer in his eyes. Mortimer was a vampire too.

"Oh God," Alex breathed again, thinking that explained why Sam had suddenly dumped a career she'd worked toward her whole life just to play den mother to Mortimer and his friends. Mortimer was controlling Sam, probably using her as a walking blood bag and sex slave too. She had to warn her.

"Alex?"

Cale watched her with such an intensity that she fancied he was trying to control her but was too weak. She couldn't afford for him to get strong enough to do it. Alex dropped the bag she held back into the cooler, slammed it closed, and scrambled to her feet, dragging the cooler out of the car as she did.

"Wait! Alex. No!" She heard the rustle and tearing again and knew he was struggling to get free and come after her. Unsure what he was capable of, and terrified that he'd succeed, she raced back along the road toward his rental car. She was only a couple of feet away when her feet slid out from under her. Alex dropped the cooler as she started to skid and was trying to stay upright when the ice patch suddenly ended. Her right foot stopped abruptly as it hit the rough tarmac, and she was suddenly falling forward. She threw her hands out, trying to brace her fall, but her head swung forward as she went down, her forehead making a bone-jolting impact as it hit the ground.

Moaning, Alex squeezed her eyes closed against the pain, but then crawled to her hands and knees and glanced back the way she'd come. Cale had dragged himself out of the car to come after her. Scrambling to her feet, she charged around the rental to the driver's side and pretty much threw herself inside, almost closing the door on her ankle in her desperation to get it shut and locked.

Grateful that she'd left the car running, Alex shifted into drive, and then glanced toward Cale in time to see his legs collapse beneath him, too damaged to carry his weight. Her heart wrenched at his roar of pain as he fell, and she hesitated, but then spotted the cooler she'd dropped. It had opened as it fell and several bags of blood had spilled out and were gleaming dark crimson in the beams from the rental's headlights.

Grinding her teeth, she spun the steering wheel and hit the gas, fishtailing to head back down the ramp the wrong way. She wasn't even going to risk driving past Cale. She just didn't know what he was capable of. Fortunately, no one appeared on the road ahead, coming in her direction, and the way was clear when she reached the highway. Alex turned on to it, tires spinning and back end fishtailing again before she got control and shot off up the highway. Her mind was now focused on only one thing; she had to get to Sam and warn her.

On his knees and panting heavily, Cale watched his rental car speed away, then collapsed onto his back and roared with pain and despair. He'd nearly ripped his own foot off trying to get out of the car. The pain was excruciating. But then his whole body had been in terrible pain since he'd woken after the accident. Without the seat belt to restrain him, he'd flown into the dashboard and had heard the crunching of bone on impact. He suspected he had a cracked skull, broken cheekbone, broken nose, a broken collarbone, several broken ribs, and he didn't even want to speculate on the internal damage. Then there were his legs and feet. He raised his head and glanced down at them, grimacing at the state of them.

The two bags he'd managed to consume had started the healing, but he needed much, much more to heal fully. And then he had to find Alex, calm her down, and try to save this situation. He couldn't lose her now, he thought, and cursed the idiot who had hit him.

Grimacing as a shock of pain ran through him, Cale dug into his pocket to find the cell phone Alex had been searching for earlier. Fortunately, she had only managed to try the one pocket and had mistaken his attempt to tell her he didn't want her calling in help, for his saying he didn't have his phone. Now he dragged it painfully out and began to punch in Bricker's number but paused when he realized nothing was happening. He turned it over and saw the large crack across the back. The damn thing had been destroyed in the crash.

Cursing, he tossed it away, hearing it skitter in the snow. He then rolled onto his stomach with a groan to peer at the cooler lying up the road. He couldn't call for help and couldn't walk, but he *would* get to that damned cooler, he thought grimly, and began to drag himself through the snow, using his arms to pull himself forward, his useless legs leaving a bloody trail behind him.

Alex pulled into the driveway of Mortimer's house, only then recalling the ridiculous level of security he had. Probably to keep anyone from sneaking in and staking one of them, she thought as she hit the button to roll down her window. Usually they recognized her car and let her in without stopping her outside the first gate, but she was in Cale's rental tonight. However, they apparently recognized that as well and before she could lean out to press the button and lie and say she was just stopping by for a visit, the first gate began to open.

Sighing, she sank back in her seat and hit the button to roll her window back up, but then began to fidget as she realized they would stop her between the two gates to glance under the car while finding out why she was there. Alex had no idea what they were capable of but suspected she should keep the real reason for her visit out of her mind. If they could control people like she suspected, they might be able to read minds too. She was pretty sure that in books and the movies vampires could read minds.

It had been stupid of her to come here. She should have called Sam and had her meet her at a coffee shop or something. Alex had barely had the thought when an SUV pulled into the drive behind her. Realizing she had no choice but to go forward now, she cursed under her breath and removed her foot from the brake, allowing the rental to slide forward into the area between the two high gates barring the entrance to the house. A glance in the mirror showed the SUV following her inside, and then pulling up beside her as the first gate began to close.

Alex watched it unhappily, wondering if she would ever leave this place . . . alive.

A tap on her window drew her attention, and Alex glanced around to see Russell smiling in at her quizzically. Her gaze slid from Russell's blond hair and golden eyes to the dark-haired man moving past him toward the back of her car to look underneath. Francis was the second man's name, and while no one had said so, she suspected the two men weren't just work partners on the security detail but life partners as well. They were the only two Sam hadn't introduced to her and Jo. Besides, there was just something about the way they looked at and treated each other that made her think there was more than friendship between them.

Alex shifted her gaze back to Russell and hit the button to roll down her window again, quickly trying to blank her mind as she did in case they could read her thoughts.

"Hi, Alex. What's up?" Russell greeted her.

Something about his stance or the way he spoke made her fear it was already too late to hide her thoughts, but she forced a smile and tried to sound casual as she said, "Nothing. I just swung by to see Sam."

"It's kind of late, isn't it?" he asked, his eyes narrowing.

"A little," Alex agreed, realizing that it was nearly dawn. Her gaze slid to the SUV to see two men getting out to talk to Francis, who had finished at the back of the car. She recalled them from other visits. They were usually on duty during the day. She'd arrived at shift change she supposed.

"I'll call up to the house and have someone meet you at the door."

Alex turned sharply back to Russell. His expression

was closed, and there was concern in the depths of his eyes. She was positive he'd been able to read her mind and considered shifting the car into reverse and trying to crash her way back out through the first gate.

Russell nixed that idea by saying, "I wouldn't if I were you. You could get hurt."

Alex swallowed. The words had been softly spoken, but they sounded like a threat to her in that moment. Worse yet, there was now no denying that he could read her mind.

"Go ahead."

Alex glanced to the front to see that Francis had opened the second gate for her and now stood waiting for her to drive through.

"It isn't as bad as you think," Russell said quietly when she hesitated. When she glanced to him again, he added, "Go on up to the house and let someone explain things to you. Everything will be all right."

Swallowing, Alex hit the button to close the window and drove through the gate, her hands gripping the steering wheel tightly. That drive, short as it was, was the worst of her life . . . because she suspected she was driving herself to her own doom.

Cale could have sobbed with relief when he finally reached the cooler. That relief just increased when he saw that it was already open, its contents spilled out onto the snow like precious rubies. Grabbing the nearest bag, he dragged it to his mouth and sank his teeth into it, waiting impatiently as it emptied, his thoughts on Alex and where she could have gone.

He should have explained everything before revealing his teeth, Cale berated himself. It must have been something of a shock when his fangs had suddenly appeared. However, he'd been in such need, and she had been bleeding, the smell and taste of the blood on her cut palms taunting him . . . It had been a case of the lesser evil, suck on a bag of blood or give in to his desperation and bite Alex. Either one would have revealed what he was; but he was in no shape to woo and caress her so that she would be excited enough to open her mind and feel his pleasure rather than her own pain. His biting her then would have hurt, and while he would never deliberately hurt Alex, with the hunger on him as it had been, he hadn't trusted himself not to. Getting her to bring him the cooler of blood had seemed the only recourse.

If he'd been in a little better shape, Cale might have thought to have her leave the cooler and go for help so that he could feed without her seeing, but once he'd seen the cooler, he hadn't been able to think of anything but the sweet relief the blood would give him.

Cale ripped the now-empty bag from his teeth and dragged another over to replace it. He fed on four bags like that before worrying about anything else . . . like the fact that he was presently lying at the side of the road where anyone might find him. And that within seconds the blood would hit his system, it would start to heal him, and he would be in so much pain he wouldn't be able to control himself. If a Good Samaritan should come by at that point, he was likely to rip into their throat without even being aware of what he was doing.

Sighing, he glanced around. There was nothing but the metal rail and a triangle of snow between the highway and the off-ramp on this side, but there was a small copse of trees starting about fifty feet from the road on the other. It seemed a long way away at that point, but Cale didn't feel he had much choice. It was that or risk hurting someone. He had already been incredibly lucky that no one had come along yet, he couldn't risk—

Cale's thoughts died as lights splashed over him. Raising his head, he saw that someone had turned onto the off-ramp and was slowing as they approached.

Fourteen

If Alex thought driving up to the house was bad, forcing herself to get out of the car and walk to the house was even worse, but she made herself do it. For one thing, Sam was in there, completely oblivious that the man she loved was a ravening vampire who was just making her think she loved him so that he could feed off of her like a parasite. She had to go in and warn her, and—if she could—get her out. Though Alex was starting to think that wasn't likely.

Pausing at the door, she took a moment to try to compose herself, and then finally raised her hand to knock. It wasn't exactly a loud rapping, it was more a timid tapping, but then she was scared out of her wits at that point . . . and really had to pee, she realized unhappily, wondering why things like that always seemed to happen at the most inopportune times. One good boo would be enough to have her wetting herself at this point, and since she was entering a vampire lair, Alex suspected she was going to experience more than a boo . . . which meant she was likely to experience humiliation on top of horror tonight, Alex realized, and was suddenly irritated. That irritation only grew as minutes passed without someone answering her summons. Geez, if she was going to be sacrificed on the blood altar of a bunch of neck suckers, the least they could do was not keep her waiting.

That last thought told Alex she was probably losing her grip on sanity. It just didn't seem all that sane to be angry that her would-be killers lacked promptness. Sighing, she shook her head and knocked again, but it still wasn't very loud. She just couldn't bring herself to pound as if she really wanted someone to come kill her. When another moment passed without the door opening, she hesitated, and then reached for the doorknob and turned it. Much to surprise, it wasn't locked.

She eased it open, feeling like some Victorian heroine entering a haunted house . . . or a vampire den, Alex thought dryly, and then muttered, "I may be about to die, but at least I haven't lost my sense of humor."

Wincing at how loud her voice sounded, she slid inside and then paused as a cacophony of sounds hit her ears: shrieks and shouts and the insistent ringing of a phone. She supposed the phone was Russell, trying to warn of her arrival. It sounded like no one was bothering to answer his call. She put that down to the fact that they probably couldn't hear it over the shrieking coming from upstairs. It was loud and agonized . . . and her sister, Alex realized with horror as she recognized Sam's voice in the tortured sound.

She started instinctively toward the stairs, but stopped abruptly as she heard other voices shouting, trying to be heard over Sam's screams.

"God damn it! Why isn't it working?!" That sounded like Mortimer, and he actually sounded a bit frantic, Alex noted with a frown.

"I don't know. We gave her the prescribed amount!" someone shouted back.

"Give her more!" Mortimer roared.

Alex bit her lip and glanced around, looking for a handy weapon. A cross, holy water, or garlic would have been nice, but of course there wasn't anything like that around. Spotting the light on in the kitchen, she hurried up the hall to it and straight to the wood block full of knives. She pulled out the two largest and turned back to the door, but then paused as she realized that they weren't likely to do her much good. Cale had taken a crap load of damage in the car accident and still been going. She needed a bazooka . . . or a stake.

Alex shifted from foot to foot, trying to think what to do, and then began tugging kitchen drawers open, searching desperately until she came across a long, wooden spoon. Pulling it out, she took a moment to sharpen the end with one of the knives. It was a very bad job, rushed and, really, she only managed to make the tip slightly pointy, but it would have to do, Alex decided, as Sam's screams grew in volume. She would just have to plunge it in with a lot of force.

Slipping the makeshift stake into her back pocket, she started for the door again, but then paused as she recalled that vampires could read minds. She needed a plan, or they'd simply take control and make her hand over her weapons, Alex realized with dismay. A sneak attack would be best . . . or some way to keep them from getting into her head.

Turning slowly, she scanned the kitchen, and then returned to the drawers. In the second or third drawer she'd opened she was sure she'd seen a box of—

"Ah ha!" she gasped as the food wraps were revealed in the first drawer she tried. Alex snatched out the aluminum foil, ripped off a huge sheet, and quickly tugged it over her head. She crunched the ends together under her chin so that it would stay, and then pulled the front forward until her entire forehead was covered. It left the back of her bare, however, and she quickly ripped off a second sheet and attached it to the other by crimping the edges together so that all of her head but her face from the eyes down was protected.

Alex felt an utter idiot in the thing, and didn't even have any idea if it would work, but she'd try anything at that point. Besides, it was what those science geeks always did in the movies to prevent space rays or whatever from penetrating their minds. There must be some science behind it. Perhaps it would keep her safe.

"I've lost my mind," Alex muttered, grabbing her knives again and stomping back across the kitchen. "I woke up this morning a boring little chef on planet earth, and somehow ended up in the Twilight Zone as a third-rate stand-in for Buffy the Vampire Slayer."

She hurried up the hall toward the stairs, adding, "And where the hell is *she* when you need her? I could use a little Buffy right now."

Alex knew it probably wasn't smart to be talking to herself when she was trying to sneak up on vampires, but it made her feel better and gave her courage. Besides, it wasn't like they would hear her over Sam's ear-piercing cries, she thought and frowned to herself over what might be happening to her sister.

It was probably some weird blood orgy, twelve of the bastards crowded around and biting into her poor naked sister's flesh. She should have run straight upstairs when she first heard them, Alex berated herself, as she reached the top of the stairs, but knew that wouldn't have helped anything. It was risky enough armed as she was.

Her gaze slid over the doors along the hall, pausing on one she knew from previous visits was a bathroom. Alex still needed to pee. In fact, the more scared she was, the more she had to go, but there was no way she would make a pit stop with Sam shrieking as she was. Stopping for weapons was one thing, but pee breaks were out of the question.

However, she was definitely going to kick some vampire ass if she wet herself, Alex decided as she followed the sound of Sam's screaming to the door of the bedroom she knew her sister shared with Mortimer. Other voices were still shouting inside, but it was harder to distinguish what they were saying now that she was so close. Her ears were so full of the sounds of Sam's agony, she couldn't seem to concentrate on the other voices.

Taking a deep breath, Alex shifted her knives to one hand and slowly turned the doorknob, easing the door open with all the eagerness of a child entering a dentist's office.

The moment Alex could see inside, she scanned the room. There were four people inside with Sam, not twelve: Mortimer, Bricker, and another man as well as a woman. None of them appeared to be biting Sam, however, though they *were* all holding her down on the bed.

Sick bastards, Alex thought with disgust before turning her gaze to Sam. The moment she spotted her, Alex's concern ratcheted up another notch. Aside from being physically held down, Sam had ropes at her wrists and ankles, tethering her to the bed, though it appeared one of them was broken. She was also fully dressed, which was good, they hadn't gotten to the orgy part yet. And they hadn't gotten to biting her either, at least there were no bite marks on the skin of her throat or what little was visible at her wrists and ankles.

However, Sam was incredibly pale, sheet white as if all the blood had been sucked out of her already. But she wasn't acting like someone weak from blood loss. Four people were holding her down, vampires, who, the movies suggested, were stronger than mere mortals, and yet they were having trouble keeping Sam on the bed as she thrashed and shrieked as if on fire.

Pushing the door farther open, Alex eased into the room, grateful that the four vampires were distracted by her sister. She might actually be able to creep up and stake one or two before the others realized what was happening.

Bricker was the nearest one. He and another man were at each corner of the foot of the bed, holding on to Sam's lower legs, while Mortimer and the woman held her arms. Alex didn't recognize the dark-haired man on the left, and was almost sorry that he wasn't holding Sam's other ankle, which would have made him the closer target. She was sure it would have been easier to stake a stranger. As she approached, she was suffering some regret at having to stake Bricker. She'd always liked the guy.

But he was a vampire and she had to save Sam and he'd probably kill her if he got the chance now that she knew his friendly mask hid a bloodsucking fiend, Alex reminded herself and slipped the knife from her right hand into her back pocket so that she could remove her makeshift stake instead. Eyes locked on Bricker's back, she raised her stake high, and then plunged it down, aiming in the general vicinity of his heart.

It didn't quite get the reaction she'd expected. Bricker merely glanced around with an annoyed frown, and then blinked in surprise when he spotted her.

"Alex. What are you doing here?" he said, or at least she thought he'd said that. She was mostly having to read his lips since she couldn't hear anything over Sam at the moment.

Confused, Alex glanced to her stake and saw with dismay that the damned thing was backward. She'd plunged it spoon end first. Alex began berating herself for not checking to be sure she'd had it the right away around before stabbing him, and then realized that Bricker had turned back to Sam as she continued to thrash. Alex quickly twirled the spoon in her fingers, cursing when she nearly dropped the damned thing.

Geez. I am such a bad Buffy, Alex thought as she frantically plunged the spoon toward Bricker again, this time with the right end of it. Unfortunately, he glanced over his shoulder at that moment and instinctively reached out and caught her descending arm with one hand.

"Bricker, stop playing with Alex and hold Sam," Mortimer roared so loudly she actually heard him, and then he added, "And Alex, go stand in the corner and behave yourself."

Alex turned on her heel and walked to the corner, then turned back and simply stood there. It wasn't by choice. Her body just did what Mortimer had ordered her to as if . . . well, as if the bastard was controlling her, she realized with dismay, and there didn't appear to be a damned thing she could do about it. Her muscles and limbs simply wouldn't take the orders she was sending to try to make them move.

"The second dose is working," the woman at the top of the bed said now, hardly having to raise her voice as Sam's screams dropped to moans.

Giving up on trying to move, Alex peered to Sam to see that she was thrashing less as well. Wondering what was working, she shifted her gaze to the woman who had spoken, taking in her long dark hair and perfect skin. She'd never seen anyone with hair as shiny and healthy-looking or skin as pure as that woman's. Porcelain dolls would have wept at their own deficiency on seeing it. The woman glowed with good health and contentment.

Definitely the Queen of the Damned, Alex decided.

"Thank God," Mortimer said, and Alex shifted her gaze to him, a little surprised to see the distress and love on his face as he peered down at her sister. A little surprised too that he would dare to use the Lord's name. Shouldn't his tongue burst into flames or fall out for that?

A soft chuckle from the woman drew Alex's gaze back to see her peering her way with gentle amusement.

"What is funny, darling?" the man down at Sam's feet with Bricker asked.

"She was just thinking that—" She paused and shook her head. "Nothing. I don't want to embarrass the poor girl."

Alex was frowning over the words when she became aware that everyone had now turned to peer at her. Mortimer was frowning with annoyance, obviously displeased at her presence. Bricker was casting her his usual grin, but the man she didn't know had turned a curious gaze on her and now glanced to Mortimer, and said, "Are you not going to introduce us?"

Mortimer merely turned his gaze back to Sam, it was Bricker who spoke.

"This is Sam's sister, Alex," he announced, straightening and moving toward her. Pausing in front of her he added, "Alex, this is Marguerite Argeneau Notte and her husband Julius Notte."

Recognition slid through Alex, and her eyes shifted to the woman again. She'd noticed that Sam always spoke of her with a bit of awe. Now she knew why . . . Queen of the Damned.

"What's with the . . . er . . . hat?" Bricker asked, drawing her attention back to him.

Alex opened her mouth but promptly closed it again, unwilling to admit that she'd hoped it would keep them from being able to control her.

"Yeah, that's not working so good," Bricker chuckled. "But it looks kind of cute in a little old lady with a funny foil kerchief kind of way."

Alex scowled.

"So?" he asked with amusement. "What are you doing here? I mean besides trying to spoon me to death?"

"Bricker," the woman reprimanded, leaving the bed to join them. "Stop teasing her. The poor girl is terrified."

Bricker was silent, but then so was Marguerite now, Alex realized, and glanced from one to the other, frowning when she saw the concentrated expressions on their faces. She slowly became aware of a strange ruffling of her thoughts, a sort of tickle as if a moth or butterfly were fluttering around inside her skull, and then she was distracted when Marguerite's husband, Julius, joined the pair to stare at her as well.

Another moment of silence passed and she began to glare back, and then Marguerite suddenly said, "Bricker, you'd better go find Cale."

"Already on it," he assured her, moving away.

"What's happened?" Mortimer asked from the bedside. Alex couldn't see him, Marguerite was in the way, but his voice sounded worried.

"Nothing to concern yourself with, Mortimer," Marguerite said soothingly. "I'll handle this. You just watch over Sam. We'll be in the next room. Shout if you need me."

"Do you want me to come with you?" Julius asked.

"No, we'll be fine," Marguerite assured him, and leaned up to kiss him before glancing back to Alex. "Come along, dear. I can see we have a lot to talk about."

Marguerite had barely finished speaking when Alex found her feet turning and moving her toward the door Bricker had just exited through. Once again, it wasn't by choice. Not wanting to leave Sam, Alex tried to stop, but her body wouldn't listen.

"Sam will be fine," Marguerite assured her quietly as they exited the room and started up the hall. "Mortimer loves her and would never hurt her. I promise."

Alex had to wonder what good the promises of a vampire were. Surely they could lie as easily as mortals?

"Of course we can, but I'm not," Marguerite said as Alex's feet led her into the next room. She heard the door close behind her. "Would you like to go to the bathroom?"

If she could have turned her head, Alex would have been glancing back with surprise though she supposed she shouldn't be surprised that the woman knew she had to go. She was reading her mind after all and that was up there among her concerns. Dying was one thing, but she'd like to go with some dignity.

"You aren't going to die," Marguerite said with exasperation. "And you can speak. I haven't taken total control of you."

"You could have fooled me," Alex muttered.

Marguerite's laugh was a tinkle of chimes in her ear, and then Alex felt her feet moving her toward a second door inside the room. "Go ahead and use the facilities. But please don't try to escape. You wouldn't get far."

Alex grimaced, thinking that was pretty obvious, and then she reached the door and suddenly felt whatever power had been making her feet move disappear.

"I think you can handle it on your own," Marguerite said quietly. "I'll wait for you out here."

Alex glanced back to the woman, happy to find she was able to. When Marguerite smiled encouragingly, she swung back and opened the door. Once safely inside, she pushed the door closed and then leaned weakly against it. She was trapped in the lion's den and pretty much done for. It seemed obvious she wasn't going to escape from these people when they could control her. Besides, even if she escaped from the bathroom and the house, she knew about the security here, the high electrified fences, motion-sensor cameras, and armed men. She wasn't going anywhere. She wouldn't even have tried without Sam.

A shout stirred Cale from the hell he was suffering, and for one moment he feared more mortals had come along to find him. That would not be a good thing. He was weak, and in agony, and just not feeling very sociable at the moment. Aside from that, he was out of blood, needed more, and didn't think he could control himself as he had the first time.

His first instinct when he'd seen the car rolling toward him was to slip into the mind of the driver and make them keep going, but then he'd glanced to the copse of trees, noted the distance, and changed his mind. He would never have been able to drag himself that distance, so he'd taken control of the driver and made him stop, which he suspected he'd been doing anyway, and then he'd had the two occupants of the vehicle get out and come to him. Much to Cale's relief it had been a couple of men in their early twenties, healthy and strong.

Once the men stood silent and still before him, Cale had collected the last two bags from the cooler, tucked them into his coat, and then made them carry him to the copse of trees. Between the snow and the uneven ground, the going had been awkward for them. It had also taken longer than he'd hoped, and by the time they'd laid him in the cover of the trees, the healing had set in with a vengeance. Cale had only had a thin thread of control over himself. The only thing that had kept him from attacking one or both of the men was the knowledge that he had the two bags of blood tucked inside his coat. He'd ripped into the bags the moment they set him down, even while sending them hurrying back to their vehicle with the thought to forget about the mangled car and him. They'd reached their vehicle and torn away just as he'd finished the last bag of blood and begun to convulse on the forest floor.

"Cale!"

Not mortals then, he thought on a sigh, as he recognized Bricker's voice. He tried to shout "here," but what came out was a parched croak. It didn't matter. He'd apparently been heard because Bricker suddenly appeared beside him, a tall silhouette in the dawning light weaving through the leafless trees.

"Jesus, you're in bad shape," the man said grimly, kneeling to look him over. When his gaze shifted to Cale's legs, he cursed. "Did the accident do this?"

Cale grunted, and the other man turned to glance at his face.

"I saw the tracks. You left one hell of a trail of blood."

That explained why he wasn't further along in his healing, he thought grimly. He'd been losing the blood as quickly as he could consume it. There were probably so many burst veins in his legs they couldn't close quick enough to prevent it. It meant he'd need a hell of a lot more blood. The best bet was probably to soak him in a tub of it.

"Russell and Francis are getting rid of the trail and taking care of the car," Bricker informed him. "They'd just finished their shift when I was leaving, so I recruited them to come help."

Cale grunted again.

"There were two sets of footprints. Who did you get to carry you out here?"

"Mortals," Cale managed to get out.

"Where are the bodies?" Bricker asked dryly, bending to slip his arms under him.

Cale just groaned in agony as Bricker lifted him off the ground.

"Don't worry, buddy," Bricker said sympathetically. "There's blood in the SUV and I'll have you back at the house in no time."

"Alex," Cale managed to get out as they headed out of the trees.

"She's at the house. She's fine. A little crazy, maybe," he added with amusement. "But fine."

Cale would have liked to ask what that meant but just didn't have the energy for it. His eyes drifted closed and he fell gratefully into unconsciousness.

Fifteen

Alex glanced in the mirror as she washed her hands and paused as she saw her reflection. She looked utterly ridiculous with the foil over her head . . . and it hadn't even worked. She ripped the silver cap off. Between that and her attempt to "spoon" him to death, it was a wonder Bricker hadn't killed himself laughing, she thought with disgust as she tossed the foil in the garbage. She was definitely a bad Buffy.

Sighing, Alex dried her hands and forced herself to return to the bedroom. She really would have liked to hide away in the small room forever, but it wouldn't accomplish much.

Marguerite was seated in one of two chairs at the opposite end of the room. She smiled when Alex appeared, and then patted the arm of the chair next to hers. "Come sit down."

Alex didn't move. "I'd really rather not."

"Oh, come now," she chided. "I don't bite."

Alex snorted. "You're a vampire."

"No, I'm not," Marguerite assured her solemnly. "I am an immortal."

She glanced at her uncertainly. "What is that?"

"You'll have to come over here to find out," she said firmly. "I do not wish to shout across the room."

Alex hesitated another moment before moving reluctantly to the chair. Squeezing herself into the far side of it, as far away from Marguerite as she could get, she eyed her warily and waited.

"First of all, you have nothing to fear," Marguerite assured her quietly. "No one here would hurt you. We do not, and in fact are not allowed to, feed on mortals. We consume bagged blood."

Alex felt some of the tension seeping from her, but then stiffened again and said, "Sam—"

"We were not hurting her," Marguerite assured her firmly. "You must have noticed how she was thrashing and convulsing on the bed. We were trying to keep her still to prevent her causing harm to herself." She tilted her head and added, "Surely you saw the love and concern on Mortimer's face? He would never allow harm to come to her."

Alex frowned. She had noticed, and it had confused her at the time. "What's wrong with her?"

Marguerite hesitated for a moment, and then said, "I think before I explain that, you need to understand who and what we are."

"I know what you are," Alex said stiffly. "You're vampires."

"We are *not* vampires," Marguerite said firmly. "We are immortals."

"You have fangs," Alex said dryly, and then frowned and added. "At least, Cale did."

"Immortals all have fangs," Marguerite said calmly.

"Right," Alex said with a scowl. "You all have fangs and consume blood to survive but you aren't vampires?"

Marguerite clucked her tongue impatiently. "Yes, I know there are similarities. The mythological vampires have fangs and feed off the living. However, they are also supposed to be the cursed, soulless reanimated dead. And I assure you I am neither cursed nor soulless. I am very definitely also not dead."

"Then what—?"

"I will explain. But you may find the explanation difficult to accept," she warned.

"More difficult than vampires really existing?" Alex asked dryly. "Go ahead. I think I can handle anything right now."

"I wish you would stop calling us that unpleasant word. It's really quite distressing," Marguerite said unhappily, but continued, "You've heard of Atlantis?"

Alex raised her eyebrows. "Yes. An ancient, mythical land that was supposedly more advanced than the rest of the world or something."

"Yes . . . well it was not just myth. It was a country on the tip of a continent, surrounded by ocean on three sides and cut off from its neighbors by a mountain range that made travel difficult. It was isolated, and *was* far more advanced scientifically than the rest of the world, to the point where the scientists had begun to work with what are now called nanos. It seems one of these scientists thought they could be a medical aid and created nanos specifically programmed to repair injuries and combat illness in the human body.

"His idea was that these nanos could be shot directly into the bloodstream, which would carry them throughout the body and take them wherever they needed to go to accomplish this. For that reason, he designed them to use blood to propel themselves as well as regenerate themselves so that they could accomplish even the largest task like fighting off cancer in a body riddled with it."

Alex raised her eyebrows and asked with disbelief, "And when was this?"

"Well before the arrival of Christ, dear," Marguerite said solemnly.

"Okay, that's a bit wild," Alex acknowledged. "But what has that to do with vamp—immortals," she corrected herself at the last moment.

Marguerite smiled at her for making the effort. "Well, these nanos were supposed to dissolve and leave the body when finished with their work. However, there are countless illnesses and injuries a body may suffer, and programming individual groups of nanos for each such ailment would have been impossible, so he, or they really," she interrupted herself to say, "because while one man started the work, others finished it.

"But anyway, to avoid that problem, the nanos were simply programmed to repair any damage, fight any illness, and keep the host body at its peak condition.

Unfortunately, the body always has something to repair. The sun, the environment, even the passage of time kills off cells and causes damage that the nanos see as something that must be repaired."

"They never dissolve and leave," Alex realized.

Marguerite nodded. "And they use blood to power and regenerate themselves as well as to make repairs. More blood than a mortal body can create."

"The need for blood," she murmured.

She nodded again. "In Atlantis, they combated the problem by giving transfusions to those who had been given the nanos before the flaws were discovered. However, when Atlantis fell—"

"How did Atlantis fall?" Alex asked curiously.

"I believe it was an earthquake. Whatever the case, Atlantis basically sank into the ocean."

"Like they say California will do someday," Alex murmured.

"Yes." Marguerite said, "And when that happened, pretty much the only survivors were those with nanos in them. They climbed over the mountains to rejoin the rest of the world and found themselves in a much-less-advanced society. There were no more doctors or transfusions."

Alex grimaced. "That must have been a bit of a shock."

Marguerite nodded. "It was apparently a very rough time for most of them. They still needed more blood than they could produce, but now had no way to get it. Some simply died, but in others, the nanos sort of forced them to evolve to adapt to this new habitat. They suddenly sprouted retractable fangs to get the blood they needed."

Eyes narrowing, Alex snapped, "I thought you said you didn't bite and couldn't feed on mortals."

"Yes, well, I should have said we don't bite *anymore*. But we cannot feed off mortals now that there is bagged blood, it's against our laws. An immortal who breaks that law can be executed."

"Can be? Or is?" Alex asked dryly.

"Exceptions are made in emergency cases when an immortal is in terrible need without bagged blood available," Marguerite explained. "But otherwise, if they are simply feeding off mortals because they want, they will be found rogue and put down."

Alex thought of Cale. He'd definitely been in terrible need . . . and she'd taken the cooler of bagged blood away. If he couldn't get to it, and a passerby stopped, would he be forgiven for feeding off the person?

"He would be more likely to control the person and have him bring the cooler to him," Marguerite said quietly.

"I think he's too weak to do that; otherwise, he simply would have made me bring it back," Alex said, and frowned as she realized he really had been controlling her this last week as she'd feared.

"An immortal is never too weak to control a mortal," Marguerite assured her. "Cale did not control you because he couldn't. He can neither control nor read you, Alex. That's what makes you special."

"You can control me," she pointed out, not believing her.

"Yes, as can any immortal on this property who wishes to." Marguerite shrugged. "But that is because you are not a life mate to any of us. Cale's inability to either read or control you is what makes you a possible life mate for him."

"What is a life mate?" Alex asked at once.

Marguerite hesitated. "I think I will leave that to Cale to explain."

"Why?"

Marguerite shrugged. "It is his place. In truth, it would have been better for him to explain all of this to you, but I did not think you would be willing to listen to it from him."

Alex frowned with dissatisfaction and stared at the other woman for a moment, and then sighed, and said, "So the nanos gave you fangs and the ability to control and read minds to help you feed after the fall. What else—"

"Not me. I was only born in 1265 A.D.," Marguerite interrupted quietly. "And I was born mortal and later given the nanos."

Alex shrugged that away. "What else can you people do?"

"Do?" she asked uncertainly.

"Do you turn into bats and fly or—" Alex paused. The woman was laughing softly.

"No," Marguerite assured her with amusement. "While I think it would be lovely to be able to fly, I don't think I would care to be a bat." Shaking her head at the idea, she explained, "The nanos only increased the natural abilities all humans have. They were programmed to keep their hosts at their peak and needed blood to do it, so they made their hosts better able to achieve that. They made their hosts stronger, faster, and increased their sense of smell and vision. Immortals also gained incredible night vision so that they could hunt at night and avoid the damaging rays of the sun during daylight."

"They became night predators," Alex said slowly.

"Essentially, yes," Marguerite agreed, "although, it wasn't by choice. They had come from a cultured society and didn't suddenly become ravening animals. They hunted and fed, but most tried not to unduly harm the neighbors and friends they were forced to feed on."

"And the mind control and—?"

"More abilities the nanos brought about," Marguerite said with a shrug. "It makes it easier to hunt and live without the constant threat of discovery if the chosen donor does not fight or even recall being bitten. Understandably, people do not like to be prey."

"No, I suppose not," Alex said dryly, and then tilted her head and returned to an earlier point. "You said you were born mortal."

"Yes. I was turned as a teenager," Marguerite said quietly.

"There were no syringes or doctors capable of shooting you up with nanos in 1265," Alex pointed out.

"No there weren't. My sire turned me by biting his wrist open and pressing it to my mouth so that I would drink his blood and the nanos with it. It is how most mortals are turned even today."

Alex wrinkled her nose with disgust at the thought. "Why? I mean I understand you had to then, but nowadays there *are* syringes and there is no need for that kind of barbaric nonsense."

Marguerite smiled faintly. "But it has become tradition."

"A painful one," Alex inserted dryly.

"Yes, but then the turn itself is painful, and I think your sister would agree that the pain Mortimer suffered tonight was little enough compared to that she is now suffering in the turn. Besides, there is some suspicion that sharing the same nanos gives an added connection, although no one has proven it yet."

Alex simply stared at her, barely hearing the last part. Her mind had stopped at the "I think your sister would agree that the pain Mortimer suffered tonight was little enough compared to that she is now suffering in the turn" part. The words echoed inside her head as she recalled Sam's agonized shrieks and the way she'd thrashed on the bed. Lifting haunted eyes, to Marguerite, she asked shakily, "Sam isn't—?"

"Yes, dear. Sam is turning," Marguerite said solemnly.

Alex started to jerk to her feet, but just as quickly found herself sitting back down. Not under her own power.

Marguerite patted her hand gently. "Sam chose to turn, Alexandra. It was not forced on her. She loves Mortimer. They are true life mates and she wishes to share her life with him."

Alex stared at her blankly, her mind only comprehending that Sam was now a vampire too, or would be once the turn was finished.

"She will still be Sam," Marguerite assured her. "She will simply not grow ill, and not age. She will also probably fill out a bit."

Alex blinked. "Fill out?"

"Well, she is unhealthily thin," Marguerite pointed out. "I suspect some sort of thyroid malfunction."

"Mother was always dragging her to doctors about that, but they couldn't find anything wrong," Alex said faintly.

"There is much doctors do not yet know, but the nanos are programmed to get their hosts to peak condition and keep them there," she reminded her. "I do not think Sam has ever been at her peak. She will be soon."

Alex simply sat there, too stunned by the news that her sister would soon be a vampire to say or even really think anything for a moment, but then she asked, "When did she decide to turn?"

"What you really want to know is how long she knew about us and did not tell you," Marguerite said quietly.

Alex didn't comment but knew that was really what she wanted to know. She was feeling a bit betrayed at the moment. Sam should have told her.

"She could not if she wished to stay with Mortimer, and Sam would not have been allowed to retain the memory had she chosen not to stay with him," Marguerite said firmly, and then added, "And she has known since the cottage last summer but has only recently agreed to the turn."

When she fell silent, Alex glanced to her curiously to see a brief struggle taking place on the woman's face, and then Marguerite grimaced, and merely said, "However, you should not allow the fact that Sam is one now to influence your decision."

"What decision?" she asked with a start.

"As to whether you are willing to accept Cale as your life mate and turn as well."

She blanched at the suggestion. "Become a vampire?"

"No, an immortal," Marguerite said with exasperation. "And please do not spout that nonsense about their being the same thing. I know you no longer think that way now that I've explained matters."

Alex stilled.

"You are not afraid of me anymore, Alex. Nor are you afraid of Cale now that you understand the basis of what we are."

"Yes I am," Alex said quickly, but could hear the lack of conviction in her voice.

"No, dear, you aren't," Marguerite said firmly. "I can read your mind, and I know you aren't afraid of us any-more . . . at least not physically afraid. The fear only returned at the suggestion of being Cale's life mate."

"So which is it? Am I afraid, or not?" Alex asked dryly, and really wanted to know what the woman thought. She was pretty confused at the moment her-self and unsure what she was feeling. Marguerite was right, she had begun to relax and stop fearing them all as she understood things. But the moment Marguerite had mentioned being Cale's life mate, abject terror had rushed through her.

"I believe you *are* afraid, but only of Cale, and not that he would hurt you physically, but that he could emotionally." Marguerite said gently, "You've come to love him, dear. I can read and feel it in your memories and thoughts. You recognized from the first that he was special, that you could come to care for him. You used needing to keep a professional footing between you as an excuse to protect yourself but couldn't make yourself stay away as you felt you should and found excuses to see him every day. But you find it impossible to believe that he could love you," Marguerite said sadly. "For all that you are an attractive, intelligent, and successful woman . . . for some reason you don't think you are worthy of love."

Alex swallowed a sudden lump in her throat and blinked her eyes rapidly as she felt them fill with tears. Marguerite's words had certainly struck a chord.

"I think perhaps you need to stop and ask yourself why," she said solemnly. "Who made you think you were not worthy of love? Who said that to you?"

Alex didn't have to think hard, her mind immediately raced back to culinary school and her first experience with adult love. A train wreck to be sure, she thought on a sigh. But surely that couldn't be affecting her still?

"I believe it compounded something that was already growing within you, an irrational fear I think, but that doesn't make it any less scary. You'll have to search farther back for it, and I'll leave you to do it. You have a lot of thinking to do. You need to know what made you the way you are today before you can move past it and accept all that Cale has to offer you. He does love you, Alexandra. I promise you that. And he can't read or control you. The two of you could share a wonderful life together if you can only accept that love. But you shall have to sort out and confront your past to do it."

Alex watched silently as the other woman stood and moved across the room, but stood abruptly herself when Marguerite opened the door to reveal Bricker carrying a limp Cale past. She hurried to the door but was brought up short at the sight of him. His injuries looked even worse in light than they had out on that dark road . . . and she'd just left him there, she thought with shame. This was a man who had been nothing but considerate and loving to her, and she'd left him to fend for himself in the middle of nowhere in that condition.

"You thought him a monster," Marguerite said quietly. "It was unfortunate, but understandable under the circumstances. He will not hold it against you."

Alex started to move to follow Cale, but her feet stopped almost at once and turned her back into the room, carrying her to the chair she'd just left. Marguerite had taken control again.

"I will help Bricker with Cale. The best thing you can do for him right now is sort yourself out so that you can love him as he deserves," Marguerite said from the door, as Alex found herself sitting down. "I should warn you that you have to be certain of your decision when you make it. It is irreversible. Should you choose not to be Cale's life mate, all memories of him will be removed from your mind, and you will never see him again lest the sight of him makes those memories return."

The door closed on that note, and Alex found herself suddenly able to move again. She stood at once, but then simply sat back down. They would just take control of her and send her back. Besides, she had a great deal of thinking to do.

Sixteen

Cale opened his eyes and peered at the ceiling overhead, waiting for the pain to return and consume him as it had every other time he'd woken in this room during the last several hours. Nothing happened. The pain was gone. He was briefly relieved, but then thought he'd better be sure before getting too excited. He tried moving various limbs and digits to test for pain, but froze and glanced to the side as a rustling reached his ears.

"You're awake." Alex sat forward in the chair beside the bed.

He took in her tentative smile with surprise, and then scrambled to sit up, forgetting all about his concern that the pain might return. "You're here."

"Yes." She hesitated and then asked, "Do you want me to leave? I'll understand if you're upset with me for leaving you—"

Cale caught her hand when she stood up. "No. Stay."

He held on to her until she sat back down, and then patted her hand, and assured her, "I am not angry about that. It must have been terrifying for you when you saw my fangs. I handled the whole thing badly. I should have sent you away before——"

"You'd just been in a terrible accident, Cale," she interrupted. "You were hardly thinking straight. I should have at least stuck around long enough to be sure you were all right and allow you to explain."

"I take it someone else has explained while I was recovering?" he asked.

Alex nodded. "Marguerite."

Cale sent a silent thank-you to the woman. It was a relief not to have Alex looking at him as if he were a monster anymore. He suspected it would be a long time before he forgot the horror that had blanched her face when he'd allowed his fangs to slide out and torn into the bag of blood. It was one of the very few times in his life he'd felt like the fiend his kind were proclaimed to be.

He glanced back to her now to see that she was peering down at her hands, twisting them nervously in her lap. The sight made him frown. While Marguerite had explained what they were, and she appeared to accept it, there was obviously something still troubling her.

"What is it?" he asked quietly.

Alex licked her lips·and then blurted, "Marguerite says you love me."

"Yes, I believe I do," he admitted. While it had been little more than a week, how long did it really take to know you loved someone? He suspected sometimes it was slow, growing like a sweet-smelling flower that buds and blossoms, but other times it could be fast. Besides, thanks to the nanos, immortals had a head start in the matter. They knew with a certainty that if the person was a life mate, they were the right one and were able to enjoy the person without all the questions about whether they would suit and so on. And that was what Cale had done this last week, enjoyed her independence, her determination, her ambition, her creativity, her sense of adventure. She was a spectacular woman and would suit him perfectly in some ways and complement him in others. While he was organized, she was a chaotic, creative thinker. They would balance each other out and teach each other things at the same time.

"She said that I love you too," Alex said quietly, and still wasn't looking up from her hands.

"Is she right?" he asked, and then held his breath, praying for the answer he wanted.

"Yes . . . no . . ." She grimaced, and then finally met his gaze. "I was pretty shook up when I saw your fangs. My immediate thought was that it just figured I'd go and fall for a monster, and the only thing I could think at that point was that you wanted me for a blood donor and sex toy."

"No, Alex, I—" Cale began, but she continued.

"Marguerite said I was using that as an excuse not to get involved and risk being hurt, and she was right. I've done a lot of thinking while you were recovering and, basically I've come to the conclusion that I'm pretty messed up," she admitted with a dry laugh.

Cale frowned with concern. "You seem pretty together to me."

"Oh." She waved that away. "Sure, I seem together, but . . ." She sighed, and said, "You remember I told you that we moved every year until I was ten, and that made it hard to make and keep friends?"

He nodded.

"Well, the thing is, I did make friends, but then we'd move, I'd make a new friend, and then we'd move again. That happened over and over so that when Gramps came to stay with us, it was just easier to be with him, for him to be my best friend and confidant. Then he died and left me too." She made a face. "It started to feel like maybe I wasn't supposed to have anyone. They all either died or left me."

"I see," Cale murmured, and he did understand how it must have seemed to a child. "You didn't have friends in high school?"

She shook her head. "By that time I'd hit the awkward teenage years and was shy . . . and it didn't help that, as the oldest, I had to look after Jo and Sam after Gramps died. It meant I could never accept invitations to do things after school or on weekends. I was pretty lonely." She grimaced, and added, "But then I went away to culinary school, and it was like the whole world opened up for me. I was in a foreign country, met lots of new and interesting people, made friends and . . ."

"And?" he prompted.

"And there was Jack." She grimaced. "I met him the

first week of school. He was from Canada too, a little town in southern Ontario. He spoke French and he was handsome, and funny, and charming, and he liked me. That whole first year I was in heaven. Everything was wonderful. Jack and I were always together and even had a lot of classes together. He said he loved me."

Cale felt his mouth tighten. Part of it was jealousy though he had no right to it, the other part was because there had been a plaintive sound to the words, a hint of very old, very deep pain that made him want to hunt down this Jack guy and break his neck for causing it.

"Then the final project came around," she continued. "We were supposed to show our personal creativity by coming up with our own recipe, something new and different. Thanks to Gramps, that was a breeze for me. He'd always encouraged me to experiment. I was used to it and quickly decided what I would do and experimented with it in my apartment ahead of time to get it perfect. I made Jack my taste tester. Big mistake it seems," she said dryly. "The day after the class when I had to create the dish, I was called in to school. It seems my recipe was an exact replica of another student's who had presented the same thing earlier in the day."

"Jack."

Alex nodded solemnly. "I said there must be some mistake, that Jack would never steal my recipe, and they began to ask me how I had come up with the recipe and why I had added this or that." She smiled wryly. "Somehow I ended up on the topic of Gramps and told them how he'd gotten me into cooking and experimenting with recipes and so on. Then they asked me to wait in the outer office. When I walked out, Jack was just arriving, and they took him in at once."

Her mouth tightened. "I still thought it must be some kind of mistake. After all, Jack loved me. But the office door was very thin, and I heard every word said. He accused me of stealing the recipes from him. That floored me, and I hardly noticed that he couldn't answer the questions on how he'd come up with the recipe or why he'd added this or that. When they called me in to join them, I was terrified that they believed I really had stolen it."

"Of course they didn't," Cale said staunchly.

"No, they didn't," she agreed. "They said it was obvious Jack had stolen it. That he was a mediocre cook at best while I had shown the makings of a first-class chef from the start. He was tossed out of school in disgrace, and they apologized for having put me through their questions and sent us on our way."

"How did Jack take that?" Cale asked, suspecting he knew the answer.

"Oh, he wasn't pleased at all," she said with a grimace. "I waited until we were outside, and then asked why he'd done what he had when he'd said he loved me. He just exploded, shouting, 'Love you? How could anyone love you? You're a stupid ugly cow. The only reason I paid you any attention was because you're good at cooking and I wanted to graduate.'" She wrinkled her nose. "There was quite a bit more, but you get the idea. He was quite unpleasant."

"And he validated your inner feeling that you weren't

supposed to have anyone love you," Cale said with understanding.

Alex nodded solemnly. "It was a new version of the old button. Anyone I loved left me, died, or didn't really love me at all and would betray me . . ." She glanced away, and then admitted, "And while I know that's irrational, that God didn't take Gramps because he loved me, and I loved him, and that Jack was a big jerk . . ." She shrugged helplessly. "It doesn't make me any less scared that if I let myself love and trust you, you won't . . ."

Cale caught her hand in his and waited for her to look at him before saying, "Then don't trust me. Trust the nanos."

She blinked at him in confusion. "I don't understand."

"Didn't Marguerite explain about life mates to you when she explained everything else?" he asked with a frown.

Alex shook her head. "She said she would leave that to you."

Cale nodded, and then took a moment to arrange his thoughts, before saying, "A life mate is that one person that an immortal can live out his or her very long life with happily. Neither will ever stray from the other, never betray the other, never stop loving each other. An immortal would sooner cut out his own heart and eat it than cause harm to his life mate . . . and you are mine."

Alex frowned. "How do you know I am? Maybe—"

"She explained our abilities to you? That we can read and control mortals?" he asked.

Alex nodded. "But she said you can't read or control me."

"Yes. That's right. That's how I know you're my life mate," he said firmly.

"That's it?" she asked with a frown.

"It's more important than it probably sounds to you," he said wryly. "You see, not only can we read and control mortals, we can also read the thoughts of other immortals if they aren't guarded. This means most immortals spend their time guarding their thoughts in the company of others. We never get to relax, we must always be on guard. But with a life mate, we can relax and not guard our thoughts."

"And you can't read or control me?" she asked slowly.

"No, I can't," he assured her.

Suspicion immediately filled her eyes. "Marguerite said that too, but I was thinking about it, and it seems to me someone did some controlling at the restaurant last night. I woke up on the couch that first time and started throwing my clothes on, preparing to make a quick escape, but then suddenly I was taking my clothes off and going for a shower."

"That was Bricker," Cale admitted apologetically. "I was feeding in the kitchen and he sent you for a shower so you wouldn't see."

Her eyes narrowed, but she merely said, "And the night you helped me out at the restaurant? I wasn't too sure about leaving you there and then all of a sudden I—"

"Bricker again. I really can't read or control you, Alex. I wouldn't lie about that. It wouldn't do either of us any good," he assured her. "But you don't have to take my word on it. There are other signs of life mates."

"Like what?" she asked promptly.

"They are usually perfect for each other, suiting or complementing each other in temperament and taste. The nanos seem to recognize like souls and match them up. And we do complement each other, Alex. You're more creative to my more logical mind, we've worked together very well since I arrived."

She nodded reluctantly. "That's true enough. You handled the business side like a dream."

"And you cook like a dream," he assured her.

She smiled faintly, but said, "How else do you know if you're life mates?"

"The arrival of the life mate tends to rejuvenate an immortal. We suddenly enjoy things more."

"What kind of things?" she asked at once.

"Food," he responded, choosing the easier subject. "I haven't been able to stand the taste or even the smell of food for more than a millennium, but after meeting you, I found my appetite for it returning. I seem to have done nothing but eat since meeting you."

"That was true at first, but we didn't do much eating Sunday night before the accident," she pointed out dryly.

"Yes well, sex is the other appetite reawakened," he admitted with a small smile, and then asked, "Surely you noticed that it was rather . . . explosive?"

Alex flushed. "Yes, but—"

"It's because of the shared pleasure that only life mates experience."

Alex eyed him uncertainly. "Shared pleasure?"

Cale patted the bed beside him. "Come here."

"Why?" she asked warily.

"It is easier to show you than to tell you," he said quietly, and when she still hesitated, added, "I promise just to show you enough so that you understand more clearly, and then we will finish our talk."

Releasing a little sigh, Alex stood and stepped to the side of the bed, and then sat carefully on the edge of it.

"Touch me," Cale said.

She raised an eyebrow, and then peered over the expanse of his wide chest. They'd removed his clothes when they'd brought him to the house. He was completely naked under the sheet covering him from the waist down. Alex peered over the available flesh, and then reached out tentatively to run her fingers lightly down his arm.

Cale stiffened involuntarily as a slow tingling ran down his skin in the trail of her touch, but Alex merely glanced to him in question. "What am I supposed to feel?"

Cale's eyes widened, and then he realized the problem. She too had to be excited to be able to experience what he'd described. Clucking under his tongue, he slid his hand into her hair, cupping her skull. He started to draw her closer, but she put a hand to his chest, stopping him.

"Wait. What—?"

"Trust me," he insisted quietly, and then grimaced and added, "Trust the nanos."

Alex bit her lip but nodded and allowed him to urge

her closer. Cale kissed her lightly at first, seducing her by just brushing his lips over hers, teasing her gently until her lips parted, inviting a deeper kiss. He gave her what they both wanted then, and briefly deepened the kiss, thrusting his tongue into her mouth. Other than his hand at her head, however, he didn't touch her, and he broke off the kiss at her first moan.

They were both breathing more heavily than usual when he pulled back. His voice was gruff when he said, "*Now* touch me."

Alex opened her eyes slowly and met his gaze. She then lowered her eyes and reached out tentatively again. This time she touched his chest, her fingers starting by his collarbone and sliding down until they brushed across his nipple before she jerked her hand back with surprise.

"I felt that," she said with confusion, her fingers going to her own breast as if to rub away the tingling she'd started in him with her light touch.

"*Oui.* Life mates experience each other's pleasure," he said gruffly. "That was why I would never let you touch me before now. You would feel this and have questions I simply couldn't explain, so I—" Cale stopped on a gasp as Alex suddenly ran her hand over his groin through the blankets. She was definitely experiencing it, he decided grimly when he saw her lips part on a small gasp too.

"Right," he said a bit breathlessly. "We should probably get back to—"

"In a minute," Alex muttered. He felt a moment's relief when she removed her hand from him, but then she simply used it to tug away the blankets covering his lap. The moment they were out of the way, she closed her fingers around his erection and Cale squeezed his eyes closed against the pleasure of her warm soft hand sliding down to the base, gently squeezing as it went. In the next moment he cried out and blinked his eyes open in shock as he felt something warm and wet close over the tip. She'd bent to take him into her mouth.

This had been a really bad idea, Cale decided, as Alex whirled her tongue around the tip and suckled firmly. Damn, he thought dazedly, they were never going to finish this conversation if she—

Alex stopped abruptly and sat up to stare at him wide-eyed. "I felt that."

"Yes," he nodded, half-grateful she'd stopped, and half-wishing she'd continue.

"I mean I seriously felt that. Not like I had a penis or anything, but every touch and lick sent shock waves of pleasure through me too."

"*Oui*. I know," he said with a grimace, tugging the sheet back into place. It was better they finish this conversation. "That's why it's called shared pleasure. Only life mates experience it."

"So you felt that every time you kissed and caressed me?" she asked with amazement.

He nodded.

"Well, damn," she breathed, and then suddenly reached out and pinched his nipple . . . hard.

Cale barked in startled pain and stared at her with amazement. "What did you do that for?"

"Sorry," she murmured, patting his arm with a frown. "I just wanted to see if I would feel your pain too."

"No, it doesn't work that way," he said dryly, rubbing the spot.

"Huh. I wonder why not."

Shaking his head, Cale now tugged the blankets all the way up to his armpits in case she was tempted to try other experiments, and said, "The point is we are definitely life mates. Only life mates experience the shared pleasure." Reaching out, he caught her hand, and added solemnly, "I love you, Alex, but I understand if this all seems sudden, and you have some doubt in my feelings for you. That's okay. You don't have to trust just in me, Alex. Trust the nanos instead until you learn to trust me."

Alex stared at Cale silently, her mind whirling. This was all happening so fast, and she wanted it to slow down. The rest of her life was at stake here, and she'd have liked more time to think, but knew she didn't have that luxury. Marguerite had explained that she had to make her decision soon, that they couldn't allow her to leave with the knowledge she had until she did. The woman had said Alex didn't have to agree to the turn right away, but she did have to decide before she'd be allowed out of the house. It was to protect their people. They hadn't kept their secret all this time by letting just anyone know about them.

Alex knew Cale was waiting for an answer, but it was so hard. She thought she loved Cale, or she was definitely headed that way. The man was gorgeous in her eyes, and considerate, and smart and sexy and the sex was to die for . . . and he was right, they did work well together and balance each other out. But she'd thought Jack loved her too. She would have staked her life on it that he had. And now was terribly afraid she might be making another mistake if she said yes.

On the other hand, her mind argued. The other choice was to never see Cale again. Ever. No more kisses, no more laughing with him, no more amazing sex, no more of his exasperated attempts to help her when she was determined to prove her independence.

Alex was teetering between a yes and a no when a knock sounded at the door. She practically leapt off the bed, saying, "I'll get it."

She heard Cale sigh behind her and knew he was disappointed at the interruption, but she was rather relieved to have an excuse to put it off. She opened the door with a small smile that turned into an "o" of shock as she saw Sam standing in the hall. They hadn't let her see her sister since her arrival almost twenty-four hours ago, insisting it would be better to wait until she was done with her turn and felt ready for it. Now Alex stared at the woman before her and just gaped. Sam had filled out. She was no longer Olive Oyle but had some curves to her, and her eyes no longer dominated her face but set it off. They were even arresting, with the silver tint now coloring them. On top of that her hair was healthy and shiny and her skin seemed almost to glow with good health and happiness. She was a perfect Sam, almost stunning.

"Well?" Sam asked with a grin. "What do you think?"

"Oh my God!" Alex screeched and caught her up in a hug. "You look gorgeous."

"I feel gorgeous." Sam chuckled and hugged her back, and then added, "And that damned ear infection is finally gone too."

"Really?" Alex asked, pulling back to peer at her. Sam had been suffering recurring ear infections for quite a while. It had been very worrisome for Alex and Jo, who had been concerned it might be a symptom of an underlying and more sinister problem.

"Really," Sam said with a happy sigh, and then glanced past her to Cale and frowned. "I came at the wrong time, didn't I? They said you'd been thinking since you got here and were going to give Cale your decision when he woke up, but you haven't yet, have you?"

"Are you reading my mind?" Alex asked with a frown.

Sam gave a laugh. "No. I can't do that yet. But Cale isn't looking happy, and I can tell—"

"He'll be fine." Alex glanced back to Cale, and said, "I'll be right back," as she pushed Sam away from the door and stepped out to join her. She pulled the door closed, and then whirled to her sister. "What do I do?"

"About what?" Sam asked uncertainly.

"Do I accept being Cale's life mate or not?" Alex said impatiently, and her sister frowned.

"Marguerite said you love Cale," she said finally with confusion.

"She told me that too," Alex admitted with a sigh. "And I'm pretty sure I do."

"Then say yes," Sam said at once, sounding relieved.

"But what if he doesn't love me?" Alex said with distress. "He says he does, but so did Jack an—"

"Oh, honey," Sam interrupted with a sigh. "Jack was an ass. Cale would never do to you what Jack did."

"You can't know that for sure," Alex protested.

"Yes I can. He's an immortal. It's different with them. It took me a long time to see that, but it is." She shook her head with disgust, and muttered, "I swear if Mom and Dad were here, I'd have a word or two to say to them."

Alex raised her eyebrows in surprise. "Mom and Dad were okay."

"Then how come we're so screwed up?" she asked dryly. "They weren't around most of the time, Alex. And when they were, they were pretty critical and demanding rather than loving and supportive." Her mouth twisted bitterly. "Do you know I left Mortimer dangling for eight months before agreeing to the turn? Why? Because I didn't feel like I could hold his attention, that it must be some mistake, that he couldn't possibly love me. I was scared silly he'd suddenly notice I wasn't good enough and perfect like Mom and Dad always insisted we had to be. It wasn't just my ex that made me feel that way. It was because Mom and Dad seemed to love that damned business more than they did us."

Alex stared at her wide-eyed, recognizing every feeling she'd just described. It was kind of shocking to realize that Sam had come out the same way. "Do you think Jo feels like that?"

"I don't think so," Sam said on a sigh. "She was younger, and we both looked after her and gave her the love and support Mom and Dad didn't."

They were silent for a minute, and then Sam said, "I know you're afraid of making a mistake, and I know it's scary. But if you love Cale, then say yes, Alex. The alternative is to lose him forever as well as—"

Alex raised an eyebrow. "As well as what?"

Sam hesitated, but then shook her head. "Nothing. Just take a chance and say yes. I know Jack hurt you, but would you really rather not have enjoyed the year you did have before he betrayed you? Do you really want to give up centuries of being with Cale on the off chance that something might go wrong in the future? He's been alive more than two thousand years and never met a life mate before this. Trust me, he will cherish you."

"Two thousand years?" Alex gasped.

"Oh." Sam grimaced. "I thought you knew."

"Two *thousand*?" Alex asked.

"Yeah, he was born in 280 B.C. or something. He's pretty old, huh?"

"That's kind of an understatement, don't you think?" Alex asked dryly. "He's fricking ancient."

"Yeah." Sam nodded. "But he still looks good."

Alex gave a snort of laughter, and then sighed and ran a hand wearily through her hair.

"You look exhausted," Sam said sympathetically.

"I haven't slept since I got here," Alex admitted.

Sam's eyebrows rose. "Why not?"

"I was thinking. Trying to decide what to do."

"Alex, you've never been any good at decision making when you were exhausted. Get some sleep. It will clear your head, and then you'll be able to decide."

"You're right." Alex grimaced. She was always a little foggy when she was exhausted, and she was more exhausted at that moment than she'd ever been in her life, in spirit as well as body. Between being attacked, taking her relationship with Cale to the next level, and then this whole vampire bit, a lot had happened in a very short time. It would have been hard enough to take it in after a good night's sleep, but without it, it seemed impossible. Sleep definitely seemed a good idea, but Cale was waiting.

"I'll tell him you've gone to rest," Sam said quietly when Alex glanced reluctantly toward the bedroom door they stood in front of.

"Thanks," Alex said with relief, and turned to move toward the room Marguerite had led her to when they'd had their talk.

"Alex."

She paused at the door and glanced back in question.

"I love you," Sam said quietly. "No matter your decision, I want you to know I love you. I never want you to forget that."

Alex smiled quizzically. "I love you too, Sam."

Sam smiled sadly and turned to enter Cale's room, and Alex turned back to her door, wishing she had a map or instruction booklet to life. She just wanted someone else to tell her what to do, which decision was the right one. Should she leap impetuously after love, or would it be smarter to stand on the shoreline and watch the love boat sail away?

"The Love Boat," she muttered with disgust as she entered her room. Now she was just getting sappy. She definitely needed to sleep.

Seventeen

Alex woke up with a little sigh of pleasure and stretched in bed. She felt fabulous, absolutely fabulous, even. She'd dropped off to sleep as soon as she'd lain down on the bed, and then had enjoyed some pretty erotic dreams, all of them featuring Cale. Damn, he was as good in her dreams as he was in real life. And he'd said some wonderful things in her dreams as he'd cherished her with his body. He'd told her everything he loved about her, from her nose to her stubborn determination to prove she could do anything she set her mind to. He'd also said that he'd love her forever.

It might have just been a dream, but Alex was going to take it as an omen and say yes. Even one night with him was worth any heartache that might be waiting. Besides, it wasn't in her nature to refrain from doing something out of fear; otherwise, she never would have taken a chance and started the first La Bonne Vie . . . or the second for that matter. She must have been incredibly exhausted after everything she'd experienced, or Alex was sure she wouldn't have been so confused and uncertain by the time Cale had woken from healing.

A knock at the door drew her attention, and she sat up on the bed to peer toward it. "Yes?"

"Morning," Cale said cheerfully as he pushed the door open and sailed in. "Or good evening, I guess. It's late in the day."

"Hi." Alex smiled, her gaze moving curiously from the tray he carried to the shopping bag hanging over his arm.

"I've brought you a snack, and these clothes for you to put on afterward," he announced, setting the tray on the foot of the bed, and then dropping the large bag beside it.

"Thank you," Alex said with surprise, glancing over the tray. It held some sort of sandwich and a cup of steaming coffee, she noted, and then glanced back to Cale, only to see that he was heading for the door as quickly as he'd entered.

"Take your time, and then meet me downstairs," he said lightly and slid out of the room pulling the door closed.

Alex glanced back to the tray and then pushed the blankets aside and crawled to the end of the bed to grab the coffee. It had already been fixed with cream and sugar just the way she liked it. She smiled faintly as she took a sip, thinking Cale had learned her likes and dislikes quickly. The coffee was delicious, but then so was the toasted bacon, lettuce, and tomato sandwich, and she consumed both quickly before reaching for the bag of clothes. It was very large, and she soon realized why. While there were a clean pair of jeans, a sweater, panties, and bra, there were also a snowmobile suit, heavy socks, a hat, gloves, and boots as well. It seemed they were going somewhere.

Alex took a quick shower before dressing. She found Cale similarly geared up and waiting by the front door when she tramped down the stairs in the heavy boots and hoped he hadn't been waiting there long.

"So what's going on?" she asked curiously as she reached the bottom of the stairs. "And where is everyone?"

"Bricker and Mortimer are in the garage at the back of the property, and Sam is in the kitchen," Cale answered, turning to open the front door. "Come on."

"Where?" Alex glanced out at the night sky, and then stepped out and paused with surprise when she saw the waiting snowmobile. "What—?"

"You said you always wanted to try snowmobiling, but never had the time, so I had the guys rent one for me," Cale announced, leading her to the machine. He removed two helmets from the snowmobile's seat and handed her one, then put on his own.

Alex merely held the helmet and stared at him silently, recalling the conversation he was talking about. She was amazed he remembered, and even more amazed that he'd gone to the trouble of renting one for her to try.

"Russell showed me how to drive it. I'll take you for a spin, and then show you how to do it so you can drive me around," he announced, and then started the engine. Talk was impossible over the loud roar of the engine after that. When Cale turned, gesturing her forward, Alex pulled on her helmet and moved forward, silently shaking her head that he'd gone to this trouble. It was really very sweet, and not the first time he'd been so thoughtful. She'd figured out pretty quickly that the man had never been antiquing in his life the day they'd gone, and suspected he'd suggested it purely to please her and keep her happy during her enforced relaxation after the head injury.

Alex didn't know how he'd known she liked antiquing, but suspected Sam had suggested it. And then there was his taking over the business end of things so that she could cook. She knew he preferred that to cooking, but the truth was he didn't have to do either. He was here on vacation but had given up his time to help her. He was a very generous and giving man.

Cale straddled the machine, and then urged her to get on behind him. Once she did, he reached back to catch her hands and draw them around his chest, and then the snowmobile engine's roar suddenly increased in volume. Alex tightened her hold on him as they jumped forward and began to fly across the front yard, but she squealed and ducked her head behind his back when he turned to send them flying up and over a small pile of snow made from shoveling the sidewalk.

They landed with a *whumph,* and then he sent the machine shooting around the side of the house to the backyard. Alex was too busy holding on at first to really pay attention to anything else, but when he started toward the trees, she glanced around and caught her breath. The branches of the thick evergreens were coated with new snow that sparkled in the snowmobile's headlights; but it was the oaks and maples that truly shone, their branches were encased in ice from previous snowfalls that had melted, and they glittered like diamonds when the light hit them. It was beautiful.

She was surprised when Cale suddenly stopped the machine and simply sat staring. Then he said exactly what she was thinking. "It's beautiful, isn't it?"

Alex smiled and hugged him tighter, whispering, "I love you."

Cale stilled, turned abruptly on the seat, flipping up the visor of his helmet so that he could see her better. "What?"

Alex raised her visor as well, and said firmly, "I love you, and I'm willing to turn."

Rather than seem pleased, he frowned. "Are you sure? I mean, this morning in my room you seemed confused and scared and—"

"This morning I was exhausted," she interrupted firmly, and then pointed out, "It's been a rough couple of days, with a lot happening and little sleep. I was a mess this morning."

"And now?" he asked uncertainly.

"Now I've had some sleep," she said gently. "And while I'm still scared I'll get hurt, I do love you, and it seems to me it's worth taking the chance."

"I wish you weren't scared," Cale murmured, raising one gloved hand to brush a finger down her cheek. "I wish I could convince you I love you and won't hurt you."

"Time will do that," she said quietly.

Cale hugged her close and sighed. "I hope I never run into that Jack fellow. It would be hard not to break his bloody neck for hurting you."

Alex laughed against his chest. "It wasn't just Jack. He was just the icing on the cake that made me this way. Besides, you already have met him. Or at least talked to him," she added.

"What? I haven't met Jack."

"Jacques Tournier," she said dryly. "Peter said that Jacques tried to hire you away from me. Didn't he?"

"Yes, he did. He called. But he introduced himself as Jacques, and now you're saying he's your Jack?" he asked with a frown.

"He's not *my* anything," Alex said with a grimace, and then explained, "He was Jack when I knew him in school. He changed his name legally to Jacques Tournier before opening Chez Joie. I guess he figured a French name would do in lieu of a diploma from a French culinary school. He always was an ass," she added dryly.

"He's your biggest competitor?" Cale asked, his voice grim.

Alex nodded. "Pretty much. He—" She broke off with surprise as he suddenly turned and started the engine again. She frowned, unable to ask what was going on. He'd never hear her over the engine. All she could do was hold on tightly as he suddenly sent the snowmobile shooting forward.

Alex wasn't terribly surprised when he headed them straight back to the house, but she *was* concerned.

"What's going on?" she asked as soon as they were in front of the house, and he shut the engine down again.

"Nothing," he muttered, getting off the machine and striding toward the house. "I just need to have a talk with someone."

Alex narrowed her eyes and hurried after him. "You are not going after Jack."

Cale didn't respond but stepped into the house, and shouted, "Sam?"

"Yeah?" her head poked around the kitchen entrance, eyebrows raised in question.

"Can you call Mortimer and Bricker down at the garage and have them come up here?" he asked as he removed his boots. "I need a word with them. It's important," he added as he finished with his boots and started upstairs in full snowmobile gear.

Cursing, Alex kicked off her own boots and gave chase. "Cale, tell me what's going on."

"Nothing for you to worry about," he assured her as he reached the hall at the top of the stairs. "I just need to check into something."

"That's bullshit," she snapped, following him into his room. "You're going after Jack, and it's stupid. He was just a childhood fling. He means nothing."

"He's still affecting you, which means you could still be affecting him," Cale said absently as he began to remove his outer gear.

Alex paused and stared at him blankly. "What are you talking about? I mean, I know I said it affected me, but it was just one more thing, not the be all and end all. And it certainly wouldn't be affecting *him* anymore. He never loved me."

"Alex, his relationship with you, and getting caught stealing your recipe is what got him thrown out of culinary school in disgrace," Cale said patiently as he tossed his helmet and gloves on the bed and began to unzip the jacket of his snowmobile suit. "Of course it's still affecting him. He probably blames you for it somehow. People like him always twist things around in their heads so that they can blame someone else for their own shortcomings."

"But—"

"Did he start Chez Joie before or after you started La Bonne Vie?" Cale asked, tossing his coat on the bed and starting to work on removing the bottoms.

"About six months after," she said, not sure what that had to do with anything.

"How close is it to your restaurant?"

Alex frowned as she watched him step out of the bottoms, leaving him in his jeans and a sweater. "I don't know. Not far. You can walk there on a nice day."

"And do you really think it's a coincidence that he started a French cuisine restaurant just like yours, here in Toronto, so close to yours, and only months after your own restaurant opened?" he asked, hands on hips.

She blinked in surprise at the question, and then admitted, "Well, I never really thought about it."

"And he's changed his name to Jacques Tournier to give himself more credibility because he doesn't have the culinary school's stamp of approval as you do," he added dryly, and then frowned. "You really should have told me this earlier."

"I didn't tell you because it wasn't important," Alex said defensively. "And it still isn't."

"What's up?" Bricker asked, leading Mortimer into the room.

"Jacques Tournier, the owner of Chez Joie, Alex's biggest competitor, is also Jack Turner, the jerk who messed with her head in culinary school and got kicked out in disgrace for stealing her recipe," Cale announced as if they would understand the significance where she hadn't, and much to her amazement they appeared to.

"Interesting," Bricker said slowly.

"More than interesting," Mortimer said dryly. "That's one hell of a coincidence."

Alex's eyes widened, and she turned on Cale with dismay. "You told them about Jack?"

"It wasn't Cale. Sam told us some guy at culinary school broke your heart and stole your year-end project," Bricker said absently, his expression thoughtful as he apparently considered the ramifications of Cale's words.

"Maybe we'd better make a visit to Chez Joie," Mortimer said quietly.

Alex turned on him with amazement. "Why? This is stupid. What—?" She stopped abruptly as she felt a ruffling in her mind and turned furiously on Bricker and Mortimer. "Cut that out. If you want to know something, ask me. Don't read my mind."

Bricker raised his eyebrows. "She's more sensitive than most. She felt me poking around."

Alex merely scowled. "What were you trying to find?"

"It's all right, I found it," he said with a shrug, and then glanced to Cale, and announced, "She hasn't connected any of the events."

"What events?" Alex asked through gritted teeth.

Cale moved to her side to take her hands, "Honey, you've had a lot of setbacks and problems recently."

"Yes, I *had* noticed," she said dryly. "It's been one thing after another for months."

"Well, I don't think it's just bad luck," he said quietly.

Alex stilled. "What do you mean?"

He hesitated, and then said, "When I first found out about all the troubles you'd been having, it bothered me. It reminded me of my family."

"Your family?" she asked with surprise, and then shook her head. "How?"

"You remember I told you my brothers were all soldiers?"

"Actually, you said warriors, and then claimed it was your English and you meant soldiers," she said, recalling the conversation . . . and then she recalled how old Sam had said he was and raised her eyes to his, and said, "You really meant warriors, didn't you?"

He nodded. "My father hired himself out as a mercenary. As my parents had sons, he trained each of us in battle, and we joined him until we had a small army. We were considered the best in the business. But we had a competitor, another immortal, Niger Malumus. He had his own small army of sons, and they vied for the same contracts. It was no big deal when both groups were small. They often ended up both being hired and fighting together and did so for centuries. But as each side grew in number, one or the other was hired rather than both, and they started competing for contracts. It was a friendly competition at first, but then it got less friendly . . . and then we started having a run of bad luck," he said grimly. "Sudden accidents, horses going wild and throwing their riders, weapons with defects, small fires starting in the stables."

Cale sighed and ran a hand wearily through his hair. "We didn't realize it at the time, but one of our men was a traitor, paid to make these accidents happen. But those accidents were just the appetizer. Niger was working himself up to removing us as competition, permanently."

"What happened?" Alex asked quietly when he paused.

Cale shook his head. "That's the hell of it. We don't know for sure. One day a messenger came with a supposed job offer. My father and eight of my eleven brothers rode out."

"Why only eight?" Alex asked.

"I had been thrown from my horse that morning. One of those accidents that kept happening," he said bitterly. "I'd broken my back in a fall from my usually faithful horse, who suddenly went wild and threw me into a tree. I was still healing. As for my two still-surviving brothers, the eldest, Darius, lived a little distance away with his new life mate and my brother Caleb was sent to collect him and catch up to my father and the others on the way."

He paused and swallowed and closed his eyes. "Caleb

and Darius caught up to them sooner than expected, a mere hour from our stronghold. They'd ridden into some kind of trap and been slaughtered down to the last man. Everyone beheaded and left to rot on the side of the road like so much garbage."

"I'm sorry," Alex breathed, squeezing his hands. She couldn't even imagine it. Eight brothers and a father lost in one night, murdered for the sake of a few jobs. "What happened to Niger Malamus and his sons? Did they ever catch them?"

Cale sucked in a deep, steadying breath. "They were taken care of, eventually," he said quietly. "But it didn't bring my father and brothers back."

She glanced down to their entwined hands and shook her head. "I'm sorry, Cale, I can't imagine suffering such a huge and tragic loss, but I really don't understand how that relates to Jacques."

"Don't you?" he asked quietly. "I see the same pattern. Competition, setbacks, accidental deliveries of the wrong supplies . . ."

"I had a really bad project manager. That's why I fired him," she pointed out impatiently.

"And the fire right after you bought the house?" Bricker asked.

"That was an electrical fire," Alex said at once. "It was an old house, old wiring."

"What about the attack at your restaurant?" Mortimer reminded her.

"A mugging attempt," she said firmly.

"And then the pickup that forced me off the road," Cale said grimly.

Alex blinked in surprise. "I'm sure that was just a drunk driver."

"Alex," he said dryly.

"I know there have been a lot of problems lately. Believe me I know," she added grimly. "But it's just been bad luck. I don't think anyone is behind it. No one has any reason to want to hurt me, especially Jacques. For heaven's sake, if anyone has a right to a grudge between him and me, that's me. And I don't."

"Well, someone does," Bricker said dryly.

"Why would you say that?" she asked with surprise.

Mortimer glanced to Cale. "You didn't tell her?"

"Tell me what?" Alex asked, turning to Cale with a frown.

He looked grim. "When I was being forced off the road, I started to try to take control of the other driver to get him back in his lane. I thought perhaps he was drunk or having a heart attack."

"He probably was," Alex said at once. "Couldn't you control him?"

"I didn't get the chance. You laid on your horn, distracting me, and I glanced around to see that I was headed for the concrete divide. I gave up on worrying about the other driver and concentrated on trying to avoid the crash. But while I didn't get to read the driver's mind, I did get the flavor of his thoughts before you honked."

"The flavor of his thoughts?" she asked with confusion.

"People's minds are . . ." He frowned. "Think of it like a dish. You smell it before you actually bite into it, and that gives you a hint of what you're about to taste."

"Our brains smell?" Alex asked with amazement.

"No." He chuckled softly. "But they have a general feeling about them that you can sense before you actually penetrate and touch on their thoughts. For instance, you would have a general sense of confusion and unconcern before penetrating a drunk's brain, or you might get a sense of panic and pain before touching on someone having a heart attack." He waited for her to nod that she understood, and then said, "The driver didn't have either of those."

Alex felt her heart begin to sink. "What did he have?"

"It was a heavy feeling. The only way to describe it would be malice," he said quietly. "I'm pretty sure he knew exactly what he was doing. He deliberately ran me off the road."

Alex frowned. "Who would do that to you?"

"I don't think he knew it was me. It was your car," he pointed out quietly.

Alex stared at him wide-eyed, floored by the possibility that anyone would wish her harm, but then shook her head again. It just couldn't be. It was ridiculous. Why would anyone deliberately try to drive her off the road?

"Bricker called around while I was healing," Cale said quietly. "No one reported the accident to the police, and no one has shown up at any of the many auto shops in town with the kind of damage that pickup must have suffered when I drove up the side of it. Do you know what kind of vehicle Jacques drives?"

Alex shook her head with a frown, and then turned abruptly and headed out of the room.

"Alex? Where are you going?" Cale asked, following her past Mortimer and Bricker. She didn't glance back to see if they were following too, but heard their footsteps as the trio trailed her down the stairs.

"Alex," Cale said impatiently, catching her arm at the bottom of the stairs.

"I'm going to find out what Jacques drives," she muttered, shaking his hand free and hurrying into the kitchen.

Sam was there and turned with surprise as she entered with the three men following. "What's happening?"

Alex ignored the question, a bit miffed with her sister for blabbing about her relationship with Jack to Bricker and Mortimer. She moved to the phone on the counter but heard Mortimer murmuring and knew he was explaining things.

It was seven o'clock on Tuesday. La Bonne Vie was closed, but Chez Joie stayed open seven days a week, and Mark would be working, so he wouldn't be available to take Bev out. Alex called her at home, relieved when she answered after only a couple of rings. That relief turned to concern as she heard the girl's watery voice and sniffles.

"Bev? Are you okay?" she asked, worried the girl was coming down sick.

"Alex?" Bev asked in a stunned voice.

"Yes, are you okay?" she repeated.

"Me?" the girl practically shrieked. "Oh, my God, I've been worrying sick about you. I was so upset I—"

"I'm fine," Alex interrupted with a shake of the head. She'd been standing right beside Cale when he'd called

Bev from the hospital after the attack. He'd told her she was all right, for heaven's sake. "It was just a bump on the head. That guy who attacked me didn't get the chance to hurt me thanks to you."

"That bastard," Bev suddenly growled.

Alex raised her eyebrows, but merely said, "Look, I was just calling because I wondered if you knew what kind of vehicle Mark's boss drives?"

"Jacques?" Bev said the name with disgust. "No I don't, and I don't want to know. What a jerk. Do you know he gave Mark some cock-and-bull story about seeing on the news that you'd been in a terrible crash? He said your car was an accordion, and it looked fatal. He asked Mark if I'd heard anything or knew what was going to happen to the restaurant. Of course Mark called me right away, and I've been a wreck ever since. I've been calling your house, and when I didn't get an answer, I started trying to find your sisters' numbers to call them. I even called the hospitals and the police to try to find information about you. I should have known when they couldn't tell me anything that the dirt bag was lying."

The phone still pressed to her ear, Alex turned slowly toward Cale, Mortimer, and Bricker. One look at their grim faces told her they'd heard everything. Jacques was out to get her, she realized with dismay. She already knew that Bricker and some other men had cleaned up the crash site and moved her car so that no one would come upon it and ask questions. No one but the people in this house knew about the crash . . . except for the driver of the black pickup. There had been no news report. Jacques had been fishing for information and made that up to get it.

"Bev, I'm at Sam's. Get the number from your call display and call me if you need me," Alex said, and pushed the button to end the call.

"Umm, our number won't show on call display. It's unlisted and blocked," Bricker announced as she set the receiver back in its cradle.

Alex waved that away, not particularly caring, and glanced to Cale. Only one word came out of her mouth. "Why?"

Cale came forward at once, taking her in his arms. Hugging her, he rubbed her back soothingly. "I don't know, honey. But we'll find out."

"Yes, *we* will," she said grimly, pulling back to stare at him firmly. "I'm coming with you."

Cale opened his mouth in what she suspected would have been a protest, but Mortimer beat him to it. "I'm afraid I can't allow that."

Alex jerked out of Cale's arms and stepped around him to glare at her sister's boyfriend. "Can't allow it?" she asked sharply. "Who the hell do you think you are? You can't stop me if I want to go."

"Umm, well actually, Alex, he can," Sam said gently. "It's his job."

Alex narrowed her eyes and then turned them onto Mortimer. "Not in a band, I take it?"

Mortimer grimaced, which made Bricker give a bark of laughter before he said, "He hated that cover."

Alex sighed. She should have known. She'd been at the house several times and never even seen a musical instrument here. Why had that never occurred to her before? Probably because they hadn't let it, she answered herself. Jesus. They were like little demigods, controlling people and arranging things the way they liked. Shaking her head with disgust, she asked, "So what are you?"

"Vampire cops," Bricker said at once making both Mortimer and Cale wince. He seemed amused at their pained reactions and told her, "The old ones don't like the term vampire."

"And you shouldn't either. Vampires are—"

"Much sexier than immortals," Bricker interrupted firmly. "Heck, they're all the rage today. We'd get a lot more tail if we came out to the world and called ourselves vamps."

"Right, because so many people are necrophiliacs looking for undead lovers," Sam said on a laugh. "I don't think so, Bricker."

"Back to the point," Mortimer said grimly, turning his gaze back to Alex. "I'm afraid you can't leave here until you make up your mind about being Cale's life mate or not."

"I already have. I told him outside that I'd be his life mate," Alex said at once.

"Oh, thank God!" Sam rushed across the room to hug her tightly with relief. More tightly than she realized, Alex thought as she began gasping for air.

"Sam, honey, you're a bit stronger than you realize," Mortimer said gently. "You might want to let Alex go before you suffocate her."

"Oh, sorry!" Sam let her go and patted her arm

apologetically. "Sorry, I'm just so happy." She hugged her again, less tightly this time, and babbled, "I was so worried you'd say no, and then they'd wipe your mind, and we'd never be able to see you again."

Alex frowned. "You mean Cale wouldn't be able to see me again."

"No. Jo and I wouldn't either now that we're immortals too. It might have sparked memories, and they wouldn't have allowed it. You'd have been lost to us forever."

Alex stared at her blankly, feeling like she'd just been punched in the gut. She then shrieked, "Jo's an immortal too?"

Sam winced, and then offered apologetically, "Yeah. Nicholas turned her just days after they met."

"Why didn't you tell me?" Alex asked furiously. "It was bad enough when you didn't tell me about Mortimer, but I can sort of understand that. But Jo? Our baby sister? You should have told me!"

"They wouldn't let me," Sam said at once. "They were afraid it would influence your decision on whether to accept Cale as a life mate and turn or not. That's why they wouldn't let me tell you that if you said no, you'd lose us too."

Alex turned to glare at the three men, but they were no longer there. They'd used the opportunity her distraction had afforded and slipped out of the house.

Eighteen

The sound of the front door opening stirred Alex from the light doze she'd fallen into on the couch, and she sat up to glance tensely toward the hall as she heard the men stomp their way inside. Sam got up at once and moved out to greet them, but Alex stayed where she was, almost reluctant to know what had happened. She didn't want to believe anyone had been behind her run of bad luck, but Bev's phone call had convinced her Jacques must have been the one who had forced her car off the road . . . which made it possible that he'd had something to do with the other problems she'd been having of late. To her it was just plain stupid. She was the one who'd been wronged in their relationship. Why the hell had he set out to make her life such a misery?

Cale appeared in the doorway, and then crossed the room to join her, and Alex saw Sam lead Mortimer and Bricker to the kitchen. They were giving them time alone. That didn't seem like good news, she decided, as Cale paused before her.

"Is it okay if I sit down?" he asked, eyeing her warily, and she found herself smiling wryly. He wasn't sure of his welcome. At least he knew sneaking out had been dirty pool.

"Yes, of course," she murmured, and waited until he'd seated himself beside her before turning to sit cross-legged facing him. "So?" she asked. "What happened? Did he do it?"

Cale blew his breath out on a sigh, and then admitted, "He wasn't at the restaurant when we got there. It seems as soon as you hung up, Bev called Mark to ask him what kind of vehicle Jacques drives so that she could pass the information on to you. She then ripped into him about what a jerk the guy was for saying you'd had a terrible accident when you were fine. Mark told Jacques about the call, and he left at once." He grimaced. "We figure he got spooked because you were asking what kind of vehicle he drives . . . which was a black pickup, by the way. According to Mark's memories, he was driving that until Monday, when he showed up at the restaurant in a rental car claiming his pickup was in the shop."

Alex ran her hands through her hair with a little sigh, acknowledging that that was pretty damning. It seemed Jacques had tried to run her off the road on Monday morning. She was just lucky it had been Cale behind the wheel. Not that she was happy that he had been hurt, but she never would have survived. "I suppose you checked his house after that?"

When Cale appeared surprised, she shrugged. "Mortimer and Bricker are vampire cops, cops would check the house next."

He nodded. "His drawers were open and half-empty, and there was a spot in his closet between a large suitcase and a small one where a medium-sized suitcase would have fit. We think he packed in a hurry and got the hell out. They're having someone check his bank records right now to try to track him, and Mortimer has sent some men out to hunt. They'll find him eventually and figure out just how many of your recent problems were caused by him and how."

"And then what?" she asked quietly. "And please don't tell me they'll hand him over to the authorities. I know the car has already been sent to the wreckers, so there's no proof he did anything wrong. What will they do with him?"

"I don't know," Cale admitted quietly. "Lucian will probably decide what should be done. He makes all the decisions like that."

"Lucian." Alex murmured the name with dislike. Sam had told her a lot about the immortal while they waited for the men to return. She'd explained that just because she'd chosen to turn didn't mean she could now go about her life. If she didn't turn right away, she would have to be "interviewed" by Lucian Argeneau. He would decide if it was safe to allow her out with the information about who and what they were. It was an effort to keep their secret and their people safe.

Alex understood but, judging by Sam's description, would rather avoid that interview. Sam had described it as brain rape. She also didn't particularly want to go weeks worrying about having to go through the turn. It had looked damned painful to her when she'd seen Sam suffering it. She'd made her decision, and as always, just wanted to get to it and get it done.

Deciding not to worry about Jacques and his future now, she said, "So . . . if you turn me tonight, will I be recovered enough to work tomorrow?"

Cale looked shocked by the question. "Tonight? This morning you weren't sure what to do."

"And then I had a nap and decided I wanted to be with you and turn," she said firmly. "I don't want to waste any time."

"Yes, but it's a big decision. If you want more time—"

"Geez," Alex muttered, and shifted up onto her knees to climb into his lap. She felt a little awkward doing it at first. It was all still new to her, but she settled in his lap and slipped her arms loosely around his neck. Looking him in the eyes, she said solemnly, "You sound like you're having second thoughts."

"Never," he assured her, slipping his own arms around her waist. "I just don't want you jumping into it before you're positive."

"I'm afraid that's my nature," she admitted, pressing her forehead against his. "I fuss, and then I decide, and then I race ahead with whatever decision I've come to. It's part of my charm," she added wryly.

"Yes, it is," Cale murmured. "And *I* think things through, calculate the pluses and minuses, and then after a suitable time has passed, decide if it is feasible."

Alex snorted. "From what Sam said, you decided I was your life mate the first night we met."

"That is different. The nanos chose you. There was no decision to be made."

"Then why drag it out and wait?" she said simply, and kissed him.

Cale responded at once, his mouth opening to allow his tongue out. Alex sighed as he invaded her, her hands dropping to run over his chest, sending little ripples of pleasure through them both as she found his nipples and began to play with them through his shirt.

"I never knew men liked to have their nipples touched too," she gasped as his mouth left hers to trail to her ear.

"Maybe they all don't," he murmured.

"You do," she almost moaned as he began to nibble at her earlobe.

"So do you," he breathed, his hands now finding her breasts through her sweater and kneading lightly.

Alex moaned as the pleasure sliding through her doubled, and then doubled again, but then gasped in surprise when Cale suddenly stood up, taking her with him. His hands cupped her bottom, holding her up, and she instinctively wrapped her legs around his hips. Alex hooked her ankles around each other as he began to walk toward the door, but asked worriedly, "Do we have time? I have to be well enough to go to the restaurant by four tomorrow."

"We'll be fast," he assured her, carrying her out into the hall.

She chuckled wryly at the promise. "We always are. But if we sleep too long afterward . . ."

Cale's response was to shout, "Mortimer, check on us in an hour and make sure we're awake!"

He didn't even wait for Mortimer's assurance that he would, but started up the stairs, his eyes moving to her face as their bodies rubbed together, sending shock waves of pleasure through them both.

Alex shifted against him with a little moan, grinding herself against the hardness growing where their bodies met, and said breathlessly, "I think you'd better hurry."

"I am," he assured her, and she realized he'd picked up the pace and was practically jogging up the stairs now. It just ground her body into his more firmly, pounding them against each other with each step. By the time he reached the top, they were both panting, and it had little to do with the exertion of mounting the stairs.

Instead of carrying her on to his room or hers, Cale groaned and bore her backward. He pressed her against the wall, allowing it to help take her weight as he claimed her lips and removed one hand from her behind to bring it around to cover a breast. Alex wasn't still. She immediately began tugging at his sweater, pulling it up to bare his chest, and then urging his arms up so that she could pull it off. Cale immediately released her, pinning her against the wall with his hips and breaking their kiss so that he could do her silent bidding and raise his arms.

"This is insane," he muttered, as she dragged the sweater over his face.

"Uh-huh," Alex agreed, tossing the sweater the moment she had it off him. She caught a glimpse of it sailing over the balustrade, and then her attention moved to the bare chest she'd revealed. She didn't think, but bent her head to lick the bare skin of his upper chest, her lower body squirming between him and the wall as she nibbled at his collarbone, sending up a maelstrom of pleasure. Who knew a collarbone could be so sensitive? she thought dazedly, as his pleasure mixed with hers.

She felt him tugging at her sweater now, and pulled back enough to allow him to remove it as well, then shivered as he tossed it over his shoulder. She saw it float over the balustrade, and then closed her eyes on another shiver as his hands, still cool from outside, slid over her heated flesh. Her eyes opened again when her bra suddenly went slack around her, and then Cale was slipping that out from between them and sending it flying as well so that he could cup her breasts, unfettered by the silky cloth.

"God, you're beautiful." He almost sighed the words as he lifted her higher to close his mouth over one now-bare nipple.

"Hey! Sam, Mortimer! You gotta see this. It's raining clothes out here." Bricker's words sounded on a laugh, and Alex heard Cale growl deep in his throat, and then his hands slid down to cup her behind again. He lifted her away from the wall to continue up the hall, still suckling at her and Alex closed her arms around his head, her body arching and twisting against his head.

"Door?" he mumbled against her flesh, not lifting his head.

Alex shivered as the vibration of his speaking went right through her, and then laughed at the absurdity of it, but glanced around.

"A couple more steps," she gasped, running her hands down his back and scraping the nails back up.

When he pressed her against the door, she reached back to open it, aware of the soft murmur of voices below but unable to comprehend what was being said. Not that she cared what they said or thought below. She didn't have the ability at that point; all she could think about was the sensation roaring through her body. She barely had enough spare brainpower to turn the doorknob, but she managed it, and the door swung open.

Cale immediately carried her inside. He turned to close the door by pressing her back against it as his lips let her nipple slip free only to nibble their way across to her other breast and claim that one. He was holding her high now, her legs around his waist rather than his hips, and Alex moaned in frustration as she writhed against him. She began to tug on his hair, just wanting him to lower her enough to allow her to rub against him again, and he did, but had to stop what he was doing to achieve it, and Alex found that frustrating as well.

She caught his face in her hands and lifted it, claiming his mouth with her own, and then tore her mouth away to glance around with surprise when he turned her away from the door.

"Bed," he gasped for explanation. "Soft surface."

Alex glanced back to him with surprise, amazed that he recalled that request at the restaurant, when she could hardly recall her own name. She'd have been happy for him to have ripped her pants off and made love to her right there against the door . . . At least until they woke up in a heap on the floor, she acknowledged, and then he was bending to the bed. He set her down gently, and then immediately kissed her again. She kissed back with all the passion only he could bring to life in her, but grabbed his hands when he reached for the waist of her jeans.

Cale paused and broke their kiss to peer down at her in question, and Alex immediately clasped his face in her hands.

"I like you," she said breathlessly.

Cale blinked in confusion. "I like you too."

"No, I mean it," she said more firmly. "I like you. I've loved people I couldn't stand to live with, my sisters for instance," she added dryly. "Sibling rivalry was hell . . . But I like you, Cale. You're funny and smart and considerate and sexy as hell, and I really like you."

He smiled softly, and then turned his head to press a kiss to first one of her palms, and then the other, before meeting her gaze solemnly. "I like you too. You're sweet and intelligent and ambitious and an amazing cook . . . Now let's get you naked cause I like you best that way."

Alex laughed and helped him undo her pants, then grabbed ahold of the bed to keep from being pulled forward when he dragged them off. Her panties went with them, and both items went flying over his shoulder, then Cale quickly shucked his own jeans.

"Mmm, soft," he murmured as he climbed onto the bed to join her.

"You or the bed?" she teased.

"The bed," he said dryly. "I don't think I'll ever be soft around you."

"That's good to know," Alex gasped as he slid into her, warm and full and definitely not soft.

"Shut up and kiss me, woman," he growled, withdrawing a little.

Alex laughed and did, covering his mouth and allowing her lips to part for his tongue to thrust in even as his body drove back into her.

"I think you can call this a success."

Alex glanced to Cale as he paused beside her. It seemed the most natural thing in the world to lean into him as his arm slid around her waist, and his lips touched her forehead.

The night of the opening had finally arrived. It was an evening she'd feared a time or two might never happen, but here it was. The restaurant was finished, everything in its place, the new cooks in the kitchen working away and the dining room and bar area full of people mingling and partaking of her food and drink. Alex had arranged it to be more of a party than a restaurant night. The regulars at the original La Bonne Vie had been invited as well as friends and family, several local celebrities, Emile, of course, and the local press, who, thanks to Emile, had shown up en masse. It was definitely a success.

"You're looking pale," Cale murmured, peering down at her with concern. "Perhaps you should slip into the office for a quick refresher. It will only take a minute, and I'll keep an eye on things here," he added when she frowned at the idea.

"All right, then," Alex grumbled with all the good

grace of a child agreeing reluctantly to take cod liver oil. It wasn't that blood tasted bad. She didn't even taste it the way they'd shown her to feed, but it was the idea of actually consuming the blood. She hadn't quite gotten used to that yet and found herself shuddering with distaste even as her fangs slid out eagerly to consume it. How messed up was that?

Chuckling, Cale hugged her close and bent to press a quick kiss to her lips. "Poor darling. You'll adjust soon."

"You keep saying that," she murmured, toying with his tie. "But it hasn't happened yet."

"It's only been a couple of days, love," he chided. "Give it time."

"Hmm." She smiled faintly. "I appear to have a lot of that now."

"Yes. You do," he said solemnly. "Not regretting it already, are you?"

"You're kidding, right?" she asked with amusement. The last two days since she'd woken from the turn had been amazing. Now that she'd stopped trying to keep him at arm's length with her professional footing nonsense and agreed to be his life mate, her life had become almost blissful. They made love every chance they got, which was amazing of course. Alex was sure there was nothing that could beat immortal sex. Except there was in some ways, and that was when she and Cale were together and unable to make love, which had been an awful lot these last two days as she'd had to cook at the old La Bonne Vie, and he'd refused to leave her alone until Jacques was found. While there had been desire and need sparking between them under the surface, there had also been witty discussions and gentle teasing and easy affection that she reveled in as he sat on the counter and watched her cook.

She really did like this man, and of course she definitely wanted him, but she also loved him, and while Alex had said that to him when she'd agreed to the turn, she thought now that perhaps she hadn't really, because what she felt for him seemed to grow stronger every day and sometimes actually hurt. She could look at him and feel an actual ache in her chest. Or perhaps that's how love was. Perhaps it just grew stronger with time, she thought, and assured him, "I'm very happy with my decision."

"Good." He smiled and kissed her nose before releasing her. "Go on. There's a surprise waiting in your office too."

"Oh?" she asked with interest. "What kind of surprise?"

"Go and see for yourself," he insisted, giving her a little push.

Smiling, Alex moved quickly through the milling crowd, thanking people as they congratulated her on the new restaurant, the food, the drink, the service. She was beginning to think she would never get to her office, when Sam suddenly appeared to grab her hand and drag her the rest of the way.

"Wooh! Thank you." Alex laughed as they escaped into the kitchen and the door swung closed behind them. "I was starting to think I'd never make it out of there."

"Yes, you did look like a damsel in distress with all your admirers fawning over you," Sam teased.

"Yeah right. Besides, I *was* a damsel in distress. I need a little pick-me-up to sustain me, and Cale says there's a surprise in my office too that I want to see," Alex said, moving away from the door.

"Did he?" Sam asked innocently.

Alex slowed and eyed her narrowly. "You know what it is."

"Who me?" She batted her eyelashes and urged Alex to keep moving.

Alex snorted. "You are such a—" The words died in her throat as she stepped into her office and spotted Jo seated in the chair, her feet on the desk.

"Finally!" Jo dropped her feet to the ground and came around the desk. "You took forever getting her here."

"Jo!" Alex gasped, rushing forward to hug her little sister. She just as quickly pulled away to peer at her, noting that while the turn had added some weight to Sam, and removed a couple of pounds from herself, it didn't appear to have changed Jo at all except that she had a healthy glow to her now. They all did, she acknowledged, and asked, "What are you doing here? You're supposed to be traveling in Europe with Nicholas. I thought you couldn't make it."

"And miss your big day?" Jo snorted. "Not bloody likely. Of course we flew back for the party."

"Oh." Alex stepped back to peer at her, and then shifted to slip her arm around Sam too and include her as well. "It's pretty awesome isn't it?"

"Way awesome," Sam assured her.

"It's the start of a chain, my dear," Jo announced. "I

predict that within the next ten years, there will be La Bonne Vie restaurants across the globe."

"Not that," Alex said on a laugh. "And I assure you I have no desire to open more restaurants. I meant us. Here. The three of us with men who love us and whom we love."

"Immortals who love us and whom we love," Sam said solemnly.

"We should have a joint wedding," Jo announced suddenly.

"Oh, God, don't start talking wedding already," Alex said with disgust. "Cale and I just got together. And I hate weddings."

"Which is exactly why we should have one big one," Jo said at once. "Less work for each of us. Besides, it doesn't have to be right away, next year sometime maybe. We can—" She paused and glanced to Sam curiously as she began to shake with silent laughter. "What?"

"I was just thinking how wonderful this is," she admitted with a grin, and then burst out with a full laugh, and said, "And they kept telling me it wasn't going to happen, that three sisters wouldn't find life mates. Ha! *Ha* I say!"

"Wait, wait." Jo pulled away and rushed to the small refrigerator in the corner. "We need a drink to toast that."

"The only thing you're going to find in there is blood," Alex said dryly.

Jo grimaced as she opened the door and peered inside to see that this was true. She wavered for a moment and then shrugged. "Ah, what the heck."

"I better get the blinds," Sam muttered, and rushed to the blinds as Jo retrieved three bags of blood.

Alex quickly closed the door as well, and then turned back to accept the bag of blood Jo was holding out.

"Okay," Jo announced as she handed a bag to Sam as well. "We say, 'Ha! *Ha* I say!' together, and then slap the bags to our teeth. It can be our own private toast from now on." She paused to glance from Sam to Alex with concern. "You *can* both bring on your own teeth without Cale and Mortimer turning you on first, right?"

Alex raised her eyebrows. "I seem to always need blood and just seeing it brings them on. Cale has never had to turn me on to get them out," she said, and grimaced at the way the fangs in question mangled her words. They had made an appearance the moment she'd seen the bag of blood.

"Me too," Sam said, the two short words coming out "me thoo."

"Huh." Jo frowned. "Must have just been me." Shrugging, she raised her bag. "Okay. Together now."

Alex shook her head at the silliness of it, but they had always got silly together, and she too said, "Ha! *Ha* I say!" as her sisters did, and then slapped the bag to her teeth. They then stood there, grinning like a trio of idiots around their bags as they waited for them to drain.

"We should have toasted to us," Jo decided with a little sigh as she tore her empty bag away a moment later.

"We'll do that with champagne later," Alex decided, ripping her own bag away. "The Willan sisters are worthy of a sparkling toast."

"Is there champagne?" Jo asked with interest.

"It's being chilled. It should be ready after the others leave. But there are all sorts of other goodies out there if you're thirsty or hungry."

"I'm starved," Jo admitted. "We came right here from the airport."

Alex arched her eyebrows as her gaze slid over Jo's slinky, long black dress. "You flew here like that?"

"Are you kidding? I flew here pretty much naked most of the time," she said with amusement, and when both sisters' eyebrows flew up, explained, "It was a company plane. Bastien sent it for us, and Nicholas and I were alone in the passenger section. I'm now a member of the mile-high club several times over. That man can't keep his hands to himself."

Alex gave a laugh. "And I suppose you wanted nothing to do with it and were trying to fight him off?"

"Oh, good Lord no." Jo chuckled. "I may even have started the getting-naked part. He, however, started the touchy-feely business. I was trying to behave myself until then."

"I didn't hear that, I so didn't hear that," Sam said, tossing her own bag away. "You're my little sister. You don't have sex. You're still a virgin, and as far as I'm concerned will be until I die."

"What about Alex?" Jo asked with amusement.

"Her too," Sam assured her. "Neither of you have sex, and that's that. When the babies come, I will exclaim with amazement over the fact that immaculate conception happened again."

Alex and Jo laughed at the claim.

"All right, Alex, we've hogged you long enough. We should let you get back to your opening," Sam said more seriously. "We can catch up later back at the house. Have one of our girly nights."

"Are you staying at the house?" Jo turned to Alex to ask with happy surprise.

Alex grimaced. "Yes. Mortimer and Cale insist on it until Jacques is found."

"Jacques Tournier?" Jo asked with a frown. "What—?"

"I'll explain," Sam interrupted firmly. "Alex, you really should get back. One of the reporters might be panting for an interview."

Alex nodded, but said, "I need to use the bathroom first. You two go ahead."

"All right, we'll hold down the fort in your absence," Sam said, ushering Jo toward the door.

Alex watched them go, smiling to herself, and then turned to open the door to the bathroom. She flicked on the light and started inside, only to pause as she spotted the man inside, seated on the toilet.

"Oh, sorry," she began with surprise. "I didn't real-ize—" She stopped abruptly as the man stood, and she realized he was dressed, just sitting on the closed toilet lid. It was then she actually looked at him. Once she'd realized someone was on the toilet, she'd immediately averted her eyes, but now she looked at his face and her eyes widened as she recognized the man with three days' worth of stubble on his face. "Jack."

"Jacques," he corrected grimly, starting forward. The gun she now noted in his hand jerked to gesture her away from the door as he walked, and she quickly shifted to the side, moving around him and trading places as he closed the door.

Eyeing him warily, Alex stopped beside the toilet and peered at him in question. "Now what?"

It seemed the most reasonable question. He had the gun, and while she didn't think he could kill her with it now that she'd been turned, he could certainly hurt her. No one liked to be hurt. However, her question seemed to irritate him. Or perhaps it was her lack of weeping and wailing in terror she realized when he sputtered with frustration.

"You don't do anything the way you're supposed to," he spat with frustration. "In France, you were supposed to love me enough that you would claim you had stolen my recipe, but did you? No. You let them believe I had stolen yours."

"You *did* steal mine," she said at once.

"But if you loved me like you said you did, you should have taken the blame. But you didn't. You let them kick me out in disgrace," he snapped. "My father never forgave me for that."

"Well, that's hardly my fault," she said impatiently. "And I did love you. Or I thought I did. Enough that if you'd asked me for help, I would have helped you, but instead you stole it."

"And then I go to all the trouble and expense of opening a restaurant near yours, and do you even notice? Hardly. You just wish me luck and go about acting as if it's fine with you."

"It *was* fine with me," she said dryly. "There are a lot

of people in Toronto, Jack, certainly, enough to support two French restaurants."

"Jacques," he snarled. "And I know you were laughing at me, thinking I wasn't real competition because I didn't graduate the great culinary school," he said bitterly.

"I wasn't laugh—"

"You even go off and decide to open a second restaurant to show me up," he added, talking over her. "And what happens when I make trouble for you there?"

"We suspected it was you behind my problems here," she said with a little sigh.

"You're damned right it was. I spent a hell of a lot of money to make sure the electrician wired things so that this place would burn down. But you live under a star or something. It didn't burn to the ground as it should have. It just suffered some smoke damage. It didn't even slow you down much. You just set to work gutting it and redoing it." He shook his head.

"I don't suppose you had anything to do with the problems I had with that too, did you?" she asked grimly. "The wrong carpet, the tile, the—"

"That cost me a small fortune for all the good it did," he said bitterly. "I was paying your project manager to bungle things and bribed everyone from the tile salesman to the carpet installers to mess things up. But again, you just kept plugging along. Even hiring Peter out from under you didn't slow you down. You just brought in another guy."

Alex stared at him with amazement, finding it incomprehensible that he'd spent so much time and money just to try to hurt her. How had he twisted his own deception in his mind to make it somehow her fault? What was wrong with him?

"The attack at the old La Bonne Vie?" she asked.

He nodded grimly, eyes burning with hatred. "Nothing else had seemed to even touch you. I realized that the only way to teach you a lesson was to just straightout hurt you. I was even looking forward to beating you senseless, but Bev came along and spoiled everything."

Alex narrowed her eyes. She no longer cared why he had done all this, she was getting angry now. "And forcing my car off the highway?"

That question made him pause as confusion slid across his face. "How the hell did you survive that? I only meant to hurt you there, but I was sure I must have killed you. Yet you don't even have a mark on you, but I saw the car hit the rail."

"It wasn't me in the car," she admitted grimly, and recalling Cale's injuries felt her anger crank up another notch. The man could have killed her. Would have killed her had she been driving as intended, but he *had* hurt Cale horribly, and all because *he'd* stolen *her* recipe when they were basically just kids?

"It wasn't you?" Jack echoed with amazement, and then shook his head. "You're the luckiest bitch I ever met."

"Yes, I am," she assured him grimly. "So maybe you should reconsider whatever stupid plan you have swimming around inside that thing you call a brain and just get the hell out of here."

He snorted at the suggestion. "You are joking, aren't you? You've completely ruined me. The cops are after me now. They know I hit your car. They were at the restaurant questioning my people."

Alex didn't doubt for a minute that the men he thought were cops were actually Cale, Mortimer, and Bricker; but she supposed they were cops, vampire cops, but cops just the same, so didn't bother correcting him. She doubted he would have listened anyway. Besides, her attention had slid to the door behind Jack. It was slowly opening inward.

"You've ruined me," Jack repeated, dragging her attention back to him before she could see who it was. "I'm out of money, can't go near my house or the restaurant to get more, the cops are after me, and I have nowhere to go. I'm done now."

She frowned at his tone. His anger appeared to be spent, and he merely sounded sad. Even so, she wasn't prepared for his next words.

"I loved you," he said pitifully. "I imagined us starting a restaurant together and having babies and . . . But I had to graduate to do that with you, and I was desperate and copied the recipe. I didn't know they brought in all the teachers to judge them and that they would all see them both. I thought your professor would see yours and mine would grade mine and no one would ever know."

Alex stared at him with amazement. All this time she'd thought he'd never cared, and he'd simply been a pitiful weak idiot. "But you said all those horrible things."

"I was embarrassed and angry," he admitted wearily. "And you didn't love me like you should have. Love means never having to say you're sorry."

Alex shifted impatiently. "What drivel! If you love someone, you *do* say you're sorry because you care enough to. And you don't steal their damned recipes," she snapped.

"See!" he snarled. "Once again you aren't doing what you're supposed to do."

"And what exactly is that?" she asked dryly.

"I believe he was hoping you would say you love him back and forgive him all, so he'd be off the hook," Cale said dryly, slipping through the partially open door to join them.

Jack jerked around, gun rising, but Cale merely snatched it from his hand, the action so quick Alex almost didn't see it.

"Unfortunately for you," Cale continued, glaring at the man. "I believe you'll find that Alex loves me now. So you're out of luck."

"Who the—?" Jack swallowed the question as Cale pushed the door open, revealing Nicholas, Mortimer, and Bricker all standing in the office, almost empty bags of blood to their teeth.

When Alex peered at them with disbelief, Bricker tore his now-empty bag from his mouth, and explained, "He talks a lot, and we got thirsty. Besides, you always enjoy a show more with refreshments."

Alex shook her head with disgust. "I'm glad you find the nightmare of my life so entertaining."

"I'd say it was more a comedy than a nightmare,"

Bricker assured her with amusement. "The guy's a real loser. I'm glad your taste in men has improved."

Alex narrowed her eyes on the enforcer, wondering if she could take him now that she was immortal too, and Mortimer suddenly ripped his bag from his teeth and gave Bricker a shove toward the door, ordering, "Go get Lucian. He'll want to decide what to do with this guy."

"Just when you start to like him," Cale muttered, watching the younger immortal leave. He shook his head, and then glanced to Alex and held out his hand. When she took the few steps around Jack to take it, Cale tugged her to his chest and frowned with concern. "Are you all right?"

"Yes." She sighed, and then glanced to Jack, noting that he stood blank-faced and still, apparently under someone's control. "What about him?"

"We'll take care of him," Mortimer assured her quietly, relieving Cale of Jack's gun. "You two go on back to the party before the girls come looking for you. We don't want to draw too much attention to this room. It would just mean a lot of work wiping minds and replacing memories."

Cale nodded and urged Alex into the office, and then on to the door.

"What will they do to him?" she asked quietly as they stepped into the kitchen.

"Probably wipe his mind, dump him in a psychiatric facility, and make sure he stays there," he said with a shrug.

"Shouldn't we just hand him over to the police?" she asked with a frown.

"For what?" he asked dryly, and then said, "Unfortunately, we don't have proof that he's done anything. I'm sure he paid his bribes in cash, and then there's no way to prove he's the one who attacked you in the parking lot. As for the incident with the car, we never reported that and can't now. The car was taken to the auto wreckers that very night. Even if it hadn't been, how would we explain my not having even a bruise on me now?" He let her think about that, and then shook his head. "No. It's better if we handle this ourselves."

"Yes, but putting him in a psychiatric facility seems . . ." Alex bit her lip unhappily and shook her head.

Cale stopped walking and took her into his arms. "Don't feel bad for him, honey. If you'd been in the car rather than me, you'd be dead now." His arms tightened briefly at the thought, and then he added grimly, "He's getting off light. If he were immortal, he'd be staked out in the sun to bake all day, and then beheaded. Besides, he's not really in his right mind, Alex. I know you can't read thoughts yet, but I read his, and he's cuckoo, trust me—" He stopped and sighed, before adding, "Or, you know, rather than trust me you could ask one of your sisters to read him and—"

Alex pulled back and quickly placed her fingers over his lips. "I don't have to. I trust you."

The tension left his face at once. "Do you?"

She nodded solemnly. "With my life, my body, and my heart. I really do love you, Cale."

"Oh, thank God," he murmured, pulling her close again. "I love you too."

"Geez, you two, not in the kitchen. It's not hygienic. Go find a room somewhere or something. Honestly."

Alex and Cale pulled apart to see Bricker leading Lucian Argeneau to the office.

"Someone's going to kill that boy someday," Cale muttered, as the two men disappeared into the office.

"Yeah," Alex agreed on a sigh. "But someone else can do it. I have better things for you to do with your time."

"Oh?" he asked, turning back to her with interest.

"Hmmm," she murmured. "I'll show you later to-night at the house."

"Sounds good," he murmured, turning her to continue toward the door to the dining room. "I can't wait."

"Well, I'm afraid you'll have to," she said apologetically. "Sam, Jo, and I are going to have some girly time first."

Cale paused again to glance at her with a frown. "Girly time?"

She bit her lip and nodded.

Cale sighed. "All right. I guess they can have their girly time with you . . . So long as I get you after that."

"You get me forever," she assured him quietly.

Cale grinned. "Hmm. I like compromise."

"Works well, doesn't it?" she agreed with a laugh, as they pushed through the door to rejoin the party.

Turn the page for a sneak peek at the next novel
in the Argeneau Vampire series,
The Reluctant Vampire

One

Drina hardly noticed the rhythmic tap of her heels as she descended the stairs from the plane. Her attention was shifting from the winter-dead trees surrounding the private airstrip to the man leaning against the back of a small golf cart on the edge of the tarmac.

With dark hair and skin and a black leather coat, he could have been mistaken for a shadow if it weren't for his glowing gold-black eyes. They peered at her, steady and cold from between his black wool hat and scarf, and he remained utterly motionless until she stepped down onto the paved runway. Only then did he move, straightening and walking forward to meet her.

Despite the cold, Drina forced a smile. A greeting was trembling on her lips, but died there when he took the small bag she carried and turned wordlessly away. The abrupt action brought her up short, and she watched blankly as the man walked away with her luggage. When he slid behind the wheel of the small, open cart and dropped her bag on the front passenger seat, she managed to shake herself out of her surprise and move forward, but couldn't resist muttering, "Hello, you must be Drina Argenis. Such a pleasure to meet you. Please, allow me to take your luggage for you. And here, please take a seat so I can get you to the enforcer house and out of this cold."

With their hearing, she knew the man must have heard her sarcastic mimicry of what she would have liked him to say, but he didn't react by deed or word. He merely started the engine on the cart and waited.

Drina grimaced. It seemed obvious from where he'd set her suitcase that she was expected to sit on the back bench seat. Not welcome in the front, apparently, she thought with disgust as she settled on the cold, stiff seat. She then grabbed the supporting bar to keep from sliding off as the cart immediately jerked into motion. The icy metal under her fingers made her think, not for the first time, that she should have researched North American winters more fully before making this journey. It was a bit late for that, however. But she would definitely need to take a shopping trip or two as soon as she could if she didn't wish to end up a Popsicle while here.

With nothing else to look at, Drina watched the small plane that had brought her here turn on the landing strip and start away. The moment its wheels lifted off, the lights on the field suddenly blinked out and darkness crowded in. For one moment, she couldn't see a thing, but then her eyes adjusted and she took in the knee-deep snow and skeletal trees lining the path and wondered how long she would be on this contraption and out in the cold.

The woods weren't as deep as they'd seemed from the plane. It only took a matter of moments before they left the woods behind to follow a small path along the side of an open snow-covered yard holding what looked like a long garage and a house. It was the garage her driver steered them toward. The tires crunched on the hard-packed snow as they came to a halt beside a small door. The man who hadn't greeted her, then grabbed her bag and slid out from behind the steering wheel. He moved toward the door to the garage without a word.

Eyebrows rising, along with her temper, Drina followed him inside and up a short hall. She spotted an office and a hallway leading to cells on her left, but he led her to a door on the right and straight into a garage, where several vehicles sat waiting.

Drina cast a quick glance over the few vehicles inside. They were all the same, SUVs, she thought they were called. She followed Mr. Tall-Dark-and-Mute to the back passenger door of the first vehicle. When he opened it, and then simply waited, she eyed him narrowly. It seemed obvious he was going to be her escort to Port Henry, but she'd be damned if he was going to stick her in the backseat like some unwanted guest for the duration of what her uncle had said would be a two-hour journey.

Smiling sweetly, she ducked under his arm and moved past him to the front door instead. Drina pulled it open and quickly slid inside, then turned to eye him challengingly.

His response was to heave a long-suffering sigh, toss her bag on the floor at her feet, and slam the door closed.

"Great," Drina muttered, as he walked around the vehicle to the driver's side. But she supposed she shouldn't be surprised at the man's attitude. He worked for her uncle, after all, the most taciturn man she'd ever met. On this side of the ocean at least. She added that last thought as Mr. Tall-Dark-and-Miserable slid behind the steering wheel and started the engine.

Drina watched him press a button that set the garage door in front of them rolling up, but waited until he'd shifted into gear before asking, "Are we heading straight to—"

She paused as he suddenly slid a letter from an inside pocket of his fur-lined coat and handed it to her.

"Oh here, I was to give you this," Drina mimicked dryly as she accepted the envelope.

Tall-Dark-and-Rude raised an eyebrow but otherwise didn't react.

Drina shook her head and opened the letter. It was from Uncle Lucian, explaining that her escort was Anders and he would be delivering her directly to Port Henry. She guessed that meant Lucian hadn't trusted Anders to pass on this information himself. Perhaps he really was mute, she thought, and glanced curiously to the man as she slipped the letter into her pocket. The nanos should have prevented it . . . unless, of course, it wasn't a physical problem but a genetic one. Still, she'd never heard of a mute immortal.

"Do you speak at all?" she asked finally.

He turned an arched eyebrow in her direction as he steered the vehicle up the driveway beside the house, and shrugged. "Why bother? You were doing well enough on your own."

So . . . rude, not mute, Drina thought, and scowled. "Obviously, all those tales Aunt Marguerite told me about charming Canadian men were something of an exaggeration."

That had him hitting the brakes and jerking around to peer at her with wide eyes. They were really quite beautiful eyes, she noted absently as he barked, "Marguerite?"

"Dear God, it speaks again," she muttered dryly. "Be still my beating heart. I don't know if I'll survive the excitement."

Scowling at her sarcasm, he eased his foot off the brakes to cruise forward along the driveway until they reached a manned gate. Two men came out of a small building beside the gates and waved in greeting. They then immediately set about manually opening the inner gate. Once Anders had steered the SUV through and paused at a second gate, the men closed the first one. They then disappeared inside the small building again. A bare moment later, the second gate swung open on its own, and he urged their vehicle out onto a dark, country road.

"Did Marguerite specify any particular male in

Canada?" Anders asked abruptly, as Drina turned from watching the gate close behind them.

She raised an eyebrow, noting the tension now apparent in the man. "Now you want to speak, do you?" she asked with amusement, and taunted, "Afraid it was you?"

He glanced at her sharply, his own eyes narrowed. "Was it?"

Drina snorted and tugged on her seat belt. Doing it up, she muttered, "Like I'd tell you if it was."

"Wouldn't you?"

She glanced over to see that he was now frowning.

"Hell no," she assured him. "What self-respecting girl would want to be stuck with a doorstop for a mate for the rest of her life?"

"A doorstop?" he squawked.

"Yes, doorstop. As in big, silent, and good only for holding wood." She smiled sweetly, and added, "At least I'm pretty sure about the wood part. Nanos do make sure immortal males function in all areas."

Drina watched with satisfaction as Anders's mouth dropped open. She then shifted in her seat to a more comfortable position and closed her eyes. "I think I'll take a nap. I never sleep well on planes. Enjoy the drive."

Despite her closed eyes, she was aware that he kept glancing her way. Drina ignored it and managed not to grin. The man needed some shaking up, and she had no doubt this would do it. Over the centuries, she'd become good at judging the age of other immortals, and was pretty sure she was centuries older than Anders. He wouldn't be able to read her, which would leave him wondering . . . and drive him nuts, she was sure. But it served him right. It didn't take much effort to be courteous, and courtesy was necessary in a civilized society. It was a lesson the man should learn before he got too old to learn anything anymore.

Harper considered his cards briefly, then pulled out a six of spades and laid it on the discard pile. He glanced toward Tiny, not terribly surprised to find the man not looking at his own cards but peering distractedly toward the stairs.

"Tiny," he prompted. "Your turn."

"Oh." The mortal turned back to his cards, started to pull one out of his hand as if to discard it, and Harper shot his own hand out to stop him.

When Tiny glanced at him with surprise, he pointed out dryly, "You have to pick up first."

"Oh, right." He shook his head and set back the card he'd been about to discard, and reached for one from the deck.

Harper sat back with a little shake of the head, thinking, *Lord save me from new life mates.* The thought made him grimace since that's all he seemed to be surrounded with lately: Victor and Elvi, DJ and Mabel, Allesandro and Leonora, Edward and Dawn and now Tiny and Mirabeau. The first four couples had been together for a year and a half now, and were just starting to re-gather some of their wits about them. They were still new enough to be trying at times, but at least they could actually hold on to a thought or two longer than a second.

Tiny and Mirabeau were brand-spanking-new, however, and couldn't think of much else but each other . . . and how to find a moment alone to get naked. And they couldn't control their thoughts either, so that it was like constantly having a radio playing in his ear, life-mate porn, twenty-four/seven.

Harper supposed the fact that he hadn't packed up his bags and moved on a year and a half ago when his own life mate had died, was probably a sign that he was a masochist. Because really, there was no worse torture for someone who had just lost their long-awaited and prayed-for life mate than to have to stand by and witness the joy and just plain horniness of other new life mates. But he had nowhere to go. Oh, he had an apartment in the city and businesses he could pretend to be interested in, but why bother when he'd set them up years ago to ensure he needn't be there to oversee them, and could travel, merely checking in once in a while. He also had family in Germany he could visit, but they weren't close, each of them having created their own lives centuries ago and barely keeping up with each other.

Actually, Harper thought, Elvi, Victor, Mabel, and DJ were the closest thing to family he now had. When Jenny had died, the two couples had surrounded and embraced him and pulled him into their little family. They had cushioned and coddled him during the first shock of her loss, and slowly nursed him back to the land of the living, and he was grateful for it. So much so, in fact, that he was glad for this opportunity to repay some of their kindness by looking after things while they went on their honeymoons. He just wished that looking after things didn't include a pair of new life mates to torture him with.

Tiny finally discarded, and Harper picked up another card, but then paused and glanced toward the window as the crunch of tires on new snow caught his ear.

"What is it?" Tiny asked, his voice tense.

"A vehicle just pulled into the driveway," Harper murmured, then glanced to Tiny and raised an eyebrow. "Your replacements, I'm guessing."

Tiny was immediately out of his seat and moving into the kitchen to peer out the back window. When he then moved to the pantry to collect his coat from the closet there, Harper stood and followed. The arrival of the replacement hunters was something he'd looked forward to. He suspected Tiny and Mirabeau would now retreat to their bedroom and not be seen much. It meant he could avoid the worst of their obsessive thoughts about each other . . . which would be a blessing.

Tiny apparently saw him coming and grabbed Harper's coat as well. The man handed it to him as he came back into the kitchen, and both pulled them on as they headed for the door to the deck. Tiny had pulled his boots on while in the pantry and headed straight out the door, but Harper had to pause to kick off his slippers and tug on the boots by the back door. It only took a moment, but by the time he did and stepped outside, Tiny was already out of sight.

Harper grimaced as the bitter wind slapped his face. He followed the big mortal's footprints in the snow, trailing them across the deck and down the steps to the short sidewalk that ran along the side of the garage to the driveway. With his eyes on the ground, he didn't see the person approaching until he was nearly on top of them. Pausing abruptly when a pair of running shoes came into view in front of his boots, he jerked his head up with surprise and found himself blinking at a petite woman in a coat far too light for Canadian winters.

His gaze slid from her hatless head, to the suitcase she carried, and then beyond her to the two men by the SUV.

"Hi."

Harper glanced back to the woman. She was smiling tentatively at him and holding out one ungloved hand in greeting.

"Alexandrina Argenis," she announced when he merely stared at her hand. "But everyone calls me Drina."

Removing one hand from his pocket, he shook hers, noting that it was warm and soft despite the cold, then he cleared his throat and said, "Harpernus Stoyan." He retrieved his hand and shoved it back into the safety of his pocket as he stepped to the side for her to get by. "Go on inside. It's warm in there. There's blood in the fridge."

Nodding, she moved past him, and Harper watched her go, waiting until she disappeared around the corner before continuing on to the SUV now parked in the driveway. Tiny and another man, this one dressed more befitting a Canadian winter, with hat and gloves and even a scarf, were still at the back of the truck. As he approached, the new man pulled a cooler from inside and handed it to Tiny.

Rather than turn away and head back to the house though, Tiny said, "Throw your suitcase on top and I'll take it in as well."

Harper smiled faintly to himself. Tiny was a big guy, a small mountain really, and very strong . . . for a mortal. He was also used to being the muscle among his own people and forgot that he was now dealing with immortals who outclassed him horribly in that area.

But the new arrival merely set a suitcase on top of the cooler and turned back to the SUV without comment. Tiny immediately slid past Harper to head for the house, leaving him to step up beside the newcomer and peer curiously into the back of the SUV. There were two more coolers left inside. The fellow was unplugging them and winding up the cords.

"Harper."

He glanced to the man with surprise at the terse greeting, eyebrows rising as he recognized the eyes that turned to him. "Nice to see you, Anders," Harper greeted in return as he reached in to retrieve one of the coolers. "It's been a while."

Anders's answer was a grunt as he claimed the second cooler and straightened from the vehicle. He paused to close the back of the SUV, hit the button to lock the doors, and then nodded for Harper to lead the way.

Harper turned away but found himself grinning and couldn't resist saying, "Chatty as ever, I see."

When the man basically told him to bugger off in Russian, Harper burst out laughing. The sound of his own laughter was somewhat startling, but it felt good, he decided, as he led the way across the deck. Maybe it was a sign that he was finally coming out of the depression that had struck him when Jenny had died.

The thought made him sigh to himself as he shifted the cooler to open the door to the house. He'd been sunk pretty deep in self-pity and gloom for the last year and a half, and while he supposed it was only to be expected when one lost a life mate, it would be a relief to feel more himself again. He was not a naturally gloomy guy but had found little to laugh or even smile about since Jenny's death.

"Here." Tiny was in front of him, reaching for Harper's cooler the minute he stepped into the house. He gave it up and watched the man carry it into the dining room, where he unraveled the cord and plugged it in. The one Tiny himself had carried in was already plugged into a socket in the corner of the kitchen, Harper noted, and supposed the man was spreading them throughout the house to be sure they didn't overload a breaker. The coolers were basically portable refrigerators and probably used a lot of juice.

Feeling the cold at his back, Harper realized he was blocking Anders from entering and quickly stepped aside for him to pass. He then pulled the screen door closed and shut and locked the inner door. By the time he turned back, Tiny had returned and was taking the last cooler from Anders. Harper's gaze slid over the dining room in search of Alexandrina-Argenis-everyone-calls-me-Drina and found her standing beside the dining-room table, shrugging out of her coat.

"If this is all blood, you brought a lot of it," Tiny commented with a frown as he turned to carry the last cooler away, this time heading for the living room.

"Lucian sent it for your turn," Anders responded, bending to undo and remove his boots.

"My God, he speaks again," Drina muttered with feigned shock. "And a whole sentence too."

"Sometimes you'll even get a paragraph out of him," Harper responded, but his gaze was now on Tiny. The man had paused in the doorway of the living room and turned back, a startled expression on his face. Apparently it hadn't occurred to him that now that he and Mirabeau had acknowledged they were life mates, the next step was the turn.

"A whole paragraph?" Drina asked with dry amusement, drawing Harper's attention again.

"A short one, but a paragraph just the same," he murmured, glancing her way. He then paused to take her in. She was petite, as he'd noticed outside, which was a polite way of saying short. But she was curvy too, rounded in all the right places. She was also most definitely Spanish, with olive skin, deep-set eyes, the large brow bone, and straight, almost prominent nose. But it all worked to make an attractive face, he decided.

"Right, of course, the turn," Tiny muttered, drawing his attention once more, and Harper shifted his attention back to find the other man looking resolute. As he watched, Tiny straightened his shoulders and continued into the living room.

Harper frowned and had to bite back the urge to tell Tiny that perhaps he should wait on turning, but he knew it was just a knee-jerk reaction to his own experience. It was rare for a mortal to die during the turn, and in all likelihood, Tiny would probably be fine. However, Jenny had died, and so that was the first thing he thought of and the worry that now plagued him.

Sighing, he bent to remove his boots. He set them beside the radiator, and straightened to remove his coat. Laying it over his arm, he then took Anders's as he finished removing it and crossed the room to collect Drina's as well before ducking into the small pantry in the back corner of the kitchen. It held the entry to the garage but was also where the closet was.

"Handy."

Harper glanced around to see that Drina stood in the doorway to the kitchen, eyes sliding around the small room. Her gaze slid back to him as he reached for hangers, and she moved to join him as he hung up her coat.

"Let me help. You don't have to wait on us." She took the second hanger he'd just retrieved and Anders's coat, leaving him to deal with only his own.

Harper murmured a "thanks," but had to fight the urge to assure her it was fine and send her from the room. The tiny space suddenly seemed smaller with her in it, a good portion of the air seeming to have slipped out with her entrance, leaving an unbearably hot vacuum behind that had him feeling flushed and oxygen starved. Which was just odd, he decided. He had never been claustrophobic before this. Still, Harper was relieved when they were done with the task, and he could usher her back into the much larger kitchen.

"So where is this Stephanie we're supposed to guard?" Drina asked, sliding onto one of the stools that ran along the L-shaped counter separating the kitchen from the dining area.

"Sleeping," Harper answered, moving past her to the dining-room table to gather the cards from his game with Tiny.

"Stephanie's still used to mortal hours," Tiny explained, returning to the kitchen then. "So we thought it'd be better if one of us was up with her during the day and the other up at night to keep an eye on things while she slept. I got night duty."

"They're concerned about the lack of security here," Harper explained, sliding the cards into their box and moving to set them on the counter.

Drina frowned and glanced to Tiny. "But isn't that backward? You're mortal, aren't you? Shouldn't you be up during the day and this Mirabeau up at night?"

Tiny smiled wryly. "That would have been easier all around, but it's only been this one day. Besides, while I can hang out with her during the day or night and keep an eye on her, someone has to sleep in her room, which had to be Mirabeau." When

Drina raised an eyebrow, he explained, "We didn't think it was a good idea to leave her alone in her room all night. There's no fence here, no alarm . . . It could be hours before we realized she was gone if she was taken or—"

"Or what?" Drina asked when Tiny hesitated. It was pure politeness on her part, Harper knew. The woman could have read him easily enough to find out what he was reluctant to say but was asking instead out of respect.

Tiny was silent as he removed his own coat, but finally admitted, "There's some concern that Stephanie might try to run away and get to her family."

"Really?" Drina asked, her eyes narrowing.

Tiny nodded. "Apparently, Lucian caught the thought in her head a time or two. He thinks she only wants to see them, not necessarily approach them, but—" He shrugged. "Anyway, as far as she's concerned, none of us know that, and someone has to be with her twenty-four/seven because of Leonius."

"So we are not only watching for attack from outside, but a prison break as well," Drina murmured. "And because of this, Mirabeau has been sleeping in Stephanie's room with her?"

Tiny shrugged. "This was the first night. We only got here the day before yesterday, and Elvi, Victor, DJ, and Mabel were here then to help keep an eye on things. But they left at four this morning, so . . ." He grimaced. "When Stephanie went to bed, Mirabeau did as well."

Drina heaved a sigh, smiled wryly, and said, "Well,

I guess that will be my gig from now on. I'll have a bag of blood, and then go up and relieve Mirabeau."

Harper had to smile at Tiny's expression. The man looked torn between shouting hallelujah, and protesting it wasn't necessary tonight and she could take over that duty tomorrow. Duty versus desire, he supposed. Tiny and Mirabeau had brought Stephanie here from New York, sneaking her from the church where several couples were being wed in one large ceremony, including Victor and Elvi. They had left via a secret exit in the church, and traveled some distance through a series of sewer tunnels before reaching the surface. They'd then driven to Port Henry, where Victor and Elvi had been waiting to welcome the girl.

While Tiny and Mirabeau were officially off duty now that Drina and Anders had arrived, Lucian had insisted they stay to get over the worst of their new-life-mate symptoms. Harper suspected they would feel a responsibility to help out while they were here. They would probably even feel they should, to pay back for staying here at the bed-and-breakfast for the next couple of weeks.

"Drina's right," Anders announced, saving Tiny the struggle. "It's better someone less distracted than Mirabeau be in Stephanie's room with her. Besides, it's our worry now. You two are off duty."

Tiny blew out a small breath and nodded, but then added, "We'll help out while we're here, though."

"Hopefully, it won't be necessary, but we appreciate that," Drina said, when Anders just shrugged. She then slid off her stool and glanced from Anders

LYNSAY SANDS

to Harper in question. "Which blood do I use? From the coolers or the fridge?"

"Either one," Anders said with a shrug. "More is coming in a couple of days."

Harper moved to the refrigerator to retrieve a bag for her, pulled out three more, and turned to hand them out.

"Thank you," Drina murmured, accepting the bag Harper offered. She popped it to her fangs, then suddenly stiffened and turned to glance over her shoulder. Following her gaze, Harper saw that Teddy was entering the dining room from the foyer.

"I thought I heard voices," the man said on a yawn, running one hand through his thick, gray hair.

"Sorry if we woke you, Teddy," Harper said, and gestured to the newcomers. "The backup Lucian promised has arrived." He turned and explained to Drina and Anders, "Teddy Brunswick is the police chief here in Port Henry. He's also a friend, and he offered to stay and help keep an eye out until you guys arrived." He glanced back to the man, and said, "Teddy, this is Alexandrina Argenis. She prefers Drina."

Teddy nodded in greeting to Drina, and then glanced to Anders as Harper finished, "And her partner is Anders."

"Hmm." Teddy raised his eyebrows. "Anders a first name or last?"

"Neither," Anders said, and ended any further possibility to question him by popping his bag of blood to his mouth.

Teddy scowled but merely moved into the small

back room with its coat closet. He returned a moment later with a coat in one hand and a pair of boots in the other.

"Now that the cavalry have arrived, I guess I'll go home and crawl into my own bed," he announced, settling on a dining-room chair to don his boots.

"Thank you for staying, Teddy," Tiny murmured. "I made a fresh pot of coffee shortly before Drina and Anders arrived. Do you want a cup for the road?"

"That'd be nice," Teddy said appreciatively, finishing with one boot and pulling on the other. Tiny immediately moved to the cupboard and retrieved a travel mug. By the time Teddy had finished with his second boot, Tiny had poured the coffee and added the fixings. He waited as Teddy donned his coat and did it up, and then handed him the mug.

"Thank you," Teddy murmured, accepting it. "I'll clean the mug and return it tomorrow when I come to check on things."

"Sounds good," Tiny said with a nod, as he walked the man to the door and saw him out.

"Well," Drina said, pulling the now-empty bag from her fangs and moving around the counter to throw it out. "I guess it's time for me to go to bed."

Harper smiled faintly at her grimace as she said it. It was only a little after one. Going to bed now was like a mortal going to bed at four in the afternoon. It was doubtful she'd be able to sleep for quite a while. In fact, he suspected she probably wouldn't be able to drift off until just before dawn, and then she'd have to get up with Stephanie in the morning.

She was in for a rough time until she adjusted to her new hours, he thought with sympathy.

"It's the room in the front right corner as you come off the stairs," Tiny said helpfully. "I'm not sure which of the twin beds Mirabeau chose, though."

"I'll figure it out," Drina assured him as she picked up her suitcase. "Good night, boys."

"Good night," Harper murmured, along with the others. He watched until she'd left the room, and they could hear her mounting the stairs. He then frowned slightly and glanced up toward the lights, wondering why the room seemed a little darker all of a sudden.

Love 👄 Sexy and 💗 Romantic novels?

Get caught up in an Angel's Kiss . . .

Vampire hunter Elena Deveraux knows she's the best – but she doesn't know if she's good enough for this job. Hired by the dangerously beautiful Archangel Raphael, a being so lethal that no mortal wants his attention, only one thing is clear – failure is not an option . . . even if the task she's been set is impossible. Because this time, it's not a wayward vamp she has to track. It's an archangel gone bad.

Enthralled by **Angel's Blood?**
Then get caught up in the rest of the series: **Archangel's Kiss**

For more Urban Fantasy visit www.orionbooks.co.uk/urbanfantasy
for the latest news, updates and giveaways!

Lynsay Sands was born in Canada and is an award-winning author of over thirty books, which have made the Barnes & Noble and *New York Times* bestseller lists. She is best known for her Argeneau series, about a modern-day family of vampires.

Visit Lynsay's website at: www.lynsaysands.net